PRAISE FOR NATIONAL BESTSELLING AUTHOR

Julie Beard

Falcon and the Sword

"*Falcon and the Sword* is medieval romance at its best. Julie Beard paints a lively and colorful portrait of the thirteenth century with vivid descriptions, sharp narrative and an engrossing, original plot. She is at the top of her form and continues to dazzle with stories that speak to the heart and the mind."

—*Romantic Times*

"A sensitive, thought-provoking story with an original plot, fascinating characters, and a vibrant setting. Another bestseller for Ms. Beard."

—*Rendezvous*

"Since her debut . . . Julie Beard has fast become known for her rich, dramatic medieval romances. There is a magical quality to Julie Beard's writing that brings to life a long-ago time of pageantry and legend, yet gives us characters who are living, breathing people to care about."

—*Heart to Heart*

A Dance in Heather

"Lively [and] endearing."

—*Publishers Weekly*

"A nice interweaving of medieval British history, pageantry, and love."

—*Library Journal*

"Julie Beard has a magical touch for bringing the Middle Ages to life with color, pageantry and excitement that never detracts from the romance. Every scene is beautifully rendered . . . [A] nonstop read."

—*Romantic Times*

"Vivid and compelling, the fifteenth century springs to vibrant life . . . From roistering festivals in ancient castles to teeming life in medieval London, she paints an astonishingly vivid picture of the times; and a bold lord, his fair lady and their love . . . a memorable read."

—Edith Layton, author
of *The Crimson Crown*

"A glorious love story in every sense—alive and vibrant, enthralling, and intriguing . . . I couldn't put it down until the last page."

—*Rendezvous*

"Beard is writing tales of love and romance that always have happy endings."

—*Chicago Tribune*

Lady and the Wolf

"Fiery passion . . . Ms. Beard captures your imagination from page one of this outstanding tale of the Middle Ages."

—*Rendezvous*

"*Lady and the Wolf* mixes the plague, primogeniture, the Spanish Inquisition, witchcraft, jousts, grave robbing and some sizzling sex scenes into a brand-new, best-selling, fourteenth-century romance."

—*Chicago Suburban Times*

"A powerful debut novel that sweeps us into the lives of a medieval family . . . [A] stunning and poignant climax."

—*Romantic Times*

"Beard is writing tales of love and romance that always have happy endings."

—*Chicago Tribune*

Romance

of the Rose

Julie Beard

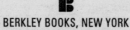

BERKLEY BOOKS, NEW YORK

ROMANCE OF THE ROSE

A Berkley Book / published by arrangement with
the author

PRINTING HISTORY
Berkley edition / May 1998

All rights reserved.
Copyright © 1998 by Julie Beard
This book may not be reproduced in whole or in part,
by mimeograph or any other means, without permission.
For information address:
The Berkley Publishing Group, a member of Penguin Putnam Inc.,
200 Madison Avenue, New York, New York 10016.

The Penguin Putnam Inc. World Wide Web site address is
http://www.penguinputnam.com

ISBN: 0-425-16342-3

BERKLEY®
Berkley Books are published by The Berkley Publishing Group,
a member of Penguin Putnam Inc.,
200 Madison Avenue, New York, New York 10016.
BERKLEY and the "B" design are trademarks
belonging to Berkley Publishing Corporation.

PRINTED IN THE UNITED STATES OF AMERICA

10 9 8 7 6 5 4 3

To Nancy Brown, a class act,
a devoted mother, and a
great sister.

ACKNOWLEDGMENTS

Only Mary Alice Kruesi truly knows how indebted I am to her for her insightful criticism and advice, so I'll leave it at a simple thanks. I'm not sure what I would have done if Donna Julian hadn't saved the day with a brilliant idea for an eleventh-hour plot change. Thanks, Donna! I also owe Suzette Edelen a big hug for a last-minute read and a strong dose of encouragement. And special thanks to my editor, Hillary Cige, for a spectacular job of polishing my prose.

I owe an incalculable debt to the late John McAdam, my eighth-grade drama teacher, who taught me to love Shakespeare and life in general, two awesome gifts I will always cherish. Thanks also to my friend Vinita Vannier, the dedicated teacher who encouraged me in my former acting career.

Thanks to Dave Murray for his three-page, single-space critiques. I cherish your letters. Thanks, too, David Boylan and David Kunzweiler on general principles. (Does this mean I don't have to use your names in my next book?)

So many women have encouraged and supported me on the long road to publication, including Martha Powers, Cynthia Brown, and Kate Bowman. And I must thank a special group of extraordinarily talented and loving women who've nourished my dream of writing forever, it seems— my fellow former singing wenches from the Kings Manor Dinner Theatre: Annie Dekom, Kitty Bickers, Cyndi Maxey, Cindi Cronin, Cindy Symmonds, Tammy De-Young, Jill Bremer, Jeanne Cerceo, Bev Buzinski, Deb Miller, Liz Pazek, and honorary wench and fellow journalist Mary Boylan.

I have an even longer history with my Stephens College buddies: Lauri Kempson, Helen Lewis Moore, Cynthia Cobb Sullivan, Kitsy Battle, and Suzanne Carbery Emery, whose dignity inspired the name for my heroine.

Thanks to all for sharing the dream!

AUTHOR'S NOTE

Avid Shakespeare readers will note that I've taken a few liberties with the Bard, including having the audacity to include William Shakespeare as a character. I simply couldn't resist. I've also rearranged the order in which Shakespeare is believed to have written his plays. The plot compelled me to make use of literary license in chronological matters.

I also want to mention the fact that the female parts in Elizabethan plays were played by men. Considering the many liberties women enjoyed under the reign of the strong-willed Queen Elizabeth, this limitation may seem odd, theatrically and socially.

Technically, women in the papal states were forbidden to act in public until the eighteenth century. But rules were made to be broken. Italian commedia dell'arte troupes started using actresses as early as 1570. And Elizabethan England was no longer under papal rule. So why the social stigma against females on stage? Historian Michael Shapiro posits two factors: the Elizabethan fear of female sexuality and its tolerance of male homoeroticism. While it may be difficult for us to imagine a boy actor dressed in a female costume playing the role of Juliet, for example, that is exactly what the first audiences of Shakespeare's classics witnessed.

An excerpt from the early seventeenth-century
book on plant husbandry entitled

Love in an Elizabethan Garden
by
ANONYMOUS

Ah, the joys of gardens! They nourish the heart, feed the intellect, and fertilize the soul.

After observing the finest English curious knotted gardens, I can recommend four basic principles of design.

First, the size of the garden and the designs of the flower beds, or knots, should harmonize with the architecture and character of the home.

Second, plant the knots with mixed flowers. Let the colors produce a rich and colorful mosaic pleasing to the eye.

Third, concoct a garden of flowers and shrubs for all seasons. Even in winter, there should be delights for the eyes, to encourage the owner to exercise and take respite amidst the beauty.

And finally, make a garden that will please the nose as well as the eyes. Blend herbs with flowers. Choose fragrances that mingle sweetly in a nosegay, or a tuzzie-muzzie. Follow these principles and you will find that love always blooms in an Elizabethan garden.

Romance
of the Rose

Prologue

❦

Outskirts of London, 1580

Lord Andrew Carbery, Earl of Dunnington, shuffled several pieces of parchment as he rose from the desk in his private parlor. He smiled with satisfaction on the boy kneeling before him in a cream-colored doublet that had been newly sewn for him.

"Stand up, child. You are not a servant. You are a welcome visitor here. No, my boy, you are much more still."

"My lord, you do me great honor," Mandrake Rothwell replied. The ten-year-old rose from bended knee with a proud arch to his supple back. His watchful eyes never roved from the gray-haired benefactor who had sheltered him and his mother for six months. "I would like nothing better than to please you, Lord Dunnington."

"You please me greatly, child."

"Hellkite!" ten-year-old Rosalind Carbery squeaked, then slapped a hand to her mouth, wide-eyed and fearful. The Rose of Thornbury House, her father's sweetest rose, crouched on a narrow ledge outside the room, watching

the private meeting through a partially open window.
Bluntly put, she was eavesdropping and could not risk being discovered.

Rosalind had nearly broken her neck running through
the Elizabethan great house to reach this spot. As soon as
she'd learned that her father had requested an audience
with their unsettling little vistor, Mandrake—or Drake, as
everyone called him—Rosalind had torn off in her stock-
ing feet, practically tumbling down the grand staircase of
her father's prodigy house. She'd burst out the front door,
down the marble stairs, and scrambled over the grassy
estate, through a row of bushes that lined the side of
the house. She'd heaved herself up a marble statue of the
Greek goddess Juno and then gingerly inched onto the
ledge outside the second-story parlor.

Fortunately, she wasn't wearing a farthingale, merely a
simple gown, the one she wore for pruning the garden.
And she gardened often now that her dear mother, God
rest her soul, was no longer alive to scold her for it.

The Countess of Dunnington had died five years earlier
while giving birth to a son—the son that Rosalind *should*
have been. On that fateful day, Rosalind had listened with
terrified awe, unnoticed in a corner of the birthing chamber, knees drawn tight to her chest. She watched in help-
less horror as her mother and newborn brother gasped their
last breaths.

Rosalind felt her breath clutch in her chest as she recalled that moment, relived the anguish of realizing that
her mother would never have died if she herself *had* been
the son her father so craved. For her frail mother would
never have risked a second pregnancy if her first child had
been a cherished male heir. Rosalind had vowed that night
as she huddled in the dark, and repeated the vow this afternoon, crouched in the shadows, that she would be the
son her father had wished for. She would be the worthy

heir of Thornbury House. Not this miserable upstart named Drake!

Her small fists clenched at the windowpane as she studied her young rival. Why did his very appearance send her insides tumbling with contradiction?

His unruly thatch of black hair looked like the devil's own. But his eyes were those of an angel, a devastating blue, just the right shade to deceive one into thinking he was kind and sweet-natured. Just look at the loving manner in which her father patted his shoulder. Everyone was fooled but her!

Wasn't Drake always pointing out her inadequacies, or making fun of her for scribbling poetry and plays, or tugging on her braids?

Those were triflings, however, compared with the greatest threat he posed. How many times had she spied him gazing at the house—*her* house—from a distance, transfixed with a look of longing so powerful it made her shiver?

"Imagine my surprise," Lord Dunnington continued, "when I found you and your mother staring up at Thornbury House from the street outside the front gate. I invited you in that day, and you've never left."

"Yes, my lord," Drake replied, swallowing thickly at the reminder of charity. "I am grateful. I will try to prove worthy of your generosity some day."

"No need. You belong here, Mandrake. Your father built this house. That is the great irony of it all."

"*You belong here,*" Rosalind repeated sotto voce. Her breath clouded the glass, and she wiped it clean with a fist until she could once again see the room and the reflection of her own troubled green eyes and tousled red hair.

Drake shrugged. "We had come to see the house and remember how grandly we had once lived. That is, before my father . . ."

"Before your merchant father went bankrupt," Rosalind whispered when Drake's voice fell away in embarrassment. She blinked and sighed, surprised that she felt sorry for him.

"That is all past now," Lord Dunnington continued, patting Drake's shoulder. "Your poor father is dead. They say he died of drink, but I suspect the cause was heartbreak. If I had built and lost a prodigy house, along with every farthing I owned, I'm not sure I would have recovered either. Unfortunately, we will never know who tricked him into investing his money in a trading company that didn't exist."

"My father was driven to his death, my lord," Drake said in a quiet, seething voice. "And I will avenge him."

"No, Drake, do not even think of it. The person who duped him is someone very powerful indeed. My own inquiries have come up short. Whoever it was, he has connections in Court and will not allow himself to be exposed. It would be dangerous to try."

"Someone in Court . . ." Drake whispered. He blinked solemnly, absorbing the shocking revelation.

"Never mind all that," Lord Dunnington said, squatting down and grasping Drake's shoulders. "You are back at Thornbury House now. For good. I have asked your mother to stay on, as a family friend. I will be like a father to you now. You will not inherit from me, but I will use every connection I have to make sure your future is bright. You, my boy, will be like the son I never had. I can't tell you how disappointed I was at Rosalind's birth."

"Zounds!" Rosalind muffled her cry, covering her face with both hands. How could her father regret her birth and still be so loving?

"I've thought of bringing you into my wool business as an apprentice, but the wool trade is on the wane," her father added, his words scarcely audible for the pounding in her head. "It is time you learn another skill. I've found a place for you with a new spice-trading operation, and I assure you this one is legitimate. It has the queen's blessing."

"It's always been my dream to be master of my own ship, my lord."

Lord Dunnington chuckled at the boy's excitement. "Dreams can drive a man to greatness. Makes me recall another bright, ambitious young man. Your namesake, Francis Drake."

A breeze swirled around Rosalind and howled in her ears like the winds of destiny. If only she knew what it all meant. If only she knew her purpose in life. She felt she had something important to say. But who would listen to a girl? She had no worth, that was clear. Perhaps if she had been a boy . . .

The wind gusted again, a high teasing wail that mercifully drowned out her father's voice. She lowered her head, clutched the folds of her gown, and shivered. She was too stunned to retreat, too numb to hold on, like a small stone gargoyle. Unanchored, she began to sway. Oh spite! She was going to fall. Whatever had possessed her to climb to such a height?

"No!" she cried out, reaching out for the window and missing it. She plummeted to the ground, landing behind a bush with a teeth-rattling thud. Struggling for breath, the wind knocked out of her, she bit her lip to stifle a groan.

"Did you hear something?" Lord Dunnington said. "I thought I heard a cry from outside. Probably one of Thadeus's yipping hounds."

"Stand aside, my lord," Drake replied. "Let me look."

As she managed to struggle to a sitting position upon her bruised derriere, Rosalind saw Drake approach the window and gaze downward. Spying her, he grinned wickedly.

"Little devil," she mouthed to him.

"Little brat," he mouthed back.

"Do you see something, Mandrake?" Lord Dunnington said.

"Nothing, my lord. Nothing at all."

"Good, good, my boy." The earl's voice grew fainter, and Rosalind guessed that he had crossed the room. So that was that. Her father had automatically trusted Drake's assessment. Of course! He was a boy. Boys were to be trusted. Whereas a girl, well, a girl could be drowned in the river like a kitten in a sack and never be missed.

"I'll show you both!" she muttered to herself, rising with angry determination.

A quarter of an hour later a winded and fuming Rosalind reached the last sloping hill before her destination—her father's fishing pond.

"You'll see what a girl can do!" she muttered as she hiked her gown to her knees and stomped up the incline. Brambles and stiff grasses snagged her stockings and pricked her fair skin, but she felt no pain. "Just wait and see!"

At the crest at the hill overlooking the pond, Rosalind stopped abruptly and swallowed hard. She gingerly inched her way out onto the rickety pier, defiance warming her cheeks. Lord Dunnington allowed Drake to drop a fishing line there, but forbade his own daughter from doing likewise. Just because she couldn't swim! It wasn't fair, she told herself as her feet skimmed inch by inch over the rotting wood. Boys took risks and so would she.

At the sound of the gentle but insistent lapping of the water below, her stomach grew queasy. She really should learn to swim, she thought as she reached the end of the pier. Then she slowly pivoted, and seeing the house loom in her sight, she gasped.

It was so enormous! She had never seen Thornbury from this angle. No wonder Drake stood on this spot for hours at a time. The house looked like a palace, with square towers rising a storey above the main facade—a mass of veined golden stone shadowed now and then by deep bays. What splendor! As the bronze light of the setting sun glistened and winked on hundreds of panes of glass, the stones seemed to congeal before her eyes into a mass of dignity, a fortress that would withstand the vicissitudes of time and nature, politics and human vanity, sorrow and misfortune. This was more than a house; it was her destiny.

Her destiny, she vowed again, clenching her fists. Yes, she was a girl. She would one day be a mere woman. Her father bemoaned that fact. But she was still his only heir. And if her father did not remarry and have a true son of the blood, she would inherit. Then no one would doubt her worth.

She would be like Queen Elizabeth. Many were the fireside tales about King Henry VIII's disappointment at the birth of his daughter. Still, Elizabeth had survived political machinations and misfortune to claim his crown. Just like the queen, Rosalind would rule Thornbury House.

She let out a low sigh, relaxing for the first time since Drake's arrival. Her breath joined the wind that swooped low over the field that lay between her and Thornbury. The breeze was like a breath from the building itself. And she wondered if it were possible for a house to have a soul.

"What in blazes are you doing, Moppet?" Drake said.

"Jesu!" Rosalind cried out in astonishment. She pivoted around and found Drake watching her from the edge of the pond, arms crossed, weight casually poised on one leg. Where the devil had he come from?

She had no time to ask this question aloud, for once again she had lost her balance. She had a way of doing that in his blasted presence.

"By Juno!" she cried out as her arms flailed through the air and she desperately tried to right herself. A moment later she landed in the water with a loud splash.

"Moppet!" Drake cried out, using the nickname she detested so.

She saw him racing to the end of the pier, frowning with what looked like genuine alarm. Then all she saw was a greenish swirl as water filled her eyes. The weight of her gown pulled her down into the pond's murky depths.

But she did not want to die! She had finally found a reason to live, something to strive for. Frantically, she clawed at the water, somehow managing to thrust herself above the surface. As she choked and sputtered in her efforts she saw Drake treading water, just out of her reach. And he was smiling at her. Just smiling.

He was going to let her die, she realized with chilling certainty. And why wouldn't he? Then there would be nothing to keep him from getting what she was now certain he wanted.

"Help!" she cried out. "Help me, Drake. Please!"

She went down again. Then suddenly he jerked her back up for air, pulling her close and dragging her to shore through cattails and tall, wild grass. Together they collapsed on the muddy shore, Rosalind panting for air.

For a moment she was too stunned and exhausted to move. She blinked moisture from her eyes and focused on Drake's profile. Half-sprawled across her, he turned his head and their eyes locked. Drops of water glistened on his black eyelashes. Who would blink first? Not she, Rosalind silently vowed.

Oddly, as it turned out, they blinked in unison. Then Drake braced himself and drew back, sitting on his heels. "Aren't you going to thank me?" he said, his handsome little cheeks dimpling with audacious charm.

She scowled and jumped to her feet. "I should rather curse you for nearly letting me drown! What took you so long? Did you enjoy the spectacle of my terror in the face of death?"

"You weren't going to die. The water only comes to my shoulders."

She turned to the pond in dismay. Could it be so shallow? Moments ago it had seemed like an ocean.

"I wanted to teach you a lesson," he said, and stood with ease and grace.

"What lesson was that?"

"That you should learn to swim."

"I have a lesson for you as well," she announced as she brushed back the wet hair plastered to her cheeks. "You'll never be master of this house. That's what you want, isn't it?"

He swallowed, his cheeks growing thin as the shadow of destiny seemed to swoop over him.

"Say it! Or will you lie to me, too?"

His countenance changed and he looked at her with a warmth and fervor that she found disturbing. "No, Moppet. I'll never lie to you." Then his face tightened, and he looked at her with calm certainty. "Yes, I want this house. And I shall have it."

"No!" she cried, her voice hoarse. "Never!"

Tears sprang to her eyes. But he wouldn't see them. She sniffled and turned. But not before seeing him smile with glee.

"I'll see you in hell first." With that, she started away. Soon she was running, as if for her very life. And all the way home she could see him in her mind's eye, still smiling that last arrogant smile.

What had she expected? The threat of hell was no deterrent to the likes of Drake Rothwell. He was, after all, the devil's own.

One

Twenty years later

"No, Uncle, I am quite adamant. I will not marry. I've reached the age of thirty without enduring those shackles, and there is no reason to do so now."

Rosalind Carbery paced with determination in the parlor once treasured by her late father. With broad hand gestures, she spouted her well-rehearsed arguments to an empty room. She was preparing for a confrontation with the man who now mattered most in her life—Thadeus Burke, her maternal uncle, only surviving relative, and trustee of her father's estate. While Rosalind was the heiress and mistress of Thornbury House she had longed to be, she could not dispose of her inheritance without Thadeus's approval. Fortunately, the old courtier had an admitted weakness for impertinent women, and had encouraged Rosalind's precocity in this area over the years.

Rosalind paused for a breath and then turned to the parlor windows. Her beloved curious knotted garden was gently yielding to wistful autumn, its brittle, barren stalks and rust-colored leaves whirling in the chilling wind. The passing of summer only added to her sorrow, and she sighed, as she had all too often of late.

Three weeks earlier her father and his dear friend the Widow Alice, Drake's mother, had perished in a shipwreck at sea. The queen had immediately released Rosalind from her duties as a lady-in-waiting so that she could assume her new role as heiress.

The news of the tragedy had been devastating. Rosalind had truly loved Alice and had grown ever closer to her father over the years. She felt guilty that she hadn't been there to comfort them at their hour of death. But then responsibilities had loomed up. Rosalind had had to make all the funeral arrangements. In truth, she had taken over the management of the estate and her father's business as well. Charming at Court and a provider of useful political information to her father, Uncle Thadeus was otherwise inept. So, putting aside her grief, Rosalind took charge, as she had prepared herself to do all her life.

Some years before, when her father had grown weary of running Thornbury House, Rosalind had assumed his responsibilities, leaving the earl to his castle in Dunnington. The only reason she had become a lady-in-waiting was to gain knowledge about politics, and to curry favor that might be useful if Drake decided to try to buy the house out from under her nose, as he had threatened during one visit.

Six years had passed since he'd swaggered through the door with his rapier swinging at his lean hips, his black hair shiny in the beaming sun, his long, strong fingers stroking his neatly trimmed and pointy black beard, and had whispered, "I'll be back for this one day, Moppet," his breath tickling her ear. When he'd made his fortune trading spices, he explained, he would buy Thornbury House, to "relieve" the old earl of the burden.

Turning from the window, Rosalind moved to the blazing hearth and held out her hands, listening a moment to the sound of music tinkling in the air. Francesca, the Viscountess Halsbury, was playing the virginals in a nearby chamber. Francesca had grown up at the great house next door. She'd played with Drake and Rosalind until her father had died and she had become a ward of the crown. Rosalind hadn't seen Frannie for years and was pleased when she'd returned for the earl's funeral. Rosalind had also been pleased by Drake's absence. He was somewhere on the high seas and it had been impossible to contact him in time for the funeral.

She fidgeted with an emerald ring on her middle finger, suddenly unnerved. Why was it that the mere thought of Drake still struck fear and anger in her heart? She was the one who had inherited Thornbury House. It would be months before word of his mother's death reached Drake. And months more before he could return. By then she would be thoroughly entrenched in her role as mistress of the house.

The door opened and Rosalind turned, smiling at the sight of Thadeus and Francesca. The raven-haired, violet-eyed viscountess crossed the long room and kissed her cheek.

"What is it, Rosalind? I can hardly wait. You said we should come at four, and not a moment before."

"Please have a seat." Rosalind indicated two chairs placed near the fireplace.

Thadeus bowed and kissed her hand. "My girl, you look enchanting as always."

"Good," Rosalind purred. "I hope you still think so when I'm done." She paused as they sat down. "I'll get straight to the point, Uncle. I've decided not to marry."

"What? Why not?" Thadeus's gray brows gathered in a disapproving frown.

"I see no reason to. It will gain me little and perhaps

jeopardize what I cherish most—possession of this home.
I am well past the age of my majority. The crown can't
claim my wardship. And I would only have to share authority with a husband. Why would I want to do that?''

"Why?" Thadeus answered indignantly, tapping his
cane on the floor for emphasis. "Because a woman can't
run an estate this size!"

"Is that so?" Rosalind's eyes flashed. "It seems to me
Queen Elizabeth is running an entire nation without the
help—or hindrance—of a spouse."

The sixty-year-old courtier raised a finger to argue, then
wilted in defeat. His eyes gleamed with confusion beneath
his gray hair, which was plastered over his forehead like
a bust of Julius Caesar.

"Please, Thadeus," Rosalind said with a cajoling smile,
"accept the inevitable. I will never wed."

Thadeus nervously tugged at the ruffled collar of his
garishly bejeweled doublet and twitched his broom-edge
mustache. "Here now, Francesca, talk some sense into
your friend."

"Never is a long time," Francesca gently offered.

"I know that." Rosalind reached for the viscountess's
hands and knelt before her, searching her amethyst eyes
for signs of their old intimacy. "But I could never marry,
dear heart. Don't you know that? I'd throw a sharp and
weighty object in a fit of temper. My groom would be dead
before the sun rose the day after our wedding."

Francesca tossed back her head and laughed, a throaty
sound that hinted at something raucous hidden beneath the
veneer of her delicate nobility. Rosalind joined in. Soon
both were weeping from merriment.

"You very nearly did kill Drake a few times," Francesca said as she dabbed at her eyes with a kerchief, then
started giggling anew.

Rosalind sighed. "Yes, and I failed." She rose and

smoothed the silken pleats of her gown. "But let us get back to the subject of marriage and put it to rest once and for all. It's a subject with which you are well acquainted, Frannie."

"Overmuch, I fear," Francesca admitted ruefully, her opinions cut short as Huthbert, Rosalind's gentleman usher, entered with a tray of muscatel. While the bald and precise man poured three goblets full, Rosalind pondered Francesca's matrimonial history.

At the age of thirty-three, Francesca had already been a widow for five years. That happy state had followed fourteen years of marriage to the Viscount Halsbury, a man fifty years her senior. To the best of Rosalind's knowledge, it was a match made by a greedy and reckless guardian and permitted by the cruel laws of wardship.

If a girl or boy who hadn't yet come of age lost a father, that child became a ward of the crown. A mother, unless she had enough money to buy her child's wardship, was without rights. The child was taken from her and essentially sold to the richest guardian, who then took the child into his home until a suitable marriage could be arranged, usually at great profit to the guardian.

Francesca had never complained about the ancient husband this cruel and unfair system had thrust upon her. But Rosalind was aware of the scars, as if they were lined upon her perfect face.

"You know, Frannie, I'm thinking about writing a play that will expose the barbarity of the wardship system."

Francesca graciously accepted a goblet from Huthbert and took a sip. "I didn't know you were still writing."

Thadeus harrumphed. "I've tried to tell her that women have never written plays."

"Until now," Rosalind added pointedly.

"Will that be all for now, Lady Rosalind?" the gentleman usher asked.

"Yes, thank you."

When Huthbert closed the door behind him, Francesca eyed her hostess speculatively. "I won't bore you with details of my woeful history, Rosalind. Tell me about yours. We've been apart too long. Why *haven't* you married in all these years?"

"It was not for lack of trying. Father first had me betrothed at the age of eleven. Do you remember, Frannie?"

"Yes, poor little Bartholomew, the Earl of Blaine's son. He died from a fever shortly after the betrothal ceremony."

"Then there was Sir Simon Vane's oldest boy," Thadeus offered. Remembering the child's awful demise, he winced. "Got tangled up in his stirrups during a hunt at Burghley."

Rosalind grimaced. "Poor little William. He was a promising match. Then came Roger Eaton. He would have been the next Earl of Luddington had it not been for that nasty duel."

"Ah, yes," Thadeus recalled. "Roger was a devoted suitor, handsome and adept with a rapier. But he took Rosalind's flirtations too seriously and ended up challenging an older man to a duel. A lamentable end, indeed."

"Poor Roger." Rosalind sighed again.

"And then there was Sir Henry Hall," Thadeus continued. "He was killed at sea."

"And the Earl of Oxborough," Francesca mused. "You wrote to me about that one, Roz. He was very rich."

"And very unlucky," Thadeus said. "He walked in front of a carriage at the most inopportune time. Oxborough was followed by—"

"Please, Uncle." Rosalind turned pleading eyes his way. "Must we go through every death in laborious detail?"

"That's nearly all of them. Seven in all."

"Seven betrothals. Seven deaths," Rosalind whispered. She had never wanted to marry, and sometimes it seemed to her that her suitors' deaths were a sign that she shouldn't. Still, it was an embarrassing record, and one that made her feel guilty. "I can't blame my father for trying so hard. He didn't want my wardship to pass to the crown in the event of his demise—a fate you suffered, Frannie. Alas, if he only knew where his good-hearted efforts would lead. No wonder no one will come near me now." She blew out a stream of air. "Perhaps some good has come of it. No one will want to marry me as long as they believe I'm cursed."

"Unless the queen decides you should marry," Thadeus noted ominously.

"The queen?" Rosalind turned to him, dumbfounded. "But surely she will not want that. After all, she threw Sir Walter Raleigh into the Tower for daring to marry one of her ladies-in-waiting."

"Yes, even in far-flung Yorkshire I've heard tales of Elizabeth's desire for every woman in her service to be as lonely as she," Francesca said.

"Indeed." Thadeus pulled out a pouch of tobacco and filled a pipe. "Though I cannot fathom why. The virgin queen could have used a good tupping long ago. The fruit of her womb is no longer a plum, but a prune, and who would have her now in her dotage is beyond my reckoning."

Rosalind choked on a swallow of wine and cleared her burning throat. "Uncle, you shouldn't be so disrespectful."

"Disrespectful? You call *me* disrespectful?" When the tiny red veins in his white cheeks darkened, Rosalind knew a lecture was about to be delivered.

"Why, I respect the queen as if she were a saint here on earth," he began, with unintentionally comic grandiloquence. "I have adored her longer than Raleigh and Leicester and Burghley put together. I was there when—"

" 'When she was locked in the Tower under Bloody Mary's reign.' " Rosalind mocked the oft-quoted sentence with her hands on her hips and a theatrical scowl on her face. " 'Why I was there when the queen was crowned! When the entire nation fell in love with Gloriana, the Virgin Queen!' "

Francesca stifled a giggle and Thadeus looked back and forth between them, his eyes narrowing threateningly. "Do you jest at my expense, young ladies? Why, I'll paddle your bums. Both of you." He shrugged against the weight of his doublet, sniffed, then plucked a burning twig from the fire and lit his pipe. As the tobacco crackled softly and began to glow, he continued.

"You believe I jest? I know better where Elizabeth is concerned. Think, Rosalind, think about the queen in all matters. You are too close to her to do anything unnoticed. Has she said anything, anything at all to you about your future?"

Rosalind stilled. She slowly inhaled a whiff of Thadeus's smoke; heard the snap of a log in the fire; felt the trickle of perspiration between her breasts as, suddenly, she remembered.

"Oh, dear Jupiter!" she cried out. "Yes, she did say something." She narrowed her gaze on her uncle, stunned anew by his knowledge of the queen and her Court. "How did you know? Who told you?"

"What is it, Rosalind?" Francesca rushed to her side in a rustle of silk.

"Shortly before I left Court, right after I learned of Father's death, I heard the queen talking with someone outside my chamber. I thought it was an idle conversation, but it was more than that, I realize now."

"What? What did she say?"

"She said the mistress of any prodigy house needs a husband at her side. At the time I thought the queen had lost her senses, for she has ruled a country without the aid of a man and has beaten a lady-in-waiting or two for secretly marrying."

"Would you want to marry if your father had divorced or beheaded a goodly number of his six wives, as Elizabeth's did?" Francesca queried.

"Of course not." Rosalind began to pace anxiously, running a hand through the sea-foam tangle of her red hair. "That's why the comment made no sense. I see now she was planting a notion she wanted me to overhear. It was the queen's way of telling me what she wanted me to do. But I won't." She stamped a foot. "Do you hear me? I won't marry. I've spent my whole life preparing to run this house. I cannot simply hand it over on a salver to someone else."

"You'd defy Gloriana, our great queen!" Thadeus bellowed.

"I will not marry!" Rosalind bellowed back, not unlike the very vocal queen she'd served so many years.

"There has to be some way to get what you want without offending the queen," Francesca said decisively, ever the diplomat. "She could compel you to do her bidding if she's of a mind. After all, Raleigh broke no law; he was legally married when the queen imprisoned him and his wife. She could do the same to you, Rosalind, if she, in all her contrariness, decided that you *should* marry."

"It's true, Rosalind." Thadeus leaned toward the fire and relit his pipe. Smoke plumed in his eyes and he squinted. "The old queen is moody these days."

"If the queen can force you to marry," Francesca continued, "then perhaps your only choice is to choose a husband before she can do it for you."

"You're right, Frannie."

Francesca's jaw dropped in astonishment at Rosalind's uncharacteristic pliability. "I am?"

"Yes, I must choose. But not a husband. Merely a suitor." She glanced at Thadeus. He was nervously twisting the carved lion head on top of his cane.

"Now go slowly, puss. I merely wanted to remind you of your duty to the queen."

"Slow doesn't win the race, Uncle Thadeus."

"I can see that brilliant mind of yours working," Francesca said, a worried frown on her forehead.

"Frannie, if the queen thinks I am serious about marrying, she will give me time to find my heart's desire. I can manage to delay the actual marriage for months, even years!"

"But she will know it is a farce." Thadeus tugged at one end of his gray mustache. Then he added, for Francesca's benefit, "Rosalind's misadventures with Cupid are legend at Court."

"But surely there is some suitor who might believably seek your hand," Frannie argued.

Rosalind rolled her eyes. "Yes, a scurvy knave, a cutpurse, an untutored churl who needs my money more than I need his. No man of equal rank will risk the curse if he already has money."

"So that leaves no one but an opportunist," Thadeus concluded.

"Or . . . an old man," Rosalind was thinking aloud. "Someone who is already resigned to his own mortality. Yes, that's it! Why didn't it occur to me sooner?"

The doors opened and Rosalind caught sight of Huthbert's shiny pate. "Perfect timing. Go fetch some mad dog. We need something stronger to celebrate my happy future."

"Yes, my lady," the usher mumbled as he bowed and departed.

"A happy future? Married to an old man?" Francesca was aghast at the very idea. "You will never be happy then. You may learn to accept your fate, but you will never know joy."

"Oh, come, Francesca." Thadeus rolled his eyes. "Do not try to dissuade my headstrong niece. If she thinks she will enjoy bedding an old cock whose comb has fallen about his ears, then let her have her way."

Rosalind flushed, but would not let him see it. Instead, she pretended to study the emerald ring that glimmered on her right hand. "You can't talk me out of this, Thadeus, so don't even try. Besides, I have no intention of marrying anyone. I'll simply go through the motions of courtship."

"You know, it's not a bad idea." Francesca drummed her fingers together. "It has possibilities, but not with an old man."

"Come, come, Francesca," Thadeus singsonged. "Rosalind will enjoy a dotty fiancé. Just imagine how impassioned she will be by his sagging flesh and his shrunken little nib."

"Really, Uncle, you're being cruel and vulgar."

"He's not far off the mark," Francesca warned her, speaking from experience. "If you must contrive a match that's unlikely to work, why don't you consider a foreigner? They are despised here in England. He would become frustrated and eventually lose interest."

"A foreigner!" Rosalind rewarded her with a beaming smile. "Now you're thinking. I'll seek the courtship of an old man who hails from a foreign country."

Thadeus began to chuckle. "I've been had, haven't I? I might as well give up now."

"Indeed you'd best," Rosalind said triumphantly. "Now, can we close the subject?" She gazed with satisfaction out the window at her beloved garden. That morning she had spent one precious hour of solitude there, writing a sonnet to the fading flowers.

"I shall have a suitor," she vowed, tapping her lips with her ink-stained fingers. "I shall plan the courtship as I would the acts of a play. The lines will be written with care, the scenes well chosen, and the ending happy." She turned to her companions with an assured smile. "Let the play begin."

$\mathcal{T}wo$

Off the coast of Quedah, five months later

"Drake," said Captain James Hillard, "you have a messenger in your cabin from one of Levy's ships."

Drake stood rigidly at the starboard side of his flagship, *La Rose*, anchored along with two of his other galleons near the island of Buto. He gripped the rail in frustration as the vessel rocked back and forth, his gaze never wavering from the barrels full of precious pepper onshore.

"Drake . . ." Hillard repeated.

"Yes, I heard you," he snapped. "I have a messenger in my quarters. You'll forgive me if I'm distracted. You see, I'm contemplating the damnedest irony I've ever encountered. Sitting before me on the shores of Buto is enough pepper to corner the market in London and make me a rich man." Drake waved an arm impatiently toward the shore. "Unfortunately, I haven't a farthing left to buy the blasted condiment from these natives. That's a humorous turn of events, wouldn't you say, Hillard?"

His words ended in a roar of sarcasm, but it was scarcely

noticed by anyone but Captain Hillard. There was too much noise swelling onshore—the strange garbled words of the natives; the shouts of the fishermen hauling nets from the water; the drunken laughter of sailors who were anxious to end this two-year expedition and return to England, preferably the richer.

"I have faith, sir, you'll find a way to get this pepper home," said Captain Hillard.

Drake snorted in derision and glared at the lanky gray-bearded seaman. "If you have any faith at all, you have more than I, Hillard."

Drake was not a man quick to despair. After earning his sealegs as an apprentice, then a boatswain and pilot to the Turkey Company—now known as the Levant Company—he soon struck out on his own, commanding his own ship and succeeding as a privateer. After acquitting himself honorably in sea battles against the Spanish Armada, he had set his sights higher and decided to forge new trading routes, as his mentor and idol, Sir Francis Drake, had done. Doing this had required raising funds through an investor, an old friend of Lord Dunnington's.

Everyone told him it could not be done without a syndicate to finance the long years at sea, but Master Mandrake Rothwell had refused to be daunted. He wanted to show the world that the Rothwells were a family to be reckoned with.

And so, starting with one ship, he had built up a fleet of six. He had pirated more than a few Spanish carracks to restock his stores along the way. He had opened up new marketplaces that the Levant Company occasionally slipped into in his wake, profiting from the relationships Drake had forged with native kings and tribal leaders.

Recently, however, he had learned that a new company was forming, one that would usurp his territories as the Levant Company could never do. It was called the Com-

pany of Merchants of London Trading into the East Indies—or the East India Company, as his sailors were
already refering to it. Its investors, more than two hundred
in all, currently seeking a charter from the queen, had the
financing to threaten everything Drake worked so hard to
achieve. They could benefit from his explorations before
he had a chance to do so himself, scooping up the pepper,
nutmeg, and other spices that Drake was finally ready to
cash in on but was sadly unable to purchase.

And that was the source of his present despair. Several
months before, in Acheen, an admiral commandeering a
Levant Company ship that happened to be one of the
queen's personal vessels, had mistaken Drake's effort at
diplomacy with the natives as an act of piracy against a
British ship. Admiral Anthony Peele had proceeded to
open fire on Drake's fleet, sinking three of his ships. As it
happened, two of them were the ones carrying the gold
and silver and trinkets Drake planned to use to buy the
condiment that was sure to fetch such a high price in pep-
per-starved London.

His intention had been to return to England after this stop
at Buto, and he had even sent word to that effect. But he
could not return with empty ships. Somehow he had to raise
the money to buy more ships before the East India company
slipped into Buto, and, in addition, he had to transport the
pepper back to London before Admiral Peele was able to report Drake's so-called raid on the queen's ship.

These two horns of his dilemma foremost in his mind,
Drake turned to Captain Hillard, raking his gaze from the
dock where tons of pepper sat waiting. "What the hell am
I going to do?" he gritted his teeth, then shook his head,
the large hoop earring in his left ear dangling in his shoulder-length hair as he did so. He wiped a broad hand over
his sun-beaten face and inhaled the salt air whirling around
him.

"Well, sir, I suggest you hear what the messenger has to say. Mayhap he brings good news."

Drake gave his loyal captain a wry smile. "Pray God he brings a miracle," he said, and turned toward his quarters. Hillard followed in his wake.

A bowlegged seaman rose, nervously twisting a parchment in his hands, as Drake entered. "Captain Rothwell?"

"Yes, what is it?" Drake sat at his desk and kicked his heels up onto it.

"A message from Lady Rosalind Carbery of London."

Rosalind. Drake sobered instantly. He swung his legs down and sat up. "Lady Rosalind? She'd follow me to the gates of hell if she could, just to torment me. Well, what is it?"

The seaman handed over the parchment. Drake stood, rapidly scanned the words, then took a deep breath.

"What does it say?" Captain Hillard asked as he poured three cups of native spirits and handed one to Drake, who sipped it, grimacing as it burned down his throat.

"It's a message telling me that my mother is dead."

There was an awkward pause, punctuated only by the lapping of the water against the boat.

"I'm sorry," Captain Hillard said. "So we'll be going back to England after all?"

Drake noticed that the missive contained not one page, but two. He crumbled the first, Rosalind's note. "No, it's too late to do any good. My mother was buried five months ago. I heard about it from Captain Goodall. Even then it was too late to return. Though this missive reminds me of my loss, it comes as no surprise."

Drake swallowed the lump that was still wont to form in his throat whenever he thought about the shipwreck. He didn't mind admitting he had shed more than his share of tears over the deaths of his mother and the beloved Earl of Dunnington.

"I didn't know," Hillard said. "Damned rotten luck. Sorry, sir."

Drake held up a hand of acknowledgment as he scanned the second document, which bore Thadeus's signature.

"Good God, and by all that's holy!" he whispered in astonishment when he finished reading.

"What is it, sir?"

"I cannot fathom this." Drake's heart began to slam against his chest like waves against his flagship in a tempest. "I never expected this."

"More bad news, sir?"

Drake's handsome visage, schooled to impassivity by a life at sea, began to melt as the meaning of Thadeus's message sank into his brain.

"I've changed my mind, Captain. We *are* going home after all."

Hillard's eyes lit up. "When?"

"Within the hour."

"Within the *hour,* sir? Half of our men are on land, drunk and unconscious. They won't be sober for days."

"Then we'll take the flagship and leave the others to follow. Keep one ship here, loaded with cannons, to guard the pepper. There's been a change of plans, a most unexpected event. I'll be coming back for it."

Sniffing intrigue, Hillard eagerly asked, "You're coming back, sir?"

"With a boatful of gold."

"Gold? But where will you get it?"

Drake smiled broadly, his white teeth flashing against his deeply burnished skin, but his eyes veiled, secretive. "I'll explain everything in due time, Captain. For now, we must move quickly. It may require as long as five months to reach England."

"Yes, sir," Hillard replied, and with a distinct air of

confusion, he nodded his head respectfully and left Drake's quarters with the messenger.

Drake waited until the captain closed the door, then let out a whoop of joy. When he thought of the consternation his return would cause Rosalind, he threw back his head and laughed long and deep.

Five months later

Rosalind had managed to stave off the issue of marriage for nearly a year after the death of her father, deftly using her obvious mourning to deflect queries about her future.

She had been living an active life within the confines of Thornbury House—gardening, and entertaining a few close friends with private performances by Master Shakespeare's troupe, the Lord Chamberlain's Men. And she had continued her own writing, in secret of course, and had completed three plays. None of them was any good, but she had started a fourth that showed great promise.

But after a year she sensed the time to act on her courtship plan had arrived. She asked Francesca to pick a foreign suitor from among her late husband's acquaintances, and then began making preparations to stage a spectacular masque.

It was a night on which she would stake her entire future. She had one evening in which to change the way people viewed her. She could no longer be thought of as the lady-in-waiting who stood in the queen's shadow. She had to be perceived of as a woman of singular purpose, a personage to reckon with. It would take a good deal of acting, a bit of scandal, and a delicious feast.

So, on an early afternoon in late summer, dressed in an elaborate green petticoat and a low-cut bodice, Rosalind watched nervously from the parlor window as nobles, courtiers, and London's richest merchants began to arrive for the spectacular event. Carriages rolled down the drive one after another, pulled by horses that snorted and tossed their manes in the fine summer breeze. The procession lasted nearly an hour.

The highlights of the party would be a feast in the old great hall and a fireworks display on the terrace. Meanwhile, there was plenty of entertainment to fill the intervening hours.

After being greeted by the hostess, some guests mounted up and rode to the deer park to hunt. The less robust betook themselves to the bowling alley in the west wing. Still others strolled through the garden, dallying amid the flowers while musicians strummed their lutes. Those who wished to remain indoors watched some young players from the Globe performing scenes in the middle of the long gallery. Others merely chatted, laughed, and drank.

An enormous high-ceilinged room that ran the length of the house on the second floor, lined from end to end with tall windows, the gallery was more spacious and sunnier than the great hall. In the winter, Rosalind walked its length for exercise and sunshine.

It was there that the female guests inevitably gathered, the most powerful of the women each staking out a corner, where others would come to seek their approval, earn their friendship or favor, or enjoy the latest Court gossip. And it was there that Rosalind dispatched Francesca, to listen to what was being said about her.

Francesca made an excellent spy. She had been so long in Yorkshire that few at Court recognized her, though she remembered some from the Court of Wards and from seeing them at masques her late father had staged.

Francesca wandered the length of the gallery and overheard her first conversation in the southwest corner, where Lady Willowby was popping kissing comfits between her red-slashed lips, as if the shriveled old dame were contemplating an assignation scheduled later that night.

"I hear that Lady Rosalind spied on the Puritans a few years back," Lady Willowby croaked to a cluster of white-faced ladies batting their fans. "She sneaked out in disguise, traveling through London alone, just to overhear the conversations of Do-Good Simplicity."

"Do-Good Simplicity?" said a waiflike young lady whom Francesca did not recognize. "You mean that Puritan who wants the queen to burn all Catholics and ban the theatres?"

"The very one." Lady Willowby sniffed. "Apparently the Rose of Thornbury House has taken it upon herself to ensure the Lord Chamberlain's Men survive plague and Puritan protests."

"How shocking!" another woman commented. "Next we hear she'll be traipsing through St. Paul's along with the cutpurses."

Francesca stifled a laugh and walked away with a satisfied grin. Rosalind would be delighted. Thankfully, rumors were more enduring than love. Perhaps Rosalind would not have such a difficult time after all convincing others that she was a woman who did not blink at scandal.

Moving on to the southeast corner of the gallery, Francesca noticed Lady Goosenby, who had connections with the Court of Wards, entertaining a group of younger women. This group of ladies was considerably less attentive than the first, each glancing occasionally over her shoulder to keep an eye on possible suitors, like hungry cats in an alley rife with unsuspecting rats. Quickly she hid behind some curtains. Lady Goosenby might recognize her, and perhaps self-consciously still her viperous tongue.

"Lady Rosalind is expected to perform in her own masque this afternoon in an outfit that will embarrass even the most notorious bawd," Lady Goosenby announced, her voice rich with disapproval.

"Perform in her own masque?" replied a young girl whose obvious penchant for sugar had left her with a black-toothed smile. "The Queen of Scotland performs in her own masques, I hear."

"Yes," Lady Goosenby replied. "But not in costumes that invite a good tupping. You mustn't miss it. You know, Rosalind has a particular interest in the theatre. I hear that Master Shakespeare has even asked his troupe to allow her to perform with them."

"No!" replied an older dame who could rest a chalice of muscatel on the plane of her bosom if she so desired. "A woman on the stage? How scandalous!"

"Yes," Lady Goosenby replied, "before we know it, she'll be loitering with players and other disreputable characters. It's a scandal what she's done to her father's good name, God rest his soul. He should never have left his fortune to a woman."

The gossip in the northeast corner was more mundane. The ladies there apparently hadn't anything new to discuss, and so they rehashed old tales.

"Lady Rosalind will never marry," said Lady Darborough. "She's cursed. She's killed seven men and boys. I knew them all. No matter how rich she is, she'll never find anyone willing to risk marriage. What good is a pot of gold if it sits upon your grave?"

The ladies who flattered the viscountess with their attention laughed appropriately.

That was Francesca's cue to move onward. The viscountess was a dreadful bore, incapable of starting the sort of infamous gossip that Rosalind was hoping for. Francesca eagerly looked to the northwest corner. Ah, yes. Lady Blunt would not disappoint.

The fifty-five-year-old widow of a prominent and distinguished knight, Lady Blunt wielded words as if they were weapons, though her verbal thrusts were not without a cer-

tain tarnished charm. While she herself was known not to
be a favorite of the queen, those who were so favored
considered her an indispensable gossip and purveyor of
bad news. Always stuffed into grossly ornate bodices and
farthingales like a sausage in a skin, she wore a hideous
black gregorian wig that she was rumored to have donned
in defeat after all her hair fell out during an attempt to dye
it red like the queen's. The blackness of her false hair
contrasted frighteningly with the white lead paint she reg-
ularly slathered on her face.

"The question remains," Lady Blunt said, continuing
what was obviously a lengthy monologue, "will the queen
bring pressure to bear and force Lady Rosalind to take a
husband?" The shrewd Court gossipmonger let the query
dangle in the air while she stroked the head of the Maltese
lapdog panting in her arms. "Eh, what do you say, Cockles?" she said in a baby voice to her pooch.

"If the queen forces one of her ladies-in-waiting to
marry, it will be a first," a tall, elegant woman ventured
to say.

"Is that so, Lady Ashenby?" Lady Blunt cried with
mock ignorance. "Whatever do you mean?"

"Remember Sir Walter Raleigh. His wife, poor Bess
Throckmorton, went to the Tower for leaving the queen's
service to marry without Her Majesty's permission."

"Indeed, but poor Bess was ripe with Raleigh's child
while still in the queen's service and before any wedding
vows ever passed her lips," Lady Blunt countered with a
triumphant gleam in her eyes. "Rosalind has been released
by the queen, and she is a powerful heiress in her own
right. I have heard the queen is eager to see this particular
heiress marry, for some odd reason. . . ."

Again, she let the notion dangle in the air, already fetid
with heavy perfume.

"Well, the heiress is squandering her inheritance," said

another. "I hear she's given the Lord Chamberlain's Men thousands of pounds."

"Thousands of pounds?" Lady Blunt pounced on this news like a vulture on fresh carrion.

"To make up for the money the players lost during the plague years. They could not play in London for the entire season a couple of years ago. And there is the expense of building the Globe."

Lady Blunt drummed her fingers on the stiff front of her bodice. "She is terribly predisposed to Master Shakespeare. I do wonder why. She's become eccentric, I hear. Perhaps her father's death sent her into a slough of melancholy. In any event, she's still an heiress with one of the finest houses in England. I believe I agree with the queen. The girl should marry."

"She's not a girl, she's a woman," the coolheaded Lady Ashenby corrected. "Besides, have you forgotten? There's the curse to consider."

"Pish!" Lady Blunt waved dismissively. "A smart man won't worry about a silly curse. I have a notion as to whom she should marry. Curse or no."

Rosalind struggled to pin two bunches of grapes to the highest points of her bodice, or, to put it bluntly, as she did in her own mind, she was trying to pin them to her breasts. The edge of the bodice, lined in pearls, barely covered her nipples. Her red hair was swept up under an elaborate headpiece, an ornate swirl of ribbons and buckram whose focal point was two carved and copulating cherubs.

The scandalously bawdy costume was a departure from her usual attire. As a lady of the privy chamber, she had always worn discreet gowns so as not to draw attention away from the exquisitely dressed queen. Now all eyes would be focused on her, and her hands trembled at the thought, which made pinning the grapes to her breasts a precarious operation indeed.

"Ouch!" she cried when a pin pricked a finger.

"Do you need help?" Francesca said as she ascended the last stair to the balcony, which overlooked the gallery. When she got her first good glimpse of the costume, her violet eyes glittered with delight. "Oh, Rosalind, you look . . . stunning."

"How diplomatic of you to say so. Thank Jove you've arrived, Frannie. I'm beginning to get nervous, and my costume isn't finished. How are the guests?"

"They're all atwitter over your latest scandal."

"Good!"

"I must say, spying on the Puritans was a stroke of genius. You'll have to tell me all about it sometime soon."

"Oh, that." Rosalind shrugged. "That was nothing I wouldn't do for any dear friend."

"No one can believe you had the audacity to venture out into the city in disguise."

"I didn't want to see Will's theatre troupe flounder. It was when they had temporarily lost their patronage at Court."

"You know, I'm beginning to think you *are* an eccentric," Francesca said admiringly. "There's nothing you won't do, is there?"

"If a man can spy, so can I."

"Perhaps you don't need to confound people with to-night's masque. You're already eccentric enough."

"No, I'm in too far now to go back. Everyone is expecting something tremendous. You will love me no matter how it turns out, won't you?"

"Of course." Francesca gave her a warm hug. "After seeing you in this absurd costume, I love you more than ever. Now let me have a good look. Turn around."

Rosalind obliged. She held out her arms, exposing the

bunches of grapes pinned to her breasts and a fig leaf fastened to a provocative point on her petticoat. Because of the hooped underskirts that composed her farthingale, the leaf was nowhere near her thighs, but its placement adequately indicated her intent. She had strawberries fixed in her hair beneath her headpiece. As she twirled around she revealed more of the walking cornucopia that she was.

There were two buns of bread fastened to her dress at the derriere, just over the bulge of her farthingale, which enabled her to sit without squashing them. And the back of her low-cut collar was lined with figs. It didn't take much imagination to grasp the meaning of those. By the time Rosalind had spun back in place, Francesca was laughing uproariously.

"Oh, my dear friend, you are bawdier than a jester in the pit of any London theatre."

"Is it too much? I'm supposed to be portraying the Goddess of the Harvest."

Francesca slipped her hands into her friend's. "Then you fit the part most meetly. Don't forget, Rosalind, you want to shock people. Let no one doubt that you will be the mistress of your own fate, and no one can shame you into submission."

"Let them try," Rosalind said with a puckish grin, and joyfully pecked her friend's cheek. "Thank you for your steadfastness. I knew there was a reason why you're my very best friend, Frannie."

"Let us hope I've added one more reason to the list. A certain Seigneur de Monteil has just arrived. I told him you were *very* interested in getting to know him better."

"Seigneur de Monteil. Is he . . . ?"

"Very old," Francesca reported matter-of-factly.

Rosalind's hesitation was of but a moment's duration. "Good. He's old and a foreigner. He'll be the perfect suitor. I'll meet him in the garden after the masque."

"Secret garden meetings?" someone said from behind. "What plots are you vixens devising now?"

At the sound of the lively, well-enunciated male voice, both ladies turned.

"Will Shakespeare!" Rosalind rushed to him and pressed her cheek to his. "I'm so glad you came."

The auburn-bearded gentleman in his fine black doublet crossed his arms, looked her up and down, then grinned. "You remind me that I haven't eaten since I left Stratford."

"Master Shakespeare, are you making an improper reference to your hostess's fruitful attire?" Francesca said playfully.

Shakespeare took her hand and kissed it gallantly. "Lady Halsbury, I would not be so impertinent. Rosalind is one of my theatre's most gracious patrons." He cast her a dubious glare. "However, I must admit, dear Rose, you surprise even me, the master of bawd."

Rosalind's resolve began to wilt. "Is it too much?"

"For the Goddess of the Harvest?" he replied. "Not in the least. Come along. I can see you need a breath of fresh air. It will be some time before the players have finished their scenes and the masque begins. Let us walk in the garden. Perhaps we can find something that will suffice as a sheaf of grain. You may need use of a fan to cool the ardor you are sure to arouse, dear goddess."

"Ardor . . ." Rosalind repeated weakly as Shakespeare led her down a back stairway that led to the terrace.

Three

Rosalind and Shakespeare strolled slowly along the stone terrace that bordered the length of the house, gazing down at the twenty-acre garden. The geometric patterns of the flower and herb beds were best seen from this height, as were the fountains and maze of shrubs, the trellises, and the neo-Roman belvedere at the far end.

The sweet scent of larkspurs, carnations, and love-in-idleness mingled with the potent aroma of marjoram, myrtle, and rosemary. Beyond the garden an orchard of apple trees was filled with ripening fruit. And encompassing it all was a vast forested deer park, where animals roamed and grazed freely, until a hunter's arrow pierced their hides.

"You have inherited one of the most beautiful estates in all of England," Shakespeare said, his keen eyes taking in all the beauty before him.

"You will have to write about it in your next play. What are you working on now?"

"It is a secret." Shakespeare's thoughtful, large-lidded

eyes crinkled at the edges. A soft breeze tugged at his shoulder-length hair, exposing the small gold ring in his left ear. He was only a few years older than Rosalind. A handsome man, but more than that, a gentle wit and a good friend.

"I thrill to even ponder what brilliant play you may next produce in your theatre."

"Dear Rosalind, my work is not so profound. I write only to bring in our audiences, you know that. If my plays sell enough penny seats, then I get a fat share of the receipts at the end of the performance. I am a mercenary at heart."

"No, you are a poet. Witness your sonnets. Your odes to your dark lady," Rosalind said delicately, wishing as she always had that he would speak of the woman who had inspired passionate volumes.

Was she a dark-skinned beauty? An exotic lover? Or a dark-haired widow who had first shown him love? Was she an apparition? Or was she a he? What went on in the mind of someone so brilliant, and so humble? But she said nothing. She knew the limits of their friendship. Shakespeare was always discreet. He rarely spoke of his wife in Stratford, of whom he saw little. Nor did he elaborate on the tragic loss of his son, Hamnet, who had died four years earlier at the age of eleven. To speak of things so intimate, she had concluded, was not only too familiar, the very act of speaking might sap him of the inspiration that made him so brilliant.

"I am simply a player who writes to support my troupe," he said as he affectionately patted her hand, which was crooked over his arm. His hint of irony led her to smile.

"I doubt that, sir," she said philosophically.

"Do you really? Perhaps, then, I am a purveyor of theatrical filth that corrupts the good people of England."

"Now you're sounding as hollow as the Puritans."

He chuckled. "I need not fear them anymore. Our new patron is highly placed at Court." Then more seriously: "But even if there were danger, I know I could trust the Rose of Thornbury to find out about it." He beamed at her, and she blushed with pride. "You're an amazing woman, Lady Rosalind."

She heard the tittering of two young ladies who strolled by on the terrace, arm in arm. They were pointing at her costume, but Rosalind refused to shrink away in embarrassment.

"I'd like to repay you for your spying one day." Shakespeare grinned naughtily at the word *spy,* as he always did. He loved to ascribe the worst titles to her, for she was known at Court as a lady of unimpeachable morals, if a little dreamy. "If there is anything I can do for you . . ."

Rosalind studied his sincere face, the glint of earnestness in his wise and observant eyes. She sensed the depth of his gratitude. But was he grateful enough to grant her dearest wish?

"What I want I'm sure no one can give me."

"What? What is it?"

She turned to him and swallowed the fear that would strangle her. She wanted so much more than anyone would guess. She wanted something that women, even most men, could not dream of possessing. She wanted pleasures so ethereal that she feared to express them.

"What, my Rose? Tell me."

"I want to see my own words coming out of the mouths of players."

He simply stared at her, a flicker of pity in his eyes.

She rushed on, defending herself. "I want to be a writer of plays, Will. Just like you. I can do it. I know I can. I've been writing for years."

He tilted his head and smiled with melancholy. "My

dear friend, you have a poet's heart imprisoned in the body of a woman."

"But that does not mean I cannot write."

"No, but it does mean even Burbage, the star of our troupe, would have a hell of a time selling penny seats using a playbill with your name printed on it."

"I don't care about selling seats." She clutched both his arms. When he gently grasped hers in kind, she saw the ink stain on his fingers and looked up with a loving smile. "I want to give life to my words, just as you do. That is all."

"That is much to ask when I have boys playing the parts of women."

"I don't want to perform. I don't want applause. I want to create." She withdrew her hands and clasped them together, as if beseeching God to help her convince him. "I want to create something greater than myself. Something lasting. Francesca says that most women define themselves by the men they marry. As a maid, I won't have that. So I must give myself over to something else. There is magic in words, Will." She caught herself and her lips curled into a self-deprecating smile. "Here I am lecturing the master. Forgive me. I must sound like a pompous apprentice."

"I pity you, Rosalind. You have been captured by the Muse. Seeing your plight, how can I turn you away? Let me see your writing, and if your plays are any good, I will have some of the Lord Chamberlain's Men act out a few scenes."

Her heart nearly stopped in her chest. The scent of carnations and larkspur seemed to die on the breeze. Or had she merely stopped breathing?

"Do you mean it, Will?"

"For a small, private audience, mind you."

"Of course."

"But I warn you, it's a fruitless venture. I would starve if I could no longer act and had to depend solely on my writing. And we cannot divulge your identity."

"No, no, I wouldn't expect that. I don't need to be paid. It would be enough to hear my words, to see the audience's reaction, to move someone to tears, and then to make them laugh. . . ." Her mind reeling with the possibilities, she impulsively hugged him.

His startled laughter rang softly in her ears. "Whoever marries you, Rosalind, will be blessed indeed."

She drew back and gazed at his thoughtful eyes as her smile faded. "I do not plan to marry. A husband would expect me to see him as my lord, my life, and my keeper."

"A right supremacy, some would say."

"Some who are fit for others, not for me."

"You are a headstrong woman, Rosalind."

"Aye, good sir, and I like it that way."

"I like you that way, too," Shakespeare admitted, chuckling as he stroked his short brown beard.

She took one of his hands in hers. "You are always so thoughtful, Will. Quicker to ask a pointed question than to spout an opinion."

"It is a poet's duty," he replied. "I am an observer of human nature."

"Master Shakespeare, the masque is about to begin!" The voice came from across the terrace.

"Oh, dear!" Rosalind cried, her nerves jumping like a frightened cat.

Shakespeare grinned mischievously and clapped his hands. "Your time has arrived, on the winged steeds of fortune." He held out his arm. "Shall we?"

"Yes, all is in order. Francesca is waiting in the audience. She said she will be my ears and eyes."

"Then she is fortunate indeed," Shakespeare observed gallantly.

• • •

A short time later in the gallery, Shakespeare literally pushed a terrified Rosalind onto the platform filled with wildly costumed musicians and dancers. Her heart was pounding so hard in her chest, she momentarily forgot her lines. But Rosalind would not admit defeat. She cleared her throat and began the performance she had rehearsed in her chamber for weeks.

"I am the Goddess of the Harvest," she began.

"Are those *grapes* attached to her . . . her . . . ?" A loud voice rose from the audience.

"Yes, they're attached to her bosom!" came another voice. The crowd broke into laughter.

Rosalind felt her knees start to give way, then rallied. Laughter was good, wasn't it? It meant that her audience was being entertained.

"I have been the hope and the salvation of plowmen and farmers, wisemen and fools," she continued, her voice stronger now. She took another step, emboldened. "Come and I will show you the richness of my store. I bring succor to starving men."

Rosalind projected her voice as if she'd walked the boards all her life. "I give of myself to replenish the land. I bear fruit—"

She was momentarily interrupted by another swell of laughter. She paused, her eyes wide through the slits in her mask, then pushed onward, realizing that she felt truly exhilarated for the first time in her life.

Down in the audience, Francesca moved lithely between the standing and gaping figures that included some of London's finest citizens. The men, she noticed, did not tsk or shake their heads, as some of the women did; they merely grinned, foolishly or in admiration. Certainly bawdier scenes had been performed in the great halls and galleries of England, but rarely had the main actor been the daughter of an earl.

Seigneur de Monteil looked nearly apoplectic with glee. His toothless mouth gaped open in wonder and he held a hand to his heart, as if to keep it from falling out.

"Well, seigneur, what do you think of the Rose of Thornbury?" Francesca asked him.

"*Elle est magnifique. Ravissante. Formidable.*"

"You might catch her in the garden after her performance. Perhaps you can have a moment alone with her."

"*Mais c'est certain.* I will greet her as quickly as possible. One never knows how long zee fruit will stay on zee vine."

He smiled at Francesca suggestively and started toddling through the crowd toward the exit. Frannie realized anew what she had known long ago, that age is no impediment to a lecher, and she wondered if she had done right by steering the seigneur in Rosalind's direction.

Four

❦

When she finished speaking her part, Rosalind exited
through a swarm of young girls who skipped onto the
makeshift stage, singing and swirling the gossamer strands
of cloth of gold they were holding. The crowd broke into
applause, whether in appreciation of Rosalind's performance or in relief at her exit, she knew not. It didn't matter. She had done what she had set out to do, and she was
elated.

She dashed down the gallery steps to the ground level
and spirited herself out a nearby door that led to the garden. She needed a moment to still her racing heart and
cool her heated brow. It wasn't until she reached the fountain in the middle of the garden that she remembered that
she'd agreed to meet the seigneur Francesca had invited
out there.

She saw an old man sitting on a bench and immediately
felt a pang of guilt about the deception she was about to
practice. She had not taken her conscience into account
when devising her scheme.

She approached the elderly French nobleman and was about to greet him warmly when he rose, a distinctly lustful flame brightening his faded eyes.

"*Bon jour, demoiselle*," the seigneur said. "It is a pleasure meeting you. Zee Viscountess Halsbury said you were a delicious female, but I am sure she underrated your charms and beauty. *Vous êtes belle comme le join,* as we say in my country."

Rosalind's eyes widened in surprise, and she forced a merry laugh. "I'm quite sure Francesca would not have used the word 'delicious.' "

He shrugged, and his thin lips widened above a pointy chin. "Perhaps I misheard her."

"Perhaps indeed. I am glad you have come to visit Thornbury House, Seigneur de Monteil. Please excuse me while I change my outfit. It won't take long."

She started away, but the seigneur gripped her arm with surprising strength for a man who looked to be seventy, and who was, in addition, a full head shorter than her.

"Ah, do not leave, *chère* Lady Rosalind. Your costume sets my blood ablaze." He firmly affixed his gaze on her cleavage. "It shows your greatest attributes to full advantage."

He tried to pull her close, but was forced away by the rigid whalebone that filled her farthingale. Rosalind had finally found a practical use for the cumbersome fashion device!

"Seigneur, I think you have misinterpreted my intentions."

"Certainly I have not offended you, Lady Rosalind," he said. "Not zee woman who wears zee grapes on zee breasts."

Before she could respond, Monteil leaned forward and nipped a grape between his teeth. He plucked it off and began to chew, grinning as if he'd just bedded her thrice over.

She gasped at his audacity. "I see you are a bawdy old cock!" Then, contemplating his extraordinary lack of manners—and her own absurd appearance—she sighed with resignation. After all, she had invited this sort of behavior by dressing so audaciously and by agreeing to this foolish meeting in the first place.

"Seigneur, I must speak plainly. I am not the woman that I might appear to be. I am looking for a husband who will let me live as I please. I do not want to be bothered by conjugal obligations. I will be a pretty ornament, a bauble for some man to show off, but I will not be a saddled mare."

She glanced at Monteil's bony figure, hoping he would not be shocked or offended; then, realizing the unlikelihood of her shocking that old roué, she continued her frank discussion.

"I mean to be the mistress of my own fate. I will bring a hefty dowry to any marriage I enter into, but I do not ever intend to share Thornbury House, or its bed, with any man."

"I think you will change zee mind," Monteil said confidently, taking her hand and tucking it through his arm. He led her on a narrow path by a knot of marigolds.

"Change my mind? About Thornbury? Never. About marriage? Impossible."

"No, I mean you will change zee mind about zee conjugal relations."

"No, no, I'm afraid not," Rosalind said patiently, as if talking to a child.

"Yes, zee mind will be changed sooner than you think."

"Oh?" Irritation thinned her voice. "What makes you think that?"

"Because you haven't yet known zee passion of a real lover. A French lover."

As if this were a cue, the seigneur then pounced. This time, though, instead of bouncing off her farthingale, he crushed through the folds of her gown and wrapped one arm around her waist.

"Seigneur!"

With surprising agility, he yanked her closer. His eyes came precisely to the crest of her bosom.

"I will show you the meaning of *amour, ma chère*," Monteil insisted. "I will eat of zee fruit of zee vine."

With that, he gripped one of the clusters of grapes that was affixed to Rosalind's bodice and ripped it off.

"Good heavens!" she shrieked, pushing at him, futilely. "Let me go."

"I will make you feel zee tenderness of zee scarlet nipple," the seigneur boldly continued. He pressed his bony fingers to one breast and squeezed determinedly, apparently unaware that the gesture forced the whalebone shafts of her bodice to dig into her tender flesh.

"Ow!" Rosalind shrieked.

"Ah, zee breasts are tender only because they are virgins."

"Damnation! Get your hands off of me."

Rosalind shoved him with all her might, but her efforts were to no avail. The scrawny French lord had obviously had plenty of experience with recalcitrant women.

"How dare you touch me in such a manner! I warned you earlier."

"You like it, *n'est ce pas*?"

He reached for her again, but this time Rosalind lunged back. "Seigneur de Monteil, I must remind you of who I am! And I must ask you to leave Thornbury House this instant. Since you have no care at all about propriety, I will be the one to remove myself from your presence."

Rosalind dashed around him and strode through the garden. She heard his steps on the gravel pathway and spun around just in time to see him reach out for her.

"Back, I say!" she cried out. But it was she who retreated, not he. Arms windmilling, she started to lose her balance and, with a cry of disbelief, went tumbling into a bed of carnations.

"Not as soft as zee bed of roses," the old man observed gleefully, "but I will not complain." So saying, he launched his skeletal body on top of her, nearly bouncing off the huge immovable circle of her farthingale.

"Help! Francesca!" Rosalind cried out as Monteil amorously assaulted her neck. She tried to roll from side to side, but the lecherous old man had an uncanny ability to counter her every move as he showered her with his unwanted attention.

"Now you're getting zee idea, *ma belle*," he murmured in her ear. "Zee hips of zee woman instinctively know how they should move."

"What in blazes!" a male voice thundered somewhere from above them. "Get off of her, you rogue, or I'll cut open your spleen."

At the sound of a rapier being ripped from its scabbard, Rosalind gasped in relief. "Thank heavens! My virtue is saved." Pressing both hands to the sides of the old man's head, she jerked the balding orb to one side for a glimpse at her savior.

He seemed to be all legs, towering over her, muscular calves in white stockings, sinewy thighs straining against his breeches. Looking closer, she noticed narrow hips—she wouldn't even glance at the codpiece, neither acknowledging its presence nor assessing its considerable dimensions—and a broad chest in nothing more than a white billowy shirt. An enticing tuft of black hair curled at the open collar. He was fresh off a boat if the scent of salt she inhaled was, in fact, wafting from him. And finally he was a face, too artfully chiseled for words . . . and too familiar by far. He was . . .

"Oh, dear God . . ."

"Yes, Moppet?"

"Drake!" she shouted, and cupped her hand to her eyes for a better glimpse.

"Yes, Moppet," he said, his voice oozing sarcasm. "Or should I say yes, strumpet? I've come back to claim Thornbury House before it turns into a bawdy house. It won't bother you if I kill your lover, will it?"

"He is not my lover!"

Rallying her strength, she shoved the seigneur to the side. He rolled off her farthingale and landed with a thud on his back. Propelled by fury, Rosalind flung herself up from the ground, despite the volume of her underskirts.

She squared off and honed in on those devil's eyes with the precision of an archer. Oh, God, she thought, blinking, pressing one hand to her forehead. She had forgotten. They were too blue to be human, too beautiful to be wasted on a man, too cruel for anyone with a heart.

"You're back," was all she could manage to say.

"As promised." His weather-roughened cheeks creased with a mirthless grin.

"This is my house, Mandrake," Rosalind sputtered, a child again, all sense of control vanquished in his heathen presence. For he was like some pagan who knew the laws of decorum yet still flouted them, or worse, didn't even know that civility existed. He'd been calculating as a child. Now he was incalculable. She'd never rein him in again, and it terrified her.

"Oh, how I've dreaded your return," she rasped through clenched teeth, aware that some of her anger would more appropriately be directed at the seigneur. But she was not thinking now. She was reacting. "I thought perhaps I'd outgrown my distaste for your presence, Drake, but I haven't.''

With his rapier still pointed at the figure huddled on the ground, he threw back his head and laughed, that rich, engaging sound that seemed to have deepened with time. His teeth flashed white in the gleaming sun.

"Oh, Moppet, how I've missed your vitriol.''

She heard the seigneur gasp, but could not tear her gaze from the terrible sight of Drake. "Seigneur de Monteil,'' she said over her shoulder, "please do not be afraid. You should not flatter this cur with your fear. He will not thrust his rapier in your heart, sir, for he prefers the feel of gold on his fingers to that of blood. He lives for money. He was so busy making his fortune he did not even return after the death of his mother.''

That remark earned her a quick tightening of the muscles beneath his beard, the flexing of his square jaw.

"Such is your opinion?'' Drake said coolly.

"Yes.''

His blue eyes gleamed beneath the wild wave of his brows, and his too perfect lips cut open in a mean slash against the blackness of his closely cropped beard. "I had my reasons for staying on the high seas,'' he said. "Not the least of which was the tardiness of your missive.''

"The tardiness of my missive!'' she countered, arms akimbo.

"Please!'' the old man rasped.

Suddenly alarmed by the tone in his voice, Rosalind turned and gasped. "Seigneur! You are as white as the flowers on which you lay.''

Seigneur de Monteil was clutching his chest, gurgling and gasping for breath.

"Oh, Saints! You poor man. Why didn't you tell me you were ill?''

"I tried!'' The seigneur gurgled one last unintelligible

response and sank back to the ground, his form limp, his eyes closed.

"Oh, dear Jupiter! You've killed him!" Rosalind cried out, turning on Drake with vicious anger. She rushed to him and slammed her fists on his chest. "You killed him. Are you happy now?"

Drake brushed her aside, sheathed his rapier, and knelt in the soft earth of the garden. He pressed his ear to the old man's chest. "He's still alive, but barely. Move aside. I'll take care of matters. As usual."

"There is nothing you can possibly do that I cannot accomplish myself. Not that you ever took care of much for me. I was—"

"Rosalind!" He glared up at her. "Quit chattering like a magpie and go fetch a doctor."

Pride hardened her spine. "Well, yes, of course." She looked down at the poor seigneur and felt her insides churn with guilt. "Damnation, Drake, you pick the worst times to make your entrances. Help! Fetch the doctor!" she cried out as she dashed back toward the house. She glanced over her shoulder and saw Drake scooping the limp form into his arms, then he jogged in her wake.

An hour later she alone kept vigil outside the yellow chamber in which a physician was examining the seigneur. Drake had escorted Francesca to the great hall so that she could act as hostess during the feast. Rosalind refused to make merry until she learned of the old man's fate.

Despite the heat of summer, her hands were ice-cold and a chill wind whistled up her spine, for she knew that the seigneur had fallen victim to the curse, just as every other poor fool who had ever courted her had done.

A grim-faced chambermaid opened the door and curtsied. Rosalind stepped in, only to find the physician rolling his sleeves back down his arms.

"Doctor?" she asked.

"My condolences, Lady Rosalind. He passed on a moment ago."

"No!" She groaned, though it was exactly what she had expected to hear.

"It was his heart, you see."

"Was it . . . was his heart broken?"

"By a woman, you mean?" the physician replied with an ironic smile.

"By the curse that haunts a woman."

"No, his heart did not break from ill-fated love. It was too weak. Did he face some fright or shock today?"

"Yes." Rosalind's face was burning with shame. "It was my fault you see. I selfishly invited him here for my— oh, never mind."

She sighed with what seemed every last ounce of her strength, then strolled forlornly to the edge of the bed and regarded Seigneur de Monteil's pale, now almost blue skin. "Poor man. Poor, poor man. Forgive me. Oh, heavens, forgive me."

"You are not to be blamed, Lady Rosalind. A man in his dotage should be rocking himself by a fire, not attending . . . bawdy masques." The doctor stole a furtive glance at the cluster of grapes, now thoroughly smashed, that still clung to one of Rosalind's breasts. Then he gathered up his tools.

Mortified, Rosalind reached down and ripped the fruit off, flinging it into the cold fireplace. She rubbed her purple-tinged fingers on her gown, ignoring the resulting purplish stain. The doctor discreetly made his exit.

"Monsieur, forgive me. Forgive me," she whispered to the dead man. Then a surge of emotions roared up in her— sorrow for the seigneur, fury at herself, fear of Drake. It all came tumbling out with a bitter sob. She sank into a chair and laid her head on the edge of the bed, crying as she hadn't since her father's death.

"Are those real tears?" Drake said from the doorway a few moments later, quietly, but without sentiment.

She heard him, but said nothing. Her despair was too deep. He would not know what moved her, would not care. In any event, nothing he did would bring the seigneur back to life.

"Go away," she moaned. Raising her head, she turned back and saw him through a blur of her tears. Funny, she didn't even care whether he saw her cry. Too much time had passed. They were too old to care about appearances and pride. There was no denying it: she was cursed. Hexed. Doomed. She lowered her head onto arms and released a new round of sobbing.

"Poor little Moppet," Drake said in a surprisingly gentle voice. She felt his shadow. He'd come up beside her. "You lost your plaything, now you're having a good cry."

Without missing a beat, or a sob, she swung her right arm out, hoping to strike a decisive blow, but his hands snapped around her wrist.

"Now, now, no need to end my chances at fatherhood."

She jerked her head toward him and saw that he'd caught her fist just before it plowed into his codpiece. "Can you only think about yourself?" she hissed. "A man is dead."

"Yes, and he died because he believed you when you flirted with him, dressing up like the Goddess of the Harvest. It's obscene, Rosalind," he lamented, leaning his hips against a table. Though his voice was laced with horror, a smirk hovered around his lips. "Disgusting, really."

"I did not flirt with him! I invited his attention, that is all. Oh, you know nothing about why he died. You wouldn't understand. I'll never tell you. You're a man. You have no idea what it takes for a woman to survive in this wretched world with any semblance of dignity or free-dom.'' She caught her breath with a hiccuping sob. Then realizing what was really bothering her, she began to weep again. ''Drake, I'm thirty years old and I'm still killing men!''

Drake pushed off of his resting place with uncommon grace for a man of his height and moved to her side. ''That sounds serious,'' he said, and catching her by the sleeve, he pulled her close. Her arm came up to her face in a defensive movement. He frowned. ''No need to protect yourself, Roz, I'm not going to hurt you. God's teeth, do you think me that much the monster?''

He tugged a kerchief from his pocket and began to dab her tears from the blur of white and pink on her painted face. With each stroke rough knuckles brushed her soft skin, somehow reassuring her that she was in good hands. He was so strong, so wrought with muscles. So much the man.

''You look like a harlequin,'' he observed.

''I'll never paint my face again.''

''Then you'll be unfashionable,'' he said, cleansing her cheeks with great care.

''I don't care. I'll never show my face in society again.''

''I doubt that very much.'' He flipped his kerchief over and put the clean side to her reddened nostrils. ''Now blow.''

When she merely glared at him, he raised a brow and tilted back his head, giving her a fatherly chuck. ''Come along, Roz. Don't be so theatrical. Just blow.''

She did so with a defiant and indelicate honk. He smoth-ered a smile and tucked his kerchief in his pocket.

''Wasn't so difficult, eh, Roz?''

Roz. He used to call her that in the old days, and his rapid reassumption of familiarity grated on her. Yet now there was no mockery in his voice, and she couldn't help rather liking the way his deep voice vibrated on the *z*. Roz. It was somehow soothing. Should she tell him about the curse? After all, he wasn't really an enemy. Just a man who wanted to steal everything that mattered to her. She couldn't blame him for wanting Thornbury House. In any event, she was the victor in that battle. Couldn't she afford to be magnanimous?

"Drake . . ."

"What, Moppet?" He gripped her chin, tipped it upward, surveying his work. "Yes, that's better. I can almost see those freckles that I used to count during lessons with our tutor."

She smiled at the memory and studied his face, which had since become so much more distinguished looking. His cheeks, almost square in their forthrightness, were ruddy and indubitably masculine. His lips were sensual scrolls of burgundy flesh, nestled enticingly in the soft waves of his black beard. She sighed with an uncanny sense of ease, then inhaled his musky scent. And for moment she didn't think at all about the past, or how much he had once threatened her very existence.

"Drake?"

"Yes, Moppet?"

She was about to say something conciliatory when she caught sight of the seigneur from the corner of her eye. She shuddered with a renewed wave of remorse and cast Drake an accusatory glare. "Why in the name of Zeus are we having such a ridiculous conversation while this poor man lies dead beside us?"

He looked down at the corpse with chagrin, then grabbed her hand and pulled her out into the antechamber. When he closed the door, he turned and shook his head with exasperation. "Do not blame me, Rosalind. You started the conversation."

"I did not."

"Somehow, whenever I'm with you, I end up having the most peculiar conversations in the most bizarre circumstances imaginable."

She waved off any responsibility. "That's because you always venture into places where you are not welcome. Speaking of which, you do not plan stay here tonight, I should hope?"

"Where?" His clever visage brightened, cunningly. His ensuing half smile brought the hint of a dimple to his cheek.

"Here. In my house."

"In *your* house?" He stroked his short beard contemplatively. "In your house, no. But I will stay in *my* house."

She smiled, but without mirth. "You've purchased a home, then?"

"No, I inherited one."

Rosalind's eyes fluttered, and a queasy foreboding feeling invaded her stomach. "Whatever do you mean?"

"Actually, I've inherited this house." He jammed his hands together behind his back and conducted a brief and light-footed survey of the circular antechamber. "A bit run-down, I admit, but so much could be done with it."

"Run-down!"

"And a bit like a hothouse in its ambience. What with the Goddess of the Harvest and all. But still, I'm glad to have it. You see—"

"Drake!" she cried out. "What are you prattling on about! You madden me so when you do that. This is my house, and you damn well know it."

"On the contrary, Moppet." He turned to her, a deadly serious expression on his handsome face, and strutted forward until he was a breath away. Leaning one arm on the wall, he whispered intimately, his voice seething with old venom, "It's *mine*. As I promised you it would be."

She tried to swallow, but her mouth was suddenly parched. "What in the name of Beelzebub are you talking about?"

He reached into his shirt and pulled out a pouch from which he withdrew a parchment. "I received this five months ago. It came with your letter. You can see for yourself."

She took the official-looking document with a trembling hand and straightened the curled edges. It was then that she read the words that were to change her life forever.

" 'The Last Will and Testament of Lord Andrew Carbery, Earl of Dunnington . . . ' " she whispered, the syllables scarcely audible against the thundering of her heart. " 'I, Lord Andrew Carbery, do bequeath Thornbury House and all its attached properties and environs to . . . ' " She gasped. " 'To Master Drake Rothwell!' "

Rosalind blinked as the words began to blur together. She scoured the document for a signature. And she found one. In handwriting that appeared to be her father's. And it had been witnessed by . . .

"Thadeus!" she shrieked.

Five

Early the next morning, long before Rosalind rose from her bed, Drake was dressed and pacing in Lord Andrew's parlor. He had been so long at sea that this stately, wood-paneled chamber seemed foreign to him. Yet it was unforgettably intimate and dear for all that. After all, this was where Lord Dunnington had once told him that he considered him to be the longed-for son he never had.

On this fine—nay, spectacular—morning, he watched the sun rise through the diamond windowpanes. Beyond the wavy glass, rays of light shot through the dark clouds of dawn, shining gold on the vast, green expanse that helped make this estate so great.

Thornbury House was among the most celebrated of the prodigy houses of Queen Elizabeth's time. A prodigy—by definition, a great house built to impress and shelter the queen on her progresses through the countryside during the summer months—contained a presence chamber, or state apartments, for the queen. Ever parsimonious, Queen Elizabeth, with hundreds of courtiers and servants in tow, and thousands of horses, travelled from prodigy house to prodigy house, living off the generosity of the host noble-man in each. The expense of hosting such visits would sometimes nearly bankrupt a lord, and indeed, it had been a visit from the queen that had begun Drake's own father's downward financial spiral.

Though not nearly as large as Burghley, or as romantic and fancifully constructed as Hardwick Hall in Derbyshire, or as dignified and palatial as Longleat in Wiltshire, Thorn-bury was, nonetheless, elegant by design and charming in all its details, both inside and out. The road to the estate was lined with ancient trees, which created a natural pas-sageway, and the house itself was half-circled by a twenty-acre garden and an enormous deer park. One felt, upon arrival, that one had traveled many miles to escape the stench of London, when in fact, the house was located just outside the western borders of the city.

And most important, the house had been built by Drake's father. It was the only surviving monument to the Rothwell family's former glory. The earl had never really understood how important that was to Drake. Or so Drake had thought until he received the will.

Sinking behind the desk into what had once been the earl's favorite high-backed chair, Drake reached out and clasped the old man's well-worn quill pen. He rifled through his tobacco box, feeling the old lord's smooth ivory pipe. Rosalind had apparently left the items un-touched for sentimental reasons. The rich scent of tobacco oozed from them. Smelling it, feeling the treasured mem-orabilia, Drake saw in his mind's eye Lord Dunnington, talking to him gently, reassuring him that he was welcome here, despite the fact that Rosalind loathed him and was in no way reluctant to say as much.

He wanted to reach out and hug the man, to tell him how much he adored him, how much the faith he had had in a fatherless boy had meant, to tell the earl that Drake would not be the man he is today if not for the lord's love and affection. And it sickened him to imagine telling the Earl of Dunnington that he was in trouble. Deep trouble.

"Dear Andrew," Drake said, pressing the pipe to his chest, which ached like a wound at the memory of his beloved benefactor. But he was hugging a mere object, not a person, and moments later the action seemed foolish. And perhaps hypocritical, he mused, tossing the pipe into the box. After all, he had not bothered to return until he learned of his inheritance. An inheritance for which, based on Rosalind's astonished reaction, he would have to fight.

The door opened with a soft creak. Drake looked up, and spotting the estate's steward, he felt a surge of affection.

"Greetings, Thomas."

"Oh, Master Drake!" said the steward, shuffling in with some accounting books under his arm. He unconsciously polished the floor with each long stride of his slippered feet.

"Did I startle you, Thomas? I hope not." He rose and rounded the desk, warmly gripping the doddering man's free hand. "I had hoped you were still here at Thornbury House. Please, let me help you." Drake took the heavy ledgers from the old man and pulled a chair forward for him in front of the desk.

"Thank you, Master Drake. Yes, I am still here. I serve the mistress now, her ladyship." Thomas pushed up the spectacles that perched precariously at the end of his nose and frowned through them at Drake. "But the servants tell me you are the master as well now. Befuddling matter."

"Yes, Thomas, I have in my possession a will signed by Dunnington."

Drake pulled out the parchment and showed it to the

steward, who perused it with the sharp eyes of one who'd handled every document pertaining to the estate over the last twenty-five years.

"Yes, it looks authentic. Almost exactly like the one naming Lady Rosalind heir. Well, I'll leave this to the lawyers to sort out. You're part of the family as far as I'm concerned."

Drake smiled gratefully as he sat on the edge of the desk, twirling the quill pen in his fingers. "Thomas," he said with the tactful tones of a diplomat, "may I see the books, by any chance?"

"Well, of course, you're the master now. You organized them for me when you just arrived all those years ago. Do you remember? You were just ten years old! Such a bright boy."

Drake scarcely breathed as the old man pushed the ledgers toward him across the desk. He wanted to snatch them out of Thomas's hands, they were that important to him. They contained information that would tell him whether there was enough gold in the coffers to finance his return trip to Buto. If sufficient funds were lacking, Drake would be forced into bankruptcy and would suffer the same ignominious end as his father. The very thought caused a lump to form in his throat. He reached for the ledgers and was startled when Thomas suddenly pulled them back.

"Now that I think of it, the mistress will have my head if I show these to you."

"Show Drake what?"

At the sound of Rosalind's imperious voice, old Thomas winced. Then he turned to where she stood in the doorway and managed to force out a feeble smile. "Why, nothing, Lady Rosalind. Nothing at all."

Drake stroked his chin as he observed the pitiful scene. He felt great affection for the old steward in that moment. Like every other man in sight, he'd been cowed by the shrewish Rosalind over the years, but he doted on her nonetheless. Drake squinted at her from a distance and recognized her appeal. Her nose was a perfect little thing; her high cheeks retained the faintest dusting of freckles, which she'd tried and failed to scrub off as a child. Her lips were sweetly formed, though imperfect. Instead of rising to two precise points, the line of her upper lip blurred slightly at the peak, hinting provocatively that her headstrong ways were not without hesitation, that her determination was tainted by beguiling doubt. All told, there was a lushness to her, a rich, yet fragile sensuality that was nearly irresistible. So why in hell hadn't she married? He would have thought men would be beating down her door.

"You are down early today, are you not, my lady?" Thomas pushed back his chair and, rising, sketched a short bow.

"What are you doing, Thomas?" Rosalind said in that sharp tone of hers.

The steward removed his spectacles and cleaned them on his doublet, obviously stalling for time. Then he looked up meekly. "I was merely showing Master Drake the books."

"They are *my* books. All the entries for the last year were entered in my hand. Drake has no right to see them."

"My lady . . . the will . . ."

"The will is a forgery," Rosalind stated icily.

My, but she was fetching in a state of dishabille, Drake thought, her hair all tousled, red and gleaming, and not a jot of paint on her face to cover her pert little nose. She must have been worried indeed to come down from her chamber without dressing first. She wore some sort of tiger-yellow robe. Her silken nightgown billowed out from beneath its hem.

He was having trouble remembering what a pain in the arse she had been so long ago, for the stubborn little girl had grown breasts, and at the present moment they peeked provocatively from the crumbled collar of her nightgown. Rosalind? With breasts? The two images did not coincide. Not in his mind. She'd had them before he'd left years ago, but apparently he had not noticed. That he did so now signaled the fact that he'd clearly been too long at sea.

"What *are* you staring at?" she said, focusing her wrath on Drake.

"At you," he replied. "I did not know that your passion for me would impel you from your bed so early in the morning. I rather like the sight of you undressed. It becomes you."

When her nostrils flared, he shot her a broad and gloating smile, then rose and cut a wide path through the room at a slow, swaggering gait.

"Fortunately, maiden—it is maiden, still, isn't it?"

Her delicate nostrils flared further.

"—I am a morning man. All I need to do to rise to the occasion is to put aside these ledger books and focus on something more . . . engaging."

He came to a stop inches from her and brazenly looked down. Her green eyes simmered up at him through orange-tinted lashes.

"Now, *that* is—or should I say *they* are—most engaging indeed."

"I would suggest that you engage yourself elsewhere, sir," she hissed. "You're proving yourself to be no better a man than that poor lecherous seigneur." She visibly winced at her own reminder of yesterday's debacle.

"I shouldn't think you'd bring that subject up," he murmured. "The seigneur is still dead, is he not?"

"Yes," she replied tersely, "and I still say you should engage yourself elsewhere." She glanced surreptitiously at Thomas, then whispered to Drake, "Why have you returned? Why do you want this house? Oh, I know it has sentimental value. But you are rich. You could buy a castle if you wanted. You are a man. You can roam the earth if you please." Her cheeks flushed with anguish, and her mouth tenderly parted in desperation. "But this is all I have. Can't you leave me be?"

He swallowed and spun away from her, unnerved that she could so easily wring pity from him. He had to remember just how cunning she was. Her determination made her so. He paced a few moments in silence, then pivoted and turned out one leg in courtly fashion.

"Has it occurred to you, madam, that perhaps I did not return for the house at all? Perhaps I've come to claim you?"

Her vulnerable expression twisted into one of scorn. "Oh, fie on you! You'd make a mockery of anything."

"You don't believe me? I'll send Thomas away and you'll see the depth of my desire for you." He whirled around and made for the steward. "Go on, then, man. Get you gone now."

"Oh, what, sir? Yes, oh, yes." Thomas closed the ledgers and gathered them up. "I won't be long, Master Drake. I'll be out of your way shortly. Just let me traverse the length of this enormous room."

"Stay, Thomas! I order you to stay," Rosalind commanded.

Having taken a half-dozen shuffling steps, the old man turned around. "Well, very well. You are the mistress."

"Go, Thomas," Drake ordered in a louder voice.

"Well, you are the master," the steward conceded, turning once again in the opposite direction.

"Drake is not the master here!" Rosalind practically shouted. She propelled herself into the middle of the parlor. "Now stay!"

"Ah, the stinging bee has taken flight from the flower

and winged her way into the thorny brambles.'' Drake
sauntered in her wake.

"No brambles, Drake. And the only thorn you possess
is in your Venetian breeches, and you can break that with
any doxy on your docks.''

"How now, mistress o' mine! Why this obsession with
my breeches?''

"The only obsession I have is this house.'' She turned
on him, arms akimbo, creamy skin flushing a womanly
pink. "I can understand you showing up at my estate,
armed with some trumped-up will, which is obviously a
forgery, and using it to turn my life upside down. Such
behavior is all I would expect from your mercenary sort.
But this flirtation is obviously of another order altogether.
I neither understand it nor appreciate it, sir.''

Drake put his hands on his hips and mimicked her. " 'I
neither understand it nor appreciate it, sir.' '' He dropped
his hands in disgust. "Your haughty little airs and up-
turned nose will not provoke me now, Roz.'' This time he
spat her nickname like an oath. "How many years did you
lead me around by the nose, lady?''

"You may go, Thomas,'' Rosalind said over her shoulder. When the aging steward was out of earshot, she placed
her hands on her hips and looked at Drake, eyes filled with
incredulity. "Lead *you* by the nose? Who came into this
house and stole my father's love, like a pickpocket at St.
Paul's? You plied your nefarious trade as skillfully as the
most hardened cutpurse.''

"Will I be nothing but a street urchin to you evermore?'' he roared.

"Will I be nothing but some frail little female you can
patronize and bandy about like a little doll evermore?
Someone you can put down in order to raise yourself up?''

Drake laughed morosely. Dimples rent his cheeks with
sardonic charm. "You are anything but frail, my dear

lady.'' He tugged at his ruff collar, sliding a finger from one side to the other. ''Do you still not know why I tormented you so? You who are so adept at unearthing the motivations of men?''

''I always thought you hated me,'' she said with a casual shrug. ''Was there another reason?''

''*Hated* you?'' He cocked his head in wonder, then threw it back with a burst of dark laughter. As the rumble in his broad chest slowly quieted, like distant thunder, he strolled to her, and with a still expression, his blue eyes placid in the sea of his handsome face, he stroked her cheek with the back of his right hand.

''Ah, Moppet, if you only knew why I tormented you.''

The last of his words were tinged with sadness. But that was not what she noticed most. It was the burning sensation she felt on her face where his fingers had been, and where warmth still lingered. She shut her eyes and swallowed, turning away so he would not see her pitiful pleasure, willing herself not to rub the spot in wonder.

''But that is history.'' Drake waved dismissively and strolled to the desk, shutting Lord Dunnington's box with a muted snap. ''We have a more pressing predicament. Why don't we argue about that instead?''

''Very well. Arguing seems to be what we do best.''

He smiled mockingly. ''At least we can agree on that. Have a seat.'' He pointed to the one in front of the desk.

When he plopped down casually in her father's chair, the hair on Rosalind's nape bristled to attention. ''I'd rather stand.'' She went to the open casements and savored the breeze that caressed her face.

''So what is the predicament as you see it, Rosalind?''

''*Lady* Rosalind to you.''

''*Lady* Rosalind.''

''The problem, as I see it, is an optical one. Or should I say a lack of optics? You have clearly deluded yourself into believing that a forged document is a legitimate one. I have sent for Uncle Thadeus. He will clear up the matter posthaste."

She turned just in time to see Drake lighting her father's pipe. Smoke billowed about him, white tendrils curling sensuously around his too handsome face. He plucked a bit of tobacco from his tongue with a thumb and forefinger as he studied her through the haze.

"You'll never be the equal of my father, Drake. Don't even try."

"Thank God for small blessings. If I ever have a daughter, she will be pliable and sweet, unlike you."

She cast him a scathing glance. "Don't you know that daughters are worthless?"

He stroked the fine black hairs that covered his forthright jaw. "Shall we keep to one argument at a time?"

She nodded, crossed her arms, and rubbed her shoulders. "Very well."

"I do not think Thadeus will be able to help you in your bid to deny me my inheritance."

"Whatever do you mean?"

"He is the one who informed me about the will when I was at sea."

"You are mistaken." Rosalind began to pace. "Thadeus would have informed me of the existence of such a will long before now. You have been deceived."

"Are you certain?" He leaned over the desk, cradling the pipe in the palm of one rather large hand. "You know Thadeus. You should know him better than I, and I know he's a creature of the Court. He loves intrigue."

Hearing the reason in his words, and surprising herself at her ability to accept it, she went to the desk and sank into the empty chair previously proffered. "Let me see the will again."

"If you look closely," he said as she took the document,

"you'll see for your—" Suddenly he fell silent, then snatched the document from her fingers.

"What?" She clenched her empty hand. "Don't torment me, Drake. Let me see the damned document."

"You wouldn't . . ."

"Rip it up?" Her upper lip curled with frustration. "No, as much as I'd like to, I won't. I swear."

He frowned dubiously, but offered the parchment nonetheless. She grasped it and perused it with a growing sense of dread, then stood abruptly and marched to the window.

"Rosalind!"

"Have no fear, coward. I merely want to see the signatures in the light of the sun."

"If you toss it out the window, I'll tan your hide."

"Just try it!"

"Don't tempt me."

She held the yellowed parchment up to the light, and no matter how long she stared, or how narrowly she squinted, or how high she held it in the beam of light, she could not deny the resemblance to her father and uncle's handwriting. If this was authentic, it was the ultimate betrayal. She was her father's heir! The majority of his possessions should pass to her.

Her hands began to tremble. She let them fall with the document into her lap. Her shoulders slumped.

"Well?"

"It is the very image of my will," she said hoarsely. "Both were dated the same day, both worded in precisely the same manner, but with one exception. Your name is on one, and mine is on the other."

"So, clearly mine is legitimate." Drake could barely suppress a gloating grin.

She raised her chin with all her might. "There is one other exception. Mine is real. Yours is a forgery. Granted, an exceptionally well-executed forgery, but a forgery nonetheless.''

When Drake growled with frustration, Rosalind treated him to a prim arch of her brow. ''Did you think I would say otherwise?''

''No,'' he admitted.

''Then I'm glad I didn't disappoint you.''

''But you don't *believe* it's a forgery.''

''What *I* believe has nothing to do with the matter. I will fight your possession of this house with every last drop of blood in my body.''

He gave a half grin, dimples and all. ''Well, I certainly hope it doesn't come to that. Killing a woman in a duel would do irreparable damage to my reputation.''

Rosalind turned to the window and bit a thumb. She looked like a forlorn child.

''There, there, Moppet, I know it's difficult.'' When he crossed the room and placed his hands consolingly on her arms, she spun around and staggered back.

''Don't touch me, you conniving thief!''

''Thief? I have stolen nothing. Yet.''

''I don't want your pity.''

''I'll be damned if you'll get it again,'' he said dryly.

''You haven't won yet, Drake. All I've admitted is that it *appears* as if my father and uncle signed that document. That does not mean they did so. And I still refuse to relinquish this house.''

Drake frowned thoughtfully and folded his arms. ''The only way we'll get to the bottom of this, *Lady* Rosalind,'' he added sarcastically, ''is to corner Thadeus and not let him get away until we learn the truth.''

She nodded. ''I quite agree.''

''The question is, where the devil is he?''

''I don't know where he is now, but I know where he'll be tonight.''

There was a soft knocking on the door.

"Come in!" Drake commanded in his best seafaring voice.

Huthbert poked his head around the door. "Are you done arguing, Master Drake?"

"Yes, I believe so. Lady Rosalind?" He arched his brows in query.

"Yes, for now."

"Well then, what is it, Huthbert?" Drake locked his hands behind his back and rocked on his toes.

"I thought you might do with a bit of muscatel about now, sir."

"Excellent idea." Drake rubbed his hands together. "A good quarrel always makes me thirsty, doesn't it you, Lady Rosalind?"

"Well . . . yes." She had to admit it did, even though doing so meant having to agree with Drake once more.

Huthbert entered with a tray, set it on the desk, and poured two goblets with a contented smile. "I heard your raised voices, and thought how like old times it was!"

He handed his master and mistress each a drink. "Will that be all, then?"

"Yes, thank you, Huthbert," Rosalind said.

When the usher departed, Drake resumed their conversation. "So, where will we find the noble knave?"

"Thadeus?"

"Indeed."

"At Lady Blunt's. She's presenting a masque tonight at Cranston House."

"Then we will be in attendance."

"I wouldn't miss it for the world," she replied.

Drake raised his goblet in a toast. "Down me right, my mistress."

Rosalind did likewise, and wondered which gleamed more brilliantly in the sunlight—her golden chalice, or

Drake's mischievous eyes. It mattered not a whit a moment later, though, for she downed her wine in one unladylike gulp, and noticed with satisfaction that her enemy had done so as well.

$\mathscr{S}ix$

∞

It seemed an interminable length of time between Rosalind and Drake's tête-à-tête and the evening masque. So she distracted herself with a trip to the Globe Theatre. Francesca had never seen the spectacular new playhouse and had been begging for a tour.

The raven-haired beauty's eyes widened with excitement when their hired carriage drew up before the splendid circular structure. She craned her neck to take in the dark timbers and white plaster that seemed to rise to the sky.

"It's magnificent," Francesca said.

"Indeed it is."

Rosalind led her through the entrance where the gatherers collected money from entering patrons. The afternoon's performance was over, the gatherers and the crowd gone home. Playbills littered the ground, as well as half-eaten fruit and nuts, bits of burned tobacco, wilted flowers, spilled ale—the usual signs of a rowdy crowd. The audiences sometimes talked and ate throughout the show and paid only intermittent mind to the players. It took a great deal of dramatic action to hold the attention of crowds here, and the troupe often resorted to such tricks as spilling gallons of pig's blood during fight scenes, lively musicians, and even gods descending on the stage from mechanical devices, as if from heaven. The upper levels of the stage were called the Heavens for that very reason. And Hell was the area beneath the stage out of which ghosts and visions rose through a trapdoor.

Rosalind led the way into the open-air yard in front of the stage, where the humblest patrons paid a single penny to stand and watch the show. Surrounding the women, in raised tiers, were the galleries, where richer patrons viewed the plays on benches. The wealthiest spectators paid sixpence to sit in so-called ''lord's rooms'' in balconies over the stage.

''Tell Master Shakespeare he has outdone himself,'' Francesca said when she'd taken full measure.

''Tell him yourself,'' Rosalind said, tucking her hand in Frannie's arm. ''Here he comes now.''

''Lady Rosalind and Lady Halsbury! What brings you to Shoreditch today?'' William Shakespeare crossed the creaking boards of the stage, wiping the remains of the day's sweat from his neck and brow. He tugged on a doublet and swept back his disorderly hair. It was obvious that he had performed in that afternoon's play.

''Halloo, William,'' Rosalind said, shadowing her eyes with a hand on the brow as she gazed up at him. ''My friend would like a tour of your new theatre.''

''Ah, so that is it.'' Shakespeare motioned for them to circle 'round and enter the stage from a side entrance. From that vantage, he quickly pointed out the backstage area, called the tiring-house, which included dressing rooms, a wardrobe area, and storage space.

''It is awe-inspiring,'' Francesca breathed, turning in a circle as she pressing her hands to her flushed cheeks.

"I'd say awe-inspiring would be a better description of our visitor from France." Shakespeare pointed to a graceful, aesthetic-looking younger man who was laughing near the entrance to the dressing rooms with some of the Globe's players. Despite his seeming absorption in the players' banter, his eyes never left Francesca.

Very French, very handsome, Rosalind noted, glimpsing his open shirt, sweat-gleaming chest, and Roman nose, and noticing as well the way Francesca's shoulders subtly straightened in attention.

"Would you like to meet Monsieur Jacques de la Vere, Lady Halsbury? He is a visiting player from France, and he cannot seem to unclap his eyes from your person."

"Very well."

Francesca smiled across the distance, and Rosalind noticed the sudden deepening of color in her friend's violet eyes. Whatever instant attraction Monsieur de la Vere felt, it was obviously mutual.

Shakespeare waved the player over. "Jacques, this is the Viscountess Halsbury."

"*Enchanté, madame.*"

"*C'est un pleasir,*" Francesca replied. Her gaze narrowed sharply when the handsome performer kissed her hand.

It was the pinprick of arousal, Rosalind realized with sudden wonder. Her friend had obviously not been living the life of a nun at her Yorkshire estate. Of course, Frannie had always attracted men like bees. It had bothered Rosalind immensely when they were younger. Now she could only admire—and perhaps envy—it.

"Jacques, would you please show Lady Halsbury the theatre?"

"*Mais bien sûr que oui.*" He offered his arm, which Frannie accepted, and the two glided off in a blur of French words and laughter.

Rosalind stared after her, aware too late that her mouth was agape.

"What is wrong, Rosalind? You do not begrudge your friend a mild flirtation."

She sighed and shrugged. "Perhaps I do."

Shakespeare came to her side, crossed his arms, and touched his shoulder to hers in a gesture of affection.

"So you are in a candid mood today."

"I am always candid with you, Will. It is myself that I lie to."

"The philosopher has come to visit, I see."

Rosalind's cheek dimpled with an ironic grin. "No, I am not so lofty as that."

"Then be candid. Why have you come?"

The great weight of the world returned in an instant to her shoulders. She'd been pleasant for Frannie's sake, but she could scarcely suppress the terror that lay just beneath the surface of her skin. As if responding to a cue from the stage prompter, Rosalind and Shakespeare began to stroll to the tiers of benches in the galleries. The silence continued. How could she tell Shakespeare, or anyone for that matter, that she feared all her happiness was destroyed forever?

She couldn't, for she would have to admit that she was not in control of her life. Instead, she chose another difficult topic, hoping to distract her perceptive companion. "I was wondering what you thought of my scenes."

"I looked them over. They're quite good, Rosalind."

She blinked. And then blinked again. She searched his unremarkable yet handsome face for signs of deceit, but found none, and her heart began to pound. A smile broke through her shroud of worries.

"Do you mean it, Will?"

He nodded, beaming at her. "I would never lie about such a matter."

"I've always wondered. I've written all my life, but in secret. I never knew if I had talent. I never really cared. I just . . . just had things I wanted to express."

"Well, you do have talent."

She nodded, trying to digest this enormous compliment. A great master was telling her she could write. "Being able to write is worth something, isn't it?"

He gripped her arms and laughed. "It's worth a great deal. In fact, if you can put the scenes together in some semblance of order, you might have the makings of a good play."

She thought of how she might do that, and it seemed an overwhelming task considering the turmoil she currently faced at home. "I'm not sure if I can."

He frowned.

"Oh, Will, you must think me ungrateful. Two days ago your words of encouragement would have made me the happiest person on earth. But now . . ."

"But now what?"

"Now I feel my world crumbling beneath my feet. What good is writing a play when your very existence is in jeopardy?"

Rosalind explained everything that had happened over the last twenty-four hours. By the time she concluded her tale of woe, Francesca and Jacques had returned to the stage. He was strutting around the boards, much to the delight of Frannie. Then he began to recite from *Macbeth* in a bellicose and heavily accented voice.

"Out, out brief candle. Life is but a poor player who frets and struts his hour upon the stage and then is heard no more. It is a tale told by an idiot, full of sound and fury, signifying nothing."

The last of the French actor's words bounced and echoed around the empty theatre. He began to laugh, as if he'd just told a joke. Then he fell to his knees before

Francesca and, with a great flourish, kissed her hand, rather lengthily for such a brief acquaintanceship, Rosalind thought with an empty feeling. Frannie did not pull away, as she herself would have done. What knowledge about men did Frannie possess that Rosalind seemed to be lacking?

"So," Shakespeare said, summarizing her long-winded explanation of Drake's return, "you must fight the man who wishes to usurp your very own home."

"Precisely." She turned to him. "I've realized, Will, that without my house, I am nothing. I have no sanctuary, no security."

"You have your father's wool business."

"Yes, but the trade has been waning for years. My greatest asset is the land that adjoins Thornbury House."

Shakespeare scooped her left hand up and cradled it in both of his own. "I do believe your soul dwells at Thornbury House, lady."

"I know it does," she whispered. "Unfortunately, so does Drake's."

"Ah, there you go, being candid again."

She turned on the bench and tucked one leg under the other, facing Shakespeare with casual ease. "I know him so well. He lives for one thing alone—revenge. He wants to find out who destroyed his father, and he wants to be master of Thornbury House. Why do you think he was driven around the world in search of spices?"

"Because he's an adventurer at heart?" Shakespeare offered.

"No. He's driven to succeed. He cares nothing for people, for ordinary affections. He does not care who he hurts. It's as if he's possessed."

She shut her eyes, and pictured Drake—those blue eyes, almost transparent at times, at times wild and bright, and his lips, exquisitely formed, a brutal flower born to crush another, to curse and rail and lie in the name of pride. His very life was a lie. He played at the gentlemen, the merchant adventurer, but at heart he was a monster, a machine bent on possessing and conquering. Why else would he have positioned himself as the one person in all the world who could take away the last bastion of her security? Her home.

"You need not fear Drake's claim to Thornbury House if your father intended for you to have it. Your lawyers will see to that."

She gave him a playful little smirk. "I thought you wanted to kill all the lawyers."

He grinned. "I've never advocated the destruction of the litigious lot. You are confusing me with one of my characters."

"Oh," she replied. "I see."

Shakespeare dwelled on her sarcastic grin for a moment, twiddling his thumbs, then frowned and scratched his short beard. "Rosalind, your father *did* intend for you to inherit his estate, did he not?"

She heaved a sigh that might have been a gale for its length and intensity. "I thought I knew the answer to that question. But now I do wonder. I cannot believe my father would have played so cruel a trick on me. Whatever the circumstances, I will fight Drake to the death for this house."

Hearing the conviction in her voice, Shakespeare leaned forward and said gently, "Rosalind, methinks there is more to your feelings toward Drake than hatred."

She gathered her pretty visage into an indignant scowl. "Whatever do you mean, William Shakespeare?"

His languid, moon-lidded eyes sparkled with something new. "What I mean," he said pointedly, "is that you may be upset by Drake because you find him . . . dashing?"

"Dashing!" Rosalind leaned back, aghast, as if he'd just

informed her he had the plague. "I've never heard anything so preposterous. What is there to find dashing in such a ruthless brute?"

At Shakespeare's persistent glare, Rosalind wilted. To maintain her reputation for fair-mindedness, she would have to acknowledge that Drake was not without his attributes—at least silently.

"Very well." Mind made up, she sat up straight and began to tick off his attributes on her gloved fingers. "I will admit the man possesses a certain amount of beauty. He is broad of shoulder, narrow of hip. His thighs are finely shaped and well muscled. His calves bulge beneath his buskins." His codpiece is generous, too, she thought with a blush, but did not say so. "Thick black hair peaks provocatively from his doublet. His face is finely honed. His hair full and rich—though it be a devil's black. All told, a half-dozen assets, a fine list of features for a scoundrel and a rogue."

Her voice had grown faint, for as she recited the list, she envisioned each attribute in her mind's eye, and she couldn't help but realize she had painted a picture of a most pleasing sort of man. One she would find attractive if it weren't for her well-grounded wariness of him.

"But I am not one to swoon over good looks." She sniffed, happy to restore her disapproval. "If ever I were to love, it would be an affair of the soul. No mindless panting and sweating like the beasts of the forest, which is what *he* would surely offer a woman." She blocked out the thought, and the frisson of pleasure that the image brought. "No, my lover and I would share poetry and longing glances."

When Shakespeare folded his arms and regarded her with an almost a pitying look, she blushed.

"I must sound like a mindless virgin, which is what I

am. Do you know, Will, that I have never been truly kissed in all my days?''

She heard laughter and saw Francesca and Jacques approaching, giggling with an intimacy Rosalind found disturbing. ''I am not like other women.''

''You are like the queen,'' he observed tersely.

She smiled, pleased. ''Yes, we virgins should take pride in our status. Especially when there is nothing we can do about it.''

Shakespeare chuckled. ''Virginity is a problem that can be solved in a passionate instant, maiden.''

''Yes, but the problems that follow take a dispassionate lifetime to solve. I am happy as I am. There is only one thorn right now, and that is Drake. And I'll do whatever it takes to pluck him from my side.''

''There might be another solution to your problems.''

Chagrined at his gentle chiding, for he was a gentle man as well as a gentleman, Rosalind forced her heart to hear him. ''What would you suggest, my friend?''

''I spoke earlier of your writing. It is only in your poetry that you will know freedom. Do not expect perfection from the mortals with whom you share the stage of your life. Look only for signs of that exquisite divinity which is conjured up by the curious alchemy of words on the page. The story matters not. *Romeo and Juliet* was an old tale. I did not invent the plot; I merely borrowed it. A tale can be old, even mundane, but when your words fill it up with life, it can be transformed. The characters are transmuted to gold.''

''How does that apply to my predicament with Drake?''

''You most fear losing your physical possessions. Yet your greatest asset is your love of words. I am now a respectable gentleman in Stratford. I have a beautiful home. But I board in simple quarters in London during the theatre season, while my fellow players live lavishly.

Why? Because my surroundings matter little when I dwell in the world of my imagination. If you truly want to be a writer, Rosalind, you will have to abandon your passion for mere possessions. Think about that, and perhaps Drake's return will not frighten you so.''

Seven

"Good evening, Lady Rosalind," Huthbert said later that evening, bowing to the lady of the house as she swept out the front door shortly before seven.

"Good evening, Huthbert," Rosalind replied. She sniffed the air, which smelled ineffably of summer, and blinked at the encroaching darkness with a determined smile before continuing to the waiting carriage.

"Master Drake," Huthbert said, bowing to the lord of the house as he strutted out the same door moments later.

"Huthbert," Drake replied. He didn't notice the air, or the time of day. He merely narrowed his gaze on the richly attired lady who was about to enter the carriage he had called for, and then he grinned.

"Lovely evening, sir," Huthbert said, brushing a bit of lint from Drake's black velvet doublet.

Drake tugged at the short skirt of the broad-shouldered garment. "Lovely evening, indeed, Huthbert. Perfect, in fact, for a disagreement." His smile turned waggish, and his cheeks dimpled beneath his beard as he quirked one brow at the gentleman usher. "Wouldn't you say?"

Huthbert looked at the familiar expression, then nodded knowingly in Rosalind's direction. "I see what you mean, sir. Lady Rosalind seemed to be ripe for a bit of fire herself. I could see it in the set of her lips. You won't be disappointed."

Drake laughed. "You know us too well."

"Never too well, sir. Lady Rosalind is still an enigma."

"To you, perhaps. I know her like I know my own soul."

Not even a determined summer breeze could whisk away the ominous tones that crackled in Drake's husky reply. He smoothed his doublet over the flat planes of his hard belly and descended the stairs.

By the time he reached the carriage door, Rosalind was already seated and neatly straightening the folds of her flame-colored taffeta gown. Her slender fingers flicked over the pearls and garnets sewn on the material in diamond-shaped patterns. When Drake leaned one shoulder against the doorway and crossed his arms, she looked up. At the sight of him, her face hardened.

"Oh, it's you, Drake. I was expecting Lady Beatrice, my lady-in-waiting."

"You'll have to wait a bit longer in that case."

"What brings you slithering to my side like a serpent of ill omen?"

"You're in my carriage."

Rosalind's sparking eyes narrowed. "*Your* carriage?"

"Not *my* carriage," he clarified, "in the strictest sense. I won't claim these possessions officially until the lawyers prove the validity of my inheritance. I speak of possession only in the polite sense that any civilized man, or woman, would recognize."

"Your point?" she said flatly.

"I ordered a carriage at noon. Huthbert told me earlier

you had called for one at six. Apparently you were late returning from the theatre. This one, therefore, the first to arrive, is mine, since I called for one first. That one—'' He pointed to a gilt carriage being drawn by a team of four horses that was just rounding a curve in the drive that led to the coach house. ''That one is yours.''

''In polite society,'' she replied archly, ''a gentleman would graciously take the second carriage regardless of who ordered what and when.''

He leaned closer and flashed his most taunting smile. ''But I am not a gentleman. I am a buccaneer.''

''A common pirate is more like it,'' she replied through clenched teeth.

Up close, he could smell the muskiness of her perfume, and wondered if she'd placed it in the luscious crevice between her breasts, or perhaps at the pulse in her slender, alabaster neck. He tried to swallow, but his throat was suddenly parched, as if he thirsted for her. Juno! What was happening to him? He shook off the effects of her spell and deepened his sarcastic grin. Her prim look withered not a jot. Ha! What did he expect? She'd hold her ground to the death, even if she were facing Satan himself.

''Move aside, *Lady* Rosalind. I'm going to commit an act of piracy, if that is indeed what I am.''

He vaulted himself into the carriage, brushed aside the folds of her gown, sat down beside her, and banged on the roof. At that signal, the driver whistled loudly and cracked a whip, and the carriage lurched forward.

''Stop!'' Rosalind cried out, but to no avail. The wheels rumbled over the gravel drive. Trees that bordered the pathway, now black silhouettes against the purple sunset, whipped by at a brisk pace.

Simmering with fury, she sank back against the satin-lined wall and crossed her arms. ''I see you are arrogantly appropriating that which is not yours—as usual, Drake.''

"And I see you are of no gentler, milder mold than you were when I left ten years ago."

"No, and I will be the same ten years hence."

Her cheeks were pinched, as they always were when she was angry. He'd seen the signs hundreds of times, always, for some reason, feeling a curious sense of satisfaction at their appearance.

"You're furious, Rosalind." His singsong voice heralded his victory.

"Am I?"

She glanced cooly at him, and in the fading light, he could just barely see her freckles; they were shadows of what they had been in younger days. Endearing imperfections. She had scarcely any paint on her face presently. He wished she would plaster the white lead on, then he could not see the remains of those enticing little dots. He would not be reminded of her as a child, when he had—

"I am not angry," she pronounced with a haughty arch of one reddish brow, prematurely ending his recollections. "And whatever are you staring at?"

He exhaled long and slow and gazed for some time at the gathering shadows of night. "Roz, do you ever think about what we were like when were children?"

"I do think about it. As little as possible."

"Do you still hate me as much as you did then?"

She smiled, but without mirth. "I never hated you, Drake. I merely felt sorry for you."

A small but razor-sharp spike jabbed his entrails.

"But I mean to be pleasant this evening."

"Do you know how?" he returned.

Her lips remained sweetly curled, but her eyes glazed over.

"Tonight I will be sweet and engage you in pleasant conversation, for I am quite sure that as soon as we meet with Uncle Thadeus, it will become clear that Thornbury

House is mine, and you will slip quietly away, like an old sea serpent sinking back into the misty waters."

"How poetic." He glared out the window as they approached Lincoln's Inn and the cluster of surrounding houses. The skyline of London loomed in the distance, a mushrooming cluster of rooftops and church spires. "Are you still scribbling sonnets?"

He heard a quick rustle of her taffeta gown and sensed that her gaze had sharpened on him. He turned to find her staring at him without guile. "I take it you are then?"

She opened her mouth as if to say something earnest, eyes searching the shadows of the carriage, then she compressed her lips and leaned back as she fiddled with the lace trim on her gloves.

"How many people do you suppose will be at Lady Blunt's tonight?" she said, ignoring his question.

"At least two hundred, if her desire to impress people remains as great as I recall." He gallantly let her drop the subject of her writing, but made a mental note to raise it later.

"I think it shall be a small affair," Rosalind rushed on, disagreeing as always. "The queen will not be there, I hear, and so a number of her courtiers will be required to stay at her side."

"I see." Drake stroked his beard and gazed out the window at a crescent moon. It glowed strongly even though the sun had scarcely set. "They shall miss this beautiful half-moon."

"I much prefer a full moon." She leaned forward to look and he could feel her breath warm his ear. "It's more majestic."

He tilted his head back until his lips were inches from her ear. "What about the sun?" he whispered. "Do you like it when it shines, or will you tell me you prefer black clouds?"

She met his gaze, her eyes bright and enormous in the shadows. Apparently at a loss for words, she swallowed thickly. He inhaled her curiously sweet scent. It was an intimacy he'd not experienced since he'd rescued her from the pond all those years ago.

"What do you prefer?" she whispered.

"Sunshine," was his husky reply.

"Then I do prefer clouds."

She raised her brows with subtle defiance, then leaned back, as if there hadn't been a moment of quiet intimacy between them. As if she hadn't felt the pull, the unseen force that tied them together like that which bound the sun and moon in their eternal dance. She was stubborn as hell, no doubt about it.

Weary of her, Drake leaned out the window for a breath of air.

"Evening, master!" a man shouted from the street at the passing carriage.

Drake looked back at the shadowy figure as it retreated into the dusk. With hides thrown over his shoulder, the man looked like a tanner. A workingman. Work that would have been above Drake, after his father had left him and his mother destitute. More memories to haunt him. Unaccountably melancholy, Drake leaned back and smoothed a hand over his wind-tousled hair.

"I remember when I first returned to Thornbury House, at your father's bidding," he said. "I entered the hall and just stood there and breathed in the majestic atmosphere. It brought back memories that must have been carved into my soul. I remembered my life before my father's fall—roasted peacock at Christmas and the delicious wassail bowl, my father's laughter echoing through the gallery, a visit from the queen, and her obvious love for Thornbury House. And then there was you. I first saw you standing by the newel posts on the grand staircase. You had a timid little smile on your face. I thought you the loveliest thing I had ever seen. You were kind to me that evening. It wasn't until the next morning that you became . . . cold. I suppose by then you realized that I had come from the streets.''

He propped his elbow on one knee and rested his chin in a splayed hand. "I can't blame you. I suppose if I'd grown up in luxury, I might have felt the same disdain for the poor."

"That wasn't it," she said emphatically, and he wondered if she was aware that she had placed her hand on his knee. *He* certainly was aware of it. Her delicate palm was like a branding iron. But instead of inflicting pain, it sent bolts of pleasure up his thighs, which had turned to steel.

"I do not spurn the poor," she continued. "Do you think me that selfish and cruel? It was that I realized after you spent the night that . . . that . . ."

"That I was never going to leave?"

She blinked slowly, sighed, withdrew her hand, and gazed back out the window. "Must we talk of the past? It is so boring. I'm sure I don't recall what was going on in my mind so long ago."

He studied the back of her head, for that was all she would show him now. Her hair was swept up in a pin wrought of intricate gold filigree and amber. Reddish coils of hair mingled with moonlit jewels. He felt the return of old memories of rejection, but they no longer hurt. He had cleverly numbed himself to them. During discouraging moments early in his career as a privateer, he had only to envision Rosalind's arrogant visage in order to revive his hopes, his determination to prove her assessment of him wrong.

"You're right, Rosalind. We shouldn't think of the past. Many years have come and gone. I once was a loving lad.

I am now a man. I have learned to be hard. I mean to take what is mine.''

"I am no longer a naive girl. I am a woman—equally determined to keep what is mine.'' Her gaze was fiery. A challenge. But he noticed the nervous flutter of her hand on the back of her neck. He felt a nearly overwhelming urge to press his lips to her nape, to feel the tendrils of reddish hair coiled softly at her neck.

Instead, he gloated. He leaned back and smiled at his victory. He'd gotten to her.

Eight

∞

Lady Blunt's magnificent home commanded a lovely view of the River Thames. Not far from Whitehall Palace on the Strand in the fashionable West End, Cranston House was near two other great estates—Arundel House and Somerset House—and west of Essex House, home of the notorious earl Robert Devereux.

When Rosalind exited the carriage, she heard music and laughter flowing from the open windows. She smelled the stinging odor of just-exploded fireworks. Lady Blunt was famous for her fireworks displays, which visitors watched from barges on the river behind the house. How she could afford fireworks, Rosalind did not know. It had been whispered at Court that the widow had spent nearly all the money left by her late husband and had no means, land or business, with which to replenish it. Surely she had some plan to prevent the sale of Cranston House. As mistress of her own great house, Rosalind was curious to know how Lady Blunt planned to survive.

"Ah, my dear, so good to see you," the lady of the

house greeted as she clutched her panting Maltese to her breasts when Rosalind and Drake entered through the front door. "And Master Drake! What a surprise. You arrived together? How now, what news is this?"

"No news," Rosalind replied as she pressed a cheek to that of her corpulent hostess. "A mere convenience, Lady Blunt, I assure you. We would not weary eight horses when four would do."

"To speed us to your happy . . . affair," Drake added, bowing low. "I attend your ladyship's pleasure."

Rosalind's stomach did a little flip, for even now, after that infuriating carriage ride, she saw charm in Drake's every move. She could tell that even Lady Blunt, her cheeks turning a pleasing shade of pink, visible even beneath her troweled-on white paint, was susceptible to the disarming twinkle in his blue eyes.

"Master Drake, my pleasure would be to see you merry at my *affair,* as you so wittily put it."

"Marry? Then it would be no affair," he replied.

Lady Blunt laughed, a throaty rush of giggles, as her eyes roved suggestively from Drake to Rosalind and back again. "By my troth, Master Drake, I should spurn you, for you are engaging the most eligible maiden in London."

"Yes, men are *dying* to meet her," Drake replied drolly. "Just ask the late Seigneur de Monteil."

Rosalind shot him a scathing glance. "I am not engaged with Drake any more than I would be with a serpent, Lady Blunt. Perhaps you can introduce him to Lady Ashenby, or one of the other available widows. You'd be doing London's maidens a fair turn by keeping him as far from their susceptible and trusting hearts as possible. Now, if you will excuse me, I must find my uncle."

"Thadeus? He's here somewhere. You run along and have a merry time, dear."

"I'll search the terrace," Drake said, and with a courteous bow of his head, he was off.

"If you find Uncle Thadeus, do fetch me immediately!" Rosalind called after him irritably. She didn't trust him to return for her until he'd poisoned Thadeus's ear, but she couldn't control Drake's every movement, as much as she would have liked to.

"I hope I have a chance to talk to you later, Lady Blunt, but I must find my uncle hastily." Rosalind started away, but the widow snatched her back with pudgy and surprisingly strong fingers.

"Rosalind," Lady Blunt hissed, her gracious manner gone, "why, pray tell, has Mandrake Rothwell returned?"

"He thinks he's going to gain possession of Thornbury House, but he's quite mistaken."

"Is that the only reason?"

"Why, I haven't considered any other motive. What had you in mind?"

The hard set of Lady Blunt's little mouth softened and she smiled again. "Oh, nothing, nothing, child. Run along and make merry. And if you see my son, do bid him greetings. Godfrey has always been so fond of you."

Rosalind nodded and then hurried away before her hostess could ask any more importunate questions. Whatever was Lady Blunt hinting at? Why else would Drake have returned? What could possibly motivate him to abandon his successful trade in the East Indies if not a great inheritance?

Passing the gallery, working her way through dozens of guests in rich doublets and gowns, Rosalind headed straight for the great hall. She could hear the resounding echo of recorders and the rustling sounds of dancing. She suspected she would find Thadeus there; he adored dancing.

Inside the hall, couples whirled around each other to the

lively melodies of recorders and lutes, and in unison the men lifted their partners in the air and shouted "Volta!" Around the dancers, ladies and men watched and laughed as a harlequin in black-and-white tights pranced about them.

When Rosalind didn't see Thadeus, she moved closer to the crowd. It was then that she got a better look at the harlequin. An enormous and erect cock made of stuffed material burgeoned between his legs where his codpiece should have been.

She gasped at the sight, and then closed her gaping mouth. She couldn't let the world know what a mouse she really was when it came to the subject of sex, not after her own bawdy performance just days ago.

"I prithee, lady, make room for your thrice-weekly portion of fish," the harlequin said to a blond lady in lavender. "You do like cod, don't you?"

When the lavender lady turned boldly to face the brazen performer, Rosalind saw that her nipples clearly crested her square-cut bodice.

"I haven't had a good piece of cod since Friday last," she said with a sensual snicker, and to the delight of a small audience of leering men, she bent over at the waist, so that her farthingale flipped up into the air, exposing her bottomside.

"Watch out, milady, it's a slithery little creature," the harlequin replied, and placed his padded cock to her skirts, humping like a dog.

The men roared with laughter. Several women turned away and Rosalind went pale. She gripped the wood panel of the wall and broke out in a cold sweat.

What was wrong with her? She'd seen similar antics before. Yes, she had quickly turned away every time. But never had she grown ill. What was different now? What had changed? She was being plagued again by the disquieting feeling she'd had in the carriage, a mysterious sensation that disturbed her to the core.

The antics ended abruptly with a crude approximation of two lovers' climaxing—with exaggerated shouts and groans and sighs of satisfaction. Then the harlequin skittered away to shock another group. Rosalind steadied herself with a deep breath and watched as the bold young lady righted herself, laughing at her own performance. How merry she was. How free on a subject so base.

Rosalind pushed through the crowd, disgust fueling her determination to find Thadeus. He was not in the great hall, and she hurried to the gallery. Before she got there, however, she was waylaid by another disturbing scene.

In a deep corner alcove, she spied Francesca engaged in a passionate kiss with the actor they'd met earlier. Jacques what's-his-name. His hands—terribly expressive hands, and strong—were coiled in Frannie's hair, which spilled about his fingers. Her mouth was open to him in a deep kiss.

I should turn away, Rosalind thought. I should not be witness to this.

But turn away she didn't. The sight was too arresting. To see her friend, a widow, embraced wholeheartedly, sensually, by a younger man. But what a child Rosalind was being. Still so naive, despite her earlier claim to Drake. What did she think? That Frannie's desire to be held had ended with her marriage? Or had desire never even been awakened during the years she'd spent with her ancient husband? Likely not.

The truth was that Rosalind simply hadn't thought of Frannie in conjunction with desire. For that matter, she had given little thought to her own cravings. She'd been so long serving a queen who cherished her own virginity, even while those around her gave themselves freely to debauchery.

Oh, surely, Rosalind had had dreams. Dreams that upon waking left her hungry for something she'd never tasted, left her damp in her sheets, frustrated over something she could not name. Now she knew what she had been wanting. What Francesca now reveled in. As much as Rosalind had put aside her feelings for greater purposes, for responsibilities, she did hunger.

"Rosalind, is that you?" Francesca said, hearing the rustle of Rosalind's skirts as she attempted to beat a hasty retreat.

When Rosalind turned, Frannie was brushing back her hair, not self-consciously as might have been expected. She smiled sweetly, but the heightened color of arousal lingered in her cheeks and made hazy the violet of her eyes.

"Did you want me for something?" Frannie said.

"*Bon soir, demoiselle,*" Jacques said, and tilted his head respectfully in Rosalind's direction.

"*Bon soir, monsieur.* Frannie . . . I was looking for Thadeus. Have you seen him?"

"I saw him when I arrived. I believe he was going out to watch the fireworks display. He might be on the river. What is it, Rosalind, has something gone wrong?"

"You mean other than the disaster that struck with Drake's return? Nothing that I can name." Rosalind smiled wanly, at a loss for words, not for the first time that evening. "I beg your pardon for the interruption."

She dashed through the crowd, ignoring greetings from friends she'd known at Court. She didn't think her life could be turned any more chaotic than it had been by Drake, but now she felt uncertain even of herself. Did she really know herself as a woman who would truly forge her own fate to know herself, as Queen Elizabeth had known herself? Even Elizabeth had not been exempt from sorrow and loss. She'd ruled with an iron hand, without a husband, but without children, too, and now without the youth and beauty she had once cherished and used to her advantage. How alone the queen was in the end. That was why she had not yet named a successor. She knew that no one would worship a setting sun when a bright new one was rising behind it.

When Rosalind finally reached the terrace, a new round of fireworks was exploding from a barge on the Thames. Other boats, filled with spectators, dotted the inky water. The crescent moon shone on the surface like a splash of milk. Up in the sky, bursts of gemlike color spewed out in glittering stars, ruby, sapphire, emerald, and gold. With each explosion, the crowd on the dock and lower terrace oohed and aahed and the muted clapping of gloved hands rose in the air.

It was impossible to discern who the figures were below, but soon that was unnecessary, for up the terrace stairs came two men, one tall and one short. Drake and Thadeus.

"Uncle, were you dallying with a young damsel out on one of the barges?" She gave his cheek a light kiss, for as much as she loved twitting him, she adored Thadeus. He was as mischievous as Rosalind was headstrong. They knew each other's foibles and accepted them.

"I was, as a matter of fact," he confessed with a glow in his aging face. "Now, what is of such importance that Drake should row out to the barge to retrieve me?"

"It's very serious—" A blast of fireworks deafened them, and Rosalind waited until the loud whistling and popping ceased before she continued. "Uncle, Drake has a will that appears to be signed by you and Father. I told him it was surely a forgery. I trust you will verify that fact."

At the guilty and furtive glance her uncle cast her way,

Rosalind's heart began to pound. "Thadeus, don't tell me . . ."

"Then I won't," he said defensively.

"Tell her what?" Drake said, and in the glare of the red fireworks, he looked more devilish than ever—too handsome by far, too confident. "What don't you want to tell Rosalind?"

Thadeus's mustache twitched as he tried to avoid answering. Dizziness filled Rosalind's head and she covered her face.

"It's this way, you see," Thadeus explained. "Your will is legitimate. It was signed by Andrew and witnessed by me. The earl *did* want you to have Thornbury House."

Rosalind pulled her hands away to see whom he was addressing. He was looking straight at Drake.

Nine

❧

"Here, Roz. I pray you, drink up."

Drake moved to Rosalind's side, goblet in hand. She was staring numbly at the empty fireplace in Cranston House's south parlor. He took one of her hands, unfurled it, placed a goblet of mad dog in her palm, then closed her fingers around the stem.

"Rosalind, *drink this*."

"Hmmm? What?" She pulled herself out of a daze, feeling the cool pewter against her palm and smelling the pungent odor of spirits rising from the cup. She brought it to her lips and sipped. It bit her tongue, but it felt good. She sipped again. Moments later she felt the liquid blazing a trail down her throat.

"Thank you," she murmured, giving Drake a grateful glance.

It was odd, but in her defeat she no longer considered Drake the enemy. He, too, was a pawn in some terrible game conceived by her father. Or Thadeus. She had yet to get to the bottom of the conundrum. And that was precisely what they would do now that they were alone, away from the noise of the fireworks.

"Well, now, my good fellow," Drake said, turning soberly to Thadeus. "What is the meaning of this confusion? Did Lord Dunnington leave Thornbury House to Rosalind or to me? And if he meant for me to have it, as you say, then why does Rosalind have a will naming her the inheritor?"

Before he answered, Thadeus poured a pewter goblet full of the potent brew and swallowed half of it with one gulp. He grimaced as he let out a pained rasp, pounded his chest once, and then smoothed dry his gray mustache.

"I can explain everything, I believe. Perhaps not to your satisfaction, but—"

"Get to the point, Uncle!" Rosalind insisted, stamping a foot. "I can bear the suspense no more."

Thadeus harrumphed. "Drake, Andrew *did* want you to have the house."

Rosalind exchanged a glance with Drake. She expected to see him gloating. But he actually looked concerned . . . about her, it seemed.

"And," Thadeus continued as he began to pace and twiddle his thumbs, "he wanted *Rosalind* to have the house as well."

Rosalind and Drake exchanged another look, this time one of shared confusion.

Drake took a step forward, finger pointing at the old man. "Look here, Thadeus—"

"Patience, my boy, patience." A deep frown furrowed his brow as he regarded them, weighted down by his responsibility. "Your father, Rosalind, had his lawyer draw up both wills and he signed them both on the same day. And I witnessed them. It was the only way he could think of to make sure his dearest wish would come to pass."

"His dearest wish? And what, I pray you, was that?"

Rosalind asked indignantly. "Confusion? Discord? Insecurity? Is this what he wished for me?"

"No." Thadeus's somber expression was replaced by a knowing smile. He hastened to Rosalind's side and put his hands on her shoulders. "Actually, my dear, what your father wanted was for you and Drake to marry."

Rosalind said nothing. All thoughts ceased for a moment while her heart missed a beat.

"What say you?" Drake barked out.

"My brother-in-law thought," Thadeus explained, "if he left the house to both of you, the only way to resolve the issue of possession would be for the two of you to marry."

"God in heaven and by Jove, too!" Drake cursed. He threw his chalice across the room. It clattered on the floor.

"Marry? *Him?*" Rosalind had finally found her tongue and it was sparking fire.

"Go softly, niece, do not emblazon the night with your anger."

"No, I'll leave that to the two-legged fireworks barge over there," she said, indicating a fuming Drake.

"Hear me now, Rosalind. Your father knew you well. He knew how stubborn—"

"And shrewish," Rosalind interjected sarcastically.

"—you are. And he knew how much you loved this house, and that you would not give it up for all the world."

"Did he know how much I have hated him my whole life?" she shouted incredulously, flinging her arms in Drake's direction. "Why, he's a domineering, arrogant, worthless opportunist!"

Drake's blue eyes churned with wrath, which he turned on Thadeus. "And did the earl know that I would rather marry a doxy encumbered with a litter of ruffian bastards than this self-righteous, coldhearted, arrogant little old maid?"

"Old maid?" Rosalind looked at him aghast.

The hard planes of his sculptured face softened. "I'm sorry, Roz, that was unfair."

She thrust her hands on her hips. "You're right. I *am* an old maid. And I want to continue to be one. I've lived too long without a man to try one now. I want to own Thornbury House by myself, with no one telling me how to run it."

"Hear, hear!" Drake intoned. Striding to her side, he gave her an encouraging one-armed hug. "Stand up for yourself, Roz."

His words caused her to feel a peculiar sense of gratification, and she beamed up at him. "Thank you, Drake. Truly. That means a lot coming from an enemy."

"Yes." He nodded, momentarily disarmed. "Yes, you're right. There is a certain pleasure in being cheered on by the other side."

When he withdrew his arm and, for lack of a better place, put it behind his back, Rosalind stretched out her entwined fingers. "Well, then, let me try."

She turned to a slack-jawed Thadeus and jabbed a finger at him. "You're not being fair to Drake, either. He wants sole possession. As much as I want Thornbury House, I must admit that it deserves a single hand of authority. Why should Drake be forced to swallow his pride and be the meacock spouse of a hardheaded woman?"

"Good point, Rosalind. Well said."

At the tone of genuine approval in Drake's voice, she flushed, but never lost sight of her quarry. "What say you, Uncle? Would you proceed with your ill-conceived game in the teeth of this opposition? We are in agreement, are we not, Drake?"

"Absolutely. I would not marry Rosalind if she were the last woman on earth."

"Nor would I marry Drake under similarly bleak circumstances. Indeed, under no circumstances at all."

Thadeus sniffed, his silver whiskers rippling beneath his nose. "Well, you're both being very selfish, I must say. And after all Andrew and Alice sacrificed for you."

Drake sobered instantly. "What of my mother?"

"She loved Andrew," Thadeus shot back. "Didn't you know that? Or were you too absorbed in avenging your father's honor to notice anyone else's feelings? Your inquiries on that matter have not gone unnoticed at Court."

Rosalind looked up sharply. What business had Drake at Court?

Drake's jaw muscles tightened beneath his black beard. "I suspected that my mother wished to marry Andrew. But we never discussed it."

"No, you didn't, did you?" Thadeus said indignantly, rising to the occasion with a well-practiced flourish. "Like Lord Dunnington, your mother had only your welfare in mind. Andrew would have married Alice, but he didn't want to interfere with a match between you and Rosalind."

"What?" Rosalind replied. "What do you mean?"

"He didn't want you two to be stepsister and brother, for fear that others might condemn a marriage between you. And so he sacrificed his own chance at happiness in a second marriage so that *you* could marry. He believed that you two loved each other."

Rosalind felt a cold wind whistle up her spine and squeezed her eyes shut. "No. He could have not have believed that."

"I'm not saying he was right," Thadeus clarified, patting the air placatingly. "But he did believe it. And he sacrificed his happiness in the hope of giving substance to his dream."

An image of Francesca, being nuzzled and kissed intimately by Jacques, flashed into Rosalind's mind. Then she imagined Drake doing the same to her. She opened her eyes, slowly focusing on the dark liquor in her goblet, and the reflection of a torch flickering orange on its burgundy surface.

"Did my father and Alice . . ." She fell silent, swallowed a hitch in her throat, then began again. "Did my father and Alice ever . . . I mean did they . . . were they . . . ?"

"Lovers?" Drake gently finished the sentence for her.

"I imagine so." Thadeus stroked his mustache thoughtfully. "But that is not the same as being married. At least, so I am told. Marriage usually brings a certain contentment that cannot be replicated under any other arrangement."

"Poor father." Rosalind placed two fingers upon her eyes, trying to force back her tears of regret. "And Alice. Poor Alice. She sacrificed her happiness for us." She blinked rapidly and looked to Drake. "I did love your mother. You must believe me. In the end we became dear friends. I'm sorry, Drake."

He strolled to her and stopped inches away. She felt his breath on her forehead, steady and strong.

"You're sorry," he whispered. "For what? For admitting to an enemy you have feelings?"

At the word *enemy*, a wall seemed to rise up around her heart. She stiffened her spine and turned to Thadeus.

"Uncle, your emotional gambit nearly succeeded. But I cannot let my future be decided now on the basis of mere sentiment. As much as Drake and I would do anything to keep this house, marrying each other is quite impossible. You see, we are as opposite as the day is to night."

"As black is to white," Drake agreed.

"As oil is to water," she added.

"She is the moon. And I am the sun. Sharing the same sky, but never at the same time."

Thadeus looked at them both with grave disappointment.

"More's the pity. Well, if I cannot persuade you otherwise, then I will inform the lawyers."

Rosalind frowned and Drake shifted uncomfortably.

"And when they are done with this matter," Thadeus admonished, "you will be fortunate if there's enough of the estate left for you to claim the privy!"

"He's right, Drake."

"Hold fast, Rosalind. We can fight the lawyers as we would any swarm of vultures."

"I'm not so sure."

"Rosalind, you can't let your very future be ripped from your hands like this."

She strolled, slowly, consideringly, to the window and scarcely noticed one last brilliant burst of fireworks sweep a rainbow of colors across the black sky.

Rosalind wasn't at all sure she would win a legal battle. And even if, finally, she did, ownership of Thornbury would be tied up in legal proceedings for years to come.

She did, however, have one clear advantage over Drake. She was intimate with the queen, as much as Elizabeth was close to any female, or at least she had been, and could appeal to her to intercede on her behalf. Since Drake had no real connections at Court, she could beat him handily on that front.

Yes, that was the solution. Forget the lawyers. She would meet with the queen tomorrow, if she could manage to obtain an audience. Rosalind would appeal to Her Majesty, telling her how unworthy Drake was to inherit Thornbury. This would solve all of her problems.

So why was she feeling guilty as hell?

Ten

⌘

It seemed to take forever for the carriage to swing around to the front door. And Rosalind couldn't enter its confines fast enough when at last it did. She kissed Thadeus on the cheek and accepted Drake's outstretched hand. He helped her up into the carriage, and when she was seated, he joined her.

"Give my farewells to Frannie, Uncle," Rosalind called out the window as the old man shut the door.

"I will."

"Tell her to wake me as soon as she returns to Thornbury House tonight."

As Thadeus nodded Drake rapped on the ceiling, the driver cracked his whip and the horses launched into a canter. Hearing their hooves smashing the gravel drive, inhaling air that was not tinged with the sulfur of fireworks, Rosalind heaved a sigh of relief and sank into her corner of the carriage for the rumbling ride home. She gazed numbly out the window at the passing trees, dark silhouettes in moonlight.

· "Thank heavens we've left Cranston House. I thought Lady Blunt would have me cornered until dawn."

Drake chuckled. "She is an imposing personage."

"In every sense of the word. Thanks for rescuing me from her. As soon as we finished our meeting with Thadeus, she spotted me on my way to the door. I couldn't escape."

"Not to worry. I was cornered by Lady Ashenby."

Rosalind's nostrils flared and she cut the distance between them with a discerning glare. "Lady Ashenby. What did you think of her?"

"She's lovely. I know her type. Pliant and undemanding."

Rosalind frowned at him, wondering for the first time just how intimately he had known women like that.

"What was Lady Blunt so intent on speaking to you about?"

Rosalind blinked and bit her lip thoughtfully. "She was terribly curious to learn about you."

"She's an incorrigible gossip."

"Perhaps she thinks you're a rich man who can give her money. She's hard-pressed these days. Her questions didn't run in that vein, however. I'd say she was fearful of your return, if I didn't know the scheming Lady Blunt needn't fear anyone except herself."

"If she is scheming, why do you speak to her with such apparent candor?"

"She was our hostess. Besides, haven't you forgotten? I spent five years at Court. I learned to tolerate everyone and trust only a few."

"Good advice, I suppose."

At the faintly disapproving tone in his voice, Rosalind felt a twinge of anger. "I suppose a swashbuckling pirate such as yourself has no need for diplomacy. Oh, that reminds me. Lady Blunt did ask about your privateering on the high seas.''

Drake's head turned slowly to her in the moonlit darkness. ''What did she want to know?''

''How successful your last adventure had been. I told her that you wouldn't have undertaken the voyage if you hadn't been sure of its outcome.''

''So you have confidence in me,'' he observed softly.

''In a perverse kind of way, I suppose I do. I'm damnably sure that you'll get whatever you want in the end, whether you deserve it or not, and by whatever nefarious means are required.''

When he did not volley back a biting retort, she sought his gaze in the shadows that hovered around his eyes. And she wondered if she'd read him wrong. Why wasn't he boasting about his success?

''Drake, I'm sure you've heard about it, but there is a new trading company forming. The East India Company. I hear they plan to follow the routes you have traced. Captain John Davys has been exploring the East Indies as well. He returned to Middlebury last month. I hear he will help the new company establish its trade routes.''

''I'm not surprised,'' Drake rasped through lips that barely moved.

''It must grate on you that you took all the risks searching out new routes and they profit by following you with bigger ships and better financing. Of course, since I'm sure you have boatloads of spices on their way back to England even as we speak, you are content to let others profit from your hard work.''

When he again said nothing, the atmosphere in the carriage growing heavy in silence, she decided to risk a more direct question. ''Drake, your mission *was* a success, wasn't it?''

His face was wreathed with an ironic half grin. ''Oh,

indeed, Moppet. A resounding success." *Moppet*. It didn't have quite the sting the moniker once had. As children, the name had been a sweet-coated insult. Now it was merely an echo of the past. "I didn't travel to so many countries for naught. I have several tons of pepper."

"Well, that's wonderful. What will you do with your cargo?"

When he didn't respond, she squinted harder in the shadows and saw the faintest outline of white teeth. He was smiling.

"What is it, Drake? Do you have a plan?"

"I shouldn't really say, Roz. You are still the enemy, remember?"

"Oh, yes," she said, bored with it all now. "I'm sure you'll find a way to turn everything to your advantage. You always have. You will never be poor, Drake. It would kill you."

"Yes, it would."

He grew very still then, and remained so for so long that she thought he'd fallen asleep. She leaned her head against the back of the carriage, and was startled sometime later when he spoke.

"You seem melancholy."

"I am," she whispered, so weary inside she could not even pretend that she was strong.

"We can find a way for both of us to get what we want, Rosalind. We'll hoist those lawyers on their own petards, as your friend Shakespeare would say."

She smiled wanly. "I don't think so, Drake."

"Is that why you're so sad?"

"I'm sad," she whispered even more softly, "because your mother and my father died without fulfilling their deepest dream. They gave us the dream instead. And we don't even want it. And I didn't even know it. I've been so selfish. So selfish that I hate myself."

Drake said nothing, and she knew he wouldn't. Who, after all, could argue with the truth?

Francesca did not return directly to Thornbury House after Jacques's carriage dropped her off. She was too full of life, in spite of the fact that she was thirty-three years of age and felt ancient in her widowhood. The body was young, but the mind and the heart were well-worn. She longed to be in the garden, to see the blooming flowers and to remember how innocently she had once strolled through the lush pathways, certain that life held only beauty and happiness. That, of course, was before her wardship had been sold.

She walked around the side of the house and through the arbor, letting moonlight guide her along the gravel paths. She strode past the rosebushes, choosing not to tarry there. Unlike Rosalind, Francesca had no patience with flowers that possessed thorns. She had shed too many tears already. Besides, roses were red, too suggestive of passion and its cruel vagaries.

She much preferred the love-in-idleness. A knot of the sweet little tricolored flowers bloomed on the east side of the garden. She knew the plot well and quickly reached it, a contented smile on her face as she admired the yellow, purple, and white blossoms.

Soon, though, she heard a whistle. Was it a bird? She turned, but saw no one in the manicured garden. Then she heard the whistle again, and out from behind the fountain in the center, a man appeared.

"Pssst! Francesca, *c'est toi, alors?*"

"*Jacques!*" she replied. When he nodded like a naughty little boy and stepped lithely toward her, as only a supremely beautiful and talented young player could, she began to laugh. "Jacques, you are scandalous. Others will think we are meeting for an assignation."

"*Ça va bien, non?* That is good, no?"

He rocked on his dancer's legs, tightly encased in his buskins, then ambled toward her in a playful way. When he took her hands in his and turned his youthful face toward hers—was he a mere twenty years of age?—she felt herself to be a very old woman.

"You should leave, Jacques," she whispered as goose bumps rose up her slender arms and along the fine hair at her nape.

"*Pourquoi?* Why?" he added, forcing himself to speak in her tongue.

"I am a widow and know better than to engage in dalliances with younger men."

"In France," he said, pulling her close, "older women are considered the best lovers."

His eyes were so sincere in their longing, so warm and wanting. His lips were like a flower, like the love-in-idleness that undulated softly in the summer breeze. When he leaned forward and moved them to her neck, to the little dip at her collarbone, she felt a place deep inside her burst into fire.

"Oh . . ."

"Lie down, Francesca." Deftly, he put a hand behind her back and began to lower her, but she struggled free and spun around. He looked betrayed. "Do you not want me?"

"That isn't it," she whispered. "You were about to trample the flowers. Love-in-idleness. My favorites."

He snorted with relief. "Is that all? Ah, *chérie*, you are sweet."

"They are my favorite flowers in all of Christendom. I've always wanted to lie in them, but I couldn't bring myself to crush them."

He knelt and plucked one. Then he rose and held it beneath her nose. She smiled and took it from him. "They have no smell, goose. Merely beauty. And many names. They are also called kiss-me-at-the-garden-gate, and kiss-me-quick.''

"I like that name. It is like Francesca. Beautiful and inviting.'' Jacques knelt and wrapped his arms around her waist, then lifted her in the air.

"Jacques! Put me down,'' she ordered him, placing her hands on his shoulders. Her hair tumbled around her shoulders, and she knew he would not let her go until they'd made love. He spun her around and the breeze lifted her hair until it billowed like a wind-filled sail. *Oh, set me free, Jacques. Set me free.* Would he be the one to do it? Could he? Was she a wicked woman for allowing herself to be seduced by youth? Just because she had lain with an eighty-year-old man in her marriage bed, was she justified in seducing youth? Did she even need such justification?

"Ma petite," he said, his voice thick with youthful desire, "I want you. I will have you.''

He let her slip down into his strong arms until he cradled her. "Where, *chérie*?'' he muttered as he slipped his lips over hers, his tongue darting in, then withdrawing to lave her temple, nestling in her ear, where she heard his panting need.

"In the pavilion, near the arbor that opens to the deer park.''

Despite the long walk to the end of the garden, Jacques carried her in his arms all the way. The pavilion was a low building, plaster and timber, with windows set low to the ground. Mostly used for storage, it was bordered by a small terrace and arbor that led to the stretch of greenery and trees sheltering the deer Lord Dunnington had so loved to hunt. Jacques rattled the door latch, and it gave way. There were garden tools lining the walls, and a pile of hay in one corner. Jacques went to it and lowered Francesca to her feet.

Wordlessly, he began to undress her, deftly unlacing her bodice, then removing her farthingale and petticoat. He was clearly adept, either from his years of working with costumes, or from working with lovers. Francesca chose to believe the latter, and the last vestiges of her guilt over stealing the passion of youth vanished. When at last she was free of her cumbersome clothing, she felt the air, slightly cooler in the pavilion than in the garden, shimmer over her warm skin. It tingled over her naked breasts, and her nipples hardened into purple buds. Jacques caught one between two fingers and squeezed lightly. Francesca let out a hissing breath and shut her eyes.

"Beautiful. *Comme tu es belle,*" he muttered.

Cradling one breast in a warm palm, he bent over and his mouth swooped down on the nipple. Then he knelt. His hands crawled down her back, over her ribs, and then cupped her derriere. As his mouth lowered and he pulled her forward, his lips descended on the silken curls protecting her womanhood. She coiled her fingers in his hair and sucked in a breath. When his tongue slipped into her dark, moist folds, a bolt of pleasure ripped through her. She jerked and moaned and then staggered back into the hay.

Jacques managed to break her fall with one hand, even as he began to tug at the hose gartered beneath his doublet. He loosened the ties and ripped them off, spread her thighs, and then lunged his hardness into her wetness.

Francesca cried out and wrapped her legs around him.

He was an excellent lover, at once tender and rapacious. He was as hard as a stone, as supple as a wave on the water, and he brought her to a climax over and over again. She was a hungry woman. Her hurt made her hunger, as did years of dissatisfaction. Her old and portly husband had been slow to rise, quick to fall, and never concerned about her satisfaction.

"Ah, *chérie,* you could teach the young girls to love," Jacques whispered much later as he sank in sweaty exhaustion into her arms.

"You flatter me, Jacques."

"No, *chérie,* I speak the truth." He propped himself up on his elbows and tenderly stroked the matted hair from her forehead and temples, his brow slowly forming into a curious frown. "You have had a child, *n'est-ce pas?*"

Her eyes widened. "How did you . . ."

"I know, *chérie.* I have loved many women. Did your other lovers never know?"

She shook her head.

"Then they were idiots who did not deserve this exquisite body," he said, truly incensed. "Why did you not tell me you were a mother?"

She forced down the sorrow that swelled in her throat. "No one knows, Jacques. And no one ever will."

Moved by her sad statement, the French actor kissed her deeply, and began to make love to her anew. But as much as he pleased her, Francesca knew when he finally heaved his last into her that he wasn't the one. She didn't know exactly who she was looking for, or what she needed, but she trusted that she would know it—and him—when he arrived.

Eleven

❧

The next morning, Drake paced impatiently in Lord Dunnington's parlor. The sun shone brightly through the diamond-pane windows, but it brightened Drake's dour mood not a bit.

When Thomas entered the door at the far end, Drake jerked to a halt. He fisted his hands at his side, eager to find out what the steward had learned.

"Thomas."

"Master Drake."

He waited until the steward had shuffled to the desk, where the ledgers were laid out.

"I see you've gone over the books," Thomas said, viewing them over the top of his spectacles.

"Yes. You didn't tell Lady Rosalind I was looking at them?" When the pink-faced and bejowled steward shook his head guiltily, the wattle beneath his chin wagging in accompaniment, Drake continued. "I scarcely slept last night, but I've tallied every number and I've done a full accounting."

"Did everything meet with your satisfaction?"

Drake could see the hope kindling in the stoop-shouldered old man's eyes and gently patted his back. "Yes, Thomas, you've done an excellent job. Impeccable as usual. However, I am greatly displeased with the conclusion I've drawn from your figures."

Thomas frowned. "The estate is not producing sufficient income for the mistress. Her ladyship is forced to dip into the profits from her father's business to pay for the upkeep on this house. But it could be worse. Thornbury estate could be *losing* money."

"Worse? For whom? Rosalind, to be sure. But this news is very bad for me." Drake sank into the straight-backed leather chair behind the desk and slumped down, kicking his heels up on the desk. "Rosalind unwittingly reminded me of that last night."

Instead of goading him, she had gently inquired into his private affairs, disarming him with her lack of usual venom. She'd been perceptive enough to guess that he was in trouble. But she could never know the depths of his financial woes. If she knew, then she would realize that all she had to do to see his total ruin was to find a way to forestall the resolution of the problem of Thornbury's ownership. Without the house, he had no income, and with no income, he could not return to Buto to pay for that blasted pepper. And time was no friend on this matter. How long would it be before the East India Company sailed ships to the island and swept the pepper up?

"Thomas, I have to have money. Quickly! I can't wait for next season's crop prices to rise."

"What is wrong, Master Drake?"

He sighed long and hard. His shoulders slumped as he wiped beads of sweat from his forehead. He wanted to tell someone about his troubles, but could he trust Thomas? He had been like an uncle in Drake's youth, and had heard all his youthful boasting, and a few of his trepidations.

"Can you be discreet, good friend?"

Thomas's soft blue eyes widened over his spectacles. "I have not told Lady Rosalind about any of our meetings. Nor did I tell her it was you who loaded her bed with toads that August night twenty years ago."

Drake grinned slyly at the memory. He drummed his fingers on the ledgers, deciding. "Very well, I have to tell someone, Thomas. Here is the situations, I lost three ships. Two of them carried the monies I needed to make my journeys profitable. To put it as plainly as I can, I stand on the brink of ruin."

"Oh, my. I am sorry." Thomas took off his spectacles, and shook his head in sympathy.

"If I don't raise money quickly, I stand to lose an important shipment of pepper. I won't be able to repay my investor. I'll end up like my father." Having said it, having voiced the worst possible outcome to his predicament, Drake was left with a sick feeling in his gut, a deep and cold emptiness.

"I swore, Thomas, I *swore* that I would succeed in business where he had failed. I would succeed *for* him, restore his honor." Drake leaned his head back and forced down the sting of moisture in his eyes. "I want this house. But more than this house, I want to conclude my own enterprises successfully. No, let me be more honest. I want not so much to succeed as to *not* fail. I will die before I fail."

"Wanting not to fail is a curious aspiration, Master Drake."

At Thomas's measured observation, the tide of despair in Drake ebbed. He focused on the steward, who was buffing his spectacles with one elbow. "What do you mean?"

"It is difficult to aim for the absence of something. Perhaps you should set your sights on a positive goal."

"It is too late!" Drake sat up and pounded the desk. A quill pen jumped onto the floor.

Thomas retrieved it, bending over with a grunt, and placed it carefully back on the desk. "It is never too late to learn from one's mistakes and to transform ignominy into greatness."

"Tell that to my father. Rather, tell that to his grave. But enough of this. Did you make the inquiries that I asked of you?"

"Yes, indeed," Thomas replied, sitting on a stool on the other side of the desk. "There is great interest in the land surrounding Thornbury House. It would fetch a fair price. There is one buyer in particular, who contacted your lawyer before about purchasing the entire estate. A mysterious agent for an unnamed nobleman."

"Really?"

"But I beg you not to sell any of the land, Master Drake. You might find someone who would buy it despite the threat of a legal battle over your right to sell it. But the risk is too grave. If Lady Rosalind is found to be the rightful inheritor, and you sell her property, or tie it up in the courts for years to come, you will cut off a valuable source of income to her."

"What of Dunnington?" Drake pressed.

"The title and property that came with the earldom of Dunnington reverted to the crown upon the earl's death. So all Rosalind has is Thornbury House and its acreage."

"I see."

"The income from the land does not cover all the expenses of running Thornbury House, but it is still necessary income. More importantly, Lady Rosalind lives for this land. She is a beloved landlord to its tenants. She would be most unhappy to lose it."

"That is putting it mildly." Drake folded his hands and propped his arms on the table, resting his chin on his thumbs. "When Rosalind and I were children, before she began to write sonnets and dramatic scenes, she would draw maps of her father's estate from memory. I remember how astonished I was when I rode with the earl to collect rents from the tenants, and realized that a bush along the road looked familiar because I had already seen it in one of Rosalind's maps. She knew every hill and every stream, every oak and every flower-bed. It was incredible."

Thomas nodded with equal awe. "She collects the rents now herself. And she insists on doing it alone."

Drake shot the steward a disapproving glance. "Alone! She knows better. She could be beaten or robbed on the way, there are so many ruffians wandering the country."

"She says she wants her tenants to know that on her property everyone is safe and trusted. Often she brings them gifts of food, and if a particular family has a hungry child, she will not collect the entire rent."

"No wonder the estate is wanting!"

"She loves this land. She loves her people."

"Yes, methinks she grows more like the queen every day." Drake did not try to hide the admiration that warmed his voice. "Queen Elizabeth wanted to be the perfect ruler, and she sacrificed her personal happiness to that end."

Admire Rosalind as he grudgingly did, he still could not change the course of fate. His destiny was already set, and it had nothing to do with Rosalind, or any other woman.

"Please, Drake, do not hurt Rosalind in this way." The old man reached out, gripped his forearm, and peered in Drake's eyes. "I beg you."

"It's too late, Thomas." Drake's voice was as rough as gravel. "Rosalind and I are hurtling toward our inexorable destinies. Unfortunately, our paths are set for collision. I have already been to see my lawyer, and instructed him to solicit offers."

"Ah." The steward exhaled, and all the life seemed to leave him. He visibly wilted.

Drake gently removed his arm from Thomas's grip, tugged meticulously at his doublet, and then rearranged some papers on the desk. "I'm sorry."

He was sorry to hurt her, but hurt her he must. He had to sell at least some of the land. For his father.

So why was he feeling as guilty as hell?

When Rosalind drew back the curtains from the windows in Francesca's chamber with a whoosh, sunlight flooded the cozy room and splashed on its still-slumbering inhabitant, snuggled in her bed.

"Wake up, Frannie. I have a visitor and need you by my side."

"A visitor?" Francesca mumbled as she blinked and stretched. "Who is it?"

"Lady Blunt."

"Ohhhh," Francesca moaned, and pulled a cover back over her head.

Rosalind chuckled. "I'd like to creep under my counterpane as well, but Huthbert says she's quite insistent on seeing me." She plunked herself down on the edge of the bed and yanked the cover back. Francesca gave her a sleepy smile.

"Frannie, what were you doing last night that made you so sleepy today?"

Francesca practically purred in response.

"How now, what is this?" Rosalind leaned closer for a better look. "A wilted flower in your hair?"

Francesca colored slightly and felt for the offending petals. She plucked the flower out of her tousled hair and held it in the sunlight. As she tilted her head back for examination, Rosalind spied a bruised spot on her friend's neck.

"And who did that? Don't tell me. I know who it was. It was Jacques, wasn't it?"

"Yes, it was Jacques." Francesca's eyes gleamed with

mischief. "And Lord Fairmont, and Master Connard, and Sir Jervais, and—"

"No!" Rosalind's jaw dropped. "You didn't. Not with all of them!"

Francesca let out a sweet peal of laughter. "Oh, you are so easy to tease. No, Jacques was the only man who possessed my body last night."

Rosalind stilled. "But there've been others?"

"What do you want me to say?"

"I want you to say no. Frannie, I don't think of you as a woman who . . . beds any man she pleases."

Francesca's wistful expression turned hard. "Why not? I am a widow. It is my right to do as I please. I've earned it, Rosalind." She sat up and brushed a lock of hair behind her right ear. "What is it? Why must you be so prudish? Is it because you are a—" She stopped abruptly and bit her lower lip.

"Because I'm a virgin?"

Francesca looked up, her gaze soft with remorse. "I'm sorry. That wasn't kind."

Rosalind sighed, refusing to let anger spoil yet another of her relationships. She took her friend's hands and held them tightly. Here was a friend who would never leave her, and whom she would never abandon.

"I love you, Frannie. I just don't want to see you hurt. After your wardship was sold, I didn't see you for—how many years was it?"

"Six."

"For six years. Next thing I knew you were a viscountess. Your husband was more than fifty years your senior. You had no children. I don't know what I thought. I suppose I imagined that you might still be a virgin, too. It sounds foolish, I know." Rosalind studied the lace on her friend's embroidered nightgown. The delicate scallops and swirls and flower buds were as complex as Frannie. "What did happen during those years after your wardship was sold? You've never told me."

When Francesca's contented gaze suddenly turned sober, Rosalind regretted her honesty. "If you don't wish to speak of it . . ."

Francesca pursed her lips thoughtfully. "I will tell you. One day. But not now. I'm too happy this morning."

"Very well. I suppose your amours are none of my business. I just can't imagine taking a virtual stranger to my bed."

"I thought writers had vivid imaginations."

"Yes, but there are some things I don't want to imagine." Having said it, Rosalind promptly envisioned Drake making love to her. She flushed with heat, turning red.

Francesca gave her a knowing smile. "Perhaps even you feel passion, my friend."

"I feel passion for my writing." Rosalind looked down at her fingers and noticed that they, like Will Shakespeare's, were smudged with ink. "When I write a love sonnet, I can possess love without ever living its unpleasant aftermath."

"Love does not always end in sorrow. Think of your mother and father. They loved each other for twenty years." Francesca reached out and caressed her cheek. "Methinks Cupid has an arrow left for you in his quiver."

Rosalind chafed at the very notion. She pulled back her shoulders in a practiced stance of bravado, cleared her throat, and changed the subject. "Speaking of arrows," she said gaily, "I suspect that Lady Blunt has a quiverful waiting to shoot at me. I'd best go see which part of my anatomy will be kindly impaled today." She leaned forward and bussed her friend's cheek. "Don't be long. Come down when you get dressed, and save me from London's gossip extraordinaire."

Francesca gave a lilting laugh, and in her gleaming eyes

Rosalind saw the admiration Frannie had always felt for her. She was one of the many people for whom Rosalind was brave.

"I just hope you don't let any man hurt you, Frannie. A heart breaks easily."

Francesca blinked her dark lashes against the flowerlike purple of her eyes. Her smile faded, and Rosalind suddenly saw her beloved friend turn into a stranger, as surely as if a dark spirit had taken possession of her body.

"I've not a heart left to break." Francesca's voice was hard. Then she broke the spell with a lilting smile.

"Frannie . . ." Rosalind started to reach for her hand.

"No, go, Rosalind. I was merely being morose. You need not worry about me, dear heart. Go. Lady Blunt is waiting."

"Very well," Rosalind replied reluctantly, and slowly turned to meet her first challenge of the day.

"Ah, Lady Blunt, you are up and about early today," Rosalind said as she swept into the front parlor with arms outstretched.

"Rosalind, my dear!"

Lady Blunt hoisted herself up from a wooden chair and waddled toward her hostess. The lady's torso was shaped like a short keg of wine, and her black hair seemed to top it like an unruly nosegay. Her eyes, which always seemed to be pressing to their outward limits, were keen and bright. She smiled broadly, and her red lips spread like spilled wine. While she seemed to any stranger benignly garish, Rosalind never forgot her father's warning that in her younger days, Lady Blunt was considered one of the more dangerous of the royal Court's scheming ladies.

"Did Huthbert attend to your needs, Lady Blunt?" Rosalind pressed her cheek to her guest's.

"Yes, he did. And please, call me Porphyria."

"Porphyria," Rosalind repeated with a hesitant nod. Oh dear, she thought, this is going to be worse than I imagined. Precisely how did one embrace a snake without being crushed to death? But perhaps she was being too harsh. Since the death of her husband, Lady Blunt had lost influence at Court and was perhaps seeking less conniving company in her waning years.

"Now, what is it that brings you here? Porphyria," Rosalind dutifully added as she indicated that her guest should sit. When Rosalind sat down next to her, Lady Blunt gripped her arm and snuck a glance over her shoulder.

"Is *he* here?" she said, sotto voce.

"You mean Drake? Yes, somewhere. I haven't seen him this morning."

"You *allow* him stay here?"

"I'm afraid, Porphyria, that I don't have much choice. Drake has always done exactly as he pleases."

"Call the constable, I say. And make haste. The man is dangerous. You know I'm personal friends with the Lord Mayor of London."

"He can do nothing. We are not within the city boundaries. Besides, the authorities and I are not exactly friends. The Lord Mayor would like to shut down the theatres. Between his efforts, and those of the Puritans, as well as an outbreak of the plague, it was very nearly accomplished a few years ago."

Lady Blunt's face flushed and the great folds of her bosom swelled against her satin bodice. "My dear, you might be willing to strike a bargain with the devil himself after you hear what I have learned about Master Drake Rothwell."

Rosalind's skin chilled at the ominous prediction. "I'm not to sure I want to hear it."

"Trust me, you do." Titillated, the grande dame sat at the edge of her chair. "I've learned that Drake is offering your land for sale through a solicitor who's been meeting with some of the richest and most discreet lords in England.''

"My land! No, you must be mistaken. Drake is headstrong and conniving and selfish, but he would never try to sell Thornbury estate without telling me first.''

Lady Blunt's amorphous lips turned hard and narrow against her teeth. Her eyes were harder still. "You don't believe that.''

Rosalind's heart began to thunder beneath her breasts. She struggled for air. When she remained mute, her tongue seemingly glued to the roof of her suddenly dry mouth, the lady continued.

"I have this information firsthand. Drake's lawyer contacted mine, on behalf of another party, mind you.''

"And he divulged information about another party's affairs? Isn't that . . . unethical?''

Lady Blunt quirked one brow. "He is a *lawyer*, my dear.''

"Are you certain it was Drake who sent the solicitor?''

"Positively.''

"God curse him for a knave!" Rosalind exclaimed. She jumped to her feet and swung her fist into her palm with all her might. It stung, but she did not grimace. She would not weep. She would never, ever reveal another honest emotion to Drake until the day she died.

"Does my news upset you?" Lady Blunt tried to sound surprised.

Rosalind knew the widow's game, and she knew that her own reaction would fuel the gossip at Court. But her fury transcended all caution or fear of consequences.

"Am I upset?" she replied incredulously. "Why should I be? Merely because an insolent, brutish, fork-tongued liar has attempted to lull my fears with promises of support when all along he has been dealing behind my back? My naive, trusting, stupid back! Oh, churl, he will live to regret this day.''

She stormed toward the door.

''Hold fast, Rosalind, I may have a solution. . . .''

But Rosalind was of no mind to listen. If Drake wanted to play games, it was time she established the rules by which they would henceforth be played.

''Drake!'' she shouted, screamed really, if the soreness of her throat moments later was any indication of volume. A half-dozen passing servants froze in place, gaping at their mistress. ''Where is Drake?'' she demanded of any and all of them.

Huthbert spoke up. ''In the lord's parlor with Thomas, my lady.''

''Thomas! The traitor.'' Her temperature surged and red spots began to dance before her eyes, so angry was she. ''Thank you, Huthbert.''

Never the improper hostess, Rosalind returned to Lady Blunt. ''Porphyria, Master Shakespeare's players are going to present a play tonight in my gallery. It will be a small affair. I would love for you to join us.''

''And my son, Godfrey?'' Lady Blunt said as she rose with a puffing effort.

''Of course, invite whomever you wish.''

''Godfrey thinks *so* highly of you.''

''The sentiment is mutual, I'm sure. Huthbert will show you out. If you will excuse me.'' With that, Rosalind turned and stormed toward the lord's parlor, ready to confront Drake as the enemy he had finally and indubitably proven himself to be.

Twelve

❦

When a liveried servant saw where Rosalind was headed, he rushed toward her, pushing the parlor doors open and nodding nervously to the surprised men inside, then stepped aside before Rosalind could run him over. She stopped abruptly at the sight of Drake and Thomas, hunched over the ledgers.

"What is this?" Her indignant voice echoed off the high ceiling. "Two traitors at work? Haven't you done enough damage already?"

"My lady . . ." Thomas rose with a look of alarm.

"I will hear no excuses, Thomas. Have you sold Thornbury estate yet? Did you find a buyer for the house as well?"

Drake stood and placed a comforting hand on the old steward. "Don't blame Thomas. It was my doing."

"You had no right!"

"As much right as you. Until matters are settled, we are joint heirs, my dear."

God, how she hated him. Just as much as she had when

he arrived here so long ago. More, for now he had not only the will to usurp her, but the wits and the knowledge and possibly the power. She hated the lazy pucker of his manly lips, the languid arch of his magnificently sculpted eyebrow.

"I am the rightful heir, Drake. I don't care what that damnable piece of paper says. I am my father's issue. This was his house, and I was his only child."

"My father built this house!" Drake roared. He dashed across the room in a few wide strides. "My father built this house with every drop of blood and every sinew in his body. He lived for this house. He died for it." Looming over her, he gripped her arms, ungently, so that Thomas gasped.

"Master Drake, no!"

"Quiet, Thomas! It's time this little magpie sees something beyond her own narrow little world."

"It is *not* a little world!" She yanked her arms from his strong grip. "Just because I am a woman does not mean my world is little. Nor does it mean you should have Thornbury House just because you are a man."

"Gender matters not a whit, God's teeth!"

"If my world is small at all, it is because I live for this prodigy house. It is everything to me." Devil curse it! Blasted tears began to sting her eyes. Don't cry! she warned herself. Damn you, don't cry!

"What is it to you?" She ground the words through clenched teeth. "I would have thought you wanted Thornbury House because you loved the place and because you wanted to restore the honor of your father. But no! You want to squeeze from it every last penny that you can. Money is all you live for. You deceived my father in its name years ago, and now you've shamelessly tried to deceive me."

He raised the flat of his hand to strike her. She braced herself for the blow and didn't flinch.

"Do it," she said gloatingly. "I want to see you stoop so low."

His hand began to tremble as his face flushed scarlet. Then he took the palm aimed at her cheek and smoothed it over his head. "Damnation take you, Rosalind, I have never in all my days wanted so deeply to turn a woman over my knee and to give a good blistering spanking."

"Try it, sir, and you'd best heed the integrity of your private parts lest some be missing when I rise from your lap."

He blinked as he imagined this unlikely scenario, then began to laugh. "Oh, Roz, I've missed sparring with you these years away from London."

"No, don't laugh. This is no jest, and you are no game-cock to spar with. You are a dangerous enemy. I momentarily forgot that. In the carriage, I listened to your words of encouragement, little knowing that I was falling pray to your charm."

"Charm?" Drake tugged on his russet doublet and began to strut around the room. "Thomas, she thinks I'm charming."

"Indeed, sir."

"Is it the pretty turn of my calf, do you suppose?" Drake turned out his legs, covered in white hose. "Or is it my demeanor—pleasant, erudite, amusing?"

Viewing his flexed calf straining against the fabric, she felt a twinge of desire, and grimaced at her own frailty.

"I didn't see it at first." With trembling hands, she poured herself a cup of watered-down wine. She took a sip and allowed herself to stare at him, like a hunter who dispassionately eyes her quarry, though to be honest, it was she herself who was feeling like a hunter's hopeless prey. "Your charm was insidious because it was not expected.

When we were young, you were merely arrogant. But now you have added an ability to elicit sympathy to your arsenal. Have you learned that that is the quickest way to part a woman's thighs?''

"Rosalind!" Drake frowned, genuinely. "You shock me with your language."

"Oh, yes. Virgins shouldn't talk so."

"I'd be happy to change your status if it vexes you so."

Her eyes widened, and not only in shock, since some perverse part of her brain was not at all displeased by the prospect. Still she managed to sneer. "I cannot imagine a more odious possibility."

"To tell you the truth, neither can I."

"Now, don't start agreeing with me again. That is how the viper first blinded me to his fangs."

"Sssss." He taunted her with the hiss of a snake, and struck at the air with two crooked fingers.

She shook her head in pained forbearance. "I pray you, save your childish gibes. I want you to know, Drake, that the truce is over. The war is on. I'm dividing Thornbury House in two. Figuratively speaking, that is. This half of the house is yours. You can remain in the lord's parlor and you can have father's sleeping chamber. I will remain in my bedchamber." She smiled sweetly and took one last sip from her chalice before heading for the door.

"You're very generous, Rosalind."

"*Lady* Rosalind."

"Keep your chin that high in the air and I'll start calling you Lady Pointy Nose before the week is out."

She shut her eyes and shook her head. "You sound like a petulant schoolboy."

"Yes." He smiled charmingly. "And it gets your dander up so beautifully."

"As I was saying," she continued, as if speaking to a half-wit, "you may also use the south half of the gallery, but not the north. And, incidentally, my half of the house contains the buttery, the pantry, and the kitchen.''

"How convenient," he replied drolly.

"I'm sure you can eat in a tavern or a victualling house, or perhaps one of your doxies can fix supper for you. Meanwhile, I promise you, Drake, that I will fight you for this house with every sinew and fiber and dram of blood in my body.''

Drake nodded thoughtfully as he rubbed his chin, not impressed, apparently, with this last vow.

"Good day, Drake."

Just as she placed her hand on the smooth wood door frame, he called out to her. "You know, Rosalind, I've just discovered the most curious fact.''

Against all better judgment, she turned back. "Yes, what is it?''

"*My* half of the house contains the privy. The only privy in the entire house.''

Rosalind bit her lip into silence, then turned and strode away before he could see the steam that she was sure was billowing from her ears.

Drake resisted the urge to use that much-coveted privy, for he had a saddled horse waiting outside and pressing matters to attend to. He watched Rosalind go, and when she was out of earshot, he let out a delighted bark of laughter and marched off to his waiting steed.

The journey into town was much faster on horseback than by carriage, and before he knew it, he was at the brick structure that housed the company of Starck, Dewey, and Cobb, Esquires. It was well-placed in a private little nook off of fashionable High Holburn Street, down from the Inns of Court, where many young men, including noblemen, pursued their legal studies.

Windham Starck had handled Drake's father's affairs,

and had seemed to be an old man even then, at least in the eyes of the child Drake had been. But a child's perception of age is always exaggerated, and Starck was only sixty now. Age had only heightened the suave professionalism he exuded, and his stately desk and book-lined office contributed as well.

"Master Rothwell, it is a pleasure to see you after so many years."

Drake took the soft hand reaching out over the wooden desk and shook it warmly. "Master Starck, thank you for seeing me on short notice."

"Please sit, my boy. Ah, but you are no longer that." Starck sank into the rich cushions of his armchair and steepled his fingers beneath his silver beard. "I suppose you have come to follow up on your inquiries. I wasn't sure when to expect you, when your latest adventure would conclude."

"Unexpected business brought me back to London early. But I hope to settle this matter now that I have returned. I have employed another lawyer to handle some matters of inheritance, but I wish to conclude with you the issues that concern my late father. In fact," Drake added lightly, despite the excitement that churned in his belly, "of all the matters that face me now, this is the most important."

Starck nodded soberly and stood. At the sound of his chair scraping on the old stones of the floor, his clerk stuck his head round the door.

"George, please bring me Master Mandrake Rothwell's papers," Starck said to the clerk.

"Yes, sir," the young man replied, and disappeared again.

"Drake, I have done as much as I can."

"Did you follow the leads I received from my diplomatic connections?"

At the lawyer's apologetic look, Drake sprang to his feet. "Master Starck, all I want to know is who killed my father? Surely you know. I've been paying you for years to gather information and to make inquiries on my behalf."

The lawyer's gray eyes widened at the hint of fury that lurked in Drake's voice. "We know only that a trading company, that existed on paper only, convinced your father to invest a large sum of money, which then led to his bankruptcy, to his despondency, and finally to his death."

Drake smoldered at the sound of these words, which he'd heard so many times before. "As I said, *who* killed my father?"

The harried-looking clerk entered with a neat stack of papers tied with a yellowed ribbon. "Here you are, Master Starck. The most recent letter is on top."

Recent? That was heartening. At least Drake knew he hadn't been sending Starck, Dewey, and Cobb his gold for nothing.

"Thank you, George. Shut the door when you go out, won't you, lad?"

The clerk nodded and quietly departed. Starck did not move until the door was shut and latched, then he untied the ribbon and shuffled through the top papers. "It seems you were right all along, Drake," he began. "This trading outfit, the Spicery Trading Company, was blessed by the favor of some very powerful men, men who were very well connected at Court. It was they who drew your unwitting father into disaster."

Drake tightened his grip on the edge of the desk. "What do you mean?"

Starck looked ominously over the top of his spectacles. "I mean that none other than late Lord Burghley himself drew up the charter."

Burghley! The lord high treasurer himself. He had been

Queen Elizabeth's most trusted adviser until his death two years before. Drake felt not only a stab of betrayal, but one of fear as well. If the misdeeds of his father's killers were being covered up by men in high places, then, as Lord Dunnington had long ago predicted, Drake's attempt to bring them to justice was a very dangerous, perhaps even deadly, enterprise.

But he did not care. He lived for revenge. He would pluck out his heart and sell his soul before he would renounce his quest.

"Lord Burghley," Drake said breathlessly as he sank back into his chair, thunderstruck. "I would never have guessed it would go that far up into the royal Court."

"Not that Burghley himself would lend himself to such nefarious dealings, mind you, but he did sign the papers, and so we cannot but infer that the person who formed the company was very well placed."

Another thought, another suspicion formed in his mind, for Drake now knew he could trust no one. "How long have you known this?"

He held Starck's gaze, which seemed to be cloudy with untold calculations. Just when Drake had concluded he would receive a lie in answer, the lawyer surprised him.

"I've known Burghley's hand was in this for the last fifteen years. I learned about it shortly after you left England for the first time on one of your adventures at sea."

"God's mercy!" Drake shouted. He heaved his fist onto the table with a resounding thump.

The door flew open and George the clerk again appeared, his eyes wide with terror. "Master Starck, is there something amiss?"

"No, George, shut the door."

"You *knew* for fifteen years?" Drake railed. "You knew and you never told me? *Why?*"

"I don't need to tell you that Lord Burghley was the

most powerful man in England. Not only was he the queen's closest adviser, he was master of the Court of Wards.'' Starck pursed his lips and looked away. ''At the time you employed me to investigate, Burghley held my niece's wardship. She was living with dozens of other wards.''

''At Burghley's home.''

''Yes. At my brother's deathbed, I promised him I would spare no expense trying to buy his daughter's wardship from Burghley so she would not suffer the fate of so many other women—being sold to some rich but unloving guardian. I could not anger Burghley at that time, you see, for he was in complete control of my niece's fate. I could not tell him that a client of mine suspected that his well-placed friends were behind an unlawful and wicked trading scheme. I admit that my love for my niece caused me to compromise my ability to best serve you. But I could not give your case to anyone else. You had sworn me to secrecy.''

''You could have written to me, told me that you were bound by other matters.''

''I had planned on such a course of action, but then I received this letter.'' Weary from years of compromise and secrecy, Starck shoved the missive across the desk. As Drake scanned it the lawyer continued. ''I can summarize its contents. It says that if I were to make any inquiries into the dealings of the by-then-defunct Spicery Trading Company, my queries would result in my death. So you see, I had been exploring as much as I could without offending Burghley. Enough to worry the company's founders. After I received this letter, I concluded that any missive I sent to you might well endanger your life as well. How easy it would have been for some hired knave to throw you overboard in some accident at sea, and no one the wiser.''

Drake scanned the faded letter, trying but failing to recognize the handwriting. "So you believe this letter was written by someone other than Burghley."

"Of course."

Drake let the letter fall back to the desk. He folded his hands and squeezed hard. "All these years I believed you were searching on my behalf. All these years I've been sending you payment to that end."

Starck pulled another paper from the stack and pushed it across the desk. "Here is an accounting of all you have paid me. See my clerk before you leave and he will write you a note."

Drake perused the sum. It would be enough to keep him in style awhile in London, but not enough to buy any significant amount of pepper.

"I don't want your money, Drake. Just your understanding."

"Why are you telling me now?"

"When Lord Burghley died, I assumed the danger died with him. I will retire soon. It would do my conscience good to end my career with a good deed."

Drake looked up, hope burning in his hardened gaze. "You plan to delve into this further?"

"I already have. And it has already yielded a response. Although the latest missive may be linked only to your return, and not my inquiries." This time the lawyer plucked the top letter from the stack and, with a worried shake of his head, handed it to his client.

Drake immediately noticed the handwriting. "It was written by the same person."

"It appears so."

" 'Tell Rothwell to return to the East Indies, or his visit will end with a terrible accident,' " Drake read, and smiled crookedly. "You know, Starck, this gives me a peculiar sense of happiness."

The lawyer looked confused. "Oh?"

"I feel much closer to my father. He must have been hounded by these wretched thieves, whoever they are, before his death. Now I know how he felt. The only difference between my father and me is that he was murdered." Drake met Starck's eyes with a gaze of steel. "And this time it is I who will do the killing."

Thirteen

Drake returned to Thornbury House late in the afternoon. He entered by the south entrance, and found his way to Thomas's room in the quarters used by staff and servants. When he knocked softly and poked his head into the steward's chamber, Thomas was seated by his only window, polishing his clock in the waning bronze sunlight.

Drake waited for an invitation. He had entered this room freely as a boy, but he had disappointed the steward today, and wasn't sure he was welcome anymore.

"Could you use some company, old man?"

"Drake! Come in, lad. Come in."

When Thomas rose and crossed the room with open arms, Drake noticed that he was limping and stopped him with both hands. "Walk no further, old man. We do not stand on formality here. Your bunions are bothering you, I can see that much."

Thomas looked up and frowned, his thin, gray brows gathering like soft clouds on a rainy day. "What? You remember?"

"Yes, and I remember how you never took your physic and applied the poultices the doctor instructed you to, you old knotty pate."

Thomas's eyes twinkled "My physic, eh?" He gave Drake's chest a soft punch. "Always bothering Lord Dunnington with such nonsense, you were."

"We were both concerned about your health. He loved you just as much as I did," Drake replied. "And do. Now sit, old man. I won't hear nay from you, no matter how many gray hairs are on your balding head."

Drake gently nudged the old steward back into his chair. When he knelt at his feet, Thomas tried to lift him up with a hand on his shoulder.

"No, Master Drake. It is not meet."

Drake reached out with a great palm and pulled the old man close. Thomas rested his head a moment on Drake's shoulder, and when Drake released him, the steward blinked back tears.

"You shouldn't carry on so."

"Hush, Thomas. I remember how you used to have me rub your feet with liniment." Drake tugged off the steward's slippers and found his feet wrapped tightly in cloth. He unbound the strips of material carefully. "I would rub your feet and you would advise me on matters of the estate. You spoke to me as if you expected me to inherit Thornbury one day."

"That I did." Thomas sank back with a contented sigh when Drake gently massaged first one foot and then the other, carefully avoiding the sore-looking bunions.

Seeing a box containing clean rags by the bed, Drake grabbed several strips and began to bind Thomas's feet up again.

"You were a good boy, Drake. A good boy."

"Was I?" Drake chuckled.

"The best."

Drake blinked hard as he studiously wrapped the steward's feet. "She hated me, Thomas. That's why I left. She hates me still. But I mean her no harm. It's in the stars, you see. Rosalind and I are doomed. This house has us both under its spell. The rest can't be helped. Don't you see?"

Thomas's brows gathered again, this time in a fervent effort to understand. "Rosalind can't hate you, boy. She has to see you as I."

"A woman doesn't have to do a damned thing she doesn't want to do. Even if men like to think otherwise."

"But if you tell her. Tell her you're in trouble. Tell her you need money."

"No. Rosalind must never know. She would use that information against me. She wouldn't want to, but she would. I can never be weak with that vixen." Drake knotted the strips binding Thomas's feet. "You won't be dancing tonight, old man."

"No." Thomas smiled as his eyelids began to droop. He yawned. "But you will be."

"I'll dance a thousand steps before this night is over," Drake answered dryly, then slipped out of the room as the steward nodded off.

By the time Drake returned from the privy, nearly all was in order for Rosalind's small supper party. The tables in the great hall were set, and servants were hustling to their posts, completing the preparations for the performance that would follow dinner.

At the top of the staircase at the front of the house, Drake heard noises floating up from the entrance hall—the clunk of clothing trunks being ferried in by the hired men and other assistants employed by Shakespeare's troupe and the rich laughter and jesting of the players traipsing in. He recognized the voices of Thomas Pope,

Richard Crowley, and the star of the company, Richard Burbage. And of course, William Shakespeare, and his younger brother, Edwin.

"Drake, what are you doing?"

He turned from his perch on the banister overlooking the entrance and saw Francesca approaching. She was draped in her finest gown, a soft azure color that made her lovely almond eyes sparkle like amethysts. Her sleeves were padded with buckram and stood high above her shoulders. Her hair was swept up and woven into an ornate pearl tiara.

"Greetings, Frannie." He smiled and kissed her cheek with great affection. "You look beautiful as always. I was just listening to the preparations for the performance that I'll be missing now that I've been relegated to half the house."

Francesca joined him as he leaned over the edge of the banister. "Hmmm. That does pose a problem. The play will be presented in the gallery. Ah, but you have half the gallery, too! You can enjoy the performance even if you must watch the players's hind sides."

Drake grinned. "You clever puss. Are you taking my side in this?"

Francesca poked his arm playfully with a bejeweled fist. "No, curse you. Once again I am forced to travel the uncomfortable middle road. I managed to get through our childhood without taking sides, or with both of you thinking I sided with you, and now I'm forced to do so again."

Seeing the faint lines etched at the corners of his childhood friend's eyes, Drake shook his head. "Good God, we've been at this a long time. If only Rosalind would grow up."

"It's not that simple, Drake. And I'm afraid it is only becoming more and more complicated the older we get.

She cannot see you but through the dusty window of the past.''

He nodded soberly. ''When you first approached me, Frannie, I was listening to the sounds of the players getting ready for the performance tonight. It reminded me of when I was a boy, before I returned to Thornbury House with my mother.''

Francesca touched his arm tenderly. ''You mean when you lived . . .'' She let her words trail off.

''Don't be embarrassed. You can say it. When I lived in a rent on the worst street in the worst district in London—Liberty of the Clink. I received my first black eye there. A sailor mistook my mother for a bawd. He tried to drag her off the street and into a nearby stew for a good romp on a straw mattress. I fought him off and he punched me in the eye.''

''How dreadful!''

''Not really. I learned then that I could survive a blow easily. That knowledge comes in handy when you live with murderers, villains, and thieves.''

''That part of Southwark has turned into a very fashionable theatrical district. Rosalind and I were there yesterday, visiting the Globe.''

''It's fashionable if you're one of the thousands of theatre patrons who hire watermen to ferry you across the Thames for an afternoon performance, and then return before dark, before the cutpurses emerge from the shadows of the rows of tenements, and the whores from the stews begin to solicit. When I was a boy, the only decent building in the area was the Bishop of Winchester's palace. I remember standing outside the Bear Garden as a child, listening to the roar of the crowd as bears fought it out with dogs inside the great circular theatre. When the mastiffs would sink their teeth into the paws of the chained bears, and the animal moaned in pain, the crowd cheered.

Then performers would leap out of some mechanical device and sing and dance. And a rocket would explode and shower the audience with pears and apples.''

''What a magnificent spectacle, especially for a young boy.''

Drake smiled sardonically. ''Yes, it must have been. I never actually saw the show. Couldn't afford a penny to get in. But I heard about it. I would sit outside and listen to the sounds floating out of the round and open ceiling. At the end of the night, as patrons left, I would ask them to tell me what they saw. And then I could picture in my mind what was happening when I heard the sounds from outside on subsequent evenings.''

''What a clever boy you were,'' Francesca replied, careful not to let pity creep into her voice, for she knew the aching depths of Drake's pride.

''That's why I was so intrigued when I discovered that Rosalind was secretly writing stories. What a remarkable gift, to enable people to see things they can't afford to witness themselves, or to allow them to travel without ever leaving England, all through the power of language.''

''So you do appreciate Rosalind, after all.''

''I appreciate her more than she'll ever know. I appreciate her determination, her temper, her stubbornness, her—''

''Don't let the list go on too long, Drake, or I shall have to give up on you both.''

''I've given up hope in you.''

She turned and leaned her right elbow on the banister. ''Whatever do you mean?''

''I've given up hope that my best childhood friend will ever fall in love.''

''Fall in love? What has that to do with anything? One minute you are talking about Rosalind, and the next you are talking about falling in love. What can I deduce from these wildly disparate topics? Is there some connection, perhaps?''

''You can deduce that I am a terrible conversationalist who would not know a bit of sophisticated repartee if it fell upon my head.''

She tucked an arm through his and tugged him close. ''Are you in love with Rosalind?'' she whispered intimately. ''Could it be? Is that what is behind your anger at her?''

''Don't be absurd, Frannie. That may have been what Lord Dunnington desired, but nothing could be farther from the truth.''

He briefly thought of all the ramifications of the earl's plan for them to marry, most particularly their wedding night. He imagined undressing Rosalind, seeing her fine white skin beneath her bodice. Seeing the subtle swell of her chest with each vibrant breath, the little gasps she would make in moments of passion.

He saw himself trailing a forefinger along the delicate little bumps of her spine from her slender neck down to the slope of her derriere. He saw the arch of her breasts, and his rough fingers upon them. He saw her mouth part in a soft cry of surprise and delight. Saw the moisture glistening on her lips, the pout of her upper lip that invited ravaging. He saw his own tongue flick and swirl over it, then delve into the moisture of her mouth, the precursor to a more inviting darkness.

And then he felt, not imagined, himself harden. His face reddened, as if Francesca could read his thoughts. Desiring Rosalind, or even thinking about desiring her, filled him with a multitude of warring emotions. How he would like to conquer her! To rip the last vestiges of pride from the aloof virgin. Make her grovel before him, begging for more.

He had not made love to a woman in five years. There

was no time for that when a man was eaten alive by ambition. And there was a certain falseness to it when the heart was not involved.

His heart was certainly involved with Rosalind, but there was too much discord between them to allow for love-making. Too many shattered hopes and spurned feelings. And there was a door he had closed on a secret longing, one so pure, so fragile, that he could not speak of it. He had given Rosalind so much in the early days, in that first instant when he'd seen her—the red curls dancing about a laughing visage, the spark of intelligence in her troubled emerald eyes, the arrogance, the power of a little girl whose promise of womanhood touches even the heart of a boy. She'd mesmerized him in an instant. Fooled him into thinking he'd found that one soul in all the world that was meant to be cherished by him alone.

A child can see it clearly, the promise of transcendent love, and then forget it entirely as he becomes a man. But before he forgets, a child can see and know more about devotion than any adult would credit, as Drake had seen it when he set eyes on Rosalind, and had *known* she was meant for him. It was a love to which all that followed would be compared and found wanting. That was the power she had had over him. And she had killed it. Could he let himself again love a woman he now hated so thoroughly because he had once loved her so dearly?

"Drake? Drake, are you still with me?"

He shook himself and gave Frannie a comical grin. "Ah, Frannie, if Rosalind were only more like you, I could marry her and all my problems would be solved."

"More like me? You mean pliant and cooperative and utterly thrown about by the world? No, my friend, I should be more like Rosalind. Strong and certain, even if a little misguided at times. I think you both should try to forgive each other for the sins of the past. Start over. See each other as you are now, not as you were when you were headstrong children.''

"Forgiveness?" He gave her one of his brash and handsome half grins. "I do not even know what that word means. I fear you are making much ado about nothing."

"They seem to pity the lady: it seems, her affections have their full bent. Love me! why, it must be requited. I hear how I am censured: they say I will bear myself proudly, if I perceive the love come from her; they say too that she will rather die than give any sign of affection. . . ."

As the player portraying Benedick spoke his lines, Rosalind leaned over to whisper in Francesca's ear. "Death would be preferable to showing affection."

"You don't mean that," Frannie replied, whispering so as not to disturb the performance.

They sat in the front row of the makeshift theatre, several dozen guests behind them. The players strutted about on a dais at the end of Rosalind's half of the gallery. No one asked why the other portion—Drake's half—had been left empty, and Rosalind did not offer any explanation.

"This is a wonderful play," Francesca whispered. She was adept at soothing Rosalind's wrath and was eager to do so now, for it was clear her friend was bubbling inside like a stew pot about to boil over. "What did Master Shakespeare say this was called?"

"Much Ado About Nothing," Rosalind replied. She felt Frannie give her a curious gaze. "Do I have a crumb upon my cheek?"

Francesca gave her a placating smile. "No, not at all. I . . . I was merely surprised by the title."

The actors' voices swelled. "No, truly, Ursula, she is too disdainful; I know her spirits are as coy and wild as the haggerds of the rock." The actor portraying Hero crept across the stage, as if to advance to an imaginary bower.

"You don't see any sign of Drake, do you?" Rosalind whispered, looking nervously over her shoulder.

"What if I did? He should not miss this wonderful performance. Really, Rosalind, you are too harsh on him."

"He's a thief and a liar. Oh, shhhh, here comes the soliloquy by Beatrice." The boy portraying Beatrice stepped forward and cleared his throat.

"What fire is in mine ears? Can this be true? Stand I condemn'd for pride and scorn so much? Contempt, farewell! and maiden pride, adieu! No glory lives behind the back of such. And, Benedick, love on; I will requite thee, taming my wild heart to thy loving hand: If thou dost love, my kindness shall incite thee to bind our loves up in a holy band; for others say thou dost deserve, and I believe it better than reportedly."

As the player swept from the stage, Rosalind felt a pang of joy at the sound of such clever language. She sat at the edge of her farthingale chair and applauded enthusiastically. Several dozen guests sitting behind her did likewise, then stopped. At least all but one lone member of the audience stopped.

Two bare hands continued clapping together, emitting loud and deliberate *thwomps*. When the sound persisted, even over the actors' pointed clearing of their throats, Rosalind turned and looked over her shoulder. It was Drake! Of course. Who else would have the audacity?

"You were asking about Drake?" Francesca whispered. "There he is."

One by one, the guests, who had also turned to gaze at the intruder, turned back to glimpse Rosalind. With coy smiles and raised brows, they were clearly waiting for her reaction.

She felt blood surge to her cheeks and clenched and unclenched her hands as she came to grips with the fact that a new performance, one without a preexisting script, was about to begin.

"What are you doing here?" she said calmly to Drake as she rose from her seat.

"Enjoying the play," Drake answered. "From my half of the gallery, of course. I would never cross the line."

His damnably inviting lips were poised with charming humor. His strong arms were crossed against his broad chest. His head was tilted, and in the torchlight, his eyes gleamed azure blue.

"This performance is being conducted in *my* half of the gallery," she tartly replied.

"But the sound is floating to *my* half."

From her seat in the third row, Lady Blunt tilted back and forth like a pendulum, trying to see Rosalind's reaction past the very tall Lord Brunwald's head.

"That is no excuse," Rosalind countered. "You are not invited to this party."

"But I just happened to be strolling through my half of the gallery."

"My lords and ladies, gentlemen and gentlewomen, Master Drake Rothwell thinks that he will embarrass me into a compromise," she announced resolutely to her gaping crowd. "But I am past embarrassment."

Drake lowered his arms and sought surer footing as a frown gathered on his forehead.

"Yes, Drake, I am beyond shame now. I am an eccentric, as anyone who attended my masque will tell you. I'm afraid you will have to find another way to tame my tongue. Ladies and gentleman, you've doubtless been wondering about Master Rothwell's return to London. It seems he has come to sell Thornbury House out from beneath my feet."

"Sell? What? Can he do that?" A chorus of voices swelled, then quieted.

"But I have no intention of selling. And if any of you here have contacted your lawyers about buying my land, I can assure you that I will tie up your efforts in the courts till kingdom come."

"My lady," came a rich voice from behind. Rosalind turned to find onstage Richard Burbage, London's greatest star, with his hands in a prayerful pose. "I beg you. Let us continue our performance."

Rosalind searched for Shakespeare. He was standing off the dais to one side, his arms crossed, a hint of a smile on his face. He was amused. Doubtless taking mental notes for use in his next play.

"The players want to get home to their wives and children," Burbage reasoned. "You'll not see a finer troupe in all of London. May we continue?"

"No, I think not," Drake said. "Rosalind is performing magnificently herself. Our guests couldn't see any better show than the one she herself is giving."

Rosalind spun on her feet, ready to launch a counterattack, when someone arrived to make a liar of Drake— perhaps the only person in London on this particular night who *could* entertain the guests more than the Rose of Thornbury House. It was none other than the Earl of Essex, Robert Devereux.

"My lady," Huthbert said, having preceded the earl, "and Master Rothwell," he added with a nod to Drake, "the Earl of Essex, Lord Robert Devereux, has arrived."

Unable to contain itself now, the audience let out a collective gasp. Rosalind turned, and catching sight of the fallen hero, she froze, and could almost hear the blood draining from her cheeks. Her heart began to pound.

Essex was a powerfully built man, with large eyes and a straight nose. He had a shock of wavy russet hair and sensually formed lips. At the sight of the handsome, bearded nobleman, once the queen's favorite, now a pariah at Court, the murmurs began again, a little more contained this time.

"The Earl of Essex," Rosalind repeated dumbly in a faint voice, seeing her connections to the queen vaporize before her very eyes. What would the queen think if Rosalind welcomed Essex? But how could she possibly turn him away?

More than a year earlier Elizabeth had sent him to Ireland as lord deputy to quell a rebellion led by the Irish leader Hugh O'Neill, the Earl of Tyrone. But instead of conquering the rebel forces, Essex had negotiated a treaty. Leaving his troops in Ireland, he had ridden back to Court, without permission, to explain his actions.

The queen had been furious to hear of his failure to conquer Tyrone's forces. And she had been stunned when Essex appeared, mud-splattered and uninvited, in her bedchamber before she had dressed for the day. It was the first time that he had seen the old queen without her red wig, spindly gray wisps of hair sticking up from her head. The flabbergasted monarch had, with great diplomacy, greeted him warmly, but later in the day ordered him to be put under the care of Lord Keeper Egerton at York House, with only two servants to attend him.

Thus confined, Essex grew anxious and became gravely ill. He begged the queen to receive him again, but was refused. Six months later he was allowed to return to Essex House on the Strand under what was essentially house arrest. There, he regained his health.

And last month he had been brought before a special commission of councillors and judges and was censured for his conduct. But he had been freed, under the condition that he avoid the Court and the queen. Essex had humbly retired to Oxfordshire.

And now here he was, making a social appearance, cleverly choosing an event that was being held on the outskirts of London and not attended by the queen. Rosalind guessed she was as stunned by his arrival as the queen had been by his appearance in her bedchamber that fateful morning.

"Ah, Lady Rosalind!" the earl said with great bluster when he spotted her in front of the others. "I hope I have not arrived too late to enjoy the entertainment."

"No," Drake answered for her, moving protectively to her side in spite of himself. "The entertainment, apparently, has just begun."

Rosalind flashed him a grateful look. The earl, seeing who had responded, narrowed his eyes on Drake, and his lips thinned with irritation. "Rothwell, I'd not expected you here. Why aren't you out on the high seas? I hear you've collected fifty tons of seashells for your pains. That should fetch a fair price at market—that is, if London's ladies take to wearing shell necklaces like bare-breasted natives instead of pearls and rubies."

The earl paused, apparently in the expectation of hearing laughter, but the room remained ominously silent. Rosalind could see Drake's chest expand with fury, and she quickly placed a soothing hand on his arm as her spine prickled with indignation. How dare the Earl of Essex burst into her home to insult her personal enemy. That was her duty!

"My lord," Rosalind said, "Drake has informed me that he has found so much pepper that should he return to London with it all at once, the market would be flooded and prices would plummet."

From the corner of her eye, she saw Drake shoot her an admiring gaze. In reality, she had no idea what his pepper would do to the market, but she'd heard enough about such matters to invent a believable fib.

"I would not want to send the economy into a dizzying

whirl of plunging prices, would you?'' Rosalind asked Essex.

The earl nodded as he digested her confidently expressed explanation. Then he nodded with grudging respect to Drake. ''It seems I've been wrong about you then, Rothwell. Ah, Lady Blunt! What a pleasure it is to see an old neighbor. Thank you for inviting me on Lady Rosalind's behalf.''

Rosalind pinned the old gossip with an astonished glare.

Lady Blunt reddened and nodded sheepishly to the earl. ''My pleasure, my lord,'' she muttered, meek for once in her life. ''We have missed you at Court.''

The earl moved on, and the crowd began to mingle, too disturbed by the commotion to sit quietly through the rest of the performance. Rosalind was grateful that Shakespeare had given the players the signal to pack their gear. They would be paid no matter how abbreviated their efforts. Shakespeare always said that he wrote long plays with the expectation that they would be cut as needed.

Someone had apparently signaled the musicians, for three recorders and a viol suddenly struck up a melody. Rosalind sighed away a bit of the tension that held her prisoner, then turned to Drake, appreciating the fact that he had rushed to her aide when Essex had entered. Her former rage over Drake's secret dealings seemed to pale beside the earl's threatening presence.

Drake studied her with great care and smiled morosely. ''Unlucky turn, eh? I'm sorry he's ruined your party.''

''Yes, now you can't ruin it yourself.'' Her words were tart, but her voice was gentle.

''You didn't have to lie about my success, Rosalind. I don't need a champion, least of all a woman. You have no idea what I plan to do with that pepper.'' He earnestly blinked and grinned. ''But I thank you.''

''Why on earth does Essex hate you? I saw it the moment he spotted you. What have you done to pique him?''

Drake's gaze sobered as he observed the queen's fallen angel working his way through the crowd. ''Perhaps I'll tell you another time. Essex is a bloated, arrogant ingrate who has bitten the hand that fed him all these years. He is more than sixteen thousand pounds in debt, and a desperate man is the first to cry rebellion. Let it suffice to say that he is someone you should not invite to your supper parties.''

''He was the queen's favorite for so long.'' Rosalind shook her head in wonder. ''I remember how he would play cards with her. They'd start in the early evening and he would not leave her chamber until the birds sang. If she hadn't been thirty-odd years his senior, and a devout virgin, I would have wondered if more than cards were being played.''

''He was too full of himself. He wants James Stuart to declare his rights to the English throne. Essex wants to become a kingmaker, to form a new parliament that will declare the Scottish king heir to Britain's throne. He is deluded.''

''The queen will have my head for welcoming him tonight.''

''No,'' Drake said with unexpected authority. ''The queen will learn of Essex's double-dealing through the proper channels.''

''How?'' Rosalind frowned up at him.

''I cannot say. But I beg you, stay away from him, Rosalind. He is the queen's worst enemy right now.''

She touched his arm, telling him without words that she would heed his advice. How did he know so much about the intricacies of Court politics? she wondered. It seemed odd for one who had been so long at sea. But his confident demeanor inspired new trust in her. A peculiar tingle met her fingers, and she stared at them as they melded with the folds of his linen doublet. What was it about him that felt different? Why did her hand want to linger there? Why did she trust him even as she hated him? Damn him for constantly soothing her tantrums. She wanted to spurn Drake, but it was becoming harder and harder to do so.

"You're right, of course. I will do as you say."

When he looked at her in astonishment, she swallowed the last of her pride. "Does my acquiescence surprise you? I am mature enough to recognize truth when I see it."

"I'd end this party as quickly as possible if I were you," Drake said ominously, then turned on his heel. "I'll leave that to you, since it is taking place in your half of the gallery." He bowed with a devilish twinkle in his eye, and started for the door.

Panic filled Rosalind at the thought of him leaving, and she snatched his sleeve. "You're not going now, are you?"

He turned and allowed a slow, wicked grin to wreathe his handsome lips. "Need I remind you that you've been trying to get rid of me for the last half hour?"

"Well, now I want you to stay. Keep an eye on Essex. *Please.*"

"No, Rosalind. You want to run this household, you handle Essex yourself. I know the difference between being wanted and being used."

He started away, just as she realized how much she needed him at her side. Damn him for a manipulative rogue. Rosalind stamped one foot. "Drake!"

He turned back again, and his smirk softened, apparently at the sight of her drawn cheeks and white-knuckled fists. "Don't worry, Rosalind. I won't be far. You'll not get rid of me that easily."

As he winked, and turned, she felt the most infuriating urge to run after him like a desperate thing and at the same time to punch him in the face for making her need him so much. She didn't know whom she should fear more. Essex or Drake.

Drake, a little voice replied. That damnable little voice that always spoke the truth when her clever mind was spouting edicts to the contrary.

Fourteen

❧

After the performance, many of the guests filed out onto the terrace to hear the musicians. With viols and lutes, they performed favorites like ''O Mistress Mine'' and ''Where the Bee Sucks.'' Such tepid fare was about as bawdy as the evening would get. Rosalind sensed her guests were expecting some surprise, something like they'd been treated to at her masque. But after the death of the seigneur, Rosalind's days of shocking surprises were over.

The weight on her conscience lifted considerably after she learned that the seigneur had a long history as a lecher and a string of notable conquests to his name. He'd specialized in adulterous liaisons, and on one occasion had nearly been stabbed through the heart by an angry husband. His heart failure, it appeared, had probably been caused by his exceeding fear of rapiers and not by the foolishness of Rosalind's escapades.

As she stood by the arbor, thinking about that awful night, she became aware of two shadows approaching on the moonlit grass. She turned and saw Lady Blunt with a young blond man at her side. A limp mustache drooped on either side of his flaccid, overly pink lips. His bulbous nose was slightly red, and an oily sheen coated his pallid cheeks.

"Lady Rosalind, you remember my son, Godfrey?" Lady Blunt gestured to her son as if presenting Rosalind with a great gift. The young man, who looked to be in his early twenties, let out a bleat of laughter and swung his hand out in what he apparently considered a debonair gesture.

"My lady, you doth teach the stars to burn bright."

Rosalind gave him a tolerant smile. "You've seen *Romeo and Juliet*, I take it."

"Who hasn't?" Godfrey answered, then emitted another bleat of inordinately giddy laughter.

"My son is quite an intellectual," Lady Blunt said as she strummed her sausagelike fingers on the folds of her hiked-up bosom. Then she added with disdain, "He wants to be a player on the stage, like Burbage or Will Kempe. He adores Shakespeare."

"And Marlowe, Mother, don't forget him. And Jonson."

"I didn't know you were so well versed in dramatic literature, Godfrey." Rosalind commented politely.

"Yes, Godfrey studied at Cambridge. Master of arts. My dear boy here would have been married by now if he'd found a woman who was his equal in intellect."

Rosalind pursed her lips. "I see." And she had thought the lad had been unable to find a mate because of the universal repugnance his bleating laughter inspired. She had met Godfrey once before. He had struck her then, as now, as an overgrown pup who did not know where to place his paws.

"Ah, Juliet, Juliet, wherefore art thou Juliet," he intoned, swinging down on one knee as he clasped Rosalind's hand in his moist ones.

"Wherefore art thou, *Romeo,*" Rosalind gently corrected him.

"Deny thy father and refuse thy name. Or if thou wilt not—"

"Godfrey!" Lady Blunt snapped. "Get up. You're making a fool of yourself."

"Oh." His bright smile fell around his large teeth and he stood, dusting his knees. "But I thought—"

"Go back into the house," Lady Blunt ordered him. "I want to speak with Lady Rosalind alone."

"Yes, Mother." He nodded dutifully. As he backed away he smiled warmly at Rosalind, and said, "O, speak again bright angel!"

Lady Blunt let out a beleaguered sigh. "How he can walk backward and quote Shakespeare at the same time is beyond my understanding."

"Godfrey seems like an earnest young man."

"He is earnestly in love with you, my dear."

Rosalind slowly turned her head in Lady Blunt's direction. "In love with me? Why, Porphyria, we've scarcely spoken two dozen words before tonight."

"Ah, but he has seen you at Court. Your beauty is hard to ignore."

Rosalind gave a morose little chuckle. "You're speaking to a thirty-year-old maid. My beauty, it would seem, is not quite as compelling as you may think."

"Drake certainly is riveted to your side."

"It is the beauty of my house he finds so compelling."

"You can fight him, Rosalind. Take it from one who has been a player of Court politics for longer than you've been alive."

Rosalind studied the hard and worldly gleam in the widow's eyes and nearly shivered. It had been said that

Lady Blunt's late husband was no more than a devoted dupe. She had once been slim and beautiful, but her girth had grown in proportion to her desire for power. She had not loved Sir Raymond, it was said, but had been grateful to him for his status and his wealth. After his death, she had attempted, without great success, to consolidate her power at Court. The queen had never been fond of Lady Blunt, but had recognized her usefulness. Rosalind recalled an incident that concerned the queen banishing Lady Blunt from her entourage for some peccadillo; it was said that she had finagled a reconciliation by entreating the aid of Robert Devereux, who had pleaded for her forgiveness; the queen, at that time still vulnerable to his whims and demands, had acquiesced.

While Rosalind viewed Lady Blunt as a dangerous woman, one who had her own agenda uppermost in her mind, she recognized as well how powerful an ally the older woman could be. If her desire to possess Thornbury House once and for all were to be realized, she would need all the help she could get.

"What would you suggest I do in my battles with Drake?" Rosalind clasped her hands over the folds of her full gown.

"If you married someone else, then you would have a husband's strong hand to guide you in your fight for your inheritance."

Rosalind breathed the air, so rich with honeysuckle. She watched the silhouettes of guests laughing and mingling up above on the terrace. "Need I remind you what happened to Bess Throckmorton? She was imprisoned in the Tower for marrying Raleigh without the queen's permission."

"Oh, that! Pish! They were eventually set free. And Raleigh has been restored to his post as captain of the guard. Besides, *you* are no longer serving the queen."

"Who would I marry?"

Lady Blunt reached out and fervently gripped Rosalind's arm. Her eyes danced as her chin jiggled. "My Godfrey, of course!"

"Godfrey?" Rosalind heard the astonishment, even disgust, that laced her voice, and tried to recover some semblance of tact. "Er, rather, I see. Godfrey. Of course he would be a candidate."

"You would have my late husband's impeccable reputation to back you in any Court fight."

"Well, Lady Blunt—"

"Porphyria."

"Porphyria, I appreciate your concern, but marriage is the last thing I want to involve myself in. Isn't there anything less . . . drastic I can do?"

"You can find Drake's weakness."

Rosalind nodded, fighting another irritating surge of guilt.

"Let me investigate his years of absence from Court. Perhaps there is something embarrassing, or worse, that I can dig up on our dear Drake Rothwell."

Rosalind swallowed. "I don't want to hurt Drake."

"No, you want to roll over and let him walk over you through the front door of *your* house."

"No, it's merely that . . ." She let her words trail off, confounded by her contradictory needs to survive and at the same time to be kind.

Lady Blunt patted her arm. "You are still innocent, aren't you? Despite your years at Court. Rosalind, I did not choose to be a hard woman. I was forced to be in order to survive in the queen's domain. I know men like Drake. They can be dashing, charming, and tender, yet as vicious as a dog in a bear baiting when it suits them. Drake will wrest Thornbury House from you before you blink if you do not find more effective means than those your lawyer can offer.''

Rosalind shut her eyes against a surge of warring emotions. Drake did plan to take Thornbury House. He was already trying to sell the land. She could not be blinded by her growing affection for him. She could not delude herself with the promise, no doubt false, of his support.

Seeing her uncertainty, Lady Blunt stepped in closer and spoke in honeyed tones. ''Isn't there anything you want to know about him? Something . . . suspect? I have men who can find these things out.''

Rosalind let out a quivering sigh. When she tried to breathe in again, it seemed as if the air about them had vanished. ''At first I wondered why he left his prospering trading efforts to fight for possession of this house. He could have sent an agent in his stead. Then I realized he had returned simply to vex me—to settle old scores. He wants to take Thornbury House simply to prove that he can. I don't think he even cares about the house anymore. All that remains is his vindictiveness.''

''Good. Very good,'' Lady Blunt purred. ''Did you ever consider that perhaps he is not quite as successful as you think?''

Rosalind gave a twitching smile. She clasped her hands and stroked the blue vein pulsing in her left wrist. ''Drake would sell his soul to succeed at business. I find it hard to believe he's in trouble.''

''We'll find out soon enough. Meanwhile, what do you say to a secret little marriage to Godfrey? I can make all the arrangements.''

Perspiration broke out on Rosalind's forehead. She was getting in too deep with Lady Blunt. She was out of her depth. ''Porphyria, isn't Godfrey afraid he will die if he courts me? There is the curse, you know.''

''Ha!'' Lady Blunt barked out a cynical laugh. ''Don't

even mention the silly curse to Godfrey or he'll keel over from fright.''

Rosalind nodded. Oh, dear. Not even the threat of a deadly curse could daunt this determined woman. "I will consider your offer, Porphyria. But do not nurture false hopes. I am most disinclined to marry. The curse, you know . . .''

"You'll change your mind soon enough, I think. But that is entirely up to you." Lady Blunt leaned over and bussed Rosalind's cheek. "I'll be going now, dear. I have work to do. We'll bring down this arrogant merchant adventurer yet, I avow. Have no fear."

"But I don't want to bring him down. I merely want to keep my house . . . and to understand his motives."

"I predict that when you understand his motives, you will want to bring him down. I've never met a man, except perhaps for my late husband, who did not have evil lurking somewhere in his heart."

As Lady Blunt walked away, her enormous hindquarters swishing, Rosalind shivered again. A wind had picked up and cooled her forehead. Lady Blunt was a viper, all right. The question was, could Rosalind play the widow's game, by the widow's rules, without herself suffering a fatal sting?

After Drake had said farewell to the last guest, in *his* half of the entrance hall, he turned and spied two figures in quiet conversation farther down the hallway. Recognizing the forms—one tall and striking, the other shorter and unprepossessing—he frowned.

"What are you glaring at?" Rosalind said from her half of the entrance.

"None of your business."

"It is my house, therefore my business."

"*Our* house, lamentably, for the time being." Even

from a distance he could smell the perfume that wafted intoxicatingly from his hostess, some floral blend that reminded him of the lush native women of the East Indies. His groin twisted with long-forgotten hunger.

He glanced at Rosalind, ready to dismiss her with a curt look. She could not know the extent to which their new-found ease together had chipped away at the stone wall encircling his heart, the fortress he had built so many years ago to protect himself from her claws. He tried to dismiss her, but was caught unawares by the provocative look in her eyes. Those spiteful green eyes were warm with some new emotion, he could tell. Curiosity? And tendrils of red hair were coiling in a charmingly haphazard fashion around her cheekbones. He wanted to slip a finger in one of the spirals, to feel its softness.

"You still haven't told me what you were frowning at." She placed her hands on her hips and tilted her head fetchingly.

Be on guard, he told himself. You've always paid a price for her moments of easy warmth and amiability.

"I was watching Master Shakespeare talking privately with the Earl of Essex," Drake said. "You must warn your friend not to be so indiscreet."

"I don't think he has much choice. Devereux is a rather dominating figure. If he desires to engage in a tête-à-tête, he's not above backing one up against a wall." She strolled toward Drake as Huthbert closed the door on the last of the departing guests.

"Ah, ah, ah!" Drake wagged a finger in mock reproof. "Stick to your half, Roz. You've got me as territorial as a dog."

"A dog? Now that is an appropriate comparison. Cur might even be better."

"Just be glad I haven't lifted my leg on your furniture."

"That's disgusting!"

"I'm glad you think so."

"If I could be so bold as to interrupt your bickering," said Shakespeare, coming up to them with the earl at his side.

"Rothwell," Essex said with a speculative frown. He stopped next to Drake and crossed his long arms. "Do you take pleasure at hunting?"

"When I can."

"Come to Oxfordshire, then, why don't you? I am staying at the home of my uncle Sir William Knollys. We will go hawking together and sort out our differences. Times are changing. Even enemies may become allies. King James will want to know who was first among those to take his side."

Drake's cheeks turned to stone. "Scotland's king will have to wait until the death of our queen before he is declared successor. Elizabeth will never name an heir while she lives."

"Elizabeth is an incompetent old woman, now as crooked in nature as she is in body."

"God's teeth! You would dishonor her so?" Drake took a threatening step forward, but Rosalind stepped in front of him. "You are not fit to kiss the hem of her garment."

Essex flushed a deep red, and his eyes flared with the wildness that had ruined his political career at Court. "You would dare to insult a peer of the realm, *Master* Rothwell. The queen still loves me. I will tell her of your disrespect."

Drake swallowed his temper and placed a reassuring hand on Rosalind's arm, letting her know he would go no further. He gave Essex a dubious glance. "There is a hangman's noose around your neck, Essex. I see it as surely as I see you standing before me."

Essex glared down his nose at Drake, and seemed to consider these words.

"My lord, thank you for coming to my supper party,"

Rosalind said, quickly filling the awkward silence.

Essex tossed a hand in the air, waving aside the discord with a mad chuckle. He bowed to Rosalind, extending a muscular leg with courtly grace, then turned to Shakespeare. "We will talk further, Master Shakespeare."

Will dipped his head in acknowledgment. When Essex departed through the front door, Drake turned on the playwright.

"Master Shakespeare, you are risking much by conversing with that man."

Shakespeare smiled stoically. "I hardly had much choice, Master Rothwell. But I thank you for your kind warning."

"It is a kindness that just might keep the hangman's noose from your neck as well." Drake nodded curtly and ascended the grand staircase.

As Rosalind watched his progress, and Shakespeare's sober expression, she recalled Lady Blunt's offer to search Drake's closet in the hope of finding some skeletons. Again, she was struck by his knowledge of the nuances of palace politics.

"Come, Will, I can show you to your bedchamber."

"For the sake of a full night's slumber, I can only hope it lies in such a manner that one half is on your side of the house, and the other half on Drake's," the playwright replied with a droll smile.

Around one in the morning, Rosalind sat up in bed, dragging herself from the tangles of the most alarming dream she had ever had. She hugged herself with a sudden chill even as perspiration trickled between her breasts.

The nightmare, if she could call it that, began with her at Thornbury House, as so many of her dreams did. But this time she was moving out of the house. She climbed into a carriage, drove away, and never looked back. There

was no sadness; instead she felt a peculiar sense of freedom, a surreal certainty that she was heading off for some-
place better. But while she was traveling down the road to
her new destination, a carriage wheel broke and she found
herself stranded. Then Drake rode by on a fine stallion. He
did not smirk at or mock her. He simply dismounted and
began to fix her carriage. Then he pulled her by the hand
into a quaint little plaster-and-timber cottage. He laid her
down by a fire and began to undress her and . . .

Rosalind shuddered. The details of the dream were
vague. All she knew was that there was no space between
them. Their bodies were one. He ignited a fire in her that
would not be bound by propriety, or logic, or even the
limitations of flesh. The flames of hunger ravaged her, and
she knew that she could not quench them. Not alone.

She woke up panting and quivering in the most intimate
part of her body, hungering with carnal need. She hadn't
known she possessed such cravings. Was this the elusive
satisfaction she'd been searching for her whole life? Had
she confused mere lust with the more acceptable desire for
creative satisfaction? Was it possible that this was really
the only thing that mattered, the fundamental urge to cop-
ulate? What a terrifying prospect.

But if so, if a sexual awakening were unavoidable, why
did it have to be inspired by Drake? Couldn't she dream
of someone else? Someone who did not have the capacity
to disrupt her carefully planned life so thoroughly?

Fearing the answer, she combed her hair back with her
fingers. The strands clung to her moist skin as if it had
been smeared with honey. Then she remembered something else about the dream. She'd felt guilty when Drake
stopped to fix her carriage, though she couldn't quite understand why.

She yawned and tried to wipe the sleep from her eyes
as she crawled out of bed. Bright moonshine lit the path

out her chamber door. Her feet glided as if of their own
accord down a familiar path to the privy.

"I shouldn't feel remorseful about anything," she reassured herself in her groggy state.

When she put her hand on the door to the privy, the fog
began to clear. But it wasn't until she sat down on the cold
stone seat, and felt the cool air of the underground trench
caressing her bottom, that she realized what was bothering
her.

"Oh, dear." The fog cleared in an instant. "I am in
Drake's half of the house."

What on earth had possessed her to do such a childish
thing as to divide the house? She was thinking only of
punishing him, unaware of how much she would incon-
venience him, and herself. She wanted to possess Thornbury House more than all the world, but she did not own
it yet. And it was unfair of her pretend otherwise.

At this moment, however, her most immediate concern
was sneaking back to her room unnoticed. She could pro-
claim her division of the house null and void in the morning, but she didn't want to be seen breaking her own rules
in the meantime.

She finished the business at hand, then slowly creaked
the door open. She heard ticking—the little creaking
sounds wooden floors made at night, almost as if ghosts
were tiptoeing hither and yon. She inhaled the faintly
musty odor of a tapestry hanging on the wall right outside
the privy. Lulled by the familiarity of her surroundings,
she forgot about Drake, until she swung the door wide.

"Greetings, Moppet," he said.

She jumped and gasped. Then, spying him, a blush crept
up her neck. She pressed her back to the tapestry on the
wall. She felt exposed. As if Drake had had the same
dream as she and knew just how wanton she was.

Curse him for being so handsome, so . . . male! He was

still dressed, though only in breeches and a billowy white shirt. His tight derriere rested on the banister. His legs were casually crossed, and his muscular arms peeked out of his rolled-up sleeves. He held a candlestick in one hand, its golden flame painting his face with pulsing light. But instead of a mocking expression, the candlelight revealed a look of suprise, as if he, too, had been wakened by a realization he had not expected. His cheeks were gaunt tonight. She longed to stroke them, to soothe them, to touch the goodness in him, for she could see it now. Her dream had opened her eyes to his kindness, as well as to her need to be touched. It was not enough to be mistress of one's own destiny; one had to share that destiny somewhere along the way.

"I thought I might find you here," he said. Then came the mandatory teasing smile.

"I'm sorry, Drake."

"For what?"

"For . . ."

When she faltered, he tilted his head a fraction, waiting. He always listened to her so closely, as no one else ever had, even when her words had borne daggers. He would never turn away from her in any real sense. How many men could she say that about?

Grateful, humbled, she felt her eyes fill with tears. In silence, they coursed down her pale cheeks.

"Rosalind, are you weeping?"

"No," she said dryly, "rain is just pouring from my eyes."

"If you miss the privy that much, you can have it. I'll just piss out a window."

She laughed, then licked at a salty tear that touched her lips. "You shouldn't talk to a lady like that."

"You're not a lady. You're Roz. Fear not, a chamber pot will suffice nicely."

She laughed again then sniffled when more tears threatened to fall. He thrust himself away from the banister and pulled a kerchief from a pocket.

"My jest wasn't that bad, I hope."

"It was abominable," she said as a tear coursed down her right cheek.

He raised the kerchief to dab it, then suddenly lowered his hand, leaned forward, and nestled his lips to her cheek. What was he doing? Kissing her? No, he was drinking the tear!

Rosalind inhaled a shuddering breath, stunned by the excruciating tenderness of it all.

"Please don't cry," he whispered, then put his lips to her mouth, covering it firmly, lovingly.

Rosalind froze, turned to stone, save for her mouth, which burned sweetly against his. So much said with no words—I care, you matter, all is forgiven.

She remained in that pose even after he ended the kiss and drew back.

"Rosalind, are you still alive?"

She blinked open her eyes and slowly thawed. And finally saying what she needed to say, she admitted, "I was wrong to divide the house."

"Yes, you were. But I'd have you do it again if it meant another chance to see you like this now."

"How now, are you restless, too?" At the sound of the voice rising up from the bottom of the grand staircase, Drake and Rosalind turned and leaned over the balcony.

"Master Shakespeare," Drake said in pleasant surprise. "You have come at precisely the right moment. What are you doing up at this hour?"

"Composing, or trying to. I was sitting out on the terrace, writing by moonlight." He held up his leather penner, a carrying case that contained his paper, goose-quill pen, and an inkhorn. "What else is there to do when you can't sleep?"

He began to climb the stairs.

"Will, what are you working on?" Rosalind said. She leaned on the banister as she watched his progress, only mildly embarrassed that Shakespeare might have seen her kissing Drake. She felt a satisfying camaraderie with her late-night companions, and a smile found its way to her face.

"In truth, Rosalind, I know not what I'm writing."

"A sonnet?"

When Shakespeare joined them, he frowned cynically at his paper. "No, it seems to be the beginning of a new play. I haven't got the plot yet, but the lines are coming to me. I may put it away for a year or two, or throw it away, depending on my humor."

"Would you read it to us?" Rosalind asked timorously.

"There are only a few lines."

"That doesn't matter."

He shrugged and squinted in the shadows at his scribbled notes. "The quality of mercy is not strain'd," he began. "It droppeth as the gentle rain from heaven upon the place beneath. . . ."

Rosalind felt goose bumps rise on her arms as her heart began to melt.

"It is twice bless'd. It blesseth him that gives and him that takes. . . ."

And then she felt Drake's hand clasping one of hers. He squeezed gently. And she did not pull away. For once in her life she did not pull away.

Fifteen

❧

The late hours she had kept the night before left Rosalind with a lack of zest in the morning. She had planned to do some gardening while she anxiously awaited word about her request for permission to visit the queen at Court. In the end, however, she merely gave some instructions to the gardeners and took respite on a stone bench beneath a trellis of roses. It was her favorite spot to write and read.

Leaning against one coiled arm of the bench, she was contentedly turning page after page of one of her favorite medieval romances when she heard a bee buzz overhead, and looked up to see it flit from flower to flower. As she watched the fuzzy yellow-and-black creature she began to think about the baffling changes she had been going through in recent days. For one, her newest play, as yet untitled, was turning out to be a comedy, quite the opposite of what she had intended. For another, she had found some measure of peace, however temporary, with Drake, and that made her feel safe again, though his kiss last night added a jarring new element to their relationship. She had not credited him with being so tender. It made her wonder in what other ways she had underestimated him.

She had begun to realize that there was much about Drake she did not know, and she wanted to know everything. She wanted to know what he thought, and wanted, and what life he was molding for himself, and whether his destiny was worthy of his talents, and whether he truly knew how great a destiny he deserved. Probably not. He was, after all, a man.

Men's brains were smaller than women's, she was convinced. Rosalind had read about this apparent fact on bills posted by a certain Madame de Gaurro del Sancho. Said to be a Spanish Jew trained by a Persian alchemist, she operated on human cadavers and had concluded that men were the inferior sex. Needless to say, the surgically minded lady kept to herself, or she would likely be drawn and quartered, if not for being Spanish and a Jew, then for offending the bloated pride of the male gender.

Rosalind was pondering this fascinating theory, gazing over the top edge of her book at nothing in particular, when Drake suddenly appeared in her line of sight. And he was heading her way!

In addition to a leather jerkin, knee-high buskins, orange hose, and a black codpiece, she noticed two pistols. At the sight of him, Rosalind sighed with unexplained contentment. Forget the size of his brain. It did not matter in the presence of so much masculinity.

She wondered if the blazing sun caused him to perspire beneath his jerkin. Did beads of sweat commingle with the coils of black hair that peaked above his collar? Did his finely chiseled thighs chafe as he walked with sure steps? Did he emanate that tantalizing musky scent that she'd noticed last night when he was tending to her sniffling nose? Where did that scent come from? Why did men and women smell so different?

And how in God's name was one supposed to behave after one had been kissed for the first time?

Pretend to be reading, she decided, and bent back over her book.

"Greetings, Rosalind," he said moments later.

"Oh, Drake! I didn't see you coming. What is it?"

"I . . . I am going to London. And I thought I would come see you before I go."

She lowered the book onto the scrolled arm of her bench. "Are you going to solicit buyers for my property?"

"Not on this particular trip."

"Then why come to see me?"

He pursed his lips thoughtfully, his blue eyes scanning the cloudless sky, then shrugged. The leather jerkin creaked at the movement of his broad shoulders. "Why not?"

"Why not indeed?" She smiled, unexpectedly, and he gave her one in return.

"Actually, I was curious to see which Rosalind I might find today."

"Is my nature so contrary?"

"Not where others are concerned, I'm sure."

"Poor Drake. I have been so nasty to you over the years."

He took a step forward and hiked one foot on the bench beside her, an arm upon his knee. "That sounds uncannily like the truth. Perhaps Francesca is right."

"What did she say?"

"That we must forgive each other's past transgressions. You and I."

Rosalind's skin tingled warily at the notion. "She sounds like Master Shakespeare." She paused, noticing how large and powerful Drake's hands were. He was fully a man; they hadn't been children for ages. A curious panic flashed through her, pinking her cheeks. She looked at him anew, and realized the past truly was the past.

"Forgiveness," she said slowly. "That is an enticing prospect. Alas, it will do nothing, however, to win the battles we face presently."

He groaned in protest. "I am weary of battles, Rosalind. Can't we pretend for at least a day that there is a truce between the warring parties?"

"Pretend? You mean as we did when we were children, playing with dolls and wooden soldiers?"

"If that is how you would put it, then yes."

"Certainly we can pretend. We are complex people. We can be enemies and friends at once, can we not?"

That apparently wasn't quite what he was hoping to hear, for his chest rose and fell with a sigh. He reached up and plucked a rose from the trellis, then jerked his hand back, pressing his thumb to his mouth.

"Ow! Do you sharpen these thorns, or do they grow like that?"

She chuckled deep in her chest. "They grow that way, silly. That's why the queen likes to call herself Rosa Sine Spina—'The Rose Without a Thorn.' Haven't you ever held one in your hands?"

"Someone told me once that they were lethal. I vowed then never to succumb to their beauty." He buried his aquiline nose in a froth of petals and inhaled the rose's thick sweetness, eyeing Rosalind all the while. "I see now what I've been missing."

Her heart began to quicken beneath his languid gaze. She held his eyes as long as she could, then turned away, no longer ashamed to be the first one to do so. She wasn't as hard as she'd once thought herself to be. Nor as strong. Besides, there was a strength in weakness. She saw it in Francesca's gentle visage, in the love she seemed to evoke without effort from the opposite sex.

"Is your thumb very much injured?" she said, distractedly fingering one corner of her book. "Would you like me to kiss it?" Scarcely believing she'd uttered such nauseating drivel, she looked at him in time to see his face beaming with a conqueror's smirk.

"You? Kiss my thumb well? Now there's an intriguing possibility. Do you bear thorns, too?"

"You didn't seem to think so last night," she said primly, then reopened the book and cleared her throat, as if to begin reading again, acting as if his flippant comment had not stung.

"What is that?"

She ignored him, turning a page. The words were a blur, but she frowned at them earnestly nonetheless.

"What are you reading?" he persisted flirtatiously, this time leaning over her shoulder, so closely that his beard brushed her bare shoulder.

His breath was warm. The heat curled down her neck, setting her skin on fire. She bit her lip, preferring pain to this damning pleasure.

"Is this some kind of treatise?" he said.

"It's called the *Roman de la Rose*." She tilted her head sideways to cast him a superior look. "That's French for *Romance of the Rose*."

"Is that a fact?" he said pointedly.

"Now that I've told you what I'm doing, why don't you take yourself off to London?" She turned her attention back to her book but could feel his eyes studying her profile. He seemed to be focusing on her ear. She nervously brushed a lock of hair behind it.

"The *Roman de la Rose* is an allegory about love, isn't it?" He plucked the book from her hands and flipped through the pages. "I would never have thought you would care for medieval romances."

"It's not merely about love," she said, a bit defensively. "The story is also about hate and greed."

"And passion?" His winking blue eyes caught hers, but then he frowned as a loose sheaf fluttered from the pages of the book. "What's this?" he demanded, picking it up.

Recognizing the document as her own writing, she reached out to snatch it from him. "Give it to me!"

He stepped back with a mischievous grin, which faded when he began to read:

"My tongue will tell the anger of my heart,
  Or else my heart, concealing it, will break . . ."

His voice trailed away at the beauty of the words. He continued reading the verse in silence. When he'd finished, he blinked solemnly.

"This is lovely, Rosalind." He looked up, pinning her with his intense eyes. "Did Master Shakespeare write it?"

She shook her head, even as her heart trembled. "No, I did. It's from my newest play. The previous scenes I showed Will weren't fitting together as I'd hoped. So I started something altogether new."

"*You* wrote this?"

She nodded and held her breath.

"So you're still writing. I thought you had given it up along with other childhood fancies."

"It is not a fancy." The strength of her voice swelled over the sound of chirping birds. "It is my life. It is all I have."

He carefully placed the parchment back in the book, gave it back to her, and sank down at her side. "Then it is a gift you should cherish."

"Drake, there is much, very much, you do not know about me. I have a fierce hunger for knowledge. While I do desire this house, I desire even more to discover something about myself, and about the world, that will be lasting. I want to learn as much as I can in the short time allotted me here on this earth.''

''And well you should.''

At the clear sound of approval in his voice, she sank back against the bench, scrutinizing the dashing man who stood before her. ''What about you, Drake? What do you want from life?'' She suddenly pushed out the palm of one hand. ''No, don't tell me. I already know. You want to avenge your father's death.''

He chuckled softly, a dark and cynical sound. ''You know me too well.''

She did know him. And he knew her, too, even if he wasn't adept at expressing it, as men so often were not. And if at least one person knew her intimately, even a longtime enemy, wasn't that one of the frontiers she'd hoped to cross before her death? Intimacy. One of the most baffling frontiers of all, at least to one so unnaturally head-strong as Rosalind.

Heartened, she spun on the stone bench and crossed her legs beneath her loose gown. ''Drake,'' she said, real urgency in her voice, ''you have a plan, don't you?''

''A plan?'' He sat up, turning to her more fully.

''To avenge your father's death.''

He sighed long and low but never wavered from her gaze. ''Yes.''

''What is it?'' She put her hand on his knee. ''Tell me.''

His eyes flicked back and forth between hers. He scowled and shook his head. ''I can't.''

''You must. I can help you.''

''No, Rosalind, you can't. The danger is too great. When I was a child, Lord Dunnington told me that the person who destroyed my father was someone connected to the queen's Court.''

''You've found out who ruined your father?''

''No, but I've discovered that whoever it was had connections with the old Lord Burghley, the late William Cecil.''

"Lord Burghley!'' Her hand flew to her mouth.

"Yes. Remarkable, isn't it? The only worse prospect I can imagine would be if the culprit turned out to be related to the queen herself.''

"Lord Burghley was her closest adviser.'' She thought for a moment, then declared, "Well, whoever duped your father, if he's still at Court, you'll need my help.''

"No, I cannot accept it.''

"Male pride?'' she snapped. "Or don't you think a woman capable of gathering the necessary information?''

He glowered at her. "Rosalind . . .''

"Then what is it?''

"I don't want you to be hurt.''

"Oh.'' She raised her brows and pondered that chivalrous notion. "I thank you.''

"You're welcome.''

"Oh, but what a waste! Do you know how valuable I could be to you?''

"Frankly, I'm afraid to find out.''

She glanced furtively over her shoulder to make sure that they were still alone, then leaned close. "A few years ago, when the old Lord Hunsdon, then lord chamberlain, died, and Shakespeare's troupe lost their wonderful patron, it seemed the lord mayor of London and the Puritans would finally succeed in shutting down all of London's theatres. I spied on them, when I could, to find out what their plans were. Fortunately, nine months later, Lord Hunsdon's son, who had taken over as patron of the troupe, himself became lord chamberlain and gained the influence necessary to protect the theatre. So my information wasn't needed. But it gave Shakespeare and Burbage some peace of mind. I even have my old costume.''

"Costume?''

"Yes, a beard, a wig, and a doublet."

His white teeth flashed in a brilliant smile. "I'd pay dearly to see you in those." He was mocking, but the light of admiration in his eyes did not go unnoticed, or unappreciated.

"I'll put it on for you. I'll see what I can unearth about the culprit who ruined your father."

"You're very generous."

He reached out to brush her cheek with his hand, and she shut her eyes, forcing herself not to reach out to him in return. Lord, what boundaries had they crossed to make such familiarities seem routine?

She drew back and stood. "I'm not generous at all. My hope is that if you can avenge your father, you will no longer crave the house he built." She gave him a wistful smile. "You don't need it, you know. You're—"

"A man," he finished for her. "And a man can do whatever he likes. He can make his home anywhere."

"I'm repeating myself?"

"Indeed."

She nodded, took a few backward steps, then thought better of it. "Drake, I still plan to fight for this house."

"Naturally."

"This house represents the only freedom I will ever have."

"So you've said."

"I *need* this house to survive."

He crossed his arms and tilted his head as he considered her with great care. "Are you certain?"

She blinked at the gauntlet he'd just thrown before her. She thought briefly of her dream, the one in which she happily left the house behind, but the details were now fuzzy, fading as all dreams do.

"There is no doubt. I would rather die than give it up." She turned and let him ponder the absolute conviction of her words. She would die if she lost the house.

But he would die if she did not. That was Drake's sad thought as he watched her graceful form grow smaller and smaller in the distance.

Sixteen

❧

"Did you love your husband, Francesca?"

Rosalind's frank question was totally unexpected. They were traveling to Whitehall, where Rosalind would finally have her audience with the queen. Her purpose was allegedly that of introducing Francesca, who had not been to Court since she was a child, but her real purpose, of course, was to talk to Elizabeth about Thornbury House, and she knew very well that this meeting might well determine her future. So why was it that all she could think about during the carriage ride was yesterday's intimate conversation in the garden with Drake?

"Did I love my husband?" Francesca turned and regarded her as if she'd just sprouted two heads.

"What I mean is, did you love him in a romantic sense?"

"No." Francesca shrugged. "I never expected to."

"You did not expect to love your husband?"

Francesca's delicate features clouded over. "No."

"Did you hope to?"

"Not a man more than fifty years older than I. Frankly, when we married, I secretly hoped he would die."

Rosalind frowned. "I see."

"Do you think me horrible for saying that?"

"No, Frannie, no! You were a virgin. You were afraid."

"A virgin." An ironic look transformed Frannie's face. "Yes, of course I was."

"You were forced into a marriage you despised by an uncaring guardian."

"Something like that. Actually, it's a long story. When father died, I was thirteen. I went to live at Burghley, with the other young wards in Lord Burghley's care. Six months later my wardship was purchased by Simon Ague, the merchant. He was a man of thirty, unmarried. . . ."

When Francesca's voice trailed away, Rosalind imagined the worst. "Frannie, if he—"

"Hush, dear." She reached out and gave Rosalind's hand a reassuring squeeze. "It wasn't as you might imagine. He was an honorable man, in his own way. He never touched me. But he paraded me before friends of his, some of whom were potential suitors. I fell in love with one of them."

"You did?" Rosalind's amazed question was barely heard above the grinding of the wheels on the cobblestones.

"I was fifteen by then. He was forty. Very handsome. Very attentive. He seemed to know how lonely I was, how much I missed my mother, how frightened I was. He brought me flowers. Love-in-idleness. He brought me sugared treats, just as my father had."

Rosalind leaned closer and gripped her friend's hand harder. "But not like your father."

"No. Though I was young, I knew that his interest was not paternal. He found more and more excuses to visit Ague's house in Surrey. He took me on long walks. He began to hold my hand, and I did not flinch. Soon I realized that I was in love with him. He was an extraordinary man. The love of my life."

"Did you . . . did you . . . ?"

Francesca leaned her head sideways. "Did we make love?"

Rosalind nodded.

"Yes, we made love." Tears began to drop from her eyes onto Rosalind's gloved fingers.

"Frannie . . ." Rosalind drew back and wiped a gloved thumb over her cheeks. "Oh, Frannie, you love him still."

She hugged Rosalind, a heart-splitting embrace, joining mind to mind and soul to soul. "Dear heart, I'd forgotten just how much I still love him. I thought I'd put that behind me, but telling you now, I realize he is the barrier that somehow keeps me from loving Jacques."

The women loosened their embrace and gazed at one another.

"If you loved him, why didn't you marry? Was he not rich enough to pay your guardian what he wanted?"

"He was married," Francesca whispered in a distant voice.

"Oh."

"He arranged for me to marry a second cousin of an aunt's great-uncle's niece . . . or something of that nature. I led him to believe that I would do it. But in the end I married the viscount. He was old, but at least he was of my own choosing, in a sense. What a fool I was to think that illusion of choice would make up for our difference in age."

Rosalind threw her arms around her friend and hugged her fiercely. "Oh, Francesca, damnation and hell. I wanted so much more for you. Oh, damn it, Frannie! You wanted to choose, God love you. Oh, sweetling, my darling sweetling."

Rosalind at last understood the missing chapter of her friend's life. She grieved for her friend, and railed inwardly at herself for not keeping in closer touch.

How brave Frannie had been! How disciplined. She had made the most of her unfortunate circumstances. But thanks to a selfish man who had used his charm and good looks to take what was not his to take, she would never be able to open her heart to another man, no matter how many she took to her bed.

"And this man you loved," Rosalind whispered harshly, "where is he now?"

"Near Scotland."

"Does he know how you have suffered?"

Francesca withdrew and shook her head. "I never wanted to admit how much he had ruined my life, for I still loved him. I still do."

Rosalind patted her hand. "Love is a terrible thing, Frannie. I'll have none of it."

"Love is a precious thing," she answered through her tears. "That's the damnedest part of it all. If given the chance, I'd do it all again."

By the time they were led through the long corridors of Whitehall Palace to the queen's bedchamber, Rosalind was thoroughly nervous, hopeful, and desperate—an excruciating combination of emotions that left her ready to jump out of her skin. And yet she put a gentle smile on her face, for the performance she was about to give would spell out her destiny.

Francesca's heartbreaking tale had only increased Rosalind's determination to be mistress of her own fate. And she felt stronger than ever, knowing that she was claiming a single state not because she couldn't love, but because love wasn't worth all the sacrifices it required. She would choose her fate, devil take it, for Frannie's sake, if not her own.

"Your Majesty, Lady Rosalind is here with a friend, the Viscountess Halsbury," said the queen's first lady of the bedchamber as she pushed open the door.

"Lady Rosalind." Elizabeth's keen eyes narrowed as she sought Rosalind's reflection in her dressing mirror.

It was obvious from the brilliant jewels that glittered in the queen's wig that her ladies of the bedchamber had just helped her dress. Rosalind wondered that she still had the courage to gaze upon herself.

Most women aged with dignity. Not so the queen, who, even now, insisted on wearing low-cut bodices to expose her bosom. Her face was pale from a cosmetic made of egg whites, powdered eggshell, borax, alum, and white poppy seeds, the mixture beaten to a froth and applied several times a week to hide her wrinkles and pockmarks. Against that mask, her lips were berry bright. Her teeth were dark, almost black, and a few were missing. And still Her Majesty had believed such courtiers as the Earl of Essex when they told her a fairer face was not to be seen in all of Christendom.

"Your Majesty, it does my heart good to see my splendid prince again," Rosalind said, meaning it, as she curtsied deeply. Francesca did likewise.

"You have been away too long, Rosalind. And who is this with you?"

When she righted herself, Rosalind permitted herself the bold smile that Queen Elizabeth had once likened to her own. It apparently had worked a kind of magic on the hot-tempered monarch, for other ladies-in-waiting had been beaten about the head by Elizabeth for standing up to her. Never Rosalind.

"Our Court gossips tell us you have become an eccentric." The queen glared at her in the mirror.

"If they call me an eccentric, Your Majesty," she said, coming 'round and waiting for a royal hand to be proffered, "then they flatter me more than I had hoped."

Elizabeth frowned at this, and Rosalind knew a moment of blind panic. Perhaps the queen had forgotten their affection. If so, she was lost.

"Ah, dear pet." The queen held out a shaking hand. "I've missed your impertinence. You were the only female in our entire Court ever to utter a thought worth repeating."

Overwhelmed with relief, Rosalind sank to her knees and pressed her cheek to the queen's hand. "My liege, I love you more than I can say."

It was true. Rosalind had nearly forgotten the magic the monarch possessed, how she and everyone else at Court had lived to please Elizabeth, how each had died a little during those times when the queen grew surly and refused them audiences.

"I still have not met your friend."

Rosalind stood and motioned for Francesca to come forward. "With your permission, may I present the Viscountess Halsbury."

"Halsbury?" She frowned at Francesca. "I have not met her before. How is it that your late husband never brought you to Court?"

"He was very old when we married, Your Majesty," said Francesca. "He could not travel well. I did not want to go without him."

The queen's piercing eyes softened. "So you were devoted to him."

"It was my duty."

The queen smiled, understanding.

"Francesca is a dear friend of mine," Rosalind added with a proud smile.

"Is Lady Halsbury the one who convinced you to leave my service?"

"My queen, you were the one who told me to go and attend my duty at Thornbury House," Rosalind said, but it was not her response that the queen was waiting for.

Francesca blinked calmly. "Your Majesty, I am not guilty of that great sin. I would have taken Rosalind's place at your side if I could have. I have been left out to pasture in Yorkshire since the death of my husband."

"Do you have children?"

When Francesca did not immediately respond, Rosalind glanced at her in surprise.

Francesca's perfect face did not move, but her eyes glistened as she intently studied the queen. "Do you wish for children, Your Majesty?"

The women, strangers until now, locked eyes, and a feeling of warmth seemed to grow and pass between them. "How perceptive you are, Francesca. My courtiers lie to us now, as young men do to an old woman. They call me beautiful and eternal. I make them think that I believe them. But I do not. I am a barren old woman."

Elizabeth's voice sounded like the croak of a raven. Rosalind was dismayed to hear uncharacteristic regret and pessimism.

"I would have you at Court, Lady Halsbury." The queen rose, a bit unsteadily, and turned to Frannie. "You are someone who would not flatter me."

"I have duties. . . ." Francesca said, suddenly panicked.

"Stay this afternoon and you will learn of your duty to the crown. I can make a match for you. I once kept my ladies-in-waiting to myself, but I see now that an old woman is lonely indeed. Perhaps you should marry again."

Rosalind and Francesca exchanged a worried look. "Your Majesty, Francesca would never forgive me if my introduction to you led to the odious state of matrimony. A widow has, after all, worked hard for the bliss of her single statehood.''

"Perhaps we should discuss the matter alone, Francesca." Elizabeth raised an imperious brow and nodded at Rosalind. "Our friend here is proving hardheaded on the matter of marriage."

"I will linger in the palace, then, madam." Francesca curtsied again and quietly departed.

When the door closed behind her, the queen cleared her throat. "So what has brought you to my chamber? Some problem, is it?"

Rosalind pictured Drake in her mind's eye, the tenderness in his eyes when he read her poetry in the garden. Oh, hell, why would tenderness come to mind now? She had to think of her survival, and nothing else.

"I do have a problem. A grave one."

The queen sat in a chair by her bed and patted another for Rosalind. "Come, tell me all about it."

Rosalind sank onto the chair and neatly folded her hands. "The problem has a name: Drake."

"Sir Francis?"

"No, Master Mandrake Rothwell." When the queen gave her a blank look, Rosalind continued. "I'm sure you don't know him. He's a buccaneer. A merchant adventurer."

"Is he one that my trading companies need worry about?"

"He is a brilliant businessman," Rosalind said, surprised to find herself bragging about him. "He has been quite successful going from market to market, sometimes outwitting captains from the trading companies. He's spent recent years discovering new markets with nothing more than a single investor and letters of marques to go a-roving."

"Ah, a rogue seaman. A freebooter."

"Quite. He's singularly willful and bullheaded. He thinks he can do anything, including stealing my house."

"Ah, Thornbury House." The queen's crafty eyes hardened.

Rosalind swallowed thickly. "Your Majesty, you know how much Thornbury House means to me."

The queen blinked thoughtfully. "As much as this country has meant to me."

Heartened, Rosalind sat erect. "Yes. Precisely. You see, Drake was a childhood . . . friend. Father took him in out of charity, because Drake's father built Thornbury House."

"Ah yes. The late Master Rothwell. I visited him at Thornbury House shortly after it was built. He came to an unhappy end, didn't he?"

Rosalind felt a twinge of guilt. She was gossiping about Drake, revealing his most private pains. "Yes, he did, unfortunately. Drake is a good man, Your Majesty. A strong man. He has raised himself up despite terrible misfortune, and I confess he did so without any help, in fact he did so despite the hindrances selfish people like me placed in his path."

"Did he?"

Like a confessor, the queen wisely said little; her favorite expression was *video et taceo,* Latin for "I see and I am silent." In the face of this sympathetic silence, Rosalind could not hold her tongue.

"There was always a great rivalry between Drake and me. I couldn't wait until he was gone from my life. I don't feel that way anymore," Rosalind said softly. "But neither am I willing to hand him over my inheritance without a fight. He has returned simply to vex me. What did I do to him to deserve this persecution?"

The queen waited patiently for further explanations.

"Your Majesty, I have come here to enlist your support in claiming what is rightfully mine. I have brought with me my father's will." She pulled the document from her girdle.

The queen perused it quickly. "It is a will much like any other," Elizabeth pronounced.

"Yes, but there is one exactly like it with a crucial difference. It names Drake as the inheritor. My uncle Thadeus witnessed both the documents on the same day."

The queen compressed her red lips over her darkened teeth. "What do you make of that?"

Rosalind squeezed her fingers until her knuckles turned white. "My father wanted Drake and me to marry. He thought the existence of two wills would force us to wed in order to solve our legal problems over the ownership of the house."

"Your father was a clever man."

Rosalind jerked her head in the queen's direction. "But he was misguided, Your Majesty. Somehow he overlooked the fact that Drake and I loathed each other."

"Loathe is a strong word."

"Yes, well, perhaps we no longer feel such intense animosity," she hedged. "Perhaps we never did. But I don't want to share the house. I shouldn't have to. It's mine!"

The queen rocked to the edge of her seat, then stood with great effort. She went to a desk where she kept her private papers and began to search for something.

"Your Majesty, surely you see the folly of what my father has done."

"You want me to side with you, instead of Lord Dunnington, is that it?"

"Well, yes. You know me. You know how I long for independence. You have been my model in that, great queen. You have written poetry. So have I. You have lived

without the strong arm and possibly mean spirit of a husband. So have I. I am too old to change.''

Elizabeth shot her a jaded look. "You speak of age? I
am nearly seventy. You are a young chick. I am an old
hen. Don't speak to me of age." Having apparently found
what she was after, she lifted a folded piece of paper and
ran a thumb and forefinger over one edge of it.

"I am sorry, Rosalind, but I must side with your father
in this."

"*What?*"

"Andrew was a loyal member of the nobility, and an
important supporter of mine, through every crisis."

"But I served you, too."

"For five years. I have been a queen now for more than
forty." Her voice grew thin and weak. She blinked back
tears. "I have seen so many of my dear old friends die. I
alone was blessed with uncommonly good health. Your
father is gone. So is Burghley, Leicester, Blanche Parry. I
owe my allegiance to the dead, Rosalind."

"I see," Rosalind said in a shaky whisper. Her hands
were trembling. She was afraid she was about to faint.

"You don't have to marry Drake, of course. I can't
make you do that. And I won't throw you in the Tower if
you displease me. I will, however, take Thornbury House
from you if there is any squabble over whom it belongs
to."

Rosalind jumped to her feet. Fury ripped through her
body like a searing bolt of lightning. "Your Majesty! How
could you?"

"I've always wanted Thornbury House for my own. If
you disobey your father, I will consider you unworthy to
inherit his cherished home."

"What will I do without it?"

"You are always welcome to serve at Court. Or I will
arrange a marriage for you."

"But why? You have always wanted your ladies to be without husbands."

The queen walked slowly to her, as if each step caused her pain, and handed her the paper. "You mentioned my poetry. Read this when you are alone, and perhaps you will understand. I do have your well-being in mind, Rosalind. Perhaps one day you will understand."

Rosalind took the paper in her trembling hands, then curtsied. She could not insult the queen with further argument. "Your Majesty . . ." She turned and ran without waiting to be dismissed. It was a faux pas that surely would be overlooked in light of her overwrought state of mind.

Outside the royal bedchamber, Rosalind flipped open the note with fumbling hands and held it up to a torch on the wall. Then she read a poem written by the queen in her own hand:

On Monsieur's Departure

I grieve and dare not show my discontent;
I love, and yet am forced to seem to hate;
I dote yet dare not say I ever meant;
I seem stark mute, yet inwardly do prate.
I am and am not—I freeze and yet I burn,
Since from myself, my other self I turn.
My care is like my shadow in the Sun—
Follows me flying, flies when I pursue it;
Stands and lies by me, doth what I have done.
This too familiar care doth make me rue it;
Nor means I find to rid him from my breast;
Till by the end of things it be suppressed.
Oh, let me live with some more sweet content,
Or die and so forget what love ere meant.

When the door closed behind Rosalind, Elizabeth turned to a screen that partitioned a small portion of the room.

"Well, what do you make of that?" she said.

Drake stepped out from behind the screen and exchanged a grim look with the queen.

"Were you surprised by Rosalind's visit?"

"No." Drake began a slow pace. He steepled his hands and touched them to his lips. "She cares more than anyone about Thornbury House. Perhaps even more than my father did."

"Do you loathe her, as she said you do?"

Drake halted. He squeezed the bridge of his nose with a thumb and forefinger. "No."

"Quite the opposite, I would imagine."

He tried to swallow, but his throat had constricted. It was a wonder he could breathe at all.

"Did you return to vex her, as she says?"

He chuckled with bitter irony. "No, I'm nearly bankrupt. I need money."

The queen blinked slowly, gratified as she always was when a subject humbled himself before her. "Then why didn't you tell Rosalind? She might have been able to find some for you."

When Drake sighed wearily, the queen motioned for him to sit, and he sank down on a backless stool. "I did not tell Rosalind about my woes because I am already the dirt beneath her boots. She may find me charming, but she will never consider me her equal."

"Perhaps she would if I granted you a knighthood."

Drake measured Elizabeth's cunning expression. Those all-knowing eyes of hers beamed with intrigue. The aged monarch was taunting him with a gift she would never give him.

"Everyone knows Your Majesty is loath to create more knights and lords. You've oft said such generosity would diminish the ranks of those already enjoying the honor."

It had galled the queen when Essex created so many

new knights in his battles against the Irish rebel leader Tyrone.

"Besides," he added with a wry grin. "Think how astonished your Court would be if you knighted me. No one knows I've been spying on your diplomats overseas, reporting back to you on their doings in secret while I conduct my business."

No one knew about all the wealth, pirated from the Spaniards, that Drake had given to the queen to ingratiate himself, as all her favorites did, for Drake's role was secret. He was the one who did not need to be at Court to serve the queen, who served her best by being content to roam the farthest reaches of her realms, unknown and unheralded.

The queen purred with satisfaction. "Not even Burghley knew about you, Mandrake, my little spy."

At the mention of her late treasurer, Drake's heart began to pound. Dare he mention to her the matter that was always foremost in his mind?

"What is it?" she said, missing nothing. "Is it a knighthood you've been waiting for?"

"If it so please Your Majesty, I would graciously and humbly accept. But in truth, that is not what I most desire."

"Then what? I've wondered what has driven you. You've never even asked for a commission."

"I have served you for the pleasure of serving Gloriana, whom God has justly placed on our throne." Drake knelt before her in a gallant bow.

"And you have served me for another reason, methinks." Her voice cut through the air with unfailing precision.

He looked up. If not now, when? If not the queen, then who? "I want nothing more than to find the man who broke my father's spirit."

Drake rose and paced as he told the queen all that he knew about his father's death and the bogus trading company that had swindled him out of his money. He would never have imagined speaking so plainly to the queen, but then he would never have imagined that the culprit had been in Burghley's good graces. The queen's eyes misted with tears at the mention of his name. She had spoon-fed her beloved minister on his deathbed, and it was clear she missed him sorely. Drake was careful not to implicate Burghley directly or insult his honor.

"I will make a few inquiries," the queen said at last, slumping in her chair as if the conversation had exhausted her. "But your life must continue. Sometimes revenge cannot be had at any price. I once mourned my own mother, barely known to me before her death." She was refering to Anne Boleyn, who had been beheaded by Elizabeth's father, Henry VIII.

"Where does one go for justice when one's own father is both murderer and monarch?" she croaked.

Drake blushed to see the pettiness of his own grievances in light of the queen's. "I will trouble you no further, madam." He rose and bowed deeply, leg turned out.

"I meant what I said about the two of you marrying." The queen slowly marched to sit before her mirror again. She grimaced at her aged face. When he didn't respond, she sought his reflection. "Drake, did you hear me?"

He looked at her in the mirror. "You want us to marry."

The queen scowled thoughtfully. "That doesn't matter to you, does it? Whether you marry or not, whom you marry, it's all the same to you? No, don't answer. Your motives are as unfathomable as your whereabouts. That's why you have served me well."

"I live to serve you, my liege." He bowed deeply.

"Poor Rosalind. A woman is always a pawn in a man's

game. That's why I never married. Now get you gone. Go out the secret door.''

Drake nodded and rose.

"And be good to her," the queen added. "She is dear to our heart."

Seventeen

෴

Drake left Whitehall Palace and went directly to the docks on the Thames. He had a nearly overwhelming urge to commandeer a sailing ship and return to the East Indies. Distance had always been a tonic for his woes. Why confront ghosts here in England when he could escape to the high seas?

He did, in fact, board a vessel, but instead of a ship, it was only a wherry, one of hundreds of the little boats that dotted the Thames, transporting people back and forth across the river.

"Right lovely day, isn't it, master?" the waterman said as he puffed a crude little pipe and rowed toward bankside.

"Yes," Drake said distractedly. Was it ever a lovely day where he was going?

"Where you heading, master?"

"Liberty on the Clink."

"Going to the theatre?"

"No, I'm going to visit a friend."

The waterman tossed a surreptitious look over his

brawny shoulder; his black eyes squinted beneath brows that looked like two caterpillars. "Liberty on the Clink, eh?"

Drake could read the man's thoughts in his craggy face. He thought Drake was going over to one of the hot houses for a good tupping.

"I used to live there," Drake explained.

"Right, master," the waterman said, nodding as he broke into a crusty grin. "Right."

Then he returned his attention to navigating the choppy river. Water lapped on the edges of the wherry. As they approached the dock fisherman were busy hauling in their catch, hundreds of flapping silver fish spilling onto the wooden dock. A fishy odor rose and filled Drake with a sense of comfort. He truly was more at home on the water.

He strode the short distance to the row of rents where he had spent an unpleasant portion of his early life. He could have navigated it with a kerchief wrapped around his eyes. As much as he had tried to forget this place— the overwhelming stench of refuse rotting on the cobblestone streets, the heat that suffocated one on days like this, when the tall and decrepit buildings shadowed the street and seemed to swallow the sunlight; when you didn't know what was worse, the scent of your own sweat pouring from your brow over the tip of your nose, or the odor of sex that seemed to waft from the bawdy houses, from the women who left one customer to seek out another without wiping the smeared cosmetics from their faces; the clucking of their tongues as a man, even a boy, passed by, thrusting out their breasts, pinching their own nipples in a grotesque effort to be provocative—this place could never be forgotten.

"Halloo, luv," a whore greeted him when he rounded the corner to the row of rents he used to call home.

He kept walking, but she followed, and grabbed his derriere with a determined grip. ''I'm feeling good today, luv, you can get it for cheap.''

''Later.'' Drake cut her off with a single, seething word.

The row of ramshackle buildings that stretched out before him made a pitiful excuse for homes. They looked as if they'd crumble if just one stick of timber were removed.

A gaunt-faced child, looking like a skeleton, peered out of one crumbling window. Drake gave him a little wave, but the child merely stared back with haunted eyes. From behind him, an unseen mother barked out some commands in a guttural, frustrated voice, and the child slipped away, leaving Drake to wonder if he'd been a ghost, an eerie reminder of his own desolate childhood days here.

A couple of boys darted in his path, kicking a ball made of a dog's skull. The boys, dirty-faced and grubby, giggled and shouted gleefully. He was relieved. Not everyone here was downtrodden. Perhaps, he mused, if he had been born to this life, he would have found happiness here as they obviously had. But he had been born to wealth, and had lost it. One is never quite the same after that. Not even when one regains one's position later on.

By the time he reached the rent he and his mother had occupied, sweat was pouring down his face. He went to the door of the row house, and realized that there was a gaping hole in it. The door was ajar. A rat skittered out of it, squeaking, pausing only long enough to give him a surly glare. He'd beaten determined rats from his bed as a child.

''Is anyone here?'' Drake called out perfunctorily. It was clear that his old home had not been lived in for some time. Probably not since the outbreak of the plague last year. Whole families had fled London in fear of the dreaded disease, he had heard. Others died gruesome deaths. The corpses had piled up until they were removed and buried in mass graves.

Drake stepped inside and marveled at the great chunks

of plaster missing from the walls. The floor was littered with broken furniture, tattered toys, unspeakably filthy clothing. He went into the middle of the main room and felt cold creep from his feet to his prickly nape.

Why had he come here for this particular meeting? How serendipitous that just before this rendevous Rosalind had mentioned Drake's ignominious childhood to the queen. It only served to remind him that Thornbury House was not his, and never truly would be, even if he won his battle for it. It had been his father's, not Drake's. His father, who had inherited the estate from Drake's grandfather, had lost it.

Grandfather Rothwell had purchased the property from the crown after Henry VIII had confiscated it from an abbot during the English Reformation. The possession of that great land had thrust Drake's merchant family into a position of new power and gentlemanly status and responsibility. And Drake's father clearly had not been up to the task.

Seeing this hovel again, the place to which James Rothwell's family had fallen after the loss of Thornbury House, Drake at last acknowledged that while his father had clearly been duped, he was a humble man who had allowed it to happen. He had been thrust too high in society for his own good. He had fallen like an angel into hell.

Drake stared hard at the shadows. So hard they began to move. Black swirls became gray. They moved toward him, until the gray became flesh. It was a man, standing in the shadows.

Drake jumped with a start. "Good God, how long have you been here?" he barked.

The man stepped completely from the dark corner. He wore a black cloak and a hood covered his long brown hair. His face was hard and riddled with care, but his eyes were sharp and discerning.

"Are you Stryder?" Drake demanded.

"I am," the man said, and his gray eyes glimmered with curiosity. "And you are Master Drake Rothwell. Your lawyer said I'd find you here."

"I had not expected you so soon. What do you want?"

"Thornbury House, of course."

"It's not for sale. My lawyer is soliciting only for the land. He should have made that clear."

"The house is not for sale *yet*." A mirthless half smile adorned the stranger's face.

"Pardon my candor," Drake said, "but I would not think your purse fat enough to buy a prodigy house."

"I am an agent. I buy property for my employer."

"And that is . . . ?"

"A secret." Stryder gave him a patronizing smile. "You know an agent must be discreet. But I hope you will not think me too forward by telling you my employer would be willing to pay you more than whatever price you set."

Now it was Drake's turn to smile with malice. "Why are you so sure I am willing to sell?" *And why does it seem I've met you before?* Drake scowled at his hardened features, but could not place the face with a name, or even a location.

Stryder went to the open shutters and gazed down the street. "I make my assumptions based on instinct. I grew up in a place like this. I know men like you."

Drake was not surprised. Stryder did not have the air of a nobleman, but he carried himself with an assurance that seemed above his apparent station. "I will consider your offer," Drake said. "But our meeting must remain a secret."

"Of course." Stryder gave a little half bow. With his hood still raised, he looked not a little like the Grim Reaper.

Drake turned and left without a farewell. Men like Stryder considered formalities a waste of time. Who could he be representing? Was he the one who had sent the threatening letter to Starck?

A chill swept over his skin at the thought. And when his thoughts returned to Rosalind, the chill turned into a shiver. Would she hate him when she learned what he really was? For Drake held close to his chest even more secrets than the mysterious agent who called himself Stryder.

Rosalind blinked her burning eyes at the numbers jotted in her own handwriting and pulled the candlestick closer to the accounting book she'd been studying for more than an hour in Lord Dunnington's parlor. Yellow light mercifully brightened the page. Not only were her eyes aching, her head was beginning to pound, her mind was numb from calculating and recalculating her assets and debits, and fury still tickled her insides. All she wanted to do was prove to herself that Thornbury House was worth fighting for. She had to be absolutely certain it was worth the sacrifice she was about to make. Her heart told her it was, but what did the ledgers tell her?

The economic situation of England was very bad indeed. She need only look out to the street beyond the front gate to see poor people trekking with their meager possessions from the country to the city and back again in a fruitless search for employment, or charity. Just last week, Fulton House, the great house next door, had been sold when its current owner hit hard times. Fulton House had been Francesca's home once upon a time.

Thornbury House, thank heavens, wasn't doing too badly. The crops had been poor for several years now, a fact that contributed to the country's economic hardships. However, Rosalind had been able to supplement the losses with modest income from the wool trade. Thornbury House was definitely viable from a monetary standpoint. Therefore, her fierce and sentimental determination to keep the place could be bolstered by financial arguments. If she were to fight the queen, as she had determined today that she would, with every ounce of blood in her body, she would need as much ammunition as possible.

Rosalind sank back in her chair with weary resolve just as the door swung open. She expected to see Huthbert carrying in a glass of port. Instead she saw Drake. Her heart picked up pace, and not merely because she found him attractive. How could she possibly break the news to him?

He was swaying in the doorway, one side of his riding outfit covered in mud. He must have fallen from his horse, she concluded with a smirk. His doublet was open to the waist; black chest hair peeked out from his open shirt. He was like a finely wrought leather saddle—hard in one way, smooth in another.

"Moppet," he fairly growled.

"You're drunk," she said calmly, and carefully placed her goose quill on the table. Perhaps it would be easier this way. He would only remember half of their conversation on the morrow.

"Moppet," he said again, his tone mocking this time. There was a wild gleam, Rosalind noticed, in his eyes, a tortured angst, a hunger for incivility. It lit a little ember inside her, a flare of excitement, and she folded her hands primly, suppressing a smile.

"What is it, Drake?"

"Did I really call you Moppet?" He staggered in, and she could not help but notice how tightly his muddy hose clung to his muscular thighs.

"Yes, you did call me that horrid little sobriquet. Recently, even."

The candle began to brighten, fueled perhaps by his larger-than-life presence? She'd always known he possessed some elusive greatness, and had been threatened by it. But it had always been veiled by his desire for revenge. Under the influence of alcohol as he so clearly was now, his true spirit soared unhindered. His cheeks were gaunt, his eyes riveting, searing her to the spot.

"I called you Moppet?" He was aghast, in the exaggerated way of someone who was drunk. "How many times?"

"Too many to count. I always considered it a loathsome word."

"It means doll. You are not a doll. You are a . . . mermaid." He slapped his forehead and rumbled with laughter, shaking his head in astonishment. "Yes, that's it. Why didn't I see that before? You are like the mermaid one of my sailors swore that he saw. It was two years ago, and we were so far from land and out of water and food. We were all delirious. Some of my sailors saw sea monsters, with great gnarled teeth and slithering limbs. Some saw land that wasn't there. But one sailor swore he saw a mermaid, flitting through the water with a tantalizing little smile, appearing and disappearing in the foam of the waves. She was a slippery thing, there one minute, hidden the next. My sailor described her with such detail that I began to think I saw her myself. Except that she had your face . . ."

When he fell abruptly silent, she finished the thought for him. "And you hated her for it."

His blurry gaze sharpened on her. She could almost hear the blade whisking over the wet stone.

"Yes, I did."

"Well, I certainly hope you can put your hatred behind you, at least outwardly."

He wiped a broad hand over his face. "Why?"

"Because I want you to marry me. And it wouldn't do to loathe your wife. Dislike her, perhaps. But not loathe."

"Marry you?" The idea served to sober him in an instant. My God, she was ambitious. She wanted this house even more than he'd thought. "We can't marry."

"We can and we must. I've been to see the queen."

He forced himself to raise his brows in feigned surprise.

"Yes, I must confess I went there to tell her how loathsome you are."

"Did you?"

Her gaze darted guiltily from his. "Yes. She agreed with me that you are a most despicable creature."

He stifled a smile. The little chit. Couldn't she ever admit that she'd found something worthy in him to praise? "And so the queen granted you Thornbury House with a promise to throw me in the Tower?"

She sneered at him. "No, you churl. She did not." She heaved a sigh. "I may as well admit it. She threatened to take the house for herself if we do not marry."

"So that's it? We marry?"

Huthbert entered quietly and set a tray of mad dog on the table.

"Thank you, Huthbert," she said. "Your timing is impeccable."

"Thank you, my lady," he replied, and slipped quietly whence he'd come.

Rosalind rose, circled the table, and poured herself a generous gobletfull of the potent so-called "double-double" ale. "I think I could use some refreshment myself." She sipped and grimaced at the burning sensation. Then she tossed back the entire contents and poured herself another. "Drake, I know you hate me."

But I don't, damn it. "Yes?" he said, prodding her.

"If we marry, it will be in name only."

So that was how she would stay above him. She would marry him but not quite deign to have him in her bed.

He moved to the desk and sat on its edge, watching as her lovely cheeks grew pink under the influence of alcohol. "How would that work, precisely?"

She tugged thoughtfully on her lower lip, the one he suddenly felt like nipping with his teeth. "Well, I suppose it would be natural to have separate bedchambers."

"*Un*natural, you mean."

She took in a nervous breath, and the lush swells of her breast rose against the square cut of her simple, purple gown. "There is, I have noticed, a certain attraction between us. It's merely a physical matter that can be contained." She took another quick gulp, and he noticed that her face was now flushed. There was a distinct slur to some of her words.

"Don't drink so fast, Rosalind."

"You're a fine one to talk!" she shot back, and swallowed the rest of her goblet.

"It's mad dog, for God's sake, not watered-down wine."

"Look," she said, and leaned forward, her muscles looser and her body more languid, "we're not married yet, so don't start ordering me about. If you think you'll be the lord and master, that's one thing I won't tolerate."

"No sex, no authority. What in blazes will I get by marrying you?"

"The house, idiot. Besides, you'll have lovers. I'll arrange for some to visit your chamber. Lady Ashenby is comely. I'll speak to her about you."

"Oh, I thank you, most gracious lady," he said mockingly, and bowed with exaggerated formality. "Will you also hold my cock when I visit the privy?"

She shot up from her seat, leaned over the desk, and

slapped him hard on the cheek. The sound cracked in the air. He gazed in astonishment at her furious, damnably sexy expression, and then grabbed her arm, pulling her close. His hand snaked around her narrow waist, pulling her to him, letting her feel his sudden hardness.

"You'll not have dominion over me, Roz. You'll not act like an irksome, brawling scold. Your little show of indignation merely sets my blood ablaze. You're playing with fire."

Awash in hunger, he ran his hand under the wisps of hair hanging about her neck. He gripped her tight and firmly pressed her lips to his, covering them with absolute authority. He plunged his tongue into the moist flower that was her mouth, plundering the softness as she moaned in protest, then wilted a moment later. For a second, one brief second, she returned the kiss. He pulled her hips to his, to the undeniable staff bulging from his codpiece. When that simple statement quieted her, letting her know just how dangerous was her proposal, he withdrew, savoring the taste of her on his mouth. He smacked his lips.

"Tasty wench." He thumped her rump playfully with the palm of a hand.

"Ow! How dare you? I'm not some sort of bawd, you know!"

"No, you'd be better than a bawd, I'll warrant. I avow you'd scream to heaven with pleasure if I got hold of you."

"Well, you'll not find out," she said, arching a prim brow. "You can do that sort of thing with someone else."

"With whom, pray tell?"

"Francesca," Rosalind said with a giddy laugh as she tucked away an errant tendril of hair.

"Francesca!"

"I've seen how intimately you two speak, arm in arm."

"As friends!"

''No, no, she is beautiful. A man needs his release. Admit it, Drake. You're little more than an animal.''

''Don't start, Roz, I'm warning you. . . .'' He took a threatening step toward her.

''Fine. Very well. It's your business. But I have no intention of losing my virginity just because I have to marry you.'' She fiddled nervously with an emerald ring, the one he knew her mother had given her, then looked up with the tart expression she'd perfected. ''I'll have someone from Court put in a good word for you with Lady Ashenby. She's a lovely widow.''

He shook his head, laughing ruefully. ''You're denying your own desire, Rosalind. When are you going to stop pretending you're above the needs every human possesses? When are you going to start living your life, instead of planning it in your books, rehearsing it in your plays, or assessing it in your ledgers? Or is it that there will never be a man good enough for the idealistic and inexperienced Lady Point Nose?''

When she frowned up at him, the light in her eyes was extinguished. He'd hurt her! Damnation, she wasn't her old self. She wasn't as tough as she used to be.

''I'll shut my blasted mouth now,'' he muttered, chagrined.

She swallowed her stung pride, and swallowed it again, until she nearly gagged, for no matter how cruel he was, she needed him. They had to marry. Admitting defeat to Drake was an odious task, but losing the house entirely would be far worse. She couldn't fathom life without this prodigy house.

''See here, good sir,'' she said, her voice trembling, ''I'd marry a troll to keep this house, if that's what the queen dictated. Please, Drake. Can't we stop this all? We shook hands before, remember? When we rallied our forces against Thadeus. We can do it again. Truth to tell,

I need you. Drake, I *need* you. I'm tired, so tired of fighting alone.''

The words scraped her throat raw, but she'd say them a hundred times over if need be.

When he responded by placing a hand on her shoulder and soothingly massaging her tense muscles, she heaved a sigh and continued. ''I won't ask for love. What woman does in marriage? But we can be friends. We must unite once again, for the sake of the house. I promise I will not be jealous when you take your lovers on the side.''

He withdrew his hand and shook his head in wonder. ''My God, you are ambitious. And relentless. If I'd half your determination, I'd be the richest man in the world by now.''

She gave a timid shrug and turned to face him fully. ''Is that good, then?''

''Good or bad, it's what you are.''

He reached out for her right hand. Wrapping his fingers around hers, he willed himself to feel nothing. ''Very well, Roz. You have a deal. I'll marry you. And God forgive us both our cynical motives.''

Eighteen

❧

"You know, Drake," Rosalind said much later, trying not to slur her words, "you're not such a pestilential knave, now that I know you a little better as an adult."

"High praise from you, maiden." Drake held his goblet up in silent acknowledgment, then swilled the last drop. "You're like a fine wine, Rosalind. You mellow with each passing year. I'll warrant you'll be ready to drink about a century from now."

"Touché." Rosalind giggled and took a slurp of her drink.

They had decided earlier to toast their marriage agreement. And then toast it again. Now, hours later, their lax bodies were heaped in two chairs, opposite one another at a game table near the dark fireplace. Drake leaned on the table with crossed arms, studying her with the abandon of one influenced by spirits. Rosalind leaned on an elbow, her chin tucked comfortably in one splayed hand.

Had she ever felt so content, so at ease, so sure of her future? She was quite certain that the details of what had come to pass this night would seem wild and fantastic on the morrow. But now it all seemed right. Now it seemed she could, or already had, conquered the world. By marrying Drake, she could bind him to her, no longer as an enemy, but as a partner.

"Do you think we can truly outwit the queen?" she said on a hiccup.

"By getting married, you mean?" When she nodded, he gave her a rascally smile. "We'll get the house, to be sure, but methinks it is the queen who has outwitted us. We are, after all, marrying against our wills, so to speak."

"But in name only." Rosalind laughed with giddy triumph, clasping his arms with urgent conviction. "Don't you see? They will think we have married as couples do, but it will be in name only. You will be free to bed whomever you wish, or to remain on the high seas. And I won't truly be constrained by the bonds of matrimony."

Drake ran the back of one hand across a few beads of ale that lingered on his neatly shaved mustache and beard. It seemed a bleak gesture, and even in her drunken muddle, Rosalind felt her mood darken.

"I know you don't like me, and therefore you will leave me to my own devices."

"Will I?" His face was a dark and chiseled bust of doubt.

The corners of her mouth tugged upward. "Of course. And the times when we are together, just for show, you will cut a fine figure at my side."

"Like Cockles, Lady Blunt's Maltese lapdog?" His voice oozed with sarcasm.

"Now, now," she said, soothing his cheek with a palm. "I mean only that you are handsome."

He blinked slowly, digesting this charitable sentiment. When Drake crossed his arms, leaned back, and looked at

her doubtfully, Rosalind would not give up. She leaned
forward to grip his massive forearm again.

"You must not doubt it. You *are* handsome, Drake.
Stunningly so. I wonder that you have not caught the eye
of the queen. She is fond of handsome young men. Oh,
but then you haven't been to Court. You should remedy
that. Elizabeth would like you."

"Would she?"

"You should be more than a gentleman buccaneer. You
should be a lord, an admiral. You should take the place
that Sir Walter Raleigh once held as the queen's favorite.
Or the Earl of Essex. Since his downfall, the queen has
been melancholy and lonely. She should know of your
great ability."

"Enough." Drake impatiently cleared his throat and
stood. Going to the hearth, he leaned on a stone and stared
at the empty fireplace. "Your kind words move me more
than I can say."

"*Why* haven't you gone to Court? Why must you be so
independent? The queen would adore you. I know she
would."

He glanced over his shoulder at her, irony gleaming in
his smoky eyes. "I'm glad you think so."

"I know—"

He cut her off. "And what of you?" He turned and
leaned against the mantel, again crossing his arms. "Let
us talk about Rosalind for a change. Why haven't you
married before?"

Married. The word always seemed to come panting in
her face like an abandoned, flea-ridden dog that always
finds its way home.

She batted impatiently at the air. "Do let's talk of something else."

"All I want to know is why? Surely you've had offers.

I remember you were betrothed several times when we were young.''

"Drake, please, let us discuss another matter.'' Her face burned. She didn't want him to think her independence had been embraced as a last resort. If he found out about the curse, he would lord it over her till his dying day.

"You're hiding something from me, Rosalind. What is it?''

"Yes,'' she improvised, casting him a provocative smile. "I *am* hiding something.''

"What?'' Drake prodded as he poured another cup of ale and brought it to his lips.

"Well . . .'' She brushed the corners of her lips with a kerchief to bide time. Then it came to her. "Did you know that while you were gallivanting on the high seas, I became a spy for Will's theatre troupe?''

Drake sneered. "That's old news. You told me that before.''

"But you haven't seen my costume.''

He stilled at the notion and arched one brow with mock lechery. "Are you offering to show me?''

"On one condition,'' she said, gulping the last of her mad dog. "You must come with me and spy on that rabid Puritan, Do-Good Simplicity. I need the practice. Besides, if you want to appreciate my talents, you must see me in action. I'm like one of Will's players, I cannot play the part unless I allow myself to become completely possessed by the role.''

Drake held out his arms in submission. "Lead me on, maiden spy. Just make sure we don't get caught.''

Drake ordered a horse with a pillion behind the saddle for Rosalind to ride, and waited for her on the front drive. But when a half hour had passed with no sign of a slender spy in a fake beard, he went in search of her. None of the servants knew where she was, but after a thorough survey of the house, Drake found her in the yellow chamber.

"What in blazes are you doing here?" he said.

She whirled around with a string of curses sailing from her lips. Her face was strawberry red, and her tousled hair was tumbling about her shoulders.

"What is wrong?" he said, trying to stifle a grin.

"I can't remove my bodice!" Her petticoat was crumpled on the floor next to her. The only thing covering her legs was her silk smock. "The bodice laces up the back, and I can't reach back there."

"Why didn't you call your handmaid?"

"Her sister is sick, and I gave her leave to visit the girl. She's the only servant in the household who knows how to help me donn my disguise. I can't ask anyone else to help me."

"I know you'd rather die than ask for help from me," he said drolly, coming to her side. "So I'll give it to you without being asked. Turn around."

Rosalind scowled at him momentarily, then acquiesced. "Very well. Simply undo the bow and loosen the webbing with your fingers."

"I know, Rosalind, I've done this before."

"Oh." Her answer was a surprised little chirp.

He gloated behind her back, but when he lifted the tangle of her hair and saw the milky underside of her neck, his mood altered instantly. A fine line of red hair swerved from the top of her neck to her nape, where a vertebra protruded invitingly. He placed his hand around her neck, his fingers splayed over the delicate bones above her breasts, and let his thumb trail down that thin, feminine line.

Rosalind shuddered, then stepped away from his grasp and turned slowly, blinking away the last vestiges of inebriation. ''That is not where the lace begins.'' Her eyes flashed like green jewels.

''No, of course not. I momentarily lost my way.''

She turned around again and this time lifted her hair for him. He hesitated a moment as he quelled the urge to place his mouth on the tempting spot where his hand had been. Then, businesslike, he untied the leather string that bound her vestlike bodice.

He loosened the lacing, and saw the quickening of the pulse that throbbed in her neck. He swallowed thickly, ignoring the stirring in his groin.

''There,'' he said, and stepped around to see her profile. Her lips were moist and parted, her gaze far off. The loosening of her bodice had freed her breasts, and they had risen, as if in relief. Their roundness swelled above the edges of her smock, which was visible under the loosened whalebone shafts of her bodice. ''Is there anything else?''

''That will be all for now,'' she said in an unnaturally high tone of voice. She cleared her throat and smiled at him with great equanimity. ''Why don't you wait outside a moment—I'll be just a moment.''

He left, relieved to be out of sight of the temptation she'd unexpectedly offered—he had wanted to rip her clothes off and take her there on the floor, for heaven's sake.

A few minutes later she pulled the door open with a whoosh and stood grinning at him. ''What do you think?''

He nearly laughed when he saw the very bad fake beard adorning her face. The laughter died on his lips, though, when he saw the white shirt that covered her chest.

The material was not thick enough to hide the nipples that crested against the white silk with a purplish hue. He had never seen her so scantily dressed. The shirt narrowed at her waist, and he could just make out the vague outline of her ribs, lean and curving.

The shirt was tucked into blue Venetian breeches. They hugged her hips and narrowed tightly against the top of her thighs. Her legs were wide-set, and her hands were plunked at her waist. She looked puckish and voluptuous at the same time.

"Well, what do you think?" Her eyes twinkled with pride.

"I think I've never seen a man who looked so damned good in breeches and a shirt."

She frowned. "I'm not supposed to look good."

"Indeed. And if I ever see you in such an outfit outside the confines of this house, I'll have your hide tanned."

She waved him off. "Fear not, I always wear a cape that hides everything. Now get you gone. We mustn't be seen leaving the house together. I'll be out in a moment."

Drake reluctantly followed her instructions, and a few minutes later was surprised to see that she was right about her costume. It was deceptive indeed. When she finally slipped out a side door and joined him on the drive, he scarcely recognized her. She'd pulled up the hood of her cape so that all one could see was a bushy beard and spectacles. When she hiked herself up on the pillion behind him, unaided, he chuckled with admiration.

"The world has not seen many women like you, Rosalind Carbery," he said, then added as he heeled his horse, "thank God."

They galloped away, down Holburn Street and into the city through Newgate, as the sun was beginning its descent. He tried the entire way to ignore the heat of her body. She seemed to mold against him in a perfect fit. She tucked her arms around his waist with a possessive grip, as if they had ever ridden thus, viewing in quiet intimacy the roofs of the thousands of plaster-and-timber homes and businesses that gleamed in the sepia light. They followed

West Cheap to a little lane off Lombard Street, and left their horse with a farrier on the corner.

Drake looked around for trouble. But there was no blood on the cobblestones, no inns from which drunken watermen or tanners would fall out of with fists flying, no apparent spies. Merely an old woman throwing out a bucket of slop from her apartment above a butcher's shop, and a curving street that ended in smoky shadows. They seemed to be safe for the moment.

"Where are we?" he whispered.

She blew out a stream of air to displace the strands of false hair that buried her eyes. She squinted up at him, cheeks flushed, lips moist with the taste of adventure. He smiled. Damned if she wasn't desirable even hidden in ten pounds of clothing. He had a nearly overwhelming urge to crush her in his arms.

No. They were to be married. That meant she was the last woman in whose arms he could lose himself. He'd take a doxy tonight. He'd spill himself in a woman with no name, who asked nothing in return but a few coins. Anything to keep him from the arms of Rosalind. Lovely, bewitching Rosalind.

How odd. Drake had waited a lifetime to be with her thus, jovial and gently sparring. He'd cynically watched, looking for a sign of humanity in her brittle heart, and now that she was waving that pennon in his face, letting him know that she'd stepped off her pedestal, he feared for her. For he was ever about revenge. Would he really want Rosalind if he could have her? Would he want her the morning after, forever after? Or had he merely been longing for the unattainable? Of course, bedding her did not mean that he would have access to her heart. Even if he managed to seduce Rosalind, she would find a way to remind him that she was his superior. Perhaps he should let her make love on top, he mused wryly.

"Why are you looking at me like that?" she said, seemingly more worried about his displeasure than about being murdered or robbed.

"Like what?"

"You have a peculiar look in your eyes. They're somewhat . . . hazy . . . glazed. Bizarre. Truly, Drake, don't look at me like that."

"God forbid that I should regard you at all. Now where the devil are we?"

"We're down the street from Simplicity's home. I know this street nearly as well as my own," she said tensely.

"*Our* own," he corrected.

"Don't begin to quibble, or you'll draw attention to us and we could end up on the point of a rapier."

Drake touched the hilt of the rapier at his side. "I'm well aware of the dangers. It's you who should be concerned."

"Really?" She grinned wickedly behind her cumbersome beard and pulled back her cloak to reveal the shiny handle of a pistol tucked into a girdle.

"Good God, Rosalind, you shouldn't carry one of those things around. It could be used against you."

She scowled at him good-naturedly. "You're not going to be one of these domineering husbands who will treat his wife like a malt-horse drudge, are you?"

"Let's discuss our marriage another time. I'm growing uneasy. This street is unnaturally quiet." He glanced up, and the woman with the slop pot, the one whose hair was bound in a rag, her breasts bulging from her tattered smock, stared at him, her face as round as a cabbage. He waved and forced a smile. She jerked her head away and withdrew, closing the shutters with a whoosh.

"It's this way," Rosalind instructed. "Walk by at your ease, and then when we pass the house with the peeling plaster, turn right into the narrow alley. That's Simplicity's home.''

In the distance, they heard the guard's cry of warning at Aldgate. Drake tensed. He reached and gripped Rosalind's arm. ''We must hurry. The city gates will be locked soon.''

''Yes, come along.''

They strolled down the street, sidestepping the puddles of waste thrown down on the cobblestones. When they reached Do-Good Simplicity's house, they noticed through a window someone lighting a candle. A flame flickered, illuminating the gaunt face of none other than the radical Puritan himself. Drake reached out and gripped Rosalind's shoulder, seeking confirmation of the man's identity. Rosalind gave a quick nod, but said nothing.

''Your plan is a good one.'' The Puritan's bass voice swelled on the breeze. ''But must you employ players? They are apes, hellhounds, pagan creatures who will destroy this city with their base and godless plays. I'll have none of them.''

''Now, now, Simplicity, if we achieve our wish, does it matter who we employ?'' came another voice. ''Southampton says he will arrange everything.''

Drake slowed a bit, searching the shadows that hovered around the candle, but he could not see another face. The voice was eerily familiar.

The Puritan turned with venom to the shadows. ''I'll avow she's a weak woman who has given in to the papists once too often.''

''All the more reason to use the players to aid us. I need your support,'' the mystery voice replied. ''I will employ the troupe only briefly, and then our desire will be realized.''

The voice took shape then as a man stepped from the shadows. In the second before the face was illuminated,

Drake thought he might see Stryder. But it was not the mysterious agent who was plotting with the Puritan. It was none other than the Earl of Essex, Robert Devereux.

"I don't doubt her right to reign, but she is being ill-advised by her council. She needs men like me running the country," Essex said, and his handsome face, which Elizabeth had once worshiped, glowed with grandeur. "I hear that her secretary has sold the succession behind her back to Spain."

As Drake and Rosalind passed out of earshot, like two casual passersby, she gasped in shock. Drake squeezed her shoulder, as if to say, Be still. Our very lives are in danger.

When they rounded the corner, they both flattened their backs against a stone wall. Rosalind gasped for air; Drake breathed hard, sweat beading his forehead. The crier at Aldgate was giving the last warning. The gates to the city would soon be locked.

"We must fly, or we'll be sleeping on Pauls Wharf to-night," Drake muttered. Dismissing his earlier resolution to find himself a whore, he grabbed her hand and yanked her away.

They slipped around the back of the building, found their horse, and rode like the wind toward Aldgate, sailing through it only moments before the gatekeeper shut it for the night.

They dashed into the lord's parlor as soon as they arrived home. Rosalind shut the door and turned to Drake, her heart pounding. She had torn off her beard and cape on the ride back, but still wore her breeches and shirt.

"What did that signify, Drake?" she asked, sotto voce, fearful the servants might hear. "Why was the Earl of Essex conspiring with the Puritans?"

"They have one thing in common," Drake said somberly. He filled a goblet with muscatel, stared at it, and plunked it back on the table in distaste. "They both want to see the queen overthrown."

Rosalind stared numbly at him. He was right, of course. She'd spied on the Puritans because they wanted to close all the theatres. But they posed a greater danger to society. They wanted to rid the country of Elizabeth, because she was head of the Church of England, and not nearly as pure as the Puritans would have her. They felt that the church retained too many Catholic traditions from Rome, from the time before Henry VIII broke all ties to the pope. Ironically, the Catholics, who also wanted to depose the queen, viewed England's church as too reformist.

"So will they overthrow the queen?" Rosalind queried in a squeak of a voice.

"She is vulnerable," Drake acknowledged. "She has no heir. Even her loyal vassals are just waiting for her to die in order to align themselves with a vibrant new prince. Her secretary, Cecil, knows that Essex is a threat. But the queen has vacillated about the earl's fate."

"But what of the players?" Rosalind queried.

Drake raked a hand through his hair. "That is a new twist. What could Essex possibly want with them?"

"To play the part of rebels?"

"Players wouldn't play any part without being paid."

"Perhaps Essex intends to pay them. I wonder which troupe he will use."

"Tell Shakespeare to beware." Drake repeated his earlier warnings about Essex.

"I will."

Drake strode across the room toward the door.

"Where are you going?" Rosalind said in a panic. He could not leave her now. Not when she was so unnerved, so excited, so happy to have shared this intrigue with him.

"I have someone I must see."

"Can't it wait?"

"No, it is very important."

"Drake!"

He halted at the door and turned back. Rosalind flew the distance between them. Had she ever been freer? She'd never imagined there could be a man confident enough in his own worth to let a woman lead him on such an escapade. She came to stop before him. She smiled at him, and his eyes darkened, as if inviting intimacy. When she reached out and grabbed his arms, the mere touch of him set her fingers ablaze. Impulsively, she stood on her toes, tugging him down by the collar, and kissed his right cheek.

"Thank you," she murmured against his tanned skin.

He slipped an arm around her waist and pulled her close. As he did so a wave of delicious warmth swept over her. She relaxed into the embrace, and met his mouth when he bent for a kiss. His lips were firm on her mouth. Then insistent. Quickly, he parted her lips and his tongue dipped into her for a sweet taste. Rosalind shivered and clutched him closely. Her blood quickly stirred, and when he drew back, gazing at her without apology, a profound realization weakened her knees.

It was just a matter of time.

Nineteen

❧

Two weeks later William Shakespeare presented Rosalind with a surprise. He told her he had a special gift, and all she had to do to receive it was to throw a supper party and prepare a stage in the gallery. He said he was going to let her play a small part in several scenes that he wanted to present before an audience, though he would not elaborate on the part or the play. When Rosalind protested, saying she had retired from her brief life of scandal, Shakespeare assured her that she would wear a boy's costume, and no one would be the wiser.

Rosalind acquiesced, and was thrilled at the prospect of sharing the stage with the Lord Chamberlain's Men. The only tricky part would be keeping her acting a secret from Drake.

He was on her mind as she prepared for a costume fitting the morning of the party. She saw him in her mind's eye as she stood in her smock before her mirror, waiting for her handmaid to put aside her farthingale.

In truth, Drake had been on her mind virtually every

hour of every day since their spying escapade. It had turned out that their first kiss was no accident. She'd tried to talk to him about "the Kiss," or "the Kisses," to be more precise, but he'd muttered something about impulses and poor judgment, and then changed the subject, going on about a new stud horse Thomas was recommending. Then he'd bitten his tongue and flushed a deep scarlet and stalked out of the room.

His embarrassment had amazed her, but it was the confirmation she'd been looking for. Drake was not as imperious, as impervious to feelings, as arrogant as she'd thought. Quite the contrary. And to think she had once found him to be rigidly overdisciplined and heartless. At the sight of his uncharacteristic discomposure, her affection for him had grown by insidious bounds.

In subsequent days she'd wandered in a daze through the garden, clutching the *Roman de la Rose,* but unable to read more than a line or two before growing distracted. The book seemed so remote from her immediate world. Words were inadequate. She'd sooner dance naked in moonlight to express herself, or flap her arms like a bird taking flight, making hideous chirping sounds in a foolish and delirious effort to sing Drake's praises. The urge to do so was absurd. Embarrassing. And yet . . .

She understood at last what Shakespeare had been writing about passionately for so long. Love is foolish, a sightless beggar who feels like a king when his object of desire casts a mere crust of bread his way, who feels with hands and heart, and does not need eyes to see or even recognize the voice of the beloved.

Not that she loved Drake. That would be impossible. She could never submit to him. If she softened, he would woo and conquer, not out of love, but because men always took what they could just for the thrill of conquest.

Rather, Drake made her feel things she'd never felt be-

fore. Not love or passion, but a prescience of both, a lushness of body, a flushing at secret thoughts, an eye for
colors more brilliant than those found in nature, a longing
for his lips and tongue, a craving for a nip of his rough
tanned skin, a yearning to write a transcendent poem, one
that would exalt her soul and make passionate love to her
mind. Actually, she'd thought a lot about making love pe-
riod in the last few days.

At the same time she'd lost her compulsion to write. It
was not a play that would make her immortal, she'd concluded. Printed words could make an author's name live
forever, but not a heart. It was love that made our brief
time here worth the living, she now knew. It was love that
transcended the ordinary, that lifted the downtrodden and
humbled the rich.

But if she did not love Drake, and could never love him
because it was too risky to do so, then what would she
do? How would her heart find succor when she was bound
to him in marriage? It was a dangerous game she was
playing. Marriage was forever, unless your name was
Henry VIII.

"There now, my lady," said Maribel, her young handmaid, interrupting her reverie. "I can help you off with
your smock. Then you must put on the breeches and doublet the wardrobe keeper gave me. He's waiting outside to
measure the outfit for tonight."

Rosalind raised her hands in the air for the girl to lift
off the undergarment. And she wondered what Drake
would think of her in such a state, naked, unadorned.

Drake whistled a merry tune as he approached Rosalind's
chamber. Lately he'd found himself unaccountably happy
whenever he thought of her, and he had been searching
for excuses to seek her out. He halted just short of her

door when he spied a little man pacing in front of it, wearing spectacles and a bushy brown beard.

"Do you have business with my lady?" he said.

The man bowed and smiled. "If it please your lordship, I am to measure her for a costume for tonight's performance."

Drake's ebullience lost some of its luster. "Measure Rosalind? Are you quite sure?"

"Quite. Master Shakespeare says she is to play a part tonight. I will do all I can to make sure she looks her best." The wardrobe keeper gave Drake his most reassuringly professional smile.

Drake grinned back malevolently "Quite."

So Rosalind planned to perform with the Lord Chamberlain's Men and she had told him nothing about this preposterous plan. Fury exploded in his veins. He threw open the door so hard it bounced shut behind him when he stepped through. "Rosalind! What is this about you playing a part in tonight's play?"

He was halfway across the room before he realized that Rosalind was stark naked.

Catching sight of her bare bottom, he halted and stepped back, as if an ocean wave had smashed over him, leaving him drenched and stunned. She was facing a mirror. Her hair was copper-colored foam on the white sand of her back; the sensual line of her spine was a trail of irridescent bubbles left in the wave's wake.

"Dear God," he could not help but whisper in awe.

She looked up at the commotion, her face pale, her eyes wide. Her handmaid whirled around and flung both hands over her mouth in shock, dropping her lady's smock to the floor.

No one said a word.

In the awkward moments that followed, Rosalind raised a hand to cover, however inadequately, her full and pointy breasts and another to cover the furry apex of her thighs, while Drake considered his options.

If the handmaiden were not here, he would walk softly to Rosalind and kneel before her. He would smooth his hands on her astonishingly full and creamy breasts; he would press her close, bury his face in her; hear her heartbeat, lay her down and—

Just then the handmaiden snapped from her daze and jumped protectively in front of her mistress. "Oh, my lady!" she blurted out.

He gave her a hostile glare. "Get out!"

The girl whimpered.

"No!" Rosalind shrieked, coming to her senses at last. She turned to stand behind Maribel and picked up the smock. "Maribel, do not move!"

The young girl was nearly apoplectic. She trembled in an awkward pose, with legs and arms splayed wide.

"Rosalind!" Drake shouted. "Get her out of here."

"Are you mad? It would be my downfall!" Rosalind tugged the smock over her head, restoring some sense of propriety. She stepped out from behind Maribel and patted her back reassuringly.

Drake's every straining muscle softened at her words— an admission, as he took them, that she would not be able resist him if they were alone. Damn her for her reticence. God, he had never wanted a woman so much in all his life. Was it merely because he couldn't have her?

"Rosalind . . ." he groaned.

Her glinting eyes caught his, showing that she knew the depth and source of his frustration. She was wiser in that way than he'd thought.

"Drake, we are not husband and wife yet."

He groaned again and gripped his hair, then laughed forlornly. "Damn you for your virtue."

"What on earth impelled you to burst into my chamber without knocking?"

Drake flung his hand toward the door, ignoring the resulting wince from the handmaiden. "A curious little fellow out there said he was to costume you for tonight's play."

Oh, dear. "Yes . . . I'm playing a small part."

"No, you are not." He took a threatening step forward, and Rosalind met him halfway, hands on hips, ready for battle.

"Yes, I am. I will not allow you to command me in this matter. This is my one opportunity to know the joys of a player on the stage. The costumer will see to it that no one will recognize me. No one will expect to see me. I'll be dressed like a boy."

"Rosalind, I will not have you wearing man's breeches, and that is final! Other men will then see you, they will see how . . . that you . . . that your legs . . . well, that they're . . . the shape is . . ." He made a sweeping motion in the air with his hands, outlining her luscious figure, then glared at her as if no more need be said.

She laughed infectiously as she crossed her arms and pronounced, "You're jealous."

"No."

"Yes, you are."

"No!"

"You don't want anyone else to see me as you have seen me."

"You're damned right about that." He jabbed a finger in the air to punctuate his point.

"But no one will know it's me!"

He closed the short distance between them and grabbed her arms, pulling her so close he could breathe in the lavender water that dappled her hair. "I will know it is you, and I will not be able to resist you any longer. I will take you without ceremony. I will have you like a whore in a hot house.''

''Oh!'' the handmaid cried in embarrassment, then ran from the room sobbing.

Rosalind's eyes flashed with alarm as she watched the girl scurry away. ''Drake,'' she muttered when his mouth nuzzled her neck. She shivered and arched against him. Then rallying every last bit of her maidenly reserve, she pushed him away an arm's length. ''You are suffering from a very serious case of lust. Clearly, you need a pliant widow to ease your suffering.''

''Don't lecture me, maiden,'' he growled, pulling her close, but again she extricated herself from his enticing arms.

''Widows are never demanding of aught else but . . . prowess.''

''And how would you know?''

''I've heard them gossiping at Court.''

Drake tossed his chin up and glared at her. ''And what, pray tell, do these widows say?''

''They say that they appreciate men with broad chests, especially when you can see thick bands of muscle straining against a doublet.''

She allowed her right hand to press seductively against his chest, keeping him at a distance and caressing him at the same time. With smoky eyes, he watched her hand like a cat would a mouse, waiting for the right moment to pounce.

''Widows also like a full head of hair, but only if it is not painted gray.'' She let her fingers smooth over his strong forehead, then splay through his dark locks. He shut his eyes. His jaw muscles flexed. But he said not a word. How powerful she felt!

''And they like a sensitive mouth on a man.''

When she brushed the back of her fingers against his parted lips, and her fingernails flicked over their beautifully carved surface, a band of tension in him snapped. He snatched her wrist, almost violently, then turned it over and nipped its silken underside with his teeth, laving the translucent skin a second later with the sensual swirl of his tongue.

Rosalind shuddered and cried out. At the mewling sound, he groaned and yanked her into his arms.

"Do they like *this*?" he muttered, eyes afire.

"I think so," she squeaked.

He gripped the back of her tumbled red hair in one hand and forced her mouth to his. Hungry lips devoured hers; his bold tongue plunged into the darkness of her mouth, plundering with boundless insistence. He kissed her so thoroughly, she could not even see straight when it was over. She could only hug him in terrified silence.

She wanted more.

Much more.

And he was more than ready to give it to her.

She pushed him away and tugged at her hiked-up smock. She wiped her mouth with the back of a hand and glared up at him with shimmering eyes. "Yes, that's exactly what Lady Ashenby would like."

Drake smirked at her. "You play with fire, madam. I think I'd best go find this widow of whom you speak. You're right. I do need some release."

He began to chuckle darkly to himself as he headed for the door. "And by God in heaven, Rosalind, if I see you on the stage tonight, I swear I will yank you off of it and spank your bum in front of everyone."

With this threat still ringing in the air, he bounded out the door and promptly bumped into Thadeus, who looked him up and down, and then looked askance at Rosalind.

"Drake? What is this? My dear girl, you are not married

yet." An impish grin rippled beneath his mustache as he inched into the chamber, looking back and forth between the flushed couple.

"Greetings, Uncle." Rosalind cleared her throat when the words seemed to stick there.

"Calm yourself, Thadeus," Drake said. "Nothing is amiss. Did you speak with the queen as we asked you to?"

"Oh, yes!" Thadeus replied, warming to his favorite subject. "I told her you planned to marry. And do you know, I think the old dame was disappointed somehow."

"Disappointed?" Rosalind said, slipping on a robe. "How so?"

"I think she wanted the house for herself. I believe she was hoping you would continue your battle so she would have an excuse to take it. Even in her twilight years, she seems to delight in getting things for nothing from the noble class. A free visit at a prodigy house here. A free gown or a pair of gloves there. Even a masque paid for by someone else. Nothing delights Gloriana more!"

"Well, she won't get Thornbury House." Drake shot Rosalind a conspiratorial smile. "Isn't that so, Roz?"

She smiled in return, relieved to be on safer territory. Conspiring was apparently the thing they did best together, though kissing might come in a close second.

"You haven't told anyone else that we plan to marry, have you?" Drake said to Thadeus.

"No, dear lad, I have been discreet."

The men continued their discussion as they exited the chamber, and Rosalind sighed with relief. Her own conversations with Drake were becoming increasingly intimate. They were dangerous encounters that titillated her as her spying once had. There was a thrill to danger, an excitement to walking to the edge of a cliff, and then stepping back just before a gust of wind could sweep you over.

She could flirt with Drake, since there was obviously a flirtatious side of her craving to be satisfied. But she had to remain in control. She would have to bend him to her will, if not through anger, then through affection. He was an animal, she told herself, and one that had to be tamed.

Twenty

Later that afternoon as Rosalind descended the grand staircase, dressed in an ornate bodice and petticoat, she was amazed at the number of guests milling around. Surely there were more than she had invited!

Thadeus huddled and joked with his protégés, a group of keen-eyed young courtiers who wanted to learn from a master of Court politics. Seeing their youth, their too eager smiles, and their dashing clothes, on which they'd doubtless spent half their year's expenses, Rosalind thought they'd much to learn from the old guard, the queen's experienced courtiers.

In the gallery, she noticed that Lady Ashenby had wasted no time in staking out a corner. That was something new. The elegant and discreet widow had apparently developed her own following, one filled, Rosalind hoped, with women who thought before speaking, and could do so without forked tongues. Eyeing the blond widow, she felt a stab of guilt. She hoped Drake would not pounce on Lady Ashenby the moment he saw her.

In another corner Lady Goosenby and her set of cunning canker blossoms were ensconced. But who had invited her? Certainly Rosalind hadn't. And there was Lady Blunt, heading toward the gallery, her obsequious son, Godfrey, who seemed to trot after his mother with more devotion than her dog, in her wake.

The vastness of the crowd was no doubt part of Shakespeare's plan. When she spied him at the other end of the gallery, where his apprentices and hired men were setting the stage, she prepared her gentle tongue-lashing and headed his way.

He turned to her just then, and when she waved over the heads of the milling guests, he smiled in his musing way, and started toward her until they met halfway.

"Will, what is the meaning of this? Did you invite all of London?"

"My Lady Rosalind," he said with unusual formality, and bowed. When he righted himself, he was grinning with great mischief. "This is your special night. I wanted there to be many witnesses. Your uncle approved of my plan."

"Are you going to debut a new play?"

"A portion of one. My fellows will be enacting a series of scenes." He leaned forward and whispered, "All of them written by a mysterious unknown writer named Rosalind Carbery. And she will even play a walk-on part."

"*My* scenes? Oh, Will!" she cried out, and hugged him with abandon. "How can I thank you?"

"Your enthusiasm is my reward. But we must not mention that you are the authoress. I will claim the scenes as my own. Then, if your completed play is as good as what I've seen so far, we can mount it at the Globe. As long as my name is attached to it, we will be able to draw an audience, and Dick Burbage will be happy. He might even play the principal male part."

Rosalind beamed with joy. "I can scarcely believe my good fortune."

He narrowed his thoughtful eyes on her and his lips puckered in curiosity. "Something is very different about you today, my Rose of Thornbury."

"Oh?" One glance at his intent expression convinced her to avert her gaze. Shakespeare was far too insightful, and he knew her far too well, to remain ignorant long. But what could she say? He would not believe her if she told him that she had agreed to marry her mortal enemy. And worse yet, that she had kissed him on more than one occasion.

"Rosalind, do you have more to celebrate than the staging of your scenes?" he wondered in a gentle voice.

She tossed her chin up and smiled broadly. "What could give me greater pleasure? Will Shakespeare, you have made a dream of mine come true. And I love you for it."

"Yes, you do love," Shakespeare pressed on insistently, "but methinks someone other than my fair self is the object of your desire."

"My dearest, most cherished Lady Rosalind," Godfrey sputtered, shoving his way through a group of people to reach her side, and stepping on more than a few toes in the process.

Shakespeare gave him an annoyed glance.

"Master Shakespeare! What a pleasure. What a pleasure. Am I interrupting?"

Rosalind turned to Godfrey with relief. "I can honestly say that I have never been more pleased to see you. I'm sure Master Shakespeare will not mind continuing our conversation at another time."

"No, let him stay! I've always wanted to be a player on the stage, you know." Godfrey nervously plied a moist hand over his plastered hair and pinched his Adam's apple with his thumb and forefinger. "Master Shakespeare can hear me recite a poem I've composed in your honor, Lady Rosalind. Shall I begin?''

"No, thank you, Godfrey, I believe we'll be witness to enough amateur writing tonight,'' Rosalind said. "But leave your poem with my usher and he'll see that I get it later.''

"Oh." His smiling, ill-defined lips turned down in disappointment as he fumbled to return his poem to his doublet. "Very well, I will try to find a way to express my feelings extemporaneously.''

"That is my cue to exit the stage,'' Shakespeare said, eyeing Rosalind with a knowing look. "I believe our hired men are nearly finished setting up the dais. If you'll excuse me." Sketching a short bow, he disappeared in the crowd before Rosalind could protest.

"Lady Rosalind, my mother says that you could use a good husband to defend you against . . .'' He paused and looked surreptitiously over his shoulder. "Against a *usurper,* if you take my meaning. My father was a powerful man. If we were to join our bloodlines together . . . why . . . that would be good, wouldn't it?''

Godfrey's pronouncement came to a sputtering halt. It was as if he'd memorized his words, but realized suddenly that he did not understand their meaning. Rosalind pitied him. Sweat trickled down his pallid temples. He wiped them nervously with a kerchief, then knelt before her, grimacing at her in a way that she realized must be his approximation of joy.

"Lady Rosalind, I would be most honored if you would agree to be my wi—''

"Stop!" she nearly shouted, and thrust out the flat of her hand to silence him. Several nearby guests hushed and whirled around in surprise. Ignoring them, Rosalind tugged on Godfrey's arm, forcing him to rise, and whispered her admonitions so as not to humiliate him further than he had already done himself. "Please, Godfrey, do not debase yourself before others in this manner."

"Debase myself? Why, I was merely going to ask you if you would marry m—"

"Hush!" she cried sotto voce, the tendons in her lithe neck straining with the effort. "Sir, we cannot discuss these matters in public. I beg you, hold your tongue. Do not say anything you will later regret."

He frowned in consternation. "How could I regret asking for your han—"

"Please! Godfrey, be silent! I must insist."

She was incensed now. It was touching that he thought enough of her to propose marriage, but she did not appreciate his lack of discretion. Courtship was a private matter, and yes, she was embarrassed that at the age of thirty she would have no other heartfelt offers than from the likes of this pathetic pup. Drake's unenthusiastic agreement to marry her did not count as a proposal. Godfrey was just a hair shy of idiocy. She would never consider marrying him. How could she persuade him to drop his suit?

"Godfrey, we must talk. Let us hie to the garden."

His eyes brightened at this. "The garden! Oh, yes. It is the perfect setting."

She led the way, and when her back was turned to him, she rolled her eyes, praying for patience.

Drake chuckled as he watched Rosalind walk through the crowd with Lady Blunt's son in tow, pitying the lad for the tongue-lashing Drake knew he was about to receive. He recognized the prim arch of her brow, the indentations beneath her cheeks that always presaged a fit of temper. Did she see or understand just how besotted the poor young man obviously was?

Rosalind, Drake had concluded, was ignorant of the ways of love, except in regard to those that were most important, the instinctive ones. She might spurn intimacy, but she could not hide her natural passion. When he kissed her the first time, it was as if she were a bundle of fireworks being ignited. She exploded in his arms, like a compound of highly charged sensuality placed too near a flame.

Drake had been hungering for her ever since. It was lust, he reassured himself. Merely lust. She was right on that score. He had a serious case of the disease. His craving for her had nothing to do with the heart, for he'd sooner cast that vital organ before the mastiffs at the Bear Garden than present it to Rosalind. To love such a woman would mean surrendering all authority, will, freedom, peace of mind. Was love worth such a sacrifice?

He thought of the queen's remarks. Poor Rosalind, she had said, as if she were giving herself to a dirty criminal from the Clink. Her Majesty thought him incapable of being distracted by such petty emotions as love.

Reminded of the queen, he glanced around the gallery, wondering if Essex would dare put in another appearance. Drake almost hoped he would. He needed to ferret out more information. After he and Rosalind had discovered Essex conspiring with Do-Good Simplicity, Drake had hastened to inform Queen Elizabeth. But she'd snorted in derision, as if she did not believe him, as if she were not in danger. She still was loath to believe her beloved Essex would dare to conspire after his reprimand from the council. So Drake had informed Secretary Cecil, who had wondered who Drake was, and how he came to be privy to the intimate details of the Court. Drake hadn't divulged his identity as the queen's spy, but he had warned Cecil, in no uncertain terms, that Essex was still a danger.

Drake began to pace through the gallery, still pondering Essex's next moves when Huthbert bumped into him.

"Oh, Master Drake! Forgive me. I've been searching all

over for you. There is a sea captain here to see you. He says it's urgent. A Captain James Hillard.''

''Hillard!'' Drake frowned down his nose at the flushed usher. ''What's he doing here? I'd sent him back to Buto to keep an eye on things.''

''He says there has been an unfortunate turn of events.''

''I'll curse him for a flap-eared knave if he dares to confirm my greatest fears.''

''He's waiting for you in the lord's parlor. I told the captain that you—''

''A pox on it!'' Drake cut Huthbert off with an oath as his eyes narrowed on a figure slipping through the crowd at the far end of the gallery. ''Hellkite, is it him? *Here?*''

''Who, sir?''

Drake hushed the usher with a squeeze on his arm. He rose on his toes, trying to glimpse the cloaked figure's face as it turned furtively to glance over its shoulder.

It *was* him! Stryder. The mysterious agent Drake had met at his old dwelling in Liberty on the Clink. Drake would never forget the cool hauteur of his eyes, the faint scars, like those of a ruffian who'd not escaped the sling of a whip or the ravages of disease.

Stryder met Drake's gaze. There was a flicker of recognition in his handsome face, then a twinge of irony, then cold determination. He continued toward his destination. Where the devil was he going?

''Is something amiss, Master Drake?'' Huthbert asked, now craning for a look himself.

''Yes, but I'm not sure what. Hold steady, Huthbert, I have to greet a new guest.''

''But Captain Hillard—''

''Can wait,'' Drake replied over his shoulder, starting through the crowd.

''But he said it was urgent!'' Huthbert called to no avail. Drake wove his way through the crush of people, gaining speed as he went. He'd not be surprised if Stryder slipped out a side door before he could get his hands on him.

"I beg your pardon," Drake said tersely as he attempted to bypass Lady Goosenby's entourage. The women tittered and scattered in his wake. He dashed through the door at the end of the gallery and followed Stryder's shadow around the corner. And then he ran straight into the man.

"Goodly Lord!" Drake muttered, stepping back in surprise.

Stryder leaned casually against the paneled wall of the narrow passageway, his face half-illuminated by a candle in a wall sconce. "I knew you'd follow me. Sometimes it is best to arrive unannounced. I did not want to draw attention to myself. It would not be . . . prudent."

The agent's eyes flared with sarcasm as he quietly punched the last word of his sentence.

"What do you want?"

"The house, of course."

Anger simmered in Drake's guts as hairs prickled on the back of his neck. "What makes you think I'm so desperate that I would discuss this matter here with Lady Rosalind present?"

"Because I know far more about you than you'd ever imagine."

Drake recoiled inwardly, fearing that his role as the queen's spy had been jeopardized.

"I will have ten thousand pounds to you by Wednesday next, as a measure of my employer's good faith." Stryder leaned against the wall and crossed his right foot over his left.

"That won't satisfy the estate's trustee."

Stryder blinked with boredom. "My employer is very well connected at Court. I'm sure Thadeus Burke can be reasoned with. He'll come around."

"Your employer would have to be *very* well connected to talk Thadeus into allowing this house to slip from his niece's fingers."

Stryder tilted his head, as if toying with a kitten. "My employer is more powerful than you could imagine."

Powerful enough to talk the late Lord Burghley into approving a bogus trading company so many years ago? Drake wondered. Was Stryder's employer the one who had destroyed Drake's father? Was it possible he had been after the house all along?

"It will take some doing to make the necessary arrangements," Drake said, trying to buy time. "What kind of reassurance do you want in exchange for the money you are so quickly and generously offering?"

"Your marriage to the Rose of Thornbury."

Drake scowled. "Marriage? You would dictate even that?"

"My employer would like reassurance that the house is yours to sell. Marriage to the mistress of the manor would provide the necessary assurance of that."

"Does your employer wish to witness the consummation of my marriage as well?"

At Drake's biting retort, the elusive agent smiled. "I can inquire of his intentions."

"You'd better go."

Stryder nodded and pulled his hood over his long brown hair. "Tuesday morning. Ten o'clock. Thirteen Hatton Street."

He turned and disappeared in the darkness of the small passageway, and moments later, when Drake roused himself from his deep thoughts, he suddenly wondered how Stryder knew he could exit that way.

"Godfrey, I am most flattered. Truly. An offer of marriage is not something I receive often these days," Rosalind said, forcing herself to take the young man's moist hands in her own. She had to let him down gently. "But a union between us would never work."

"Why not?"

"Well, for one thing, I am much older than you."

Godfrey shifted on the stone bench beneath the rose trellis, where the two of them were seated. "Older than me? There is a mere eight years' difference between us."

"Eight years!" she explained. "Why, I'm old enough to be your . . . your . . . older sister."

His expression remained dull. She could tell that he was unimpressed by this argument. Rosalind heaved a sigh as she fished in her mind for another.

"The union would be ruinous." Losing patience, she withdrew her hands from his. "I can't put it more plainly than that."

"Amen, amen!" he began, a bright, almost maniacal look in his eyes. "But come what sorrow can. It cannot countervail the exchange of joy that one short minute gives in your sight."

Rosalind frowned slowly. She'd heard these words before.

"For stony limits cannot hold love out!" he said with growing fervor. He fell to his knees, wincing when one kneecap landed on a stone. "And what love can do that dares love attempt; therefore thy . . . age . . . is no stop to me."

"Pish!" she said when she realized where she'd heard these words before. At the theatre. He was quoting from *Romeo and Juliet* again! Or at least his mangled version of the play.

"Godfrey, are you capable of any thoughts of your own?"

"She speaks! Oh, speak again, bright angel."

"It seems, dear sir, that you never speak for yourself.

You are either quoting Shakespeare or your mother.''

"Neither, fair maid, if either thee dislike.''

"Godfrey, stop it, for God's sake! I'll hear no more of this. I had hoped to learn your heart's desire, but I'm wasting my time, I see. I will tell your mother that I cannot possibly consider a match with you.''

The thought of Lady Blunt settled uneasily in Rosalind's mind. There was something nagging her thoughts. Something to do with Lady Blunt. But what? Then it came to her.

"O immortal gods!'' she gasped.

She had asked Lady Blunt to dig into Drake's past, and then forgot about her request in the tumult of all that had come to pass. She had set the intrigue in motion before she'd agreed to marry the rogue. What if Lady Blunt had found out something terrible? Or more likely, what if she had contrived some plan simply to ruin Drake? Knowing Lady Blunt, Rosalind was sure she would not give up until she found something. She had to seek out Porphyria immediately. She had to tell her to stop her secret investigation.

"Godfrey, I'm going back to the party. I suggest you gather your wits and pretend we never had this conversation.''

"Rosalind!'' Godfrey called out in a surprisingly strong voice. His resolve caught her unawares, and she turned back in curiosity. A new clarity gleamed in his usually vacuous eyes. "If you cannot love me, then who can you love?''

Drake, a little voice in her head answered without hesitation. But then she gathered her wits. "No one, Godfrey. I can love no one. No man is worth the sacrifice.''

"Just like our queen,'' he replied. "Then there is no hope for me.''

Rosalind sighed in relief. She'd finally gotten through to him. "No, Godfrey, there is no hope."

She reached out and patted his folded hands consolingly, then turned again to flee. But she halted when she heard Godfrey crying shrilly, "Eyes, look your last! Arms, take your last embrace!"

Rosalind turned to him and rolled her eyes. He was reciting Romeo's final soliloquy at Juliet's deathbed. "Not more Shakespeare, Godfrey, I beg you."

"And, lips, O you the doors of breath, seal with a righteous kiss a dateless bargain to engrossing death!" he declaimed tragically. He ran to her then and pulled her to him, giving her a slippery kiss and then darting away before she could box him on the head.

"For the love of Juno!" she cried out, staggering back and wiping her wet cheek. "You're getting to be as bad as the seigneur. Need I remind you what happened to him?"

"Come, bitter conduct," Godfrey continued, undaunted, backing away, brushing away the sandy-colored hair that had fallen over eyes, "come, unsavoury guide! Thou desperate pilot, now at once run on the dashing rocks thy seasick weary bark! Here's to my love!"

Godfrey pulled a small glass vial from a pocket and held it up to the winking light. When Rosalind realized what it was—a potion of some sort—an ominous shiver coursed down her back.

"Godfrey, what is that in your hand?"

"O true apothecary!" he cried histrionically. He unstoppered the tiny bottle, and a desperate look twisted his homely face. He put the bottle to his meandering lips, just like Romeo drinking his poison.

Rosalind stepped forward and held out her hands in alarm. "No, don't drink it! It's not worth your life. There

will be other women. Don't, Godfrey, I'll not have one
more suitor's death on my conscience!''

But he ignored her, tossing back his head and swallowing the vial's contents in one gulp.

He gagged, dropped the bottle to the ground, and
gripped his neck with both hands, making a little strangling
sound.

''Thy drugs are quick,'' he croaked as his eyes bulged.
''Thus with a kiss I die.''

He collapsed into a crumpled, apparently lifeless heap.

''Godfrey!'' Rosalind cried out. She ran and knelt at his
side, shaking him, but he did not stir. She whirled around
and felt the earth for the container he'd cast away. The
little brown bottle was nestled in a clump of grass.

Holding it to her nose, she inhaled, expecting some foul
odor, but it was oddly sweet. It smelled more like a drop
of muscatel than a dram of poison. Scrunching up her nose
and furrowing her brow, she cast Godfrey's limp body a
suspicious glare. She touched a finger to the mouth of the
bottle and then placed it on her tongue. It *was* muscatel!

''Why, you impudent rascal. You false hound. You
knotty-pated idiot!'' Rosalind tossed aside the vial and
gripped Godfrey's doublet, shaking him. ''Open your eyes,
you lying cur. Do you know that you nearly sent me into
a state of apoplexy with that poorly played death scene?''

His eyes blinked open at this insult. ''Poorly played!''

He sat up, and his hurt expression slowly transformed
itself into one of anger. Apparently his talent as a thespian
was the one subject on which he prided himself.

''If you had fallen into apoplexy, dear lady, it would
not have been because of my playing. It would be because
of the curse.''

Stung, Rosalind drew back. ''So your mother told you
about that. She said she wouldn't, that you were too frail
to hear of it.''

"My mother does not know me as well as she thinks," he said gloatingly, then let out a bleating burst of laughter.

Rosalind stood and brushed her petticoats as best she could. "And I know you well enough to last me a lifetime. It is most unchivalrous of you to mention the curse to me in such a manner." She hoped he wouldn't blather on about it in front of Drake. "I'll forgive you this time, but I pray, never speak to me with such intimacy again."

She turned on her heels and marched away, angry at herself for indulging his ridiculous antics. Clearly there was more to Godfrey than she'd suspected. Lady Blunt had apparently underestimated her son. He contained hidden depths—of malice.

What audacity, to mention the curse. She'd nearly forgotten about it. As she strode past the roses, the knots of sweet williams, lady-smocks, bachelors'-buttons, and the marigolds, another niggling thought seemed to cloud her vision.

The curse. Drake. Oh, Pluto and hell! She'd never thought about Drake in regard to the curse. His very engagement to her could have placed him in grave danger. If he died, as the seigneur and all the others had, just because of her, she would never, ever forgive herself.

Rosalind blinked and the great house coalesced into view. The hundreds of diamond-pane windows gleamed white in the sunlight. The mossy gray stones rose steadfast and solid against nature's changing backdrop. And somewhere inside that vast prodigy house, Drake was standing, unaware of the danger he was facing. She had to find him immediately and warn him. Before it was too late.

"Drake!" she shouted as she began to run, praying he could hear her thoughts if not her voice. "Drake, be careful!"

Twenty-one

Drake did not have to go far to find Captain Hillard. The old sea dog had grown impatient, and was crossing through the entrance hall when Drake spotted him.

"Hillard, what the devil brings you here?" Drake put a hand on his arm, urging a quick and quiet response.

"It's not good news I bring," the lanky sailor answered.

"I didn't expect it would be. Come, let us stroll. That way no one person can overhear our entire conversation."

Drake touched the captain's elbow and the men meandered through the great house, nodding politely at occasional passersby.

"What news do you bring?" Drake said.

"We lost another ship."

Drake bit back a foul curse. When he spoke, his voice quietly seethed. "How in God's name?"

"A Spanish carrack appeared out of nowhere with cannons blazing. Our crews chased the ship away, but not before it had managed to sink *Le Beau Monde*. Now we have but two galleons at Buto. It's not enough to transport the pepper back to England even if you do manage to raise the money.''

Drake's eyelids closed as tight as tombs. "So I must now raise not only a fortune, but a fleet of new ships as well.''

They'd wended their way through a maze of chambers and stood at the entrance to the gallery. The mood here had grown festive. Men and women were laughing and talking animatedly. In the black mood Drake was in, they looked like puppets, silly gaudy playthings.

"Yes," Hillard agreed. "And you'd best do it quickly. Word has it that the East India Company has sent a ship to explore Buto. When it discovers the pepper, it will return to London with a boatload, and a fleet will follow for the rest.''

"That means I must launch a fleet of my own within the next fortnight if I am to have any chance of getting that pepper before the East India Company.''

"Not much chance of that, eh?''

"On the contrary, Hillard.'' Drake crossed his arms and stroked his beard. "I just met a man who offered me a fortune. All I have to do to get it is sell my soul, and Rosalind's as well.''

Hillard's haggard face kindled with interest. "So there's hope yet?''

"Have you ever known me to give up?''

"You'll need hope aplenty when you hear what other news I bring.''

Drake shot him a scathing look. "You mean there's more?''

Hillard nodded soberly. "I've been saving the worst for last.''

"Out with it, then.'' Drake waited impatiently, wondering what on earth could be worse than the news he'd just heard, when he saw the captain cast a startled look to the ceiling. Hillard's eyes widened in horror. In what later would seem to have occurred at half the speed of ordinary events, Hillard reached out for Drake with terror gleaming in his eyes.

"Watch out!" the captain cried.

Drake froze in place, and the captain leaped through the air, knocking him to the ground. Drake's head flew back and smashed against the wooden floor. Hillard fell on top of him and then rolled away.

"What, God's bread, are you doing, Hillard?" he muttered, then fell silent when he heard a thunderous crash near his head.

When he opened his eyes, Drake noticed a three-foot-high stone Cupid sculpture that normally rested at the top of the balcony stairs was now lying shattered a mere few inches from his head. Chips of stone were setting in the air, and people were crying out and scattering. A large chunk of stone—the tip of one of the Cupid's wings—hit the ground and then ricocheted toward Drake just as he raised his head. It thudded into his skull, knocking him back to the ground again. Warm, sticky blood began to drip into his eyes.

"Drake, are you all right?" he heard Hillard say in the ominous silence that had overtaken the gallery. He heard, but could not see him, for everything was turning black.

Drake fought the loss of consciousness; he propped himself up on one elbow, blinking against the blood trickling in his eyes. He had to rise and see who had pushed the Cupid over the balcony, for the statue hadn't taken flight on its own. Someone had wanted to kill him. Someone who was still in this room.

He tried to look around, to see if Stryder was still here, or if Essex had arrived, but his head was swimming.

"Drake!" came Rosalind's shriek from across the room.

She dashed toward him and fell to her knees in a rustle of silk.

She tried to pull him in her arms. Sweet Rosalind. She was strong for a woman. So strong.

"Drake, I knew you were in danger. What happened?"

Her words sounded distant, like the voice of an angel calling through a web of clouds. He sank into her arms and watched her pretty teeth flashing from behind her red lips as she tried desperately to make him hear her.

"Don't worry," he whispered, then all went black.

"Put him there," Rosalind ordered like a general, and a veritable army of servants carried Drake's unconscious form to the bed in his chamber.

"Huthbert, send for some hot water, poultices, and my cache of healing herbs," she went on in a crisp tone that just barely hid her terror. "And send for the physician. The rest of you go to your duties, and do not indulge in idle gossip. I do not want to hear from a stranger that another suitor of mine has died at my hands, do you hear?"

The wide-eyed band of servants all nodded, the ladies curtsied and the men bowed, and they shuffled out, all at once it seemed. It did not dawn on Rosalind that she had just announced that Drake was courting her.

"Rosalind, how is he?" Thadeus said, bustling in the room, a look of alarm on his ever-ruddy face.

"What has happened?" Francesca asked, rushing in on his heels. When she saw Drake's blood-encrusted forehead, she gasped. "He's not . . ."

"No," Rosalind snapped as she ripped a piece of linen. "He's not dead, merely unconscious. Now do not melt into a puddle, Frannie. Our dear boy here will live if I have anything to say about it."

The new arrivals gathered around the bed while Rosalind nursed Drake's wound. She dabbed the blood away where a ghoulish bruise was forming on his forehead, muttering all the while.

"Come back to me, Drake. You've survived worse, I've no doubt. Come back to me." She blinked hard at the perspiration stinging her eyes, and kept her voice steady and strong, ignoring the howl of desperation that clamored for release. There would be time for regrets later. Now she had more serious business. She would not let him die.

"Drake, damn you, come back. You will not bow out of this performance yet. I will not allow it!"

"There's my Rosalind," Thadeus announced, grinning in relief. "Glad to see our beloved virago has returned."

"Please, Uncle!" She glared at him over the bed. "We have but one goal here, and that is to keep Drake from dying. I swear by God in heaven I will not claim the life of another man."

"Better than the moon-eyed female whose been wafting around the house of late," Thadeus whispered for Francesca's benefit.

Huthbert returned with a string of servants in tow. Rosalind quickly ordered them about and set to work mixing herbs for a poultice. Her work served to still her trembling hands. She resisted the urge to drag Drake up by the collar and shake him back to consciousness. She could not force her will on God. But she could do everything in her power to keep Drake alive.

By the time she had thoroughly cleansed and treated the wound, wrapping his head with bandages, she was much relieved. "I do not believe we'll need the physician," she told the others. "The wound was deep, but already the bleeding has stopped. His breathing is steady. He'll come to soon, I avow."

"Thank the saints in heaven," Francesca said.

Drake's eyes began to flutter.

"Your patient is rousing," Thadeus observed, coming once again to the edge of the bed. "The touch of a woman always stirs a man."

"What is this?" a mellifluous voice came from the doorway.

"Master Shakespeare," said Francesca, "you're just in time to see our hero stirring. Drake was knocked unconscious by a falling Cupid."

Rosalind glanced up in time to see Shakespeare's grin. "Sometimes," he said, "Cupid must go to great lengths to get a man's attention."

Rosalind smiled, feeling the return of her humor now that the crisis had passed. "We can only hope that Cupid has an arrow in his quiver strong enough to penetrate Drake's leaden heart."

"I heard that," Drake muttered as he blinked open his eyes. Everyone laughed, except for Rosalind. Only she knew the meaning of this near tragedy. "I'm glad to see my predicament is so amusing."

"Nonsense, my boy." Thadeus tapped his cane on the floor for emphasis. "We are relieved you chose not to leave this earthly vale."

"What happened?" Drake reached for his injured forehead with a look of bewilderment.

Rosalind clasped his other hand. "Don't you remember, dear?"

He scowled, whether at her term of endearment, or in recollection of his brush with death, she could not tell.

"Your life, my man," Thadeus said, eyes ablaze with intrigue, "was very nearly squashed by a fat little cherub with wings."

"Someone tried to kill you, Drake." It was Francesca, wise and courageous Francesca, who voiced the suspicions hanging over the room.

Rosalind rose abruptly and turned away from the others.

She didn't want anyone to see her trembling lower lip.

"Couldn't it have been an accident?" Shakespeare said, joining Thadeus at the foot of the bed.

"That statue weighs two hundred pounds," Thadeus answered. "It had to have been pushed. It would never have fallen simply because someone bumped into it."

"So who hates you enough to want you dead, Drake?" Francesca scurried to the other side of the bed and touched his shoulder. "I might have said it was Rosalind, but it is clear you two have learned to tolerate one another."

Drake's gaze searched for Rosalind across the room. Finding her, he gave her a half grin. "She's a tolerable wench at that."

"Who hates Drake?" Rosalind returned and mustered a teasing grin. "Let me think. Where do I begin?"

Shakespeare clasped his hands neatly at his waist and smiled morosely. "I do not think it was an accident at all."

Rosalind's blood turned cold. Even gentle Will knew it was her fault. The others turned to Shakespeare.

"What do you mean, Master Shakespeare?" Francesca asked.

"Perhaps that falling Cupid was intended merely to end this party before the play could begin," he suggested. "What if this were the act of a Puritan spy who wanted to send me a message about the continued success of my theatre troupe?"

"No, Will." Rosalind shook her head. "That cannot be. I spied on Do-Good Simplicity recently." She exchanged a look with Drake. "I cannot tell you what he said, but his attention is focused elsewhere now. I think the Puritans are more concerned about the succession to the throne than about the prosperity of the theatres right now."

Shakespeare shrugged in acquiescence. "Then I am much relieved, for I know I can trust information from the spy of Thornbury House."

"The statue very nearly fell on your head, Drake," Thadeus said. "We must conclude that you are the target. As for potential assassins, Essex would love to see your entrails on the tip of his sword."

"Concisely put." Drake tried to sit up, winced, and sank back onto his pillow.

"But why?" Francesca said. "Why does he hate you so?"

"He knows I am completely loyal to the queen."

Rosalind tilted her head, considering this. "Yes, you are, and without any obvious reason. That is very noble of you, Drake."

"Nonsense!" Thadeus growled. "It is a subject's duty to be loyal to his sovereign. It is only knaves like Essex who try to make treason fashionable."

"I think Essex is too absorbed in his own visions of grandeur to bother to kill our Drake," Francesca offered. Then she added with a teasing grin, "Not that you aren't important to the realm. Why, without your adventuring on the high seas, the East India Company wouldn't know where to drop anchor."

Drake smiled grimly. If Francesca only knew how close to the mark she was. The thought stirred recent memories, and it all came back to him in a rush. He'd been struck on the head just after Captain Hillard had told him that the Spanish carrack had sunk one of his ships, and that the East India Company was sending an exploratory ship to Buto.

"Hillard," he croaked, then cleared his throat, sitting up slowly, his head pounding all the while, "where is Captain Hillard?"

"Captain who?" Rosalind looked at the blank faces that surrounded her for some explanation. "I saw no one who bore the appearance of a ship captain, Drake. Are you sure you're all right? Perhaps you should lie back down."

"No! I know what I'm talking about. Captain Hillard came to the supper party. He told me some . . . news," Drake added in a bleak voice. "He said he had more information to tell me. Something very important. But I was knocked unconscious before he could divulge it. I must speak with him." He threw his legs over the edge of the bed, and was greeted by a chorus of disapproval.

"No!" Rosalind cried out. "You must rest, Drake."

"Sit down, lad," Thadeus said forcefully, "or you'll provide further entertainment for our guests when you collapse in a heap at their feet."

Drake's vision started to blur, and he sank back onto the bed, obeying against his will. "I must talk to Hillard."

"I'll tell Huthbert to find the man if he exists." Thadeus stepped outside to find the usher.

Rosalind began to pace, spurred by anxiety. For she knew that contrary to all the theories supplied by the others, she was the key to this unhappy event. She had to confess her secret to Drake, for his own safety. Could she humiliate herself before him by admitting the truth? Oh, what sacrifices the heart required!

"I know why the Cupid fell," she said, so softly the others had to strain to catch her words.

"What?" Drake managed to prop himself up with pillows. "Why?"

She glanced self-consciously at the others. "May we be alone?"

"Of course." Francesca tucked her arm in Shakespeare's and they made a hasty exit. When the door clicked shut behind them, Rosalind turned and moved quickly to Drake's side.

"There is something I must tell you, and when you have heard it, you will no longer want to be my husband."

Twenty-two

~∞~

"I know why you were almost killed." She sat beside him with a tortured sigh.

He reached out and stilled her fidgeting hands and caressed her with the tranquility of his sea-blue eyes. "Tell me."

"I am cursed."

When he said nothing, she looked away. "I am cursed, Drake. I have been betrothed seven times. And every single one of the men or boys betrothed to me has died." Sparing no detail, she elaborated on the misfortunes of the men who had chosen to court her. It was a cathartic experience, admitting her peculiar dilemma to the one person from whom she had wanted most to keep it secret. When she was finished, she moistened her lips and focused on him. "So there you have it. Seven poor hapless victims. And I am not even counting Seigneur de Monteil."

"The seigneur." Drake scowled good-naturedly. "He lived past his prime. You had nothing to do with his death."

"Perhaps. But all the others were young. How can I in good conscience proceed with this farce of a wedding if I know it will endanger you?" She paused, resting her hand on his sleeve. "You are not just any suitor."

"To hell with the curse." He entwined his right hand with hers and gave it a squeeze. "I don't give a fig about such nonsense."

"You should," she shot back, withdrawing her hand from his.

"There is no curse, Rosalind."

She frowned at him, wondering at his certainty. "You arrogant rogue." She shook her head and stood indignantly, flinging her arms at him in exasperation. "I have lived nearly my whole life with this curse, and yet you know about it less than an hour and then suppose that you are the expert on the matter! So like a man! What gives you the right to be so cavalier?"

"Because I care for you."

"No, that's not it." She began to pace. "It's because I am a woman and more easily dismissed. Or . . . or is it because you saved my life?" She put a hand to her deeply furrowed brow, trying to fathom the depth and breadth of his audacity. "You think merely because you saved me from drowning you have some hold over me, that you know me better than anyone else."

"I do know you better than anyone else, but not for that reason."

She blinked at him, trying and failing to understand the openness that poured from his clear blue eyes. Even if he did want to gloat over that incident, would it matter? Would that erase the dangerously intimate knowledge they now possessed of each other? Would that make all their history inconsequential?

"I'm sorry," she said, wiping a fingertip over her brow, smoothing the lines of worry. "I just cannot tolerate the notion that there is something beyond my control. There have been only two forces in my life that I've been unable to bend to my will—the curse and you.''

He gave her a lopsided grin and sat up without apparent ill-effect. "So you'd let those two conundrums deprive you of happiness? You'd rather remain a virgin all your life and deny yourself your natural passion?''

"It's the safest thing to do, isn't it? In the mayhem that followed your return, I forgot about the curse. I suppose I thought that our scheming reasons for marrying nullified the danger to you since it wasn't going to be a real marriage. I never intended to consummate the union. By Zeus, I cannot surrender *everything* to you. But this afternoon, seeing that cupid nearly fall on your head . . .'' She covered her eyes with the heels of her palms and shivered. "I realized the curse is alive and thriving at Thornbury House.''

He stood, found his footing, and came up behind her. Putting his hands on her shoulders, he softly said, "Why didn't you tell me about this supposed curse before?''

"Because then you would know for certain that I was as terrible as you had always said I was.''

"I never said you were terrible.''

"As a child, you said it often . . .''

He rasped out a rueful laugh and pressed his cheek to her ear, where tendrils of hair dangled in soft coils. Her hair was drawn up with gold pins, arranged on top of her head in a confection of red-gold curls.

"I only said it because I knew you would think the opposite. I never thought you'd take me seriously.''

"I never wanted to,'' she whispered. "But you confirmed what I already knew.''

"What was that, dear heart?''

"That I was unworthy.''

He turned her shoulders around until she faced him. He

pulled her close at the waist with one hand and stroked her flushed cheeks with the other, gently, like a father would soothe a child.

And she wanted to be soothed. She desperately needed it. For too long she'd been stoic and lonely. But could she give up enough control to let him have her heart, her body? Dear Lord, then she would be giving up the rights not only to this house, but to her soul as well. Could she trust herself to give and still be whole when it was over? Did she have enough heart to share and still survive?

She gripped his hand as he caressed her and kissed his palm. Hot tears flooded her eyes. They sprang from a well so full of sadness she could not even sob or weep. All she could do was let the river flow.

He pressed his hand to her heart, gently massaging it.

"Let that sadness take flight, madam. It was not meant for you," he murmured. "It would have been mine if I'd not been so bent on vengeance."

"No, you were what my father had been waiting for. I was a mere girl. Less than useless."

He pressed his lips to her forehead, then murmured, "You are the most extraordinary woman I have ever known. How could you think that?"

"My birth meant the death of my mother. She died trying to have the son I should have been. I would have died for her if I could have. I loved her so."

He smiled sadly, crows feet gathering on his weather-beaten cheeks. "So you think you killed your mother?" He scooped both hands around her neck, cradling her head. "My darling Rose, you are fully a woman. I see the markings of time in the creases where you smile. I see a little wrinkle on your forehead where you frown that wasn't there before. I see a fullness in your figure that is utterly divine. And it tells me that you are more magnificent, wiser, and more vibrant than the girl you once were could ever have imagined possible.''

She nodded with chagrin and acceptance, knowing where he was leading her.

''You are much too old to cling to childhood myths. You did *not* kill your mother. Your father *adored* you. I *never* hated you. And you don't *need* this house to be the brightest star in England.''

She shut her eyes, moved beyond words.

''You are a woman. That is enough. Let yourself be that—a woman—while there is time.''

''I can't . . .''

He lowered his head, hovering over her trembling lips.

''Surrender to your own passions, my love.''

''Drake . . .''

''Surrender . . .'' His mouth covered hers and the rest of his intention poured into the kiss. She sighed and he delved deeper, parting her lips to satisfy his hunger.

The more he tasted, the hungrier he grew. His hands pressed her against his chest as his kiss deepened. He wanted to draw her into him, to make them one. One hand moved to her derriere and squeezed the softness in his palm. She arched against him, the swell of her breasts a tender offering to his other searching palm.

He had wanted to take her crudely before, to be rash and quick and feed his raging hunger. But that would make him as low as any animal. It would make her feel all the more unworthy.

No. He wanted to raise her on an altar and anoint her body with oils. To show her how worthy she truly was.

He dragged his lips from hers and spread his fingers over one cheek and down her slender neck while he brought his ragged breath under control. Under his fingers he felt her pulse beat wildly, a sweet betrayal of her un-controlled passion. He smiled and brought his trembling hands to the delicate valleys at her collar, where her white skin was splattered with the faintest remains of freckles. Her shoulders were so delicate he felt the bones would crumble in his hands. But strength and weakness were deceptive, often existing hand in hand.

"Drake . . ." she muttered, blinking up at him through murky green eyes, not unlike the color of the pond from which he'd once saved her. "Drake, teach me to be a woman," she said in a rush. "Teach me."

His heart lurched at the prospect. A lifetime of dreams were about to be realized. In a flash of passion he clutched her to him possessively, then shuddered as a lightning charge ripped up his arm. What was it about her that cut through him like a knife? Why was it he had never really wanted any other woman?

Unleashing some frustrated, neglected hunger, he pulled her up to him and smothered her neck with kisses, teeth nipping, tongue swirling. When she melted in his arms, he smoothed a hand down to her breasts. Her bodice was low-cut, thank the saints, and with a yank he pulled it below one nipple. He twirled his finger around the pink bud, softly at first, then more firmly until her mouth parted in a startled gasp.

"Your wound," she whispered on a snatch of breath. "Your wound—"

"Is fine." He reached back to deftly loosen the laces that bound her bodice, giving them a good yank.

At the same time, Rosalind started tugging at his doublet, frantically unfastening the front and helping him to pull it over his head. She wanted to see him naked. She wanted him unhindered.

The moment he was free, she ran her hands up under his remaining shirt, hungry for the massive muscles that wove a pattern of strength over his back.

"I've dreamt about this," she muttered against his chest

at his collar, giving him little kisses everywhere she could. "Drake, I need you to touch me. But only you. No one else would do."

Her admission sent him straight to Heaven. For Drake knew what it took for Rosalind to admit she wanted any part of him, much less *that* part.

"And I need you more," he whispered in her hair, coiling his fingers sensually through the strands, as if bathing in a tub full of silk. He bent down and kissed her ear, his tongue darting inward, a promise of more intimate forays to come.

"I want to see you without clothes," she whispered.

He kissed her temple and smiled. "Whatever madam wants."

She sank on the bed and watched while he tugged off his shirt. Sweat glistened in the black hair that carpeted his manly chest. Muscles in his shoulders rippled with each movement. He yanked off his shoes and slipped out of his breeches and hose. The he pulled down his last defense, his braies.

She shivered at the sight suddenly exposed. Drake tossed his head, flipping back the hair beneath his bandage as he rose to full height. What a picture! Broad shoulders, narrow waist, lean hips, muscle-braided thighs, sinewy calves, and something she had never seen before, his engorged manhood.

She must have been gaping, for he said, "I will be gentle."

Somehow she doubted that. She shrank back as he approached the bed. He slipped down beside her and she learned the comfort that came with holding another. He kissed her deeply, and she gave in return, her tongue flicking into his hot mouth, which seemed to lash him on.

Emboldened, she pushed him on his back and smoothed her hand over his chest. Then she put her mouth to one nipple and nipped and tugged with a sensuous swirl of her tongue.

Drake sucked in a hissing breath and gripped her shoulders. "Pluto and hell, madam," he cursed as he tossed his head back into the pillow. "You'll drive me mad yet."

She giggled with the pleasure of conquest, and shocked even herself when she reached down and grabbed the staff straining between his legs. He shuddered and groaned. The closer she felt to him, the more pleasure she wanted to give. It was a kind of intimacy that made her want to fall down on her knees and thank the saints in Heaven.

"Zounds, Roz!" he said with a shuddering gasp. "Are you sure you haven't done this before?"

"Yes," came her husky reply, "I've just heard widows gossip."

She mercilessly tightened her grip as he rocked into her hand. When his breathing grew short and sweat gathered on his temples, he pushed her away and sat up, dragging her up with him. He knelt behind her and finished what he'd started—removing her bodice. Without waiting further, still working from behind, he yanked down on her smock, pulling the low collar of the undergarment over her breasts. They protruded with the weight and delicacy of ripe pears. Drake kissed her ear with carnal intimacy as he ripped off her petticoat and yanked her smock down around her knees, but then he stopped abruptly.

She glanced over her shoulder and watched him rake both hands over his head.

"What is it?" she whispered.

No answer. Just labored breathing.

"You may touch me. I want you to."

"And I want to touch you, believe me. But we are not yet man and wife. I know you wanted to wait. To feel worthy."

"I don't—"

"Perhaps it is *I* who am unworthy," he interrupted in a fiery confession. "Roz, you are a lady. And I . . ." His expression was pained. "I am the urchin."

She turned until they were kneeling face-to-face.

"I never truly thought you were an urchin," she said reaching up to gently cup his chin in my palm, to redirect his gaze to hers. The fire in his eyes kindled when he saw the love shining in her own.

"I knew your worth even when I was a child. That was what frightened me. I knew my father would rather have had you. What father wouldn't want a son like you? Take me, Drake. I want you to be the one. I realize now you're the one I've been waiting for. There will never be another. Please show me what it's like to be a woman. A woman at last."

His face hardened with fierce emotion as he raised himself up on his knees and pulled her up as well, pressing her against his chest. His hesitation faded. She would be his at last, and he hers. It was time to fulfill their destiny. To fill her with all he had. He reached forward and kissed her possessively, cupping her breasts, kneading them until she arched her back against him, as soft and pliant as a willow branch.

He skimmed one hand down the flat plane of her belly and gripped one thigh in turn, squeezing it as he swirled his tongue in her ear. His hand inched higher and higher until he cupped her womanhood.

Rosalind was shaking now, and when he pressed his fingers to that point of fire, she writhed in his arms until, at his insistent stroking, she exploded.

She cried out, and gasped, and held her breath as wave upon wave rocked through her. When she was spent, she sank back against him, wanting to thank him, but too loose, too other worldly to put more than a word or two together.

"Yes, my Rosalind," he murmured, smoothing back her hair. "You've waited a long time for that."

He laid her down on her back and stretched his great length over her. He pinned her arms above her head, his chest pressed against her breasts. He kissed her, artfully, drinking from her pool of lust. Then he ended the drugging motion with a peck and a grin. She smiled in return.

"Oh, what have I been missing?" she whispered. "What have I been missing all these years?"

She *was* a woman. She *did* feel passion. She *could* share herself with another. With Drake.

Attuned to her thinking, he dug his knees down and parted her thighs, poised for entrance. It was time she submitted to the fire they both had watched and tended from afar; that burning knowledge of each other that had frightened them when they were young, that taunted them as they grew older; that, in their hearts, purified them.

When he slipped partially inside he paused, allowing her time.

"Are you all right?" he said, his voice hoarse with control. He throbbed inside of her, but did not move.

"Yes," she said as a soft whisper.

"I'm in you now."

"Yes . . ."

"How long have I been waiting for this?" His lips were inches from hers. His eyes penetrated hers. Sweat dripped from his forehead to hers.

"Shh . . ." She closed her eyes. "There is no past."

"No," he agreed, "there is only *this*," and he pushed himself further.

She gasped with the suddenness; he held himself still until her face began to glow. When he began to gently rock, she groaned with a new pleasure. The feel of him driving into her, into a place she had no idea existed, was a marvel. Soon she caught the rhythm of his rocking as-

cent. She arched up to meet his thrusts. And when he unexpectedly pulled her up into his lap, he sank as deeply
into her as possible, holding her down to take him fully
in. She cried out and flung her head back as a new round
of ecstasy held her captive.

When his panting was so fierce it was like an animal's,
he lowered her back to the bed, hiked up her legs, and
rode home, like a wild stallion seeking shelter.

He heaved his last offering and stared at her in that
moment of limbo with fierce, distant eyes, as if he were
glimpsing immortality. Then he crumbled into her arms.

Silence. Long, intimate, perfect silence. Eventually he
rolled over with a contented sigh.

"I should have known," he muttered. "I should have
known."

She flushed with pleasure at the praise that oozed in his
voice. Then she propped herself on one elbow and touched
his bandage.

"Drake, are you all right?"

"My head?" He touched the bandage, suddenly remembering the earlier accident.

"We shouldn't have done that. I could kill you yet."

He opened one eye and offered a cocky grin. "Aye,
perhaps now I believe you might. And I shall die a happy
man."

She laughed lightly and cradled her head against his
broad shoulder as he drew her back in his arms. She was
far too happy to contemplate such things as a curse.

Moments later, Drake's eyes shut and a soft bluster of
air whistled through his lips in an even tempo. He was
asleep, as well he should be. Rosalind sat up and in the
fading light of dusk examined the bandage wrapped around
his head. It was dry. There had been no more bleeding.
Drake would be fine. He was not so fragile. On the con-

trary, he was strength and life personified. How could she ever thank him for this night?

For the first time since their lovemaking had begun, she heard the sound of distant applause.

"My scenes!" she whispered to herself. She'd forgotten about the role she was to play.

Rosalind donned a robe and slipped quietly through the private chambers to the small balcony overlooking the gallery. The party was still going strong. Down below a crowd was seated around a dais, where players were acting out Rosalind's scenes. Shakespeare must have despaired of her returning to the party and began without her for the sake of the guests. Apparently, one of the players took over her minuscule part.

Any disappointment she felt was quickly replaced by the wonder of seeing her scenes played out, as well as the audience's reaction. She mouthed the lines silently, anticipating each nuance, each double entendre. And to her delight, the crowd laughed numerous times, and in all the right places.

When the last scene was over, and the players took their bows, the audience rose to give them a standing ovation. Rosalind began to clap as well, even as tears of joy poured down her cheeks. She applauded for the performers and their generosity, she clapped for joy, and for life itself, for she had never been so alive as in this moment.

Today she had experienced two great joys—that which is found in the arms of a man, and that which is won only through creativity. She did not know which joy was greater. She only prayed she would never be asked to give up one pleasure for the other. Either way, she could no longer doubt her worth. A woman's worth.

Twenty-three

❦

Rosalind returned to Drake's bedchamber and slept as though it were she, and not Drake, who had been knocked on the head with a chunk of stone. At ten o'clock the next morning she was still snoozing blithely, and might have slumbered longer if Drake hadn't thrown open the door with an enthusiastic bang.

"Good morrow, sunshine!" he fairly thundered.

"Is it good?" she queried with a yawn, creaking open her eyes. "When did you rise?"

"Long ago," he said as he sat beside her on the bed. "And yes, indeed, it is a good day."

"You removed your bandage," she observed.

"It's already healing over." He touched the bruised gash. "Must have been your healing touch."

He wore a white shirt that was open at the collar and brown breeches that hugged his lean hips. She felt an unfamiliar sense of possessiveness about his enticing masculinity, and boldly slipped her hand through his shirt and caressed the silken coils peeking out.

"This must be a good day," he continued after a soft groan of approval.

"Why?" she coyly replied.

"This is our wedding day."

"What?" She was suddenly fully awake. She sat up, pulling a blanket to her naked breasts. "Our wedding day?"

"We are to be married near your favorite rose trellis in the garden in one hour. I've made all the arrangements. The vicar should be arriving soon."

"Why didn't you wake me earlier?"

"I didn't have the heart. You looked so peaceful."

"Drake, we can't be married so suddenly."

"Why not?"

"Perhaps the more pertinent question is *why*?"

"Do I need to remind you? I took your maidenhood last night."

She caught his frank stare and blushed. He didn't look at all remorseful. And she didn't feel a jot of regret. "So this is your attempt to be honorable."

"Yes. Besides, we agreed we would be married. Why wait?"

Why wait, indeed? It was an excellent question. Despite his reassurance, she still worried about the curse, even though she knew it was foolish to do so. But more important, she still wondered what would become of her as a married woman. What freedoms would she sacrifice? It was one thing to embark upon a sexless *mariage blanc* with Drake, but last night they had broken all the ground rules. Having tasted the delights of physical intimacy, Rosalind knew there was no going back.

"Are you afraid?"

His murmured question held a challenge. She heard it, recognized the bait for what it was, but rose to it and bit nonetheless. "No, I'm not afraid. One hour is fine. Now get you gone. I'll not have you watching me get dressed. That caused enough trouble last night."

He grinned and pecked her cheek. "There's a good lass. I'll meet you in the garden. Oh, I nearly forgot." He reached into the waistband of his breeches and pulled out a telescope. He handed it to her. It was warm on the side that had been pressing against his body.

"What is this?"

"A wedding gift. A new-fangled invention I picked up from an Italian fellow. I used it on my journeys. I want you to know I will never abandon you for a life at sea. Even if you hope I do."

He winked and bounded out of the chamber. If she didn't know better, she might think he actually wanted to marry her.

When Rosalind breezed into the east parlor wearing only a robe, her hair in scandalous disarray, she found Francesca working on her embroidery with Lady Beatrice and two of the lady-in-waiting's nieces, who were visiting from North Kent. Coils of yellow curls neatly framed the little girls' innocent faces.

"Good afternoon, my ladies," she called out with nervous gaiety.

They looked up simultaneously, then grew utterly still. Finally Francesca expressed their collective astonishment. "Why, Rosalind," she began, "your hair is disheveled like an overgrown topiary garden, your cheeks are pinker than I've ever seen them, and your eyes are burning as bright as flames. Either something very good or very bad has happened. Which is it?"

"I'll let you be the judge of that," Rosalind said. "I'm getting married."

"*What?*" Francesca and Beatrice cried out in unison.

"Married!" the girls cried out in glee.

"How much time do ·we have to prepare?" Francesca asked after she had recovered her wits. "A year? A month? A week?"

"Actually, an hour." Rosalind shrugged and started for the door, perfectly content to leave the ladies to their bafflement. "I'm meeting him in the garden by the rose trellis in one hour. Less, really. Time is wasting."

"Him?" Francesca queried delicately. "Who is *him*?"

Having voiced the question that was hanging in the air at that moment like the sword of Damocles, Francesca dipped her head forward, her eyes wide with anticipation.

"Why, *him* is Drake!" Rosalind exclaimed at the doorway. "Whoever else would I be marrying?"

"Indeed," Francesca replied, a relieved and triumphant grin spreading across her porcelain face, "who else but Drake? By my troth, an hour may be too long. Hurry, Rosalind! It would take only a moment for one of you to change your mind."

Rosalind extravagantly tossed back her skein of red-gold hair and hugged herself, loving life. "I knew you'd understand, Frannie. You always do."

"Hurry! We must prepare!"

As Francesca watched Rosalind's disappearing form she rose with an air of dismay. Although she couldn't imagine happier news, she was nonetheless stunned by Rosalind's state of dishabille, knowing very well what it signified. Rosalind had already given to Drake the gift that can be given only once. Her virginity. While Francesca knew she should be relieved that Rosalind had finally toppled off her pedestal, she was somehow uneasy.

Drake had changed since they were children, more than she and Rosalind had, for he had been the most pure-hearted of them all, and now he was the most calculating. He was not marrying for love. Francesca knew that much.

Few men did. She only hoped that once Drake became master of the house, realizing at last the aspiration that had always driven him, he would allow himself to be in love with Rosalind again.

She hoped this because of Drake's sake, but hoped even more because of Rosalind. For whether Rosalind knew it or not, it was clear to Francesca that her friend was deeply in love with him. Deeply and dangerously.

They gathered in the garden an hour and a half later, the delay caused by the necessity of weaving a garland of flowers in Rosalind's hair and by all the time it took for the dotty vicar to inch his way across the twenty-acre knotted garden.

Francesca stood on one side of the couple as they joined hands before the Reverend John Harwood, and Lady Beatrice stood on the other. Drake wore his very best doublet, which was of a weave a bit too thick for the weather. He was perspiring, though Francesca wasn't sure whether that this was because of the heavy clothing, or because of the weightiness of his impending marriage vows.

Rosalind had donned a flowing, almost fairylike gown of gold that Francesca had brought back from her trip to Yorkshire. The bride looked like a lush and strawberry-haired sea nymph.

Vicar Harwood was a kindly old man whose back was as hooked as his nose, a man so ancient that he frequently forgot the beginning of a sentence before he reached its end.

"You found the perfect man for this job," Rosalind whispered to Drake as the vicar opened his prayer book. "He'll forget to ask us why we're marrying in such haste, or why we didn't wait for the crying of the banns."

"I think he's already forgotten who we are."

The vicar looked up reprovingly over his spectacles, as

if he had overheard Drake's remark. "What did you say, Master, er, Master, uh . . ."

"Master Rothwell," Drake offered, smothering a smile and winking at Rosalind. "It was not important, good vicar. Please proceed."

As the old man mumbled his way through the marriage ceremony, Francesca looked on, beaming with pride. She had prayed for this moment for more than twenty years.

Like Drake, she had always seen the great potential in Rosalind. Likewise, she had been aware of Drake's adoration for the Rose of Thornbury, from the moment he'd entered the house, with his torn and scruffy little doublet and his dirty, unkempt hair. Angry, defiant, and full of wounded pride as he had been that day, Francesca still remembered the startled glow of love that had lit up his handsome little boy's features.

On that day, Francesca also recalled, she herself had felt her first stab of jealousy. Everyone had always told her how beautiful she was, and all the little boys who had ever visited Fulton House had tugged on *her* braids, not Rosalind's. Rosalind had been a tomboy, always digging in gardens while Frannie practiced needlework. Frannie had been praised for her girlish behavior, while Rosalind had been reprimanded for speaking too boldly, running too quickly, and even cursing now and then like a sailor.

But when Drake arrived, it was Rosalind, not Francesca, who became the object of the sort of attention Francesca had always yearned for, but never experienced—and still hadn't to this day. Drake adored Rosalind, not in the way Lord Dunnington adored her, but with his whole soul; a soul forged in an excruciatingly hot fire. Young as she had been at the time, Francesca had often felt scorched by the heat, the ferocity of Drake's love.

Though she would later deny it, Rosalind had felt it, too—and responded to Drake with equal fervor. That,

Francesca was convinced, was why Rosalind had hated him so. It was her only protection, the only way to spare herself impending heartache. Sometimes love can be too pure. Sometimes two souls can be too close.

Now, though, as she watched the erstwhile enemies exchange wedding vows, Francesca no longer envied Rosalind. Instead she shivered at the thought of the terrible emotional damage Rosalind and Drake could cause if they did not cherish and nurture the burning love they felt for each other.

"I now pronounce you man and wife," the old vicar mumbled, breaking Francesca's dark reverie.

She stepped forward to take from Rosalind the single rose the bride had been clutching. As Rosalind turned to her, joy and excitement lit up her face. Her eyes had never been greener, her smile never so heartfelt. She was clearly eager to kiss Drake, to seal their bond. But when she handed Francesca the rose, she looked down at her hand and gasped.

"Blood," Rosalind whispered in dismay, frowning at red drops that spotted on her palm.

Francesca's eyes widened, and she quickly pulled a kerchief from a pocket and pressed it into Rosalind's hand. "You were holding the rose too tightly. Did you not feel the thorns?"

Rosalind looked up with blinking wonder as her face drained of color. She bit her lower lip and shook her head. "I felt nothing at all."

"Don't worry," Francesca reassured her. "Just hold the kerchief in your hand. The bleeding will stop." Rosalind smiled again, shaking off the momentary dread, and turned back to Drake for a kiss.

Francesca stole a glance at the rose, at Rosalind's blood on the offending thorns, and frowned.

•   •   •

That night Francesca had trouble sleeping. At first because she had dreamed of Jacques. Graceful, young Jacques, so handsome, so tender and skilled as a lover. It was time for her to end their liaison. He was too young for her, and he lived his life without the urgency that marked her own. She knew the worst that life could offer, and was determined to seize the best. It was no longer enough to frolic with an eager and passionate lover. She wanted to find *the one*.

She tossed and turned in her sheets, which were moist with perspiration that beaded on her skin. It was one of those windless August nights when a wall of humidity seemed to encircle the estate, and lie like a heavy blanket on her body.

Francesca gave up the notion of sleep around three in the morning. She was dreaming about her child, who was calling to her with desperation. "Mama, Mama, please come to me. Come to me, Mama." The dream was always the same. And always it ended with her bolting upright in bed with a shuddering gasp, reaching out to him with clawing fingers, but grasping only air. "My baby! Oh, my baby!"

Her own voice woke her. She always thought for a moment that someone else had been speaking, some other desperate mother who had lost her child, but when the dream images faded, Francesca realized that she was the one who would never see her child again. She alone would bear the guilt of abandoning a beloved child.

But wasn't it for the best this way? Her child was with his father—Malcolm, the nobleman who had seduced her while she was in the care of her guardian—and Malcolm's barren wife. She had seen the boy only once after his birth. She had smoothed his dark hair with loving tenderness and placed her lips to his forehead in a gesture that was more a fervent prayer than a kiss. And then she had handed him, all swaddled in blankets, to the midwife. The same woman who told Francesca the following morning that she would never be able to have another child. Something had gone wrong during the delivery. She was lucky to be alive, the midwife said.

Francesca sighed at the memory and sank back into her pillows. She had no regrets. She had done what was best for her child. He would be eighteen now. A man who doubtless no longer cared about mothers and lost childhoods. He would never know that he was born of an improper union. And that was more important than knowing his mother . . . wasn't it?

She wiped away a trickle of perspiration on her neck and tried to return to her dreams. Not so that she might feel more pain, but so that she could understand a strange new element that had entered the recurrent nightmare. Tonight someone sinister had appeared for the first time. A man with two faces, a man who wanted to take something from her, something nearly as precious as her son.

Someone with dark hair, like Drake's.

No, it couldn't have been Drake. What would he take from her? If he took from anyone, it would be Rosalind.

Disturbed anew, Francesca woke her handmaid, who was sleeping on a bed in the corner of the chamber, and got dressed. When she reached the downstairs entrance hall, the sun was just beginning to rise. Pink rays filtered through a heavy mist and gleamed through the windows. Hearing voices and the whicker of horses, she rushed out the door just as Drake was mounting a horse.

"Tell Huthbert that if Lady Rosalind stirs, he should inform her that I've gone for a ride and will be back by noon."

"Yes, master," the hostler said, then headed back to the stables.

"Drake!" Francesca called before he could heel his mount.

He turned to her and smiled, but there was a falseness to it. "Frannie, what are you doing up so early?" His mount pranced impatiently beneath him, eager to be off and running.

"I couldn't sleep." She descended the front stairs and stopped near his right boot. She crossed her arms and gazed up at him, studying him with the same perceptiveness with which she'd first viewed him so long ago. "You're going to see your lawyer, aren't you?"

Drake's lips thinned. "No, Frannie, I'm going to see someone on Hatton Street."

"You're going to sell off the land surrounding Thornbury House, aren't you?"

The glance Drake darted from the half circle of the pink sun rising on the horizon to Frannie was filled with resignation. "You don't know the half of it."

Francesca's heart began to beat more urgently. Was there more? What could be worse? "You're not . . . you're not going to sell the *house.*"

Drake smiled. "Don't worry yourself, Frannie. I know what I'm doing."

"Do you? I'm beginning to wonder if I really know you, Drake."

"Frannie—"

"Does Rosalind know where you are going now? The morning after your wedding, for the love of God!"

"No, she doesn't need to know. It will disturb her. I assure you, Frannie, I plan to take good care of my wife."

"I've had my fill of men and their good intentions," she spat, taking a step back to better see his guilt-ridden face, to put some distance between them. She wanted to see his face very clearly, for his response to the question she was about to ask would tell her everything she needed to know about Drake Rothwell's motives.

"Did you marry Rosalind just so that you could make this trip into town, as the new owner of Thornbury House? Did you wed her merely to rob her of all that she loves?"

Drake's eyes flashed with anger, and his mouth pressed into a thin line, but he did not respond immediately. And in that moment of hesitation, Francesca had all the answer she needed.

"I see," she whispered. "Don't be gone long, Drake. Rosalind will be looking for you the moment she arises. She's in love, you know, like I've never seen a woman in love. She carries her heart in her hands. Did you know that?"

Drake did not take the time to answer, but heeled his horse and bounded away. Francesca turned back toward the house with heavy steps, contemplating how she might explain to Rosalind the bitter disappointments that were a woman's lot in a marriage.

Twenty-four

⬦⬦⬦

A week later Drake and Rosalind held a grand feast to officially celebrate their nuptials. Word of their union had quickly spread throughout London, and everyone was eager to attend the celebration party, if for no other reason than to gawk at the unlikely pair. Stories of Drake and Rosalind's enmity had become legion, and now everyone wanted to view them as if they were an exotic pair of animals at the zoo at the Tower of London. Rosalind simply hoped no one would expect them to couple before an audience, as the monkeys sometimes did.

The morning of the party, Rosalind was in a peevish mood and asked Francesca to accompany her for a walk in the garden. With baskets in hand, they set out to pick the flowers that would be arranged in vases for the evening festivities. But first they visited the topiary garden.

"Frannie, I've been married only a week, but it's beginning to feel like a year," Rosalind said as her feet skimmed over the dew-laden grass. Bushes sculpted in the shapes of giant rabbits, camels, and horses eavesdropped on their conversation.

"I hope you are not referring to what goes on between you after the candles have been snuffed out," Francesca replied. "If so, you are in for a very tedious marriage. I speak from experience."

"On the contrary. Every night he makes love to me with the extraordinary passion and skill with which he first seduced me. I couldn't imagine a better lover, and every night I fall asleep assured that I am the most fortunate woman who has ever lived, and that I've made the right decision in marrying, as my father had wished.

"But then the sun rises, and by the time it sets again, I am convinced that marrying Drake was the worst mistake of my life. It's as if he turns into another person by day, as if I have married a man with two personalities. By day he is so damnably precise and polite."

"I've noticed a certain disquiet between you," Francesca remarked as she ducked under the wings of a dove carved out of dark green shrubbery.

"And his distance seems to increase with each trip he takes to London," Rosalind continued. Her basket, hooked over her arm, rocked as she idly plucked the leaves from a twig.

She wanted nothing more than intimacy. She didn't cherish the ecstasy she felt in his arms nearly as much as the closeness, the quiet oneness that always followed their passionate encounters. Marriage had done nothing to anchor her in the wild seas of Drake's whims. Where before she had disdained closeness, she was now driven mad by the knowledge that he still kept a great measure of himself apart from everyone, even her. Especially her. It didn't seem fair after she had given up all control of her own emotions.

Drake had been exceptionally moody since the visit of Captain Hillard. What news had the captain brought? And where was he now? Whenever Rosalind asked about the status of his company, Drake seemed to wince, and a look of guilt crossed his handsome face. He would say, "Do not worry about that, my dear. As soon as I find Captain Hillard, I will know much more." Drake had been tearing London apart in his futile attempts to find the missing captain. His suspicion that Hillard had been kidnapped gained greater substance with each passing day.

"Rosalind, have you ever wondered why Drake is going into London with such frequency?"

"He wants to find his missing captain."

"That may not be the only reason."

Rosalind stopped to consider this. "You think he's continuing with his plan to sell part of the estate?"

"Yes, I do." Worry shimmered beneath Francesca's dark lashes.

Rosalind gave her a thin smile. "I've wondered about that, too. Before we were married, I hired London's best lawyers to see to it that Drake could not sell off the property. But I can't believe he would be so callous as to sell the estate days after our marriage."

"Why don't you ask him?"

"No, I have to show Drake that I trust him. I have to make up for all the years I tried to undermine him. Trust was the basis of my parents' wonderful marriage. Drake and I may have acted impetuously and foolishly when we bound ourselves to each other in marriage. But now that we are tied to one another, we must fight like hell to forge some measure of happiness. Don't you see?"

Francesca put on one of her brave smiles. "Of course I do. And you are absolutely right."

"He's still an arrogant boar," Rosalind allowed with a wink as they headed toward the knots of flowers. "On Wednesday he announced that he would be collecting the rents with Thomas. I could accompany him if I wished, but I am no longer *allowed* to do it alone. I nearly bit my tongue through to silence myself. You would have been proud of me, Frannie.''

"I'm very impressed.''

"On Thursday, when I was rereading the *Roman de la Rose,* he harrumphed and asked me why I hadn't yet completed the damn book. When I explained that I was rereading it, he ranted and raved about how I should be organizing the servants and the gardeners instead of wasting my time reading. By God, I will never give up my reading or writing. Not for any man.''

"That's my Rosalind.'' Francesca hugged her and patted her back. "It's foolish of me to ever worry about you.''

"I've been trying to avoid a fight our first week of marriage, but I feel like a barrel of ale whose lid is ready to pop.''

Francesca let out a lilting peal of laughter. "Just warn me before you do. I want to make sure I'm nowhere in sight when the keg explodes.''

Drake and Rosalind dressed in separate chambers, but they reached the top of the grand staircase at the same time. She saw him coming before he noticed her, and she allowed herself a brief glance of admiration before his gaze met hers.

He wore a bloodred satin doublet embroidered with scorpions of Venice gold and a white ruff collar, and his hair flowed out beneath a fashionable floppy hat of ginger taffeta in soft, black waves. Even from a distance, she smelled his soap, and the thought of him bathing made her thighs tense with longing. She could just picture him in a tub, water lapping on the ripples of his stomach, around his generous manhood, caressing his finely carved buttocks.

She forced herself to see him as he was—fully dressed, and very distinguished looking. Though his status had in-

creased by virtue of his marriage to her, the daughter of
an earl, there was no denying that Drake was a striking-
looking man in his own right. She saw it anew when his
cerulean eyes met hers and flashed like hewn silver.

"Are you ready to present your new husband?" he said
mockingly, coming to a stop before her and taking her
hands in his.

She ignored the tingle his fingers aroused. "I'm as ready
as I'll ever be." When he leaned over to kiss her cheek,
she was grateful that he seemed to be in tame spirits.

"Good afternoon, Lady Ashenby." The usher's voice
wafted up the stairs from the entrance hall. Rosalind followed the sound with her gaze, glancing down the stairs
with irritation. The lovely Widow Ashenby made her elegant entrance.

Rosalind felt a twinge of jealousy when Drake craned
his neck for a better look as well.

"That's the widow you want me to bed?" he said.

"I mentioned her, yes. *Before* we were married."

"I see why you made the recommendation." He
winked. "I may finally be ready to take your advice."

His white teeth flashed with a devilish smile.

Rosalind simmered, but took his outstretched arm nonetheless. She would ignore his provocative comments. He
was simply trying to unnerve her again. He apparently
couldn't help himself. Apparently old habits couldn't be
broken in a week. She smiled with forced sweetness.

"Shall we?"

He nodded and they descended the stairs to greet a horde
of guests. Lady Blunt arrived fashionably late with Godfrey in tow, and at the sight of them, Rosalind was momentarily speechless. She had not thought of how the
scheming woman and her awkward son would take the
news of her marriage and their own disappointment in that
regard.

Rosalind rallied a pleasant smile as Lady Blunt enveloped her in a fleshy embrace.

"Oh, my dear," she exhaled in her ear. "I can't tell you how *surprised* I was to learn of your marriage."

When she stepped back, her eyes were flat and cold. "Godfrey was surprised as well."

"Oh?" Rosalind forced herself to smile at the young man. His face was a blank, but his eyes bored into her with something less than kindness. "Good afternoon, Godfrey. I surprised even myself, Lady Blunt. Do forgive me for not taking you into my confidence. But not even Francesca knew until the last moment. You did receive my note, did you not, Porphyria?"

Rosalind had sent Lady Blunt a note asking her to cease her inquiries into Drake's past.

"I did receive it." The widow snapped open her ivory fan and began to flap it in front of her face. "Sadly, it arrived too late."

Rosalind swallowed a growing sense of uneasiness. "I sent it to Cranston House a week ago. The very day Drake and I married. I—"

"The note," Lady Blunt said coolly, "is something you and I should discuss *in private.*"

Drake placed a protective hand on Rosalind's shoulder and she flashed him a look of gratitude. "How I'm prattling on! Godfrey, why don't you start a game in the bowling alley. I'll send some *young* men your way."

At this pointed reference to his age, he glared at her, but lumbered off as instructed, his rage over his rejection, it seemed, momentarily forgotten. Lady Blunt followed behind him with an indignant waddle.

Just as Rosalind was heaving a sigh of relief, Huthbert announced the arrival of a guest who went by the sole name of Stryder. She felt Drake stiffen the moment the man, dressed in black, bowed and kissed her hand.

"My lady," Stryder said. He straightened, the elegance of his movements a strange and unsettling contrast to his mirthless grin and the shrewd, almost immodest penetration of his gray eyes. "I wish you the best in your marriage to Master Rothwell. He is more fortunate than he deserves."

Seeing the cold look this mysterious guest exchanged with her husband, Rosalind's curiosity doubled. Who was he and what did he want?

"I thought our business was complete," Drake said tersely.

Stryder's brows rose over jaded gray eyes. "Not by a furlong. But I'll not bore you with business tonight. This is a day of celebration." He bowed curtly and walked without a moment's hesitation into the great hall, where the guests were mingling.

Rosalind glared up at Drake. "To what business did he refer?"

Drake shrugged and ran a finger under his hot collar. "Honestly, I do not know."

"But you know him."

"I suppose you could put it that way."

"Drake, what the—"

"Rosalind . . ." He gently gripped her arm and put a forefinger to her lips. "Didn't you hear what he said? No business. Tonight we celebrate."

Just as they were about to join the festivities, one last guest arrived, hurried and out of breath.

"Rosalind! I hope I'm not too late." Will Shakespeare dashed through the door with a prompt book tucked under one arm. He kissed her hand and patted Drake's shoulder good-naturedly. "I was waylaid by the gatherers at the Globe. There was a squabble over how much money they had collected at this afternoon's performance. Being a sharer of the company is sometimes more responsibility than I'd like. I have a share in the profits, yes, but at times it seems I carry more than my share of the work! I'd best join the players in the gallery. Did they arrive?''

"Huthbert tells me they've been straggling in through the rear entrance. Be at ease, William, there is no rush. We will feast first in the great hall as usual. And thank you again. I can't wait to see the new scenes.''

Shakespeare's knowing eyes crinkled with fondness as she leaned forward and kissed his cheek with heartfelt gratitude.

As Shakespeare dashed off, Drake turned slowly to Rosalind. His cheeks flushed red, as if a hurricane had just blown through the house. "What is the meaning of this, Rosalind?''

She felt a prickle of the old enmity start up in a place deep inside her belly. She hated the look of superior knowledge that always managed to gleam in Drake's eyes when he thought he'd caught her at some mischief.

"What do you mean, what is the meaning of this?'' She bit each word with anger.

He rolled his eyes, as if seeking patience from the gods. "I should think my meaning would be clear. Is Master Shakespeare's troupe going to perform scenes written by you?''

At that, her patience, already stretched thin, snapped. She thrust her hands on her hips. "Yes, they are going to perform my scenes. What of it?''

"What of it?'' He swept a hand over his face to quell his fury. "You are my wife. I will not have you scandalizing all of London by writing plays. Before I know it, I'll be seeing you traipsing across the stage at the Globe.''

"And why not!'' Rosalind shot back. "Women perform in commedia dell' arte in Italy.''

"This is not Italy. And you are not some vagabond player.''

"Are you calling Master Shakespeare a vagabond?"

"No! But he is a man. You are a woman."

"And somehow the less for it, I suppose. I only wish you knew our queen, Drake; then you would understand just how powerful a woman can be."

"God's teeth!" His voice punched against the surrounding walls. "I know more about the queen than you could ever imagine. This has nothing to do with your sex. It's a matter of propriety. You are my wife."

"You mean your slave?"

"No, God's teeth!"

"How dare you!" she shouted back, releasing a week's worth of anxiety and frustration. "First you tell me I cannot collect the rents and visit with my own tenants, then you tell me to stop reading and start working in the garden. And now you tell me I cannot write! What next, in God's name? Shall I shut myself in my chamber until you bid me come to your side each day?"

"I didn't mean that you cannot write. You simply cannot let your scenes be performed before an audience. Someone will recognize you as the author."

"Ah, such a humiliation for the great master of Thornbury House! He has a wife who is creative at heart, who devotes herself to something other than her lord and master. What a dreadful blight upon your exalted reputation."

"Now you're starting to sound like the scenes from your play," he said through clenched teeth.

"And that's really what bothers you, is it not? That someone will recognize you in my work. And you have lived your whole life, Drake, hiding behind your masks. The greatest being the mask of the avenger. Well, what if you get what you're after? What if you avenge your father's honor? What will you live for then? Will there be anything left of you?"

He gripped her arms so hard she winced and bit back a

cry. She met his eyes with her own blazing fury. "You're hurting me."

His fingers sprang away from her arms as if they were made of acid. He took a deep steadying breath, and raked her with a sad and tortured look. "I'll be sleeping on *La Rose* tonight."

"Are you going to seek Lady Ashenby for consolation before you go?" she cried out to his back. "She doesn't write plays. She's merely beautiful and pliant. The best sort of woman."

He twisted around with an enraged grin. "I thank you for the suggestion. I shall do just that."

He turned on his heels and was gone an instant later. She started after him, but seeing the shocked expression of the servants scurrying by, she drew back her shoulders and tipped up her chin.

"Go about your work," she commanded, trying to hide the pain she was feeling. He could not have hurt her more if he had beaten her. He did not want to sleep with her tonight. That was her punishment for speaking the truth, for reaching past the masks. He would reject her lovemaking if she dared, if she presumed, to be equal to him in matters of the heart.

Oh, churl! What mistake had she made? Had she ruined her life? Was living with a beast the price she had to pay for the ecstasy she had learned to crave? She had seen the devil in him as a child, and had feared him. Why had she allowed herself to see, or imagine, more? She had imagined him a tender, loving man. She had imagined him someone who would cherish, rather than rule her. She had imagined that Drake was capable of feeling something more than the desire to restore his wounded pride. . . .

In her imagination, she had conjured up a man who had no counterpart in reality.

Twenty-five

∽

Francesca was passing through the great hall when Drake brushed past her, knocking her shoulder with his arm without a backward glance. She gave a startled chuckle, ready to tease him for rough-and-tumble ways, but then saw the furious set of his every muscle and pressed her lips together. Pushing through the crowd, heading for the corner where Lady Ashenby was holding court, he was clearly unaware of the startled glances of those whose greetings he ignored.

Had Drake and Rosalind had another row? Francesca wondered. She would seek Rosalind out later to find out. But right now she had more pressing business. Moments earlier Huthbert handed her a note that merely said: *Meet me in Lord Dunnington's parlor*. The note was unsigned.

As she hurried through the private chambers and stepped into the parlor, Francesca was startled to discover the author of the note.

"Jacques, I did not expect you tonight."

He was standing at a window, and had turned when he

heard her cross the threshold. His fine-featured face brightened with an uneasy smile.

"Ah, *chérie,* I knew you would not disappoint me."

Francesca crumpled the note in her hand, dreading this confrontation. She had ignored a half-dozen missives he'd sent around to Thornbury House in the past week. Apparently, in the ardor of youthful infatuation, Jacques was incapable of understanding that she was no longer interested in their dalliance.

"Francesca . . ." His voice, so deep and expressive, so full of hot-blooded youth, faded when he saw her cool smile. He shrugged his shoulders and raised an arm. "I offer you a simple gift." His hand held a bouquet of fresh flowers.

"Love-in-idleness," she whispered, her voice wilting as the blossoms soon would. Crossing to the center of the room, seeking to avoid his penetrating look, she took the flowers from his hands. "They're my favorites. You shouldn't have plucked them. They'll only die now." She pressed the blossoms to her face and felt their velvety texture.

"Francesca, why are you so sad? Speak to me, *chérie.* Do not turn away from me. Francesca, *je t'adore.* I love you."

"No! You mustn't!"

He visibly shrank at the hardness in her tone. Beneath her soft, gentle exterior, there was a woman made of steel, forged in the fires of suffering and annealed in the furnace of loss. Never having seen this side of her, the young Frenchman was startled.

"Jacques, I told you not to fall in love with me. You have been very precious, very loving. But I am not the woman for you. I can love no one, my dear boy."

"I am not a boy. I am a man!"

His outraged indignation combined with his heavily accented English made him only more adorable than he already was, and Francesca felt a stab of guilt. She had toyed with this young man. Was she any better than those who had toyed with her? Was she any better than Malcolm? She pressed the flowers to her heart, which ached anew at the thought of the man she loved. Was it wrong for her to want someone to hold her, even if she no longer had a heart to give?

"Jacques, I must tell you something, something very painful." Still clutching the flowers, she went to him and wrapped her arms around his back. She stroked his hair and spoke soothingly in his ear. "If I were any other woman, I would give my very life to you. I do love you, Jacques, but not in the way that you deserve. I am waiting for something, something I am not sure even exists. Or perhaps it existed once, and I lost or squandered my chance to possess it. All I know for certain is that you must go now and never come back. If you love, do this for me."

"Is it because I am a player?" he whispered in her ear. "That I am beneath you?"

"No, no, of course not. Do not ask why, Jacques. Just turn and walk away. I beg of you."

"Francesca—"

"Please. *Please.*"

She felt the energy drain from his body, and he sagged in her arms. Then he withdrew and kissed her chastely on the forehead. She dropped her chin to her chest in a brief prayer of thanks. He was making it easy for her. Thank God he was an actor. His heart would bleed, but it would be stage blood.

"I will never forget you," he whispered, his eyes glimmering with tears. He stroked her face, and she tried to remember how many times this farewell scene had been played out in her life. How many lovers had there been? How jaded and brittle had she become?

She did not watch him go. Instead, she gazed at the flowers in her hands—the delicate little velvet petals, the deep purple, richer than any monarch's robes or prelate's vestments. One day she would sleep in a bed of love-in-idleness with the man who would be true. One day.

As she brushed aside a single tear a sudden sound made her look up. A dark figure was looming in the doorway. "How long have you been standing there?" she gasped.

"How long would you have liked me to be standing here?" said the dark stranger.

He wore a black doublet, and she noticed a scar slashed one cheek. His brown hair fell about his shoulders like a dark angel's. He looked worn-out, world-weary, like a horse that had been ridden to lameness and still could not find a stable to bed in.

"What do you want?" Francesca inquired icily. After her tête-à-tête with Jacques, her nerves were thin. She was in no mood to be charming and gracious.

"I want a moment with you." He leaned against the doorway, his pose not so much cocky as past caring.

"You've had more than a moment already. What is it you wish?"

He quirked a tired smile. "You should not waste your time on callow youths."

Francesca's jaw opened in astonishment at his audacity and a bolt of pure rage caused her spine to stiffen. She was a woman who never allowed herself to show anger, who never screamed in her own defense. But at this particular moment she, too, was past caring.

She marched toward the rude stranger, close enough to smell the scent of leather he exuded, then slapped him hard on the cheek. Her hand left a red imprint that covered and blended with his scar. As if he were used to such blows, his eyes never flinched. She felt a pinprick of remorse, until he glared at her, eyes hard as rocks.

"That's a fine greeting, my lady," he murmured.

"How dare you presume to eavesdrop on my conversations?" she hissed. "How dare you further presume to offer ignorant opinions about that which you have seen?"

With unexpected gracefulness, he suddenly knelt before her, lifting the scalloped border of her gown to his lips. Then he glared up defiantly. "I dare because I kiss the hem of your gown." He pressed his lips to the soft fabric, his eyes never leaving hers.

Francesca broke out into a cold sweat. Her heart began to pound. What did he mean? What did this outrageous, dark man mean? Was he jesting? No. *Get thee gone, Francesca,* a little voice inside urged, *get thee gone.*

She spun around, dropping the flowers, the train of her gown slapping up at his face. He smiled sardonically and rose.

"I see you are a courtier, an apt pupil of the gallant gestures practiced at Court."

"I am not welcome at Court."

"Oh," she said with forced lightness. "Are you perchance a Spanish ambassador, then?"

She turned expectantly, but he did not laugh.

"What I am is far worse than any Spanish ambassador."

"Your name, good sir?"

"Stryder."

"Master Stryder?"

"Just Stryder. I am an agent."

"May I inquire whom you serve?"

His gray-green eyes glinted. "Such a question, in this case, my lady, would be most indiscreet."

She smiled. "Ah, one of those kinds of agents. A double-dealer. A *spy.*"

He was unmoved. His veiled expression seemed to suggest that he'd heard himself called far worse.

"So why did you interrupt the final scene of my tawdry

love story, Stryder? Could your business not wait?''

''No. Your friend—Drake Rothwell—is in trouble.''

Francesca stopped her idle pacing and turned on him sharply. ''What do you mean?''

''He should pack lightly. A man doesn't need much in the Tower of London.''

''In the Tower? What are you talking about? And how came you to know of such a matter?''

He smiled mirthlessly. ''I know. Even before he does. The queen cares for Master Rothwell. In spite of what she will do to him. I came here to warn you, because she will not. She is old and cantankerous.''

''She? You mean the queen?''

''Take care of your friend.''

''What do you know? Tell me!'' Francesca took two steps forward, then halted in frustration. ''What about Drake? If you mean he's trying to sell Thornbury House, I've already learned that much myself.''

''That!'' Stryder scoffed, heading for the doorway with a bored chuckle. ''That is nothing. He would survive that. His lovely and besotted wife would overlook him selling the clothes off her back, if I'm any judge of appearances.''

''I would hardly think you were a judge of much of anything, particularly concerning matters of the heart.''

He stopped abruptly, as if stung. Then he turned to her, assessing her with his cold eyes. He nodded then, an acknowledgment, a tip of a nonexistent hat, and then it was as if he vanished from the room, leaving a cold wave of dread in his wake.

Not long after Drake stormed away from Rosalind, she encountered Lady Blunt. The widow was lying in wait, ready to pounce in the hallway that led from the entrance to the great hall. She gripped Rosalind's silk sleeve with pudgy fingers, pinching the skin.

"Pssst! We must talk."

Rosalind winced. "What is it, Porphyria?"

"I couldn't help but overhear your argument. I can't imagine why you married that rogue! He's only after one thing, you know."

Rosalind's cheeks flushed with indignation. "No, I didn't know."

"You'll understand everything when I share a few facts with you, my dear. We must speak in private."

Lady Blunt's expression was altogether too smug, too knowing, and Rosalind had to fight the urge to turn and run into the garden. There would be no reprieve now. She had to gather the crops she had sown, however bitter the harvest.

"So you spied on Drake?" she queried in a faint voice.

"Just as you asked," came Lady Blunt's icy reply.

"But I sent you a note to cease your . . . explorations."

"It was too late. You asked me to open Pandora's box, my dear, and I complied. Now you cannot ask me to forget what I have learned."

Rosalind nodded. "Come into the lord's parlor. We can speak in private."

When they arrived moments later, Rosalind inhaled a whiff of flowers. She glanced around and saw a bouquet of love-in-idleness scattered on the floor. "Francesca must have been here," she commented to herself. "Please sit, Porphyria. I will join you by the window."

They sat at a game table where chess pieces were in place and ready for a game. Rosalind was known for her skill at chess, but she would trade it in an instant for some insight into the less savory games that Lady Blunt played.

"What have you learned about Drake?" Rosalind spoke frankly, folding her hands, telling the woman without words that she should waste no time getting to the point.

"Well, where shall I begin? Let me start with the least of Master Rothwell's deceptions."

Rosalind idly fingered a black pawn, rubbing the polished wood against her palm. Time seemed to stand still as Lady Blunt drew a deep breath and her lips spread like the Red Sea, preparing to spew forth her venom.

"It seems, my dear Rosalind, that your new husband is a spy for the queen."

Rosalind blinked, then choked out a laugh. "What? A spy? For the *queen*?"

"That's correct. He is a buccaneer, and now a landed gentleman, thanks to you, but first and foremost, he works for the queen."

"No, that can't be. He has never met the queen. He has no connections at Court. *I* do. I am the queen's friend, not Drake."

"He's been playing you for a fool, my dear. But you're not alone. He's managed to arrange countless secret meetings with the queen of which those of us at Court were in total ignorance. Did you never wonder why he knows so much about royal politics when he's been so long away at sea?"

Rosalind could not answer. She herself had wondered this on several occasions. And now she knew. He was a spy. That was why he had left her so abruptly after their visit to Do-Good Simplicity's home. He was in a hurry to report to Queen Elizabeth.

"A spy," Rosalind said in a reedy voice. She tried to swallow, but her tongue was too dry, and her head was beginning to pound. "A spy."

"Yes, one of Her Majesty's most intimate spies. He reported to her on the loyalty, or lack thereof, of her ambassadors in countries that dotted the trading routes. No one knew. Not even I." Lady Blunt sniffed at the indignity.

If Drake was intimate with the queen, what did this signify about Thornbury House? Rosalind quickly scanned
her memories of the conversations she'd had with Elizabeth about the house. Then it all became heart-stoppingly
clear. The queen had *pretended* to want the house simply
to force Rosalind to marry Drake. That way Elizabeth
could reward Drake for his spying with a prodigy house,
without ever having to dip her parsimonious fingers into
her own pocket to pay for it. And Drake had been in on
the scheme all along.

What a fool Rosalind had been! What a fool! And what
was the result? Drake was now the master of the house.
He was already proving himself to be a tyrant. Clearly his
words of passion had been designed merely to render her
pliant. Perhaps the queen had even advised him on the
endearments he should use to smooth Rosalind's ruffled
feathers.

"Lady Rosalind, say something!" Lady Blunt urged
her. "You're not going to faint, are you?"

Rosalind was too stung, too betrayed to cry out in anger.
For the first time in her life she felt defeated. Fate had
dealt her a crushing blow, knocked her to the floor, and
she could not rise.

"Say something, dear girl, or I shall have to call a physician."

Rosalind blinked back tears of humiliation and forced a
laugh. "No, I'm fine. I knew all along that Drake was a
spy. I was just pretending not to know, in the hopes of
maintaining my husband's secret. But since you clearly
cannot be fooled, Porphyria, I will . . . I will drop my silly
pretense." She cleared her throat, struggling to find more
convincing words. "You see, Drake told me just before
. . . just before we exchanged our vows."

"Oh?" Lady Blunt frowned dubiously. "Did he also
tell you that he was more than a merchant seaman? That

he was an interloper who raided one of the Levant Company ships at Acheen.''

"An interloper?"

"Actually, it's worse than that. He attacked and boarded the queen's own ship. It is one thing for a sea dog to sneak into harbor pretending to be with the Levant Company and convincing a native king to trade goods. It's another matter when that sea dog actually raids a ship belonging to the queen. And that, my dear, is what will land Master Drake Rothwell in the Tower, once the queen finds out."

"I'm sure Drake had good reason," Rosalind said, defending him in spite of her feelings of sick betrayal.

"His good reason, if he had one," Lady Blunt continued, "was his ruthless desire for success. But in fact, he's a total failure. He's been touring the high seas for ten years, and has apparently made just enough money to pay his sailors' wages. Oh, he raided rich Spanish carracks and amassed fabulous wealth at various points. But his overwhelming ambition always ended up emptying his coffers. Instead of returning to London and repaying his investor and putting away a little money for his old age, Rothwell always sought more ports, more ships, greater glory. Furious at finding that he had managed to squander his good fortune, he boarded the Levant Company ship in an act of outrageous piracy. As it happens, it was one of the queen's own vessels flying the Levant Company flag under the care of Admiral Anthony Peele."

"How do you know this?" Rosalind snapped. "Who told you?"

Lady Blunt smirked. "I heard it directly from the lips of a messenger that Admiral Peele sent to herald his imminent return. The messenger is staying at Cranston House, where I can keep an eye on him. We do not want the news about Drake's crimes to reach the royal ears before we have a chance to deliver it ourselves."

"The queen won't send Drake to the Tower," Rosalind argued. "Not if he is her spy."

"Don't be naive. Drake boarded the queen's own vessel with unmistakably hostile intent. Admiral Peele's sailors attempted to defend the vessel, and in the ensuing skirmish the ship caught fire and sank. Drake committed the ultimate sin against Queen Elizabeth. He placed his own ambitions before hers."

"Oh, dear." Rosalind's sense of betrayal was rapidly yielding ground to a sense of dread on Drake's behalf.

"As you know, Rosalind, the queen has encouraged buccaneers and sea dogs to pirate Spanish ships, and she won't even wag a finger at them if they share their booty with her. But she will not tolerate her own goods being threatened. Admiral Peele and most of his sailors safely escaped the sinking ship and continued on the trade route aboard other ships in their fleet. They're expected to return to London any day."

"How did you get your hands on Peele's messenger?"

"One of my . . . employees . . . on the docks alerted me to his arrival."

"You mean one of your spies," Rosalind said in a voice full of loathing. She rose abruptly, jarring the gaming table with her knee. The chess pieces clattered to the carpet.

"Where are you going?" Lady Blunt heaved herself up from her chair with a grunt.

"I'm going to find Drake."

"Don't be a fool! He doesn't deserve a warning."

"I won't stand by and watch him dragged to the Tower. I don't care what sort of beast he is. He is still my husband." Rosalind strode across the room, picking up pace as she went.

"Rosalind!" Lady Blunt squealed, but to no avail.

•   •   •

Rosalind dashed through the private chambers at a run until she reached Drake's chamber. She halted, out of breath, and raised her hand to knock, but then noticed the door was ajar. She lowered her fist, stretched her fingers out, wondering if she knew her husband well enough to enter unbidden. Just when she decided that she did, she heard a ripple of dulcet laughter coming out of the room.

"Oh, Drake, you are an amusing man." This gushing statement was followed by more feminine laughter. Rosalind recognized the voice instantly, and her hands grew clammy with dread. Drake was alone with Lady Ashenby. Rosalind could not see them, but she pressed her ear to the door to hear their conversation.

"I wish Rosalind found me so humorous," Drake replied with a soft chuckle that seemed to indicate ongoing familiarities.

"If Rosalind does not recognize your humor, then I should be rewarded for my perceptiveness."

"A reward?"

"You know what I want." Her voice was husky, intimate.

Rosalind's face burned, and her heart pounded in her chest. Had she happened upon Drake at the very moment when he was about to commit adultery? Even if she had all but pushed him into the widow's arms, he had no right to follow through with the affair!

"I am not a lady to mince words," Lady Ashenby was saying. "Give it to me, Drake. Put it in my hand. Here, I'll take it myself."

"Careful," he murmured playfully. "Let me help you."

Tears blurred Rosalind's eyes. Once again she was spying on Drake, but what she heard now was worse than any conversation she had eavesdropped on as a child.

"Here," Drake murmured. "You can hold it now."

"Hmmmm," Lady Ashenby purred. "It's so hard."

"Made of steel," he boasted.

"But it's so short."

Rosalind frowned to herself. How dare that insufferable woman . . . ! Wasn't it enough that the greedy widow was taking liberties with another woman's husband? Did she then have the audacity to find him wanting!

"It will get longer if you pull on it," Drake instructed. "There, that's better."

"You're right. It *is* long. I hope Lady Rosalind appreciates this."

"She does," Drake replied confidently. "Trust me."

Rosalind let out a hissing breath of outrage. How dare he discuss their intimacies with another woman!

"My lady," Huthbert said, coming up from her and tapping her on the shoulder.

"Oh!" Rosalind jolted in surprise. She gasped and spun around, accidentally knocking the door open when she stumbled back.

"Forgive me, my lady," the wide-eyed gentleman usher pleaded. "I did not mean to startle you. Lady Blunt asked me to—"

"Well, well, well," Drake's smug voice rang out.

Huthbert and Rosalind both turned to find Drake standing with crossed arms in the middle of his chamber. Lady Ashenby was standing at his side.

Rosalind strained to see any naked body parts, but nothing seemed to be exposed, except for her lack of trust in Drake. She did not know what he and Lady Ashenby had been up to, but had assumed the worst. Their conversation had been positively scandalous.

"What are you doing outside my doorway, Rosalind?" she heard Drake ask her, sounding like a scolding father. "Not spying, I should hope. I thought we were beyond that stage."

"I came to tell you something very important," she replied with clipped words. How dare he act as if she had been the one who was at fault! "But I see you are otherwise engaged. I'll keep counsel with myself. And Lady Blunt. She is waiting for me in the lord's parlor, as Huthbert has so kindly reminded me. Now if you will excuse me . . ."

Rosalind turned in a huff and sailed away, her gown flowing behind her. The befuddled gentleman usher followed.

Drake turned to Lady Ashenby with a sardonic grin. "I'm married to a curious, intelligent woman."

Lady Ashenby's even brows rose together in sympathy. "What a curse."

"Actually, it's a great blessing. I don't deserve her. Though she is a pain in the arse now and then." He held out an open palm. "Now give me back my telescope."

She flirtatiously laid it in his hand. "I can't keep it?"

"Not a chance. I gave it to Rosalind as a wedding gift. She'd have my hide if I gave it to another woman for safekeeping." He compressed the telescope to its most compact size and placed it on his clothing trunk.

"Speaking of your wife, I'd best go. I'm afraid she quite misinterpreted our little tête-à-tête."

"The jealous vixen." His voice was soft with affection.

"If there is anything else you wish to learn about the Earl of Essex," Lady Ashenby said as she started for the door, "I can provide you with the most intimate details. Did you know he has a star-shaped mole on his right inner thigh?"

Drake shook his head. "The only details I need concern his whereabouts. Keep me posted, won't you? The queen will reward you for your loyalty when all is said and done. For we have not heard the last of Robert Devereux."

Lady Ashenby winked conspiratorially and quietly slipped away.

• • •

"Do I seem jaded to you, my pet?" Lady Blunt cooed after Rosalind returned to the lord's parlor with her proverbial tail between her legs. "If so, I promise you that I won't seem so for long. You see, Rosalind, I have provided you with the means to escape your ill-thought-out marriage. I have an audience with the queen in the morning. Come with me. I'll let you break the news to Her Majesty. You be the one to tell her of Drake's betrayal, and she will reward you with an annulment. She always did like you, Rosalind."

"I loved the queen," Rosalind said as she paced the room. "But I see now that I never really knew her."

"Who does? No one knows all of the queen. Just bits and pieces of her. She is a complicated woman."

Rosalind knew far less of Gloriana than she'd ever realized. To think that her own husband had been spying for the queen all along, and Rosalind herself never even knew it.

Meanwhile, Lady Blunt was beginning to wax philosophical. "Full revelation is a luxury Her Majesty could never afford. Her own mother, Anne Boleyn, was beheaded when Elizabeth was an infant. And Elizabeth watched her stepmother lose her head as well. Can you imagine such a dreadful childhood? Would you trust anyone if your father was in the habit of executing his own wives?"

"Marriage, it seems, is no place for trust," Rosalind mused.

"Certainly not."

For once, Rosalind and Lady Blunt were in total agreement. Rosalind could never truly be open with Drake again. He had deceived her in the most stinging fashion. He had been using her on the queen's behalf, and she could never forgive him for that. Heavens, could she ever even make love to him again?

"I will accompany you tomorrow morning to your meeting with the queen." Rosalind turned to the aging gossip with a ruthless smile. "I would like that very much."

She would confront Elizabeth, rage at her for making Rosalind a pawn in a game she and her spy were playing. And after she had raged to her content, risking the royal wrath, she would betray Drake, as he had betrayed her.

Twenty-six

✦

∽◦∾

After giving Lady Ashenby enough time to return to the great hall alone, Drake left his chamber and descended the grand staircase. At the bottom, he noticed Huthbert opening the door to one last late arrival.

"Good evening, sir," Huthbert intoned. "May I tell the master who is calling?"

"Starck. Master Starck," the older man said, tugging at the sleeves of his somber doublet. "Ah, there he is now."

"Greetings, Master Starck," Drake said. "I would say welcome, but I doubt that you've traveled all the way from London to grace my ears with good news."

"I cannot say whether it is good or bad." Starck's brow wrinkled with bemusement. "But I do have news, and business to attend to."

"Come with me. I'll serve you some port in the book chamber."

Drake led Starck to a cozy library on the first floor. Candles in wall sconces flickered against the shadows of the dim-lit chamber, illuminating the spines of dozens of leather-bound volumes. Inhaling the rich, musty odor of aged parchment, Drake felt warmed by the sense of tradition and stored wisdom that the room exuded.

He pondered the magic of the chamber as he poured two beakers of port. Master Starck watched him in silence, then accepted a glass, which he raised in a silent toast.

When each man had swallowed a smooth sip, Drake sat at the edge of a desk while Master Starck settled onto a bench.

"What news do you bring?"

"I have the papers on Thornbury House drawn up as you requested," the lawyer enunciated precisely. "All you have to do is sign them and the transaction will be official."

Drake crossed his arms, his heart aching. He leaned his head back and stared at the rafters, smoothing one hand over his beard and down his throat. Then his sober gaze returned to the dignified lawyer.

"Stryder is still interested in the property?"

Master Starck raised his brows in mild surprise. "Of course. No change there. If you've had a change of heart . . ."

"No." Drake sighed in resignation. "No, I've made up my mind."

"You can come to my office tomorrow then and sign the necessary papers?"

"Of course."

Master Starck gazed at Drake speculatively in the flickering candlelight. "Drake, if I may be so bold . . ."

"Of course."

"Have you told Lady Rosalind of your intentions?"

Drake unfolded his arms and gripped the desk with both hands. "No, I have not."

"Don't you think that would be advisable? She will be shocked, to say the least. After all, Thornbury House means the world to her, by your own account.''

Drake grinned darkly. "It's best that she be surprised."

The lawyer shrugged in bafflement. "I have a surprise myself. This came for you today. You asked me earlier if I brought bad news. Frankly, I cannot say. But this bears the same handwriting as the previous missives you've received.''

Drake snatched up the letter, scowling as he recognized the hand that had scribbled his name. "Yes, I'd say the same scoundrel is still at work." He ripped open the seal and read the letter silently. "By Jove!"

"Eh? What is it?"

"Whoever sent you that letter so long ago, telling you to mind your own business, Master Starck, has written with a new threat. This letter tells me that my colleague Captain James Hillard is imprisoned in a shack down by Pauls Wharf.''

In the dim light, Starck's face registered surprise. "Is that all the note says?"

Drake folded the parchment and tucked it in his doublet. "No."

"What does it say? You mentioned a threat."

Drake blinked hard, trying to make sense of it. "It says the queen shall die."

"Evenin', Admiral," an old woman said as Drake passed by. At the sound of her guttural, somehow familiar voice, Drake's boots halted on the creaking boards of the dock at Paul's Wharf. He turned and immediately recognized the matted thatch of hair, the brightly rouged cheeks, and the sagging breasts loosely bound in an obscenely low-cut bodice that belonged to the aging prostitute everyone knew as Doxy Doll.

"Greetings, Doll." Drake tossed her a penny and continued on his way. He expected to hear a "bless you, milord,'' for Doxy Doll was too old to ply her trade and had to rely on charity. But she surprised him by limping after him and clutching his arm.

"Do not fly so fast, Admiral," she lisped through a handful of black teeth.

Drake stopped and noticed the urgency—or was it fear?—gleaming in her eyes. "What is it, Doll? I have an important matter to attend to."

"I'll attend to it for ya, Admiral. I know what yer lookin' for."

Drake glanced over her head. A couple of galleons rocked rhythmically in the water, including *La Rose,* Drake's flagship. It had been docked without a captain ever since Hillard had been kidnapped. Fishing boats dockside creaked and groaned. Sailors shouted. Fisherman laughed. Watermen called out to potential clients looking to be ferried across the Thames. All seemed normal. Except Drake knew it was not.

"What am I looking for, Doll?" he said as his eyes lowered expectantly to hers. "If you can tell me that, I'll follow you anywhere."

She chortled and slipped her arm through his. "I've been waitin' twenty years to hear ya say that, Admiral. I'll take ya to yer Captain Hillard. That's who ya want, ain't it?"

When Drake nodded and grinned, she chortled again and led him to a tiny, dilapidated shack off of Thames Street. Drake took one look at its rotten boards and caving roof, then looked aghast at the prostitute.

"Captain Hillard is here?"

Doll nodded. "So I'm told, Admiral."

Drake's feet crunched through broken glass and the remains of a rotting boat to reach the boarded-up door. "Hillard! Are you in there?"

There was a rustling inside, a cough, then Hillard answered, "Yes! You found me. Thank the sea gods and serpents alike!"

"Be patient, Hillard, while I pry open this door." Drake tugged on the boards nailed to the doorway.

"I'll be on me way then, Admiral."

"Wait! Doll, who sent you to me? Was it Essex, or one of his men? Are they the ones who imprisoned my captain?"

The old doxy shrugged and scratched the mottled skin of her well-worn breasts. She looked westward down Thames Street, and Drake followed her gaze. The thoroughfare reached a dead end at the Black Friars, and beyond that, though too far to be seen, was the River Fleet, Bridewell Palace, and Middle Temple, where the Knights Templar dwelled until their persecution more than a hundred years before. And just beyond Middle Temple was Essex House.

"Don't know about the Earl of Essex, Admiral," Doll said with a shrug. "Some cove with a pocketful of coins told me to look out for ya. That's all. I look out for me men, Admiral."

She winked at him, hiked one hip in the air in what would have been a come-hither gesture in younger days, then strutted off into the shadows of the street.

"Hold fast, Hillard!" Drake turned back to the task at hand, and after fashioning another board as a makeshift crowbar, he loosened the door and freed the white-faced, but otherwise healthy, captain.

"Bedlam!" he muttered, dusting himself off as he looked back at his dark and rat-infested prison. "By Jupiter, I've never been so glad of a visit from you, Rothwell."

"Are you well?"

"They kept me well fed. I can't speak highly of my lodgings."

"*They?* Who did this to you?"

The gray-haired sea dog scratched the back of his head. "I'd as lief you told me, Drake, for I do not know myself. It could have been Essex's men. Or anyone who wanted to keep me from telling you my news. Whoever it was, he was at your supper party. Someone grabbed me right after that blasted statue nearly flattened you."

"So what of your news? What did you come to tell me? For that will likely hold the key to this mystery."

"Admiral Peele is soon to arrive in London."

That was all that Captain Hillard needed to say. Drake instantly understood its full import. He ran a hand over his face and squeezed the bridge of his nose. "O hellkite! Not now!"

"Once he tells the queen of your raid on his flagship, Drake, I'll warrant we'll be visiting you in the Tower. What then? What do you want me to do with your remaining ships at Buto? Sell them and try to bribe your way out of prison?"

Drake lowered his hand, for suddenly his limbs seemed to weigh a thousand stone. Fate had a peculiar way of playing itself out. And thoughts had a funny way of forming. In this moment, when he saw his entire future tumbling into an abyss, all he could think of was Rosalind. Poor Rosalind. She was finally married, and it was to someone who might spend the rest of his life in the Tower. Perhaps she was cursed after all.

"I'm not giving up yet, Hillard," he said, turning to his captain with a look of fierce determination. "Stay here at Pauls Wharf on *La Rose* until you receive further word. I should be able to send news by tomorrow."

When Drake started off, Hillard called after him, "Where are you going? Where will you be?"

Drake stopped and turned. "At Court. With the queen."

''The queen! How do you propose to gain audience with her?''

Not even Hillard knew about his spying. Drake grinned sardonically. ''Oh, I'll see her one way or another. Not tonight, I avow. She'll be playing cards with Lord Buck-hurst. The lord high steward is her favorite now that Essex has fallen out of favor. But I'll be waiting. And before the sun sets tomorrow, I will have seen the queen, I avow. Maybe for the last time, but I will have seen her.''

Twenty-seven

Rosalind arrived at Whitehall Palace early the next morning. She did not want to be tardy for Lady Blunt's audience with the queen.

After a sleepless night, she had concluded that neither she, nor Lady Blunt, would utter a word to Queen Elizabeth about Drake's raid. And when Rosalind left this audience with the monarch, she would find a way to keep Lady Blunt quiet about the matter until Admiral Peele's return.

Rosalind could no longer trust Drake, and she had decided there was no choice but to annul their sham of a marriage. But she refused to see him thrown into the Tower by her own actions. If Drake was doomed, as Lady Blunt predicted, his long fall from grace would have to occur when Admiral Peele himself informed the queen of the raid. Besides, who knew how Lady Blunt may have exaggerated or misconstrued Drake's crimes? she asked herself sensibly, despite the hurt she was feeling.

This, at least, had been Rosalind's intention before Secretary Cecil escorted her into the privy chamber. But the unexpected sight of Lady Blunt, already standing before the queen, and already in deep conversation with Her Majesty—the two of them alone, the queen obviously having dismissed her ladies of the privy chamber for this interview—blasted her intentions to bits.

"How long has Lady Blunt been talking to Her Majesty?" Rosalind whispered to Cecil.

"A half hour," the hunchbacked minister replied. He was Lord Burghley's son, and had trained all his life to replace his father. What he lacked in stature, he more than made up for in efficiency.

"A half hour," Rosalind muttered, her mind awhirl.

The fate of the entire world could be divulged in that length of time. In a half hour a hoary old Templar could sputter out the secrets of the Grail, the tide of victory could swing from one warring nation to another, the head of a queen could be severed from her shoulders. More to the point, in a half hour someone with Lady Blunt's malignant tongue could draw and quarter the reputations of half of London's finest citizens.

"Your Majesty, Lady Rosalind Rothwell," Cecil announced when they reached the circle of candlelight spilling on the floor around the throne. He then bowed and returned to his work.

Rosalind was too dismayed by Lady Blunt's intimidating presence to curtsy as propriety dictated. The conniving lady had obviously arrived here early to report the news of Drake's raid herself. Once more Rosalind had been duped.

"Your Majesty," she said, trying without success to keep her voice from trembling in rage, "you must not believe a single word Lady Blunt says."

"*What?*" the gossip cried.

"What impertinence is this?" the old queen added in her cracking voice.

"Forgive me, Your Majesty," Rosalind said, curtsying in a flurry of garments. She sank to the ground, then looked up, her expression desperate. "I mean no impertinence. I bow before you always, but not before the scheming Lady Blunt. She has no doubt been filling your head with scandalous stories about my husband's exploits."

"Your husband?" The queen ran a knotted forefinger over her red-splashed lips, settled her chin in her hand, and raised her eyebrows, two black arcs drawn across the otherwise white-painted mask of her face. Rosalind held her attention utterly.

"My husband is . . . your spy," she began carefully as she rose from her deep curtsy. "This I have recently learned. I also know that you and my husband together planned my marriage to him, counting on my naïveté and my good faith, which I gave to him utterly and completely."

"Is that so, Lady Rosalind?" Queen Elizabeth said.

Rosalind met her haughty eyes, her own full of pain, but try as she might, she could not hate the queen. She could only love her, despite the knowledge of her betrayal.

"Drake told you he wanted Thornbury House," Rosalind continued. "And he told you that the threat of your seizing it from me would so devastate me that I would be willing to do anything to keep it, including marry him. And you were right. You got what you wanted. You were able to reward Drake for his spying with a house that cost you not a farthing. And he got what he wanted: he is now my lord and master, which has been his ambition since we were children."

Elizabeth folded her hands and frowned, genuine concern in her eyes. "Is that what you think happened?"

"But no matter how angry I am at Drake," Rosalind

added, "I cannot betray him. I came here to speak of
something that Lady Blunt has obviously already divulged.
But you cannot believe her. It is not true. No matter what
the circumstances, Drake would never betray you. He
would never raid what amounted to a royal ship. At least
not without good reason."

At last, the silently fuming Lady Blunt turned on her,
hands fisted at her side, and raked Rosalind with eyes filled
with loathing and disbelief. "I've told her nothing, you
idiot. We were discussing the weather!"

Rosalind's eyes fluttered. Her breath stopped. "What?"

"Lady Blunt was telling me about the progress of the
repairs on her dock at Cranston House, and how the
weather has been cooperating," Queen Elizabeth explained. "But I think I'd be much more interested in what
you have to say, Rosalind. What is this about a raid on
one of my ships?"

Oh, Lord, what have I done? Rosalind railed at herself
silently. Color drained from her face; her mouth went dry.
What a fool she was!

"I wasn't going to be so bold as to introduce the subject,
Lady Rosalind." Lady Blunt's lips puckered with indig-
nation. "But now that *you* have done so yourself, I would
be most happy to inform Her Majesty of Master Drake
Rothwell's indiscretions." She turned to the queen, an-
nouncing quietly, "He raided and sank one of your ships,
Your Majesty. The one flying the Levant Company flag.
You are an investor in the Levant Company, are you not,
Your Majesty?"

"Of course I am," the queen muttered, eyes snapping.
"I'm not senile, you overstuffed lump of sugar!"

"Yes, of course." Lady Blunt didn't even blink at this
example of the queen's renown temper. "It seems Master
Rothwell was frustrated in his attempts to gain his share
of various foodstuffs, and so he raided Admiral Peele's

flagship at Acheen. He boldly boarded it with muskets firing, and in the course of an ensuing battle, the ship caught fire and sank. Admiral Peele should be arriving in London any day with more details."

"You show yourself to be as well informed as ever, Lady Blunt, in the matter of scandal," Elizabeth said. "And you are still living up to your name."

"To make matters worse," Lady Blunt continued, impervious to the queen's snide remark, "the king who rules the natives at Acheen turned hostile after that incident. He will no longer let any English ships drop anchor in his ports. So, as it turns out, the loss to the Levant Company is far greater than one ship."

These words caused a heavy silence to descend on the privy chamber. Rosalind studied every wink, every nuance, every twitch in the queen's face. And it seemed in the moments that followed Lady Blunt's revelation that Elizabeth aged another decade. She squeezed her wrinkled eyelids tight and thrust out her lower lip in defiance of sorrow. Then she glared at Rosalind, almost pleading, as if asking her former lady-in-waiting to deny the charges, to find a way to prove Lady Blunt wrong.

"Your Majesty," Rosalind whispered, and rushed to her side. Kneeling, she grabbed the aging monarch's paper-skinned hands. "You must hear Drake out. He surely had good reasons for what he did. You know him. Probably better than I. You know he has a noble soul. He is sometimes impetuous and ruled by his quest for revenge, as I know all too well, but he is a good man at heart. He had his reasons, I'm sure of it. His intentions are good."

Elizabeth squeezed Rosalind's hands in kind. "I fear that his intentions do not count, Rosalind. Only his actions. If this is true, if he attacked a chartered ship, if his actions led to our loss of trade at Acheen, then he must be punished."

"But you are the queen. You can do whatever you wish. You can forgive. You can wink and nod and turn the other cheek."

"No, Rosalind." Elizabeth let go her hands and leaned her head wearily against the tall back of her throne. "If I were a man, I could do these things. But I am a woman, and the men in my Court are always looking about for signs of weakness. They have never seen it. Oh, they have seen me vacillate. For I have the heart of a woman, and I feel more deeply than they do. But my alleged vacillation has always been a tool I wielded to my own ends. These men I rule have never seen me fail as a leader. Not in all my forty-two years on the throne."

"You have nothing left to prove, Elizabeth," Rosalind said, breaching the wall between them and calling her by her Christian name. "Your authority has never been in doubt."

The queen's wrinkled lips parted in a sardonic smile. She laughed, as if at a private joke, no sound emerging from her lips. Then she heaved a sorrowful sigh.

Elizabeth looked at Rosalind again. "When the sun is setting, my dear, the courtiers start for the door. My, how this audience has wearied me. Leave now. But come back." She held out a hand and pulled Rosalind close. "And be more careful of the company you keep."

The queen's wary gaze traveled across the distance to Lady Blunt, who was fidgeting with her pomander ball. The corpulent widow darted a look at Rosalind, obviously jealous of her close proximity to the monarch.

"Yes, madam." Rosalind curtsied again, this time in defeat, and departed with Lady Blunt in silence.

Through a crack in the door behind the throne, Drake watched Rosalind's back as she retreated from the privy chamber. Even in defeat, his wife had held herself tall. But how much starch would there be in her spine five or ten years from now, he wondered, after her husband had dragged her through the pits of hell?

He could not think of that now. He could not think of how undeserving he was to have such a lady as his wife. He would not think about the tears that had spilled down his cheeks when she'd humbled herself before the queen on his behalf, even though she had surely felt betrayed to learn that he was the queen's spy.

He was not angry at her for revealing his secret. With Peele's return, the queen would have found out anyway. No, the revelation of this day would serve a greater purpose. Suddenly everything had become clear. The house, his desire for revenge, the true spirit of his wife, his spying—it had all fallen in place, and he had awakened from his groggy web-filled dream, aware that his destiny was hanging in the balance, and the time to decide its course would be brief. But seize it he must. For Rosalind's sake. He would not drag her down with him.

As soon as the door shut behind Rosalind and Lady Blunt, Drake pushed open a hidden door and stepped around the throne. When the queen caught his gaze, she neither frowned nor smiled. She merely blinked wearily.

"Mandrake, you heard all of that conversation?"

"Yes, madam," he said. His voice brimmed with remorse, for he had saddened her. And he would never willingly sadden the queen in her waning days.

He knelt before her, and when she offered her hand, seeking consolation, he took it in both of his and kissed her ring, then the back of her hand, where her parchment skin gleamed white like a pearl. "Your majesty, I am so sorry."

"Not nearly as sorry as I am." She smiled bravely, but he saw the depth of her loneliness in her misty eyes. "Long ago, when I was imprisoned by my half sister,

Bloody Mary, as they later called her, I thought I would die of loneliness. There was one person who kept me company, who reminded me of my destiny. Robert Dudley, who was also imprisoned. And later, when my sister the queen died, and I was crowned, my sweet Robert became my master of the horse, and I named him the Earl of Leicester. Sweet Robin. He is gone now, as so many are. He loved me to the end, you see. He wanted to marry me. But as much as I loved him, I could not agree to a marriage. I could not risk marrying any man. Not after seeing my own father marry six times and behead or divorce so many of his wives.''

Her eyes blazed into Drake's, as if she could see the past reflected in them. ''Robin, of course, married my cousin, Lettice Knollys, when he gave up hope of having my hand. And then his stepson, Lettice's son, Robert, came to my Court like a blazing star, outshining his stepfather, whom I had loved so dearly.''

Drake tried to maintain a neutral expression, for as he knew only too well, Lettice Knolly's once-beloved son was none other than the notorious Robert Devereux, Earl of Essex.

''Dear Robert, how I miss him. So many are gone now. Kat, my old chief gentlewoman. Lord Burghley, my treasurer. And Lord Hunsdon, my cousin. And now you, Drake. Now even you are lost to me.''

''I am nothing to you, madam. Merely a willing agent of your royal will.''

''Yes,'' she admitted lightly, then smiled as flirtatiously as she could still manage. ''But you are so very handsome. Like Walter Raleigh. And you were my little secret. Not even the late Lord Burghley, or Walsingham, the great spy master himself, knew you were reporting to me. I like to keep my men guessing. But now you have ruined our little game with this ill-considered raid at Acheen.''

Drake gently withdrew his hands from her grip and stood. "I committed the ultimate sin of a spy. I had ambitions of my own. But it was not ambition that forced me to board that ship. I had good reason. Rosalind was right about that. Would you hear me out, Your Majesty?"

She studied him through half-lidded eyes. She was growing tired. He recognized the signs. Her slowed breathing. Her nodding head. She would be asleep soon, even though it was still morning.

"Your Majesty, I beg you, may I explain myself?" he said a bit louder.

Her head bobbed up and she blinked in surprise. "What? Oh. No, no, Drake, your reasons do not matter. The deed is done. And now you are gone."

She flicked her fingers in the air, as if shooing away a fly. He did not need to ask for clarification. She was sending him to the Tower. Drake would follow in Sir Walter Raleigh's footsteps. Perhaps he would stay in the same prison cell. And if he were lucky, in time he would be restored to the queen's favor, as Raleigh had been.

"May I have the day to put my affairs in order?" he asked as he carefully straightened the ruffles on his sleeve.

"Yes, yes, of course. Till the end of the day."

"Don't keep me there long, my queen," he implored her, falling again to one knee with bowed head. And while he knelt he said a quick prayer that Elizabeth would not die while he was imprisoned. He could rot in the Tower before the next monarch assumed the throne. For the childless queen still had not named a successor.

Twenty-eight

༄ঌঌঌ

When Drake returned to Thornbury House hours later, Rosalind fairly flew down the grand staircase. Remembering anew how he had deceived her, she paused at the bottom step. Then she closed the distance, throwing her arms around his shoulders and pressing her head to his chest.

"I thought you'd never return. Where have you been?"

"I've been to see my lawyer, Master Starck."

She pulled her head back and took in his dusty forehead, creased with care. "We must talk. Alone. Something terrible has happened."

He took her hand in his and kissed it, then nodded, following as Rosalind hurried through a series of rooms to their favorite parlor. Drake shut the door behind them and sagged against it.

Rosalind stopped in the middle of the room, her hands fluttering at her sides as she searched for the right words. How could she tell him that she had betrayed her own husband? Just as he had betrayed her.

"Drake, I have been to see the queen." She tossed up her chin, as if ready to receive a blow.

"So have I."

"I went with Lady Blunt."

"I know."

"Drake, you must believe me, I went there to prevent the very thing I caused. Unfortunately, I—" She stopped mid-sentence, frowning. "You *know*? You know that I told the queen about the raid at Acheen?"

"I was standing behind the queen's throne. I heard everything. And I know you did not mean to betray me."

She froze in place; her fingers grew numb. She forced a brittle smile, and it was as if someone else were smiling. Someone stronger, someone less likely to wither and die as a result of betrayal.

"I see. Of course you were." She rubbed her forehead. "I am such an idiot. I once thought myself clever. Now I realize I've been duped by you all my life. And the greatest embarrassment is that the older I become, the more gullible I seem to be."

"Rosalind, I did not conspire with the queen to force you into marriage." He pushed away from the door and strode purposefully toward her. "I didn't even know she remembered visiting my father there. You have no idea how cunning she can be."

"I do know her just a bit," Rosalind shot back, eyes flashing with sarcasm. "I was a lady-in-waiting, after all."

He gripped her arms and yanked her close. "I married you because I took your maidenhead, and it was the honorable thing to do."

She let out a bitter bark of laughter. "Zounds! I feel so honored."

"Would you rather think that I married you for this house?"

"You mean you didn't?"

"No, God's teeth!" He let her go and rubbed the back of his neck, then ambled to the window. "Your father set that little intrigue into motion, and the queen played the game like the master player she is, but I had no part in it. I was just as manipulated by Elizabeth as you were, except that you had more to lose, and I had only to gain. If I sinned against you, it was by letting you marry a man who no longer has a heart to give.''

"No matter your intentions, Drake. You were a spy. All this time. And I was the last to know. That burns like bile in my mouth.''

Drake held out his arms in supplication. "Forgive me, but secrecy was essential. I became a spy out of a sense of duty, and out of my desire to learn as much as I could about politics.''

"And I sought knowledge of politics to protect me from men like you,'' she mused.

"You must believe me when I say everything I have done was to avenge my father's honor. If I could get close to the queen, I thought, then I could learn something about the people who betrayed him. Ironically, it was my lawyer in London who has learned the most. I've been halfway around the world for naught.'' He sank down in a chair by the window and kicked one heel up on the sill, burying his forehead in one hand.

Rosalind's heart melted. He had tried so hard to bury the ghosts of his past. She went to him and stood behind him, combing her fingers through his hair. He closed his eyes and surrendered to her skillful caresses.

"That feels good.''

She kissed the top of his head and placed her hands on his rock-solid shoulders. "I once thought that your desire for revenge was a waste of your talents, but I see that this mission is all that matters to you. You must find out who destroyed your father, or you will never be happy or successful yourself.''

He reached over his shoulder and gripped her hand,

squeezing hard; he'd never felt closer to her.

"How can I do that now when I am headed to the Tower?"

"You must not go." She plunked down on a chair in front of him. "I will not allow it."

He chuckled, half in cynicism, half in admiration. "You think you can actually keep me out of prison when the queen has decided to incarcerate me?"

"The queen's guards will arrive in a matter of hours. We must come up with a plan."

"You mean a miracle!"

"Explain yourself to Elizabeth."

"She would not hear me. She does not care. You know her, Rosalind. She is not ruled by logic. A year from now she may decide she's no longer angry at me, but by then she may be dead."

Rosalind steepled her fingers and pressed them to her lips, contemplating the unfortunate truth of his words. "I was right about your motives, wasn't I? You did have a good reason for your raid?"

A slow, triumphant grin spread across his face. "By God in heaven, you were right, wife. You did not doubt me. You didn't trust me, perhaps even hated me, but you never doubted my honor."

Rosalind flushed with pride and reluctantly allowed a grin. "No, husband, I did not."

He stood and pulled her up, wrapping his arms around her and twirling her around, laughing richly. "You're a damned fine woman, Rosalind. If I live to be a hundred, I'll never forget how you stood up to the queen. That alone was worth the years of grief we've caused each other."

When he set her down, she did not let go. She held his shoulders tight. His lips stole across her forehead. When he breathed in her sweet scent, he groaned.

"Rosalind, however will I live without you?" He nibbled at an ear and rubbed his cheek in her hair. "You are an angel of mercy."

A shiver worked its way up her spine, and she soothed her cheek against his, heart fluttering. But it was not enough. Making love would not save them.

"No!" She drew back, pinning him with her arms. "You must tell me everything. If I am to stand beside you, I must know all your secrets. Did you have an affair with Lady Ashenby?"

"No, God's teeth! When you happened upon us I was grilling her for information on Essex. And I showed her my telescope. That was *all* I showed her."

Rosalind hesitated, then nodded her acceptance of his explanation. "So what happened at Acheen?"

"What didn't happen at Acheen?" was his droll reply. He went to a table bearing refreshments. He poured two beakers of port and gave her one. Sipping, he retold the fateful event.

"There had been trouble in Acheen before the incident with the Levant Company. Captain Davys took his ship, the *Lion,* into port a year ago. Negotiations ran afoul, and the King of Acheen sent Davys away. I followed in his wake, and learned the native king was unhappy with the progress of trade negotiations. He felt cheated. I pacified him with the promise that I would guarantee him quality goods in any deal he made with the English. I implied that I was acting on the queen's behalf."

"Were you?" Rosalind asked.

"No. But it is not uncommon for English naval officers to act as diplomats abroad."

"You didn't pretend to be a royal officer!"

"Not really." Drake gave her a sly smile. "But who is to say what the king understood and what he did not? I did not speak his language, and he did not speak mine. We muddled our way to an agreement. And just when he was prepared to let more English ships back into his ports, the Levant Company sent in a fleet. They left with boat-loads of goods, but the king felt he had been cheated again. He was demanding the return of Peele's fleet when I reached harbor. I tried to commandeer Peele's flagship, to make him understand what was at stake for England. Peele misunderstood my intentions and opened fire. A battle broke out. His ship caught fire and sank.''

Rosalind shook her head. ''Surely you knew you could not board an admiral's ship without suffering dire conse-quences.''

''But what of the consequences of that fleet leaving Acheen without adequately compensating the natives? You see the results! English ships are no longer welcome in Acheen. That is a great loss to England. Of course, the queen doesn't care about the hopes for the future, only the transgressions of the past. It happened months ago. I was hoping that Peele would not return to England until I sorted out my financial troubles.''

''So Lady Blunt was right on that account. Your trading adventures have fared poorly.''

Drake heaved a sigh. ''Disastrously. I need more ships, more bullion, more time. None of which I have. I have failed. Just as my father failed before me. I had thought if I could succeed at a trading venture, the very sort of busi-ness that had been his ruination, it would be the best re-venge. If I could just succeed, I thought, then I would not have to kill the men who killed him. Success would be my revenge. But I would have been better off hunting the vil-lains down and cutting their throats.''

''And if you had sold Thornbury House and used the money to buy more ships and goods, all your troubles would have been solved?''

''Yes.''

She lowered her head, and for a moment he thought she

was praying, but then she looked up, pride etched on her noble features.

"You have spoken to me, Drake, as a husband to a wife. You have been honest, and I cannot ask for more. That is all I have ever wanted. I may not have been the best wife, but I can be a best friend, as I should have been a long time ago."

He stood and ambled to her, his eyes never wavering from hers. "I can be a friend as well."

He reached into his open doublet and pulled out a parchment bound with a blue ribbon. Rosalind recognized it immediately. It was one of the wills signed by her father. "Open it."

"I don't need to. I know what it is."

"Open it. I want you to read it again."

With trembling hands—hating the document for all the misery it had brought them—she untied the ribbon and unfolded the paper. She perused it and shrugged. "This is the will my father wrote naming you the inheritor of Thornbury House. I've seen it before. I no longer doubt its authenticity."

Drake nodded. Then he took the parchment and ripped it in two. Rosalind gasped. When he placed the two pieces together with the clear intention of ripping it again, she gripped his wrist.

"Stop it, Drake! You don't know what you're doing."

"Yes, I do. I'm nullifying the one thing that has threatened your happiness from the start."

He ripped the parchment again. The tearing sound splintered the air. He placed the four pieces together and ripped them in half again. And when the pieces were too small and thick to tear anymore, he nonchalantly tossed them in the air. For a moment tiny pieces of parchment rained down. As the yellowed bits fluttered to their feet, Rosalind looked down incredulously, then up at Drake, too stunned to speak.

"I'm going to the Tower, Roz. I may never return. Thornbury House is yours. I made all the arrangements the day after we were married. You gave yourself so sweetly to me, I knew I had to give you something of equal value in return. Why do you think I was so churlish in the days that followed our wedding? I did not give this house up lightly. That agent, Stryder, tried to buy it from me, but I could not sell it. No one has loved this house as much as you. Not even my father. I've just returned from Master Starck's office. I've signed the necessary papers. He assures me that everything is in order. You will not lose this house, no matter what the future may bring."

Rosalind's mouth parted, but no words or breath would come. What could she say that would not be hopelessly inadequate? She grew light-headed as she tried to fathom her husband and her relationship to him. She could not reconcile Drake the usurper with Drake the benefactor. How could anyone give so much? What could she possibly give him in return?

And then the answer came. She could give what she herself wanted in spite of everything—the touch of flesh to flesh, the meeting of lips to lips, the melting of body into body, the loss of control, the cry of submission.

Love wasn't required. It had never even been mentioned. It was hinted at, but never voiced. The guttural, gut-wrenching cries of passion were never quite as expressive as the single syllable: love. But the intimation was there. If they'd had more time, perhaps they could have learned to speak of it. If they'd had more time together, they could have practiced with the unschooled tongues of babes. But time was running out. There was just enough of it to touch again, as they were so good at doing. There was time to lie down, to abandon their objections at the threshold of the bedchamber, where their best moments always occurred.

She reached up and kissed him with aching tenderness. Shakespeare was wrong about one thing: parting was not sweet sorrow. It was torture.

"Drake, I swear I will not let her harm you, for it is all my fault."

He pressed her head to his chest. "It is not your fault. Our destinies were dictated by the stars long ago."

"Make love to me," she whispered. "Please."

He scooped her up in his arms and carried her to his chamber, where they would not be disturbed.

A pewter blanket of clouds kept the sun from gleaming through the windows. A light rain began to thud against the glass. And it seemed the haunting mist that rose from the ground met the gray clouds halfway, so that nothing was visible outside their chamber.

Drake placed Rosalind on the bed and then threw open the windows. A metallic scent of rain swirled through the room, leaving a hint of cleansing moisture. It billowed through his hair, as it must have done on the sea, she thought. How dashing he must have been, braving the dangerous main for treasure, for adventure, to forge routes lesser men dared not seek. Before, she had seen him as greedy and ruthless. Now she saw him as brave, a visionary. Every bit as much the creator that she had tried to be.

"Come to me." She held out her open hands, straining to narrow the distance. "Quickly. There is not much time."

As he turned from the window to regard her, she noticed that his smile was dark and sad. Silently, unhurriedly, he pulled off his doublet and then tugged off his shirt. He dropped them to the floor and began yanking off his boots and breeches. Soon he was a gleaming bronze statue of muscles and tanned skin and desire, for already he had risen in anticipation.

"Why did we let so much time go by?" he said as he approached the bed.

"We were fools." She reached up and embraced him as he tumbled into her arms. She was fully clothed, but felt no distance between them.

He hiked up her soft gown and the smock beneath it, wasting no time. He didn't want to ravage her or drive her to the heights of ecstasy. He wanted to feel her envelop him, to know the serenity, the sanity that their joining always brought him.

He guided his staff to her parted thighs, and finding nothing there but moist softness, he slid into her, and all was right with the world. He cupped her face and kissed her mouth, touching and then withdrawing, then returning again, like a bee to the flower. He wanted to memorize everything about her—what it was like to taste her lips, to inhale her breath into his lungs, to feel the cushion of first contact, to melt into it, to delight in the velvet texture of her tongue, to plunge deeply into her mouth, to reassure her that there was no place to which he would not, or could not accompany her.

And it was their kisses that now spoke louder than words ever could—I adore you, I will never forget you, I will never take another, I will never dream of another. This, this is life; this is what I have been waiting a lifetime for. Thank you. Oh, dear God thank you for giving me this gift.

They rocked together in a steady rhythm that seemed to match the rain. There was a softness to it, a gentle watering of the soul. A desire not to feel the heights, but rather the depths. They climaxed together, unexpectedly, almost as an afterthought. And when it was over, they clung to each other forlornly, wondering why lovemaking, like life, always came unfairly to an end.

Twenty-nine

❦

A few hours later hand in hand, Rosalind and Drake descended the stairs and walked out the front door to where the queen's guards were waiting in jackets adorned with the Tudor rose and black beret-style caps.

Rosalind tersely ordered Huthbert to tell the servants to stay away from the windows. She did not want them to see Drake hauled off to the Tower. Francesca, Uncle Thadeus, and Thomas stood behind them at the bottom of the front stairs, a somber little audience, and she was careful not to let her shoulders shake. She would pretend that Drake was only leaving temporarily. And if she believed it, perhaps others would as well.

"Drake," she whispered one last time. A single tear coursed down her right cheek.

He tipped up her head and kissed it before it fell.

The simple, gentle gesture was a perfect parting gift. She clutched his arms, knowing she should give him something in return.

I love you, she wanted to shout. I love you. I love you. I need you.

Where were the words? Why couldn't she say them? Why was she mute? And why did he stare at her with such sad, gleaming eyes? Where were his protestations of love?

"Come along, Rothwell," a yeoman of the guard said.

Drake squeezed her arms reassuringly and then mounted his horse.

No more was said. They rode away in a cloud of gravel dust. Rosalind turned on her heels and marched into her chamber where she sobbed hysterically, like a character in one of her tragedies. But as she put on her sleeping gown later that night, she questioned her right to shed a single tear.

Hadn't she contributed to Drake's downfall from the moment she'd set eyes on him twenty-odd years ago? Hadn't she been adamant in her insistence that he was an evil-hearted person, though no one else agreed with her? Hadn't she been the one to enlist Lady Blunt's aid in order to undermine Drake by looking into his past? Hadn't she been the one who confirmed what Drake had always suspected—that he would never belong in her class of society?

After undressing and lighting a candle, Rosalind marched sadly to the long-unused sunny bedchamber. It had been hers as a child and now served as a storage place for childhood memorabilia. Both of their possessions littered the floor, and she longed to be close to what Drake had been close to.

When she opened the door, a wall of hot, dusty air struck her face, rife with the odors of the past: the cool smell of the feather bed, the earthy and ancient dust from little feet that long ago had splattered mud in the cracks in the floor, the clothing trunks filled with musty mementos of childhood: shredded ribbons, yellowed undergarments threadbare at the knees, dirt-stained petticoats, all permeated with the scent of cloves and the pale remains of dried flowers in a pomander ball.

The smells, the sights, even the remembered sounds— the giggles and shouts of futile rage—all seemed to congeal into a knife that plunged into her aching heart, but that instead of producing a drop of blood brought only soothing clarity. Stripped of the past, and now the future, she could see things as never before. She had loved Drake even as a child. He had been so stunning, so pure and frightening, so intelligent and maddening. So Drake.

She threw open the window and sucked in a misty blast of air. Then she crawled into bed by the light of her single candle, and in great stillness she closed her palms over her heart and embraced the past.

An hour later she was roused by a soft knock on the door. As her eyes jerked open she realized she'd been dozing.

"Who is it?" she called, sitting up. The candle had shrunk by a third.

"Francesca," a voice replied. "And Uncle Thadeus."

"Come in."

Her uncle and friend entered with grave expressions, which sobered further at the sight of Rosalind.

"Are you all right? You look like a specter," Francesca said, rushing to her side and sitting on the bed. She stroked Rosalind's forehead with her long, lithe fingers. Rosalind took them in her own and studied them. Francesca had creamy pink nails bordered with perfect little white half-moons. Her knuckles were small and delicate, as was everything about her.

"You've always had the most graceful hands, Frannie. Mine were always caloused and mud-stained."

"They were, and are, strong and useful," Francesca said in her dulcet voice.

"Well, my girl," Thadeus said, coming directly to the

point, "our boy is in the Tower. What do you propose to do?"

"I have a hundred plans, and not one is any good."

"Matters could be worse," the old courtier said.

"How?" Francesca frowned up at him over her shoulder.

"Drake could be dead." Thadeus's impish eyes glinted. "If you were truly cursed, Rosalind, he would be dead by now. It appears the curse has been broken."

Rosalind sighed. "Why don't I feel better about that?"

"The only way you'll get Drake out of the Tower is through bribery," Thadeus mused as he stroked his mustache. "And then he'll have to escape the country and live elsewhere. He may be able to return after Elizabeth's demise. Maybe not. All that will take money. None of which you have to spare."

"I could sell the house," Rosalind whispered, frowning again at the candle. "Then I'd have more money than we could use. He could save his company. He could establish himself as a gentleman in another country. I could buy a small place in London."

"Sell the house?" Thadeus scowled at her. "Are you daft? Drake is not worth this house."

"You thought it worth my while to marry him for this house!" Rosalind shot back.

"Every woman marries for a house."

"That was not why I married Drake!"

"Wasn't it?" Thadeus asked cynically. "Oh, come, puss, do be honest."

"She *is* being honest," Francesca argued. "Uncle Thadeus, must you be as thick-skulled as all the other men in Christendom when it comes to the heart? Rosalind loves Drake. Tell him."

Francesca gripped Rosalind's forearm, quiet desperation shimmering in her lovely violet eyes as she waited for her friend to validate the belief in romantic love that she herself still cherished in her heart. It was what Francesca had longed for, sacrificed for. So why was Rosalind not speaking? Why did she look so bereft and tongue-tied.

I love him. The words were poised on the tip of Rosalind's tongue. *Say them! Say them!* she ordered herself. But was it true? Did she really love Drake if she could not give up Thornbury House for him as he had for her? Was she too much like Thadeus, like Lady Blunt, willing to sacrifice her very humanity for the sake of security and position and power?

"Rosalind, say it." Francesca was frowning now.

Rosalind sank down and wrapped her arms around her drawn-up knees. In the pregnant silence that followed, she heard the pounding of her heart. The words were not going to come.

"I'm not sure I can give up this house. Not for anyone." She raised her head at last, looking at Thadeus with a mixture of love and loathing.

He smiled smugly. "I've always known that."

When Francesca physically recoiled from her, Rosalind looked at her with a whimsical smile. "Did you know he gave me the house, Frannie?"

"What?"

"Drake gave me Thornbury House. Or should I say he renounced his own claim to it. He ripped up the will. He says he's drawn up all the papers to ensure that no one doubts his intentions in this matter."

Francesca blinked slowly as this stunning turn of events registered in her mind. "So that was why he went to London the day after you were married. To see his lawyer."

Rosalind nodded.

"And I thought . . ."

"What?"

"I thought he was going to betray you." Francesca

pressed a hand to her heart. ''I thought he was secretly selling the house behind your back.''

Rosalind gave her a quizzical frown. ''You thought that and still you would have had me pronounce my love for him? Even to a man you believed was betraying me?''

''Yes, for your sake, not his,'' Francesca snapped. ''If you cannot love, Rosalind, then what good is life? If you cannot give your heart wholly, even to an imperfect man, then, when you die, won't you regret never having given yourself fully to another?''

Rosalind turned her head sharply away. ''You are too sentimental.''

''And you are not sentimental enough!'' Francesca rose and started for the door.

''Where are you going?'' Rosalind called after her.

''To the Tower.''

''At this hour?'' Thadeus asked.

''Yes.'' She turned on them both. ''I'm going to tell Drake that I've misjudged him. Whether you think him deserving or not, Drake needs us. I'll be at the Tower until I can gain entrance. I'll tell Drake you both send your love,'' she added, her voice laced with sarcasm.

The next day, an hour after the Lord Chamberlain's Men's afternoon performance, Rosalind sat with Will Shakespeare at a table in the Silver Stallion pub on Maiden Lane near the Globe.

Shakespeare wore a handsome goose-turd-green doublet with an enormous white ruff collar. Rosalind wore a popinjay-blue bodice and petticoat, and an elaborate feathered hat. They were among the finer dressed of the pub's humble patrons, and the tapster wisely left them to their privacy at a corner table.

''Does love necessarily mean you must sacrifice all for

your beloved?'' Rosalind said as she took the first sip of
her second pint of ale.

''If you truly love, then giving is no sacrifice.'' Shakespeare pondered his own maxim as he sipped his brew.
Then he raised a finger. ''However, if I knew anything
about love, Rosalind, I would not spend so much time
writing about it. I would be living it.''

''Drake was a dastardly rogue the week we were married,'' Rosalind mused, weary from her mental torture, her
examination and reexamination of Drake's motives, and
her own.

''Marriage can do that to a man.''

''Then a man should not marry if he is the worse for
it.''

''But isn't marriage's worst better than solitude's best?''

''Is it?'' she demanded of him. ''Is it better to be married to a man who would take your very home, your very
soul, your talents, your time, than it is to live as idle mistress of your own fate? That was what I was.''

''Too idle, methinks,'' the playwright observed.

''I was in utter control of my destiny.''

''But you never felt the joys, the sorrows, the heights
and depths one feels when one dances *à deux*.''

''Nor the pits of despair, the anger of discord, the bitter
sorrow of enforced dependency.''

Shakespeare leaned back, crossed his arms, and studied
her in the shadows of the dimly lit pub. Wisdom always
beamed in those half-lidded eyes of his, quietly, indubitably. ''By your own account, Rosalind, Drake has given
you the house. He could not have wanted to lord it over
you if he has done such a generous deed.''

''Oh, Will, you're right. I am just babbling because I
am terrified by what I finally know about love. You cannot
have it and hoard little parts of yourself. You cannot be at
once miserly and enjoy the bounty of the heart. I have

never truly given to anyone in my life. I never had that luxury—what did I have worth giving, I mistakenly assumed. And now I am faced with the prospect of giving all to a traitorous spy who may well live the rest of his days in the Tower!''

"Love has ever been illogical, dear lady. Yet it is worth the fight. Do you remember what I said about possessions?''

She blinked, feeling the relaxation wrought by ale. "Yes. You said that the greatest possession was my creativity, and that if I focused on the intangible gifts of life, I would not fear the loss of the tangible.''

Shakespeare grinned as he sipped, then wiped a trace of foam from his gently carved lips. "Something of that nature.''

She frowned through the smoky haze that billowed from a dozen clay pipes being puffed by surrounding patrons. "You speak of creativity. Loving another human being is a kind of creativity. It certainly bears the likeness of creation—the tremulous beginning, the spark of insight and wonder, the rush of power, the sense of infinity, the expectation that it will never end. And the gratitude that comes in its wake, the knowledge that however painful, it was a blessing.''

She sagged against the wall. What was she arguing? There was no choice. She knew what she must do. But it would take planning, and patience. She would have to rally Thadeus, her trustee, to her side. For once, Rosalind must temper her impatient nature. For Drake's sake.

Thirty

⌇⌇

Over the ensuing months, Rosalind visited Drake at the Tower as often as the Yeoman Warders would let her through. She brought him sweetmeats and books to occupy his lonely hours, and news from the Court. Drake was most interested in learning about the Earl of Essex's latest escapades.

As Rosalind reported, the earl's house on the Strand was open to all malcontents. Such hotheaded young men as the Earls of Rutland and Bedford, Lords Cromwell and Mounteagle, gathered to vent their individual spleens over the queen's poor treatment of Essex, their exalted leader. The debt-ridden and spoiled young noblemen did not possess their fathers' memories of the glorious queen whose magnificent reign had endured for nearly half a century. They could only see Elizabeth as an aging monarch whose time had passed. And it was clear they were working themselves up toward some kind of showdown with the queen's council. They were unjustly accusing some of the queen's closest ministers of conspiring to name the Spanish infanta as heir to Elizabeth's crown.

When Drake grew gloomy at hearing such news, as he invariably did, Rosalind, admiring his continued devotion to the queen, would try to distract him, recounting amusing stories and chatting about her plans for the garden. Once, Drake broke the subdued silence he usually maintained during her narrations.

"Have you written any new plays?" he asked, his blue eyes fixed intently on her, as if her answer was crucial to his existence.

Drake's query startled her into silence. Did he really want to know about her writing? Wasn't he the one who had insisted—unreasonably—that she keep her literary aspirations private? But he seemed genuinely concerned. And so she told him truthfully that she did not have time to write, nor the inclination, but that she hoped to resume one day, the unspoken words hanging in the air: *When you are free again.*

"Good," he said emphatically. "You should write. We should all do what our hearts dictate."

She took this as an apology, or at least a change of heart, and was surprised at how relieved it made her feel. She was coming to realize that her husband was a man of many surprises.

The holidays proved to be an especially trying time. Rosalind struggled valiantly to be merry, and she ensured that Thornbury House was appropriately decorated for the twelve days of Christmas. But even then, unbeknownst to Drake, she remained busy attempting to arrange his release from the Tower.

Christmas Eve found her pacing nervously in the gallery, hugging herself against the chill that oozed through the leaded windowpanes. Outside, large white snowflakes fell silently against a dull gray sky. The smell of pine needles burning in the fireplace permeated the large room.

She and Francesca, Thadeus, and the servants were all

set to gather round the virginals, sing carols, and drink hot spiced wine. But Rosalind knew that only a part of her would be present. Her heart and soul were in the Tower of London.

"My lady," Huthbert called out from the end of the gallery, and hastened to her side, his booted feet clicking on the wooden floor. "My lady, a gentleman is here to see you. He says Master Starck sent him. Should I send him away?"

"Because this is Christmas Eve? No, Huthbert, I asked Master Starck to arrange the meeting. Did he give his name?"

"No, my lady. He was quite mysterious. He said you knew him."

"Indeed I do." She straightened the ruffs at her wrists and gathered her wits for a meeting for which she'd been preparing herself for months. "Send him to the lord's parlor. And throw another log on the fire."

"Yes, my lady." Huthbert bowed and departed to do her bidding.

When Rosalind reached the lord's parlor, she hesitated. Then taking a deep breath, she pushed open the door.

She saw the back of a man standing before the fire, warming his hands. Melted snow glittered in his dark brown hair, reflecting the golden hue of the flames. For an instant she imagined it was Drake, that somehow he had escaped and come home for the holidays, but she quickly shook off the impossible thought, and quietly said, "Good afternoon, Stryder."

He turned slowly. He did not smile. Did he ever? He merely gave a terse nod.

"Good afternoon, Lady Rosalind. Master Starck said you wanted to see me."

She crossed the length of the long, high-ceilinged cham-

ber and retrieved two goblets of spiced wine, which Huthbert had thoughtfully left for them. 'Yes,'' she said, taking
her time before answering. ''I did.''

She handed him a goblet, and noticed the scars on his
fingers as he accepted it, the less dramatic brethren of the
jagged slash that crossed the left cheek of his darkly handsome face. She looked up and held his gaze. ''I wanted to
know how much your employer would be willing to pay
for Thornbury House.''

His eyes glowed with unmistakable excitement. ''Very
much indeed, my lady. My employer, though fond of
money, has a great deal of affection for this house. I cannot
say the exact sum, but I can assure you, you will receive
more than you're asking.''

Rosalind felt herself beginning to quake inside. She was
actually setting in motion the series of events that would
lead to her loss of her greatest inheritance, her safe haven,
her pride and joy.

''Are you well, my lady? You look a little pale.''

She sipped from her goblet to hide her discomposure.
''I'm fine, Stryder. Just a little affected by the wine. When
clearly I should be much affected.''

He came as close to smiling as she'd ever seen him do.
Holding his goblet up in a silent toast, he drank, and then
wiped his mouth with the back of a hand. ''Why did you
decide to sell? I was given to understand that you fought
desperately for this home.''

Rosalind shrugged and gazed at the fire. ''Let us say
I've decided to make some speculative investments in foreign trade.''

Stryder's gaze narrowed. ''The East India Company is
about to set sail. They will doubtless corner several spice
markets.''

Rosalind forced her demeanor to remain as cool as his.

"It's no matter. There are other spices to be had. My husband will succeed yet. Mark my words."

Her seeming confidence won her another salute with Stryder's raised goblet. "Your husband is a fortunate man."

"How nice of you to say. But please I beg you, do not tell him what I just said should you see him. He would try to prevent me from doing it."

"Will your trustee agree to your decision?"

Rosalind smiled wanly. "Uncle Thadeus doesn't approve, but he has, shall we say, acquiesced in the face of my relentless resolve. He wants only my happiness, and I've convinced him this will make me happy. Until all of this is settled, I hope the transaction can remain a secret."

As Stryder drew the goblet to his well-shaped lips, Rosalind wondered about his station in life, where he was from, how he had lived. And when she could draw no conclusions, she smiled blandly.

"Fortunately, I can tell you are a discreet man."

"Without discretion, I would be a beggar on the streets," Stryder replied, placing his drink on the ornately carved dark-wood mantel and reaching into a pocket. He pulled out a piece of paper and handed it to her.

Rosalind unfolded the note and found a name written in elegant script. "Jack Rowling," she read, and shrugged, puzzled.

"That is the name of a Yeoman Warder at the Tower of London. He may be of some use to you. I should be going now. It is Christmas Eve. Your news about Thornbury House is a holiday gift. One day my employer will thank you . . . royally." Stryder bowed elegantly. "I fare you well, madam."

As he headed for the door Rosalind studied the name on the paper. Then she called out. "Why have you given me the name of a guard at the Tower?"

He turned, and she saw the shadow of disappointment cross his face. "Do you truly not know?"

When she shook her head, feeling lacking in wits, his hard gaze softened. "Then it is bravery that guides your actions, and not cunning, as I had thought," he observed. "Jack Rowling holds an important post at the Tower. He recently lost an enormous sum of money in a game of dice. I know. I beat him fairly."

A slow smile of gratitude began to inch its way up her face.

"That is why you're selling Thornbury House, is it not? To bribe your husband's way out of the Tower?"

When she remained smiling and mute, he nodded. "Just as I thought. Jack Rowling will help you. There is no more agreeable man than one who desperately needs to pay off his gambling debts."

He bowed and departed, leaving Rosalind feeling grateful to the strange and mysterious Stryder, and more than curious to learn the identity of his rich employer.

It took some time for the sale to inch its way through the official channels. But by February, the transaction had progressed to such a point that Rosalind had received the money she needed to proceed with her plans. She still did not know who was purchasing the property, but ultimately she did not care. It could be the Earl of Essex himself and she would not blink.

Nevertheless, uncertainty about the ownership of Thornbury left the household in turmoil. Decisions about its disposition were being made by the new owner's lawyers. Lifelong servants, fearful for their future, sniffled, sometimes even sobbed, as they packed Rosalind's precious heirlooms and personal items. She had much of it sent to Francesca's home in Yorkshire for safekeeping. There was not enough room for all her possessions in the elegant but small mansion Rosalind had purchased on the Strand.

By early February, all the arrangements had been made. Rosalind had given Jack Rowling enough money to set himself up in a little shop on the Continent. Once it was discovered that he helped free Drake, the prison guard would be considered a traitor to the queen. If he valued his head, he would have to depart the country.

Rosalind had also asked Captain Hillard to outfit a rig with enough food and water to last half a year. She visited the dock to ensure that all was in order before she hurried to the Tower of London for one last visit with Drake.

"Greetings, Rowling," Rosalind said when she entered the Tower.

The tall, brown-haired Yeoman Warder winked at her knowingly. "Good day, Lady Rosalind."

She nodded slowly, a silent acknowledgment that all the plans were in place. She patted the satchel at her side, which contained the costume necessary for Drake's escape.

"Follow me, my lady."

The warder led her to Drake's quarters, a dismal but decent-sized chamber.

"Hello, Drake," Rosalind said nervously as Rowling shut, but did not lock, the door behind her.

"Hello, Rosalind." He rose from his chair, quickly closed the distance between them, swept her into his arms, and gave her a drugging kiss. His hunger for his wife these long months in prison had only grown more ravenous. Kissing her now was not merely a pleasure, it was a necessity. As his lips ravished hers, as his tongue plundered her mouth, he was feasting on the assurance that his life would go on.

Why she submitted to, even sighed happily at, his displays of affection, he could not imagine. But he did not question her generosity. Her pity over his imprisonment must have assuaged her anger over the discovery that he had been a spy. She did have a heart after all. A great compassion-filled heart.

He pressed her head to his chest, marveling at the silky feel of her hair. "I do not know what I'd do if you stopped coming here."

She hugged him tightly and tilted her head back to gaze up at him. "I will never come here again." She paused for effect, then whispered her precious secret. "This is the morning you will escape."

"*What?*"

She dropped her satchel on the floor. "Here is your costume. Put it on. The guard will see us out a secret passage to a waiting carriage that will transport you to a ship that is anchored down at the river."

Drake frowned, suddenly prey to a tumult of emotions. "But how? How did you arrange it all?"

"If there's one thing I've learned in this lifetime," she said flatly, "it's that one can accomplish anything one wishes if one has enough gold."

"Where did you get it?"

When her eyes fluttered with indecision, he gripped her arms and gave her a shake. "Where, Rosalind?"

"I sold the house."

"You *what?*"

"I sold Thornbury House. I had to. I can't let you rot here any longer."

"To whom did you sell it?"

"I don't know."

When he merely stared at her, dumbfounded, pale and angry, she tried to explain herself. "The agent was Stryder. He did not say on whose behalf he was acting. Frankly, I didn't care. I told Master Starck to handle all the details. I would have sold it to the devil if that's what it took to win your freedom."

"Stryder," Drake repeated, turning away, stroking his beard as he thought about this information. "There is something odd about him, Rosalind. I know I've met him before. If I could just remember where. What did he say when you dealt with him?"

"He was very much the gentleman. In fact, it was he who supplied the name of the guard who will set you free. When I told him I planned to sell, he said his employer would one day thank me royally."

Drake stopped his soft pacing and turned on her. "Royally. Did he use precisely that word?"

"Yes. At the time I thought his emphasis on the word odd."

"Royally." Drake felt his heart begin to pound against his chest. "Good God, she got us after all, Roz."

"What do you mean?"

"The queen." Drake kicked a stool, sending it hurtling against the wall. "Damn her! Stryder is acting as agent for Elizabeth. She is the one who bought the cursed house!"

"How can you be sure?"

"Because I finally remember when I first saw the blasted man. It was more than a decade ago. At Tilbury camp, when I was presented to the queen along with a half-dozen other seamen who had shown great valor in thwarting the Spanish Armada. It was after that audience that the queen sought my services. It would seem that Stryder caught her eye as well. And he's been acting as one of her agents ever since. How she loves her intrigues!"

"Drake, it doesn't matter who owns Thornbury House now. We must get you out of here."

"Yes, damnation, it does matter. Her Majesty has forced you into a marriage you didn't want, she has imprisoned me, and now she's taking the house she wanted all along. I will not stand by and be so abused."

"Hush, Drake! Put this costume on, quickly. We must

leave." Rosalind scrambled to pick up the satchel. "There is something afoot in London. I do not want you to be waylaid. Yesterday Essex's lot managed to convince the Lord Chamberlain's Men to stage Will's old play *Richard II*. The queen learned of it and is demanding that Essex appear before her council. He's refusing to go, and there is talk that he may raise arms against her today."

"*Richard II*." Drake stroked his beard. That play, a cause of much controversy when first staged, was about the deposing of a monarch. It hadn't been performed in years. "We heard Essex talking about employing the players when he was conspiring with Do-Good Simplicity. We should have known he would want to stage *Richard II*. Essex's intentions couldn't be more clear if he'd written them in the sky with a dazzling show of fireworks. He's finally going to lead his rebels against the queen."

"Yes, and it could be happening as we speak. So hurry!"

She yanked the costume out of the satchel with a snap of her wrists and held it aloft.

Drake scowled. "What in blazes is that?"

Her lips thinned. "Your costume. What is wrong with it? Don't you like the color?"

"It's a bodice and petticoat, Rosalind."

"Yes, I know. And there's also a blond wig. Trust me, I went to great lengths to find one that would fit you."

"I will not wear a lady's gown," he snapped.

"You will if you want to live," she returned hotly. "No one will expect it is you if you're wearing female garments. I've brought a razor to shave your beard. Now get undressed and stop arguing."

He glared at her. "Are you doing this to humiliate me one last time?"

She began to giggle and gave him a quick hug. "No,

my husband, I'm trying to save your stubborn arse. Now get undressed!''

"Very well." He yanked the lavender silk outfit from her hands with a snarl. "But I will not leave London until I make sure Essex's rebellion has been quashed."

"What does it matter to you now?"

"I want to make sure Queen Elizabeth remains on the throne long enough to account for her sins against us. I will reclaim that house for you if it's my last act on earth."

"As it may well be if you put your pride before your desire to live." She pulled out the razor. "Now come close so I can shave you, and hurry!"

Thirty-one

❧

In subsequent years historians would write much about the Essex rebellion. They would tell how on that very morning the earl slipped out a back door at Essex House on the Strand when the queen's men came for him, and how he and his mob, wielding pistols and rapiers, surged toward the city. The citizens of London peered at the passing mob with gaping jaws and wide eyes. Some hurried into their shops and homes, slamming doors and windows behind them. Others cheered. But not a single one joined the mob of three hundred. Historians would tell how Essex traveled down Poultry and Lombard streets in search of the one thousand armed soldiers supposedly promised to him by the sheriff. But Sheriff Smith was nowhere to be found. He had heard of the rebels' approach and vanished. Much would be written about the earl's crushing realization that his rebellion was a disaster, and how, desperate, he returned to Essex House to devise some way to beg the queen's forgiveness. How he was arrested, tried on treason charges, and convicted. Two weeks later the thirty-four-year-old Robert Devereux, dressed in a scarlet waistcoat, laid his head on the block and stretched out his hands, and the executioner struck his neck three times before he was able to sever Devereux's head from his body.

Much was said of these events, but nothing would be said of a man dressed in a lavender bodice, petticoat, and blond wig, who preceded the earl's mob through the streets of London, warning its citizens to hide and to pay no heed to the coming rebels.

Drake rode a black steed. He charged over cobblestone streets, shouting that Essex was coming. He wasn't sure what surprised the astonished Londoners more—news of the rebellion, or the sight of a man decked out in flowing lavender satin—but he was too intent on performing his duty to the crown to worry about it. And until he ran into Godfrey Blunt, he thought that he had handled his duties rather well.

Godfrey was traveling with a dozen lords and lesser noblemen who had joined together to fend off the rebels. When the older and more experienced men continued toward Whitehall to protect the queen, Godfrey stayed behind. Recognizing Drake, he suddenly removed a pistol from his waistband and trained it on Drake's heart.

"My mother told me I might find you among the rebels, Rothwell," he said. He was sweating profusely, and a wild gleam danced in his eyes.

"Did she also tell you to go to the privy before you left to save the queen?"

Godfrey's only response was to cock his weapon. "For some reason, Master Rothwell, I do not find you as humorous as Lady Rosalind does."

The men, both drenched in sweat despite the winter chill, glared at each other as their horses pranced beneath them.

"You are supposed to be in the Tower, Rothwell," Godfrey barked.

"I escaped."

Godfrey's shapeless lips spread in an unkind grin. "No, you did not. For I shall take you to Sheriff Smith. He is presently with the lord mayor. I wonder what sort of reward the queen will give me for catching one of the rebels. Perhaps I will be knighted like my noble father."

"But didn't your father do something worthwhile to earn his knighthood?" Drake smiled. "Very well, Godfrey. Take me to the sheriff. I welcome the chance to explain myself to the queen."

Godfrey emitted a bleating laugh and the mist swirled around his red nose. "You won't get to see Gloriana. You'll be tried like all the other common traitors who joined Essex today. If you're lucky, you'll rot in the Tower. If not, you'll be drawn and quartered at Tyburn, and Lady Rosalind can bid you good morning when she passes by your head strung up on London Bridge."

Drake considered how right Godfrey might be. Then, suddenly aware of his absurd appearance, he ripped off his blond wig and tossed it on the street. "You're just as short-sighted and selfish as the rebels, Godfrey. The only difference is that you do not have the backbone or intelligence even to conceive of fomenting a rebellion."

Godfrey jerked his arm higher, his index finger trembling, clearly aching to fire his weapon. But he thought better of such an act, since no blood had been shed thus far in the revolt.

"Save your insults for your executioner, Rothwell. Perhaps your wife will join you on your journey to hell."

Hell, as it turned out, was another stay at the Tower of London, and this time Rosalind was imprisoned there as well, though in a separate chamber. Contrary to Godfrey's prediction, however, the couple was not tried for treason, along with the rebels.

They had no inkling of what their fate would be until a month after the earl's execution. Then, on a bright and promisingly warm day in late March, Drake and Rosalind found themselves being escorted to the queen. She had been eager to prove herself unmoved by the betrayal and execution of her once-beloved courtier and had continued with the affairs of state as if the rebellion had never happened.

Rosalind and Drake saw each other for the first time in nearly two months at the door to the privy chamber. Rushing toward him, she saw how haggard he looked after so many months without sunshine. As Drake took a step toward her and opened his arms, the guard escorting him jerked him back. Rosalind sagged in disappointment, but then stiffened her shoulders. This was the end. Today, everything would be resolved, for better or for worse.

The doors opened then, and they were greeted by Lord Buckhurst, the lord high steward. "Rothwell," the distinguished lord said. "And Lady Rosalind. The queen is waiting."

Rosalind exchanged a quick look with Drake. Buckhurst was smiling. Surely that was a good sign.

"Your Majesty," he announced in his deep voice, "I present Master Drake and Lady Rosalind Rothwell."

Rosalind squinted at the crowd of courtiers that was standing around the queen's throne, arrayed in velvet hats, glittering jewels, and dazzling clothes. They turned and hushed, staring eagerly as the couple entered.

Once again she felt like a monkey on display in the queen's zoo. Only this time, the prospect of mating before a crowd seemed much preferable to the humiliation she was sure the queen had prepared for Drake and her.

"Master Drake and Lady Rosalind Rothwell," the

queen said. "Come and humble yourself before your queen."

Drake took Rosalind's hand and escorted her to the dais. Together the sank to their knees.

"Get up," the queen snarled.

Rosalind was trembling as she rose, and Drake touched her elbow in support.

Queen Elizabeth stroked her lips with a gnarled finger and cocked her head, eyeing Drake shrewdly. "No, I do not think lavender would become you."

There was an astonished silence, then the courtiers and ladies-in-waiting standing near the throne began to chuckle. As the laughter swelled, joined by that of the queen herself, Drake turned red. But by the time the merriment had settled, a grudging smile was beginning to form on his again-bearded, if untrimmed, face.

"Godfrey Blunt tells us that you joined the rebels, and that your lavender bodice and petticoat was a disguise you donned for the occasion," the queen said.

"And he wore a blond wig," Godfrey piped up, stepping out from the crowd.

The queen frowned. "You should have worn a gregorian wig, Drake. Black would better highlight your blue eyes."

"Drake did *not* join the rebels, Your Majesty," Rosalind interjected before Lady Blunt could elaborate on her son's fabrication.

"I know that," the queen answered with pained patience. "Godfrey was lying."

Rosalind blinked in surprise and looked to see Godfrey's reaction. He stood next to his corpulent mother. They were both oddly subdued.

"Witnesses tell us that Mandrake Rothwell raced through the city warning citizens to beware of the rebels," Elizabeth continued. "An exceptional display of loyalty to the queen who imprisoned you. But you are still guilty of escaping the Tower, Drake. And someone helped you do it.''

The queen glared at Rosalind.

''I escaped, Your Majesty,'' Drake interjected, putting a protective arm around his wife, ''to try to prevent the overthrow of our great queen.''

''Is that so?'' Elizabeth gave him a smirk. ''And who was it that helped you?''

When Drake did not immediately reply, Elizabeth answered for him. ''You were set free by a Yeoman Warder named Jack Rowling, a traitor to the crown. He escaped the day of the rebellion and has not been seen since. One of my agents tells me that Rowling was seen purchasing a lavender bodice and petticoat the day before your escape. If he ever shows his hide in our country again, it will soon be without a head.''

Rosalind frowned in wonder. *She* had procured the lady's outfit for Drake, not Rowling. ''Your Highness, who was the agent who made this report?''

The queen merely smiled. ''We'll discuss these matters later. But first, Lady Blunt and her son, Godfrey, have something they wish to confess.''

The courtiers standing near the mother and son stepped away from them.

''Well?'' the queen snapped, her eyes shooting fire at the aging widow. ''Say it and be done.''

Lady Blunt cleared her throat. The folds of flesh beneath her chin jiggled. Her eyes bulged as she looked at Drake, standing half-shadowed in the middle of the torch-lit room. ''It was my late husband who lured your father to invest in the Spicery Trading Company.''

''Jesu!'' Rosalind gasped. She turned to Drake and found his face stony and stoic. She gripped his arm, horrified at the realization that she had conspired with the woman who had ruined Drake's father.

"My husband was in debt," the scheming lady continued. "I convinced him that there would be no harm in seeking charter for a company, even if one did not exist in fact. Your father was eager, too eager, to win glory at sea. He said he had a son who, even at the age of four, wanted to emulate the great English sea dogs."

Drake's arms stiffened beneath Rosalind's hand. She saw in his face the same look of raw pain that had marked his features as a boy.

Lady Blunt paused, fidgeting with her folded fan. "My husband was a good man. But he took the money and could not afford to return it when the company failed even to set sail. When your lawyer made inquiries on your behalf, I threatened him, for fear that my husband would be humiliated. The trading company was, after all, my idea."

"So you wrote the letters," Drake said in disgust.

She lifted her chin defiantly. "Yes."

"Even the recent one that threatened the queen's life?"

Lady Blunt's eyes widened and she flushed. "That was . . . that was just a ruse. I meant no harm to Her Majesty. I wanted you to think it was Essex who had written the letter. All I was trying to do was to end your quest for vengeance. I wanted to frighten you off. To save my husband's reputation."

"You would let a man live in infamy and ignorance his whole life when he was so close to the truth?" Drake roared. He started for her, but the queen's guards held him back.

"I had to think of my son's future," the widow replied indignantly, as if she had no idea why Drake was so distressed. "I didn't want Godfrey's reputation to suffer for my mistakes."

"He made mistakes of his own," the queen interjected with a tart tone.

When it was clear that Lady Blunt had said her piece, Drake exhaled with a burst of anger. "Why in God's name are you telling me now?"

The queen stirred, smoothing out her diamond-encrusted gown. "Because I threatened to have her drawn and quartered if she didn't. I promised you, Drake, that I would look into this matter. But that is not all. Godfrey, speak your piece."

The tremulous youth stepped forward and licked his drooping mustache. "It was I who nearly killed you, Rothwell." His eyes darted around, as if still seeking some escape. Then he twisted his hands and rushed on. "I pushed the Cupid over the balcony. I didn't plan to kill you. I wanted to frighten you off. I hoped the accident would convince you that you were destined to be the next victim of Lady Rosalind's curse. That would leave Rosalind, and Thornbury House, to me." He let out a bleating laugh, then winced. "You see, I . . . I want to be a player, a great performer like Burbage."

When a low snicker rose from the crowd, Lady Blunt looked around in embarrassment. "Hush, you fool."

"No, Mother," he said defiantly. "That was the only reason I went along with your plan for me to court Lady Rosalind. You wanted me to marry her so that I would become rich and save Cranston House for you. But I wanted to be rich for other reasons. I knew that if I became wealthy by my marriage to Rosalind, I could afford to dabble in the theatre, if not as a player, then as a patron. As eccentric as she is, Lady Rosalind would not object to a husband who took to the stage. And with her connections to Master Shakespeare, the possibilities were limitless."

"Poor Godfrey," Rosalind whispered, taking her place by Drake's side again.

"Take them to the Tower," Queen Elizabeth commanded, shaking her head sadly.

And there it might have ended. But when two guards stepped forward, Godfrey skittered away from them. He stumbled in front of Rosalind, reeking of fear. He gave her one last melodramatic look of longing, and then pulled out a knife.

"Yea, noise? then I'll be brief," he shouted, wide-eyed.

"Good Lord, he's *still* reciting Shakespeare," Rosalind whispered to Drake.

"O happy dagger!" Godfrey held the knife high. A collective gasp rose up in the chamber.

"Godfrey!" Lady Blunt cried. "What are you doing?"

Before any of the lords or ladies could move, Godfrey thrust the dagger in his belly. He groaned and doubled over. "This is thy sheath," he croaked, reciting Juliet's last lines, "there rest, and let me die."

As his legs began to buckle, the spell that gripped the presence chamber broke. "Take him!" Lord Buckhurst ordered, and a half-dozen men carried the wounded man away. "Call the physician!" A hysterical Lady Blunt followed in the wake of the crowd.

"Go see to Lady Blunt's needs," the queen ordered her remaining ladies-in-waiting. "Keep her company until she is escorted to the Tower."

Rosalind started after them, then realized happily that her place was beside Drake. She tucked her arms around his waist and nestled close to him. Somehow, whenever he held her she felt blissfully alone, as if the rest of the chaotic world did not exist.

Moments later Drake and Rosalind found themselves convened to a private audience with the queen.

"Drake, I've met with Admiral Peele," the queen began evenly.

Drake took a step forward. "Your Majesty, if only I could explain."

She held up a gnarled hand and smiled, her eyes kindling with kindness. "In due time. Admiral Peele recounted the circumstances of your battle, and then he handed me a sealed missive from one of my diplomats serving near Acheen. Sir Edward Harcourt wrote to me of the troubles with the King of Acheen, and of your diplomatic efforts to reopen trade there. I judged you too swiftly. Lord Peele is a noble and valiant admiral, but he is not the most tactful of diplomats. I believe I understand what you thought was at stake when Peele's fleet left Acheen that day. Considering that, as well as your valiant efforts to secure my throne during the recent rebellion, I've decided to release you from the Tower. And Lady Rosalind, I hope your father in heaven will forgive this old queen for your brief stay in those unpleasant surroundings."

Rosalind, overcome by the queen's humility, knelt before her. She kissed the royal hand that was proffered so generously. "Thank you, Your Majesty. God save our queen."

She looked up at Elizabeth and was rewarded with a gentle smile. Rosalind knew she should let the matter end there. But she couldn't resist asking one more question.

"Your Majesty, who was the agent who reported to you on the treachery of Jack Rowling?"

"I think you know the answer to that." The queen turned her head and nodded. "You may come in now."

Out of the shadows behind her throne stepped Stryder. Rosalind drew a sharp breath. He never failed to startle her. His long dark hair was in such vivid contrast to his pale face with its jagged white scar. His gray eyes were as cold as ever, but she was sure she saw the hint of a smile curving the edges of his strangely sensual mouth.

"Stryder," Rosalind exhaled. "It *was* you." *It was you who lied to the queen on my behalf, blaming everything on Rowling when it was all my doing.* At least Rowling would enjoy some wealth in exchange for taking the blame.

"Yes, my lady. I keep an eye on many matters for the queen."

Elizabeth smiled approvingly. "Stryder spent as much time learning law at Gray's Inn as he spent at St. Paul's learning about thievery. He serves me well. He takes care of matters that great lords consider to be beneath them. This kingdom survives because of men like Stryder. And Mandrake."

"Is there anything we can do to repay you for your kindness and generosity in this matter?" Rosalind asked the agent as she joined Drake.

Stryder cocked one brow. "Perhaps supper at your home in the presence of Lady Halsbury?"

Rosalind slipped her hand in Drake's and gave it an excited squeeze. They exchanged a curious look, and Rosalind nodded. "If it so pleases Francesca—"

"It won't," Stryder said flatly.

"I'll talk to her," Rosalind reassured him. Perhaps Francesca needed a man like Stryder to break through her finely woven coat of mail that protected her heart.

"No, Stryder, I have other plans for Francesca. Meanwhile, Drake," Queen Elizabeth said, turning her sharp old eyes on him, "have *you* nothing to say? Perhaps it will spark your tongue to learn that I am going to grant you a knighthood for your devotion to me. I have learned much in the past few months about the price of misplaced trust. You are no Essex, Drake. You've scarcely asked for anything from me but justice. And so I will honor you with much more than you even dared hope for."

"A knighthood!" Rosalind exclaimed, turning to him

and gripping his arm. "Did you hear? You will be Sir Drake henceforth."

Drake looked down in wonder at this devoted wife, then up at his noble queen. Overcome, he knelt on the dais and reached for Elizabeth's hand, pressing it to his lips with deep emotion. A knight of the realm! It was beyond anything his father could have imagined for his son.

"Oh, my liege . . ." But his heart beat with a great, dull thud. For he knew this was not how the drama was supposed to end. While he had gained so much more than he had hoped for, Rosalind had lost everything. He looked up at Elizabeth with a tortured expression. "I would give back the honor, my queen."

Hearing the angry, gruff refusal, Rosalind grew pale. "Drake, what are you—"

"I would give the honor back to you, Your Majesty."

"Why?" Rosalind gasped.

"I would give you back my knighthood and my freedom if you would just give Rosalind a chance to buy Thornbury House from you."

"Drake!" Rosalind whispered harshly. Gods, he was stubborn! "It is enough. Take the honor and be grateful."

The queen let out a hissing breath of frustration. "Damn you and that house, Drake, you are like a snarling dog with a bone. Will you never leave it be?"

"Never, madam," he swore.

She let out a beleaguered sigh. "You may purchase the house from me on one condition: you must remain married as Lord Dunnington hoped you would."

Rosalind turned to Drake, and then froze in place when she saw disappointment wash over him.

"But, Your Majesty . . ." he said, taking a step forward.

"Enough!" she shouted. "Do not ask for more. I am aware that you have requested an annulment of your marriage. I suggest you reconsider." With that, the queen rose, and when her arthritic knees wobbled, Stryder rushed to her side and escorted her from the privy chamber.

Rosalind, heart pounding, head spinning, turned to Drake. Seeing the cold resolution that molded his features like a mask of stone, she remembered her father's favorite observation about human nature. Once the devil is in a man, he always said, you can never get it out.

Thirty-two

❧

Two days later Rosalind sat in the garden at Thornbury House. It was a brilliant spring day, bone-chillingly cold when the sun slipped behind the clouds, but fresh and brisk and full of the promise of life. The air was thick with the scent of loamy earth being churned in the pastures, and little green shoots were sprouting in the barren garden, teasing Rosalind with memories of the rich mosaic they'd formed the year before—lady's slippers and daffodils, lilies of the valley and sweet williams.

Bundled in a cloak, Rosalind leaned against the stone wall that bordered the garden near the sundial. Her penner beside her, filled with ink and paper, she was scratching in the last lines of her newest play, the one that she'd put aside before Drake's first incarceration in the Tower.

For some reason, she had been feverishly writing ever since her release from prison. She and Drake were once again sharing Thornbury House, but she felt so separate from him that she hardly dared speak. They shared a bed at night, in silence, without touching. And he left in the morning before she woke. The pain of his rejection was like a dagger twisted in her already-wounded heart.

In that quiet, desperate state of limbo, she had turned once again to the well she thought had run dry—her imagination. There she found comfort and healing. And once she set pen to paper, the ending of her play, which had so frustrated her till then, had poured out as if in a dream. She wrote as if her life and her marriage, now one and the same, depended on the play's completion. If only the happiness that reigned at the end of her play would carry over into her life . . .

After she dotted the *i*'s on the last words of the last scene, she looked up and sighed with profound contentment. She thanked God for the gift of words. Then she saw Francesca approaching, looking like a veritable confection in her ice-blue silk cape, her raven hair studded with jewels. When the viscountess caught sight of her, she waved and strolled in her direction.

"I thought I might find you here," Francesca said through chattering teeth. "Don't stay long. You'll catch your death of a cold."

Rosalind smiled up at her, unfazed by the temperature, then blew on her manuscript to dry the ink. "It's not bad when the sun is shining."

"What's that you're holding?"

"I'm finished, Frannie. This will be my last play. And it's my best."

"Your last?" Francesca sat on the stone bench nearby. "Why? Has Drake told you again that you cannot write?"

Rosalind snorted in derision. "No, Drake does not care whether I write or not. He wants our marriage annulled. I simply mean that I have poured my heart and soul into this. I have nothing more to say or give."

Francesca's lips curled upward. "I doubt that very

much. And I doubt that Drake truly wants to end your marriage.''

''He made his intentions very clear.''

Francesca leaned forward and rested her forearms on her knees. ''I spoke with your husband last night. As old friends.''

Rosalind's gaze shot to her face. Her heart skipped a beat. ''I'm afraid to ask what transpired.''

''He said that an annulment was the only honorable course of action. He said that you married him under duress and that you should have your freedom as you have always wanted.''

''My *freedom*?'' Rosalind looked at her aghast. ''Why the knotty-pated, dim-witted fool!''

''That's exactly what I said.''

Rosalind set aside her manuscript and jumped to her feet. ''Does he think a woman can give her heart, her soul, her body, and then turn around and blithely walk away simply for the sake of freedom?''

''Apparently so.''

''Does he think I want to be alone? Does he think I could ever again sleep without him by my side, *knowing* him as I have?''

''I believe so.''

''Doesn't he know that I love him and would give him the world?''

''No.''

Rosalind scowled at her. ''How could he not?''

''Have you ever told him you loved him?''

''No!''

''Why not?''

Rosalind thrust her hands on her hips and threw back her shoulders. ''Because *he* has never told me that he loves me.''

''Oh, Rosalind! How childish!''

"It is not! If I were the first to tell him I loved him, he'd lord it over me the rest of my days."

"Then you must not love him as much as you say if you'd let such a petty concern get in your way."

Rosalind pressed her palms to her forehead, fearful that her head would explode. "Oh, Frannie, I'm not that petty. But I made love to him! What did he think that signified?"

Francesca waved a hand in the air. "What does making love mean to any man? For men, the act has about as much significance as a trip to the privy."

"I refuse to believe that." Rosalind began to pace. The mulchy leaves of the previous autumn crunched beneath her feet. "It meant a great deal to him. He sacrificed this house because of what we shared. So why doesn't he realize that he could leave me now and I would mourn not the loss of the house, but the man who dwelled in it?"

Francesca smiled wanly. "I don't know. He's not thinking clearly. Frankly, I'm worried about him, Rosalind."

"I'd give him the annulment without protest," Rosalind said, "if it would make him happy. I know that he's miserable."

"An annulment wouldn't solve his problems," Francesca observed.

"Oh?" Rosalind looked up hopefully.

"Your husband is a defeated man. He has been a merchant seaman all his adult life and he has nothing to show for it—no pepper, no booty, no ships, no single outstanding achievement."

"Should that matter so much?"

"To a man, yes." Francesca's violet eyes glittered with wisdom. "Remember, they are different creatures from us."

"How could I forget?"

"Drake also knows who ruined his father, but he himself was not the one who solved the mystery. It was the queen who did that for him, so once again he feels thwarted. And since the culprit turned out to be a lady, he wasn't even given the satisfaction of calling anyone out for a duel.''

"I see what you mean." Rosalind chewed her lower lip, considering her husband's dilemma.

"And while he adores the ground you walk on, he never properly courted you. He was forced into your arms by the queen. Once again he was a pawn in some larger game. He feels impotent."

Rosalind marched to Francesca's side and sat. "So what is a wife to do?"

Viscountess Halsbury sighed. "He needs to feel like a man again, and not just in the physical sense. He needs to know that he is a success."

"But what will that take?"

Hearing footsteps rustle through the rotting leaves, Rosalind looked up, shading her eyes from the sun, only to find Drake approaching. "Hush, Frannie, here he comes. Talk about the weather."

"As I said," Francesca smoothly replied, "you should return to the house soon before you catch your death of a chill."

"Only the faint of heart would allow joy-killing caution to ruin a spring day such as this," Drake announced as he joined them. His cheeks were ruddy from the crisp air, and he was smiling, but his eyes looked dull, clouded with worry.

The sight of him sent Rosalind's heart spinning. She wanted to throw herself in his arms and kiss him, console him, but he would sooner eat a sour apple than accept a woman's pity. She knew him well enough to know that. It would require all her skills, and her deepest insight into the male gender, to revive his sad soul.

"Drake, could you sit with me for a while?"

He frowned at her, as if she were asking for the world. Or, she thought, as if he didn't understand why she would want to waste the time with such a wastrel as he.

"Very well," he grumbled.

Francesca rose and hugged him. "Good to see you about. I'll leave you two alone. I'm afraid my dear friend Rosalind has arranged for some sort of visit from that brute named Stryder. I must be prepared for the worst." Laughing lightly, she turned on her heels.

Drake watched her go, then turned to face Rosalind. "You can't possibly believe that Stryder is any match for our beautiful Francesca."

Rosalind raised her eyebrows and shrugged. "Who's to say? Sometimes opposites attract. Not in our case, I'll grant you."

A heavy silence greeted the pronouncement. Drake gazed at the papers scattered on the ground. "Is that a new play?"

"An old one I've just completed. My best ever." In the silence that followed, birds chirped frantically as they prepared their nests. "Is that what ruined our marriage, Drake? My writing?"

His blue eyes, haunted and sad, focused on her, then looked away. "No. I was wrong on that matter. You have talent. You should not waste your God-given gifts as I have done. Please don't ever stop writing." He kicked a pebble and sank down onto the bench.

She was just beginning to feel sorry for him when she remembered that he had approached the queen about an annulment. How dare he threaten their promising union without consulting her! How dare he lose heart after all they had been through.

"Drake Rothwell, I've about had my fill of your dark moods and equivocations. Where is the Rothwell I have always known and feared? Where is the man who swore he would conquer the world and choke me with the dust that followed in his wake?''

He raised his head to nail her with a jaded glare. ''You speak of an arrogant youth I no longer know. I am now an old and all-too-wise man.''

''But a wise man would not be so downcast. Come, come, put aside your gloom.'' She sat beside him and put her arms around his shoulders.

When he merely stared at her as if she'd gone daft, she gripped his arm. ''Drake, you frighten me when you're like this. If you aren't confident, how can I be? You have always been my anchor, my guiding star. I measured my progress by my distance from you. Granted, the more the distant you were, the better . . .''

She hesitated. Her speech somehow wasn't going exactly as planned. ''Let me find a different way to put it.''

He put a firm hand on hers and gave her an affectionate squeeze. ''Rosalind, save your rallying speech for the troops. You don't need me. You never did. You just thought you did, and then used every dram of your power to make me think the opposite. Hear now, Rosalind, we said it a long time ago. We are oil and water. You are the moon and I am the sun. What will happen to us when the first bloom of love has faded? Will we be left with nothing but vitriol and sharp words? You would never have married me unless you were under duress. I have no illusions about that.''

''Stop!'' She gave him a good shake. ''Do you realize what we have stumbled upon? Do you realize how fortunate we are, that despite our stubbornness and hardheadedness we have found the kind of joy together that lovers find but once in a lifetime, if ever?''

''Do you think that love is enough?'' he returned sourly.

''Yes.''

''Well, I don't.''

She sank back as if she'd been slapped. He was wrong and she had to make him see it. "How can you say that love is not enough?"

"I am a failure, Rosalind. You would not love a failure for long."

"That is not true! You are not a failure. You have found out who was culpable in your father's death. Lady Blunt is now in the Tower. Godfrey, as it turns out, stabbed himself with a fake stage knife. He's now recovering from nothing more than wounded pride in the comfort of his home. You were the one who followed their trail. You were the one who became indispensable to the queen and eventually found the answers you were looking for. It was all your doing. And you may not have much to show for your years of exploration, but you have the respect of the legions of sea dogs who followed in the routes you forged. That has to mean something to you."

He frowned at the garden as he pondered her words. Then he turned his handsome, rugged face to her. "Did you mean what you said about the power of love? You see, I don't think I have a heart left to give. I've ignored it too many years. I don't think I can feel much of anything anymore."

"You can," she said emphatically. "And I can prove it."

He gave her a cynical half smile. "Oh?"

She grabbed his hand and tugged him along until they reached the barren rose trellis. She searched among the pruned rosebushes until she found a stem with the shriveled remains of a flower. She plucked the thorny spike, careful not to prick her fingers, and held out her other palm.

"Give me your hand."

He grimaced and glared at her dubiously, a long-lost glimmer of humor awakening in his eyes, but complied.

Opening his fist, she placed the thorny stem in his palm, then wrapped his fingers around it and squeezed hard.

Drake let out a hissing breath. "Somehow I knew you were going to do that."

"Does it hurt?" Her eyes danced with the excitement of a mad alchemist hot on the trail of gold.

"Yes, it hurts. Are you happy?"

"Of course it hurts! Thorns always hurt. But no one destroys the rosebush simply because he is stuck by a thorn or two. The beauty that the flower brings to the gardener is worth the pain. The exquisite velvet petals, the distinctive elegance of the blossom, and the rich, sweet scent more than outweigh the pain of being pricked. And every gardener will be pricked once or twice, to be sure."

Again opening his fist, she removed the rose stem and pulled a handkerchief from her pocket. It was the same cloth Francesca had used to dab Rosalind's thorn-pricked hand during their wedding. Rosalind pressed it into his hand to blot his tiny wounds.

"Will your nose not inhale the sweetness of spring's blossoms even as your hand stings with pain?"

His mouth twitched and then burst into a smile even as his eyes burned with cynicism. "Yes, wife. Even a rogue such as I cannot deny the sweet smell of a rose."

She smiled more sweetly than any of nature's creations. "Then so will love survive, like the sweetness of the rose."

"Here he is. Drake!" Francesca called out.

Rosalind and Drake turned at the sound of approaching feet and voices.

"We're here!" Rosalind called out, and frowned when she saw that Francesca was escorting Captain Hillard.

"Rothwell!" the sea-worn captain called out excitedly.

"Greetings, Hillard. What brings you back to Thornbury House?"

"Good news, Rothwell. Damned good news."

Francesca and the captain stopped when they reached the trellis. "The good captain came all the way from London, so I did not want him to wait a moment longer. He was quite anxious to see you."

"Well done, Frannie." Drake smiled warmly at her. "What is it, Hillard?"

"An unbelievable turn of events." The grizzled seaman pulled from his cloak a scrolled parchment. "I have here a commission from Queen Elizabeth. I am to take *La Rose* and two other ships supplied by the queen herself to Buto to gather up every last bit of pepper on its docks. She says I will sail on behalf of Sir Drake Rothwell. And for one year, said Sir Drake will have a monopoly on every bit of pepper transported from that country. The East India Company be damned!"

"But the queen is an investor in the East India Company," Rosalind pointed out.

"I'll warrant she can afford to be generous." Hillard slapped his knee with glee. "What say you, Rothwell?"

"Damned good news indeed, Hillard." Drake smiled broadly, his face alight with excitement. "When do we sail?"

The captain scratched his head. "Er, well, there is one catch. The queen says you won't be sailing. She needs your services at Court. But you'll take half the profits of whatever I bring back. She, of course, will get the other half."

"Hurrah!" Drake cried out, leaping in the air.

Rosalind looked at him as if he'd gone daft. He turned to her, laughing, and picked her up in his arms, swirling her around. "Did you hear what he said, Roz! I'm to be a rich man. I'll fill London with so much pepper they'll be sneezing all the way to Cornwall!"

"Wonderful," she muttered, and managed a thin smile when he set her back down.

"I've got to talk more with Hillard. You don't mind, do you, sweetling?"

She shook her head. "No, of course not. Go back to the house. I want to walk some more. Frannie, won't you see to the captain's comfort?"

"Of course."

Rosalind watched the trio head back to the house with an odd sense of disappointment. She should be happy for Drake. He was finally going to succeed at trading. But somehow the news made her feel empty. Why? Why did it seem as if this good news was somehow bad?

Thirty-three

❧

Drake joined Rosalind two hours later. She was down by the fishing pond. When he didn't find her in the garden, he knew she'd be at the pier. He crested the hill that led to the isolated spot, and paused to admire her beauty. She stood at the edge of the pier, gazing up at the house in all its magnificence. With her cape blowing in a taciturn breeze, she looked mystical, like an ancient druid priestess, or King Arthur's lady of the lake.

There had always been something about Rosalind that was larger than life, like this house. It had been their curse and their joy. It almost had a life of its own, a meddling, mischievous spirit. Drake sometimes wondered if its destiny had been to bring them together. Had Lord Dunnington known that on some level?

Drake strolled onward, eager to see Rosalind, to touch her, to share the estate's beauty with her. Her cape blew in the cutting wind about her statuesque form, and it seemed as if she were a sea nymph luring him to the water's edge, just as she had twenty years before when he'd followed her little footsteps there.

When he reached the edge of the pier, she stirred from her wistful trance and looked at him. He put his hands on his hips, and remembering their last visit here, he grinned. "Did you ever learn to swim?"

She smiled as she shared the memory. "No, I haven't learned to swim. I've been too busy running this estate."

"Perhaps we can share that burden now." He cocked his brows in query. She shrugged noncommitally.

He strolled to her. When he reached the end of the pier, he wrapped his arms around her and kissed her forehead. "Why aren't you happy for me?"

She embraced his waist and sighed. "You really shouldn't be so perceptive. It's not healthy for a man."

He smiled as his chin rested on her head. "Don't you want me to be a success?"

She didn't answer immediately. At length she tilted her head back. "Of course I want you to succeed. What I object to is that you can't seem to be happy unless you do."

When he frowned doubtfully, a fire kindled in the emeralds that were her eyes. She was never so impassioned as when she had something or someone to win over. God, he loved her.

"What is outward success?" she said. "Shouldn't our marriage be stronger than the rise or fall of our fortunes? You had every reason to be happy before, but you could not muster a smile until Hillard delivered his good news."

He winced at the accuracy of her words, the pointedness of her observation.

"Drake, I have to be enough for you. You have to value my company regardless of our circumstances. At last I know my worth. I will not live with a man who does not appreciate it as well."

Drake swallowed hard. Rosalind still didn't know just how much he cared for her. But then, how could she? He'd

never told her. He'd never really known for sure just how
constant he could be. Misfortune had taught him much. So
how did a man tell a woman how very much she meant
to him?

He stroked her face with one hand, studying her perfect
countenance. Clearing his throat, he gave it his best shot.
"Rosalind, you are the arrow Cupid impaled in my heart.
You are the fire that burns my soul. You are the exquisite
torture that was denied me so long. When we first made
love, I knew at last and without doubt that heaven did
exist. I knew there was a God, and His greatest creation
was a stubborn little woman with tousled red hair whose
heart throbbed with blood so pure it could feed the earth
for eternity with its richness."

She shook her head, fighting tears. "Don't say these
things if you don't mean them."

"I do." He pressed his lips to her cold cheeks. "My
darling, believe me, it's all true."

"Then tell me you love me," she demanded, her voice
shaking.

He froze, then drew back, one eyebrow dubiously
cocked. "You first."

She gasped in disbelief. "No, you!"

"Rosalind," he goaded, cheeks dimpling with a devilish
smile, eyes winking with mischief. "You love me, now
admit it."

She put her hands on her hips. "Why should I be the
first to say it?"

"Because you proposed to me!"

"Damn you, Rothwell, you never forget a thing, do
you?"

"Not when it comes to my Rosalind."

"You are a man. You should say it first. It's the only
chivalrous thing to do."

"Ladies first. Besides, you don't want to risk missing

the opportunity to pledge your heart to a man as dashing, as charming, as irresistible, as—''

''You arrogant prig!'' she said, and gave him a sound shove.

''Great Juno!'' he cried as he lost his balance.

''Drake!'' she cried out, reaching for him, but it was too late. He fell into the icy green water with a loud splash. When he came up for air, spite was burning in his face.

''By God, Rosalind, you'll pay for this.''

She put her hands to her mouth, stifling a giggle. ''I won't pay for a blessed thing until you admit you love me.''

''We'll see about that.''

When he started for shore, Rosalind began her escape. She raced over the pier and ran back toward the house.

''Come back here, vixen!'' he shouted.

She ran with all her might, soon panting for air, but could hear his footsteps gaining on her. At last he tackled her and rolled her over on her back. Wet, dripping, laughing, he climbed on top of her and gave her a noisy pond-wet kiss.

''There,'' he said tartly. ''I love you. And let it always be remembered that I was the first to say it.''

She sank back into the grass with a contented smile. ''You always were the adventurer.''

He looked at her askance. ''Isn't there something you want to say to me?''

''I love you. I have never loved another. I never will.''

A great grin spread across his face. ''Well said, madam. Now put *that* into one of your plays.''

She smiled smugly. ''I already have.''

They went to bed that afternoon to warm Drake up, and two days later they still had not emerged from their sanctuary. Alone, Rosalind and Drake had everything they needed—the privy; of course, and the *Roman de la Rose,* which Rosalind read by day; and the soothing sounds of passion, to which they abandoned themselves by night.

When morning came, they ate from bowls of fruit and cheese and Rosalind joked that she would never let Drake leave this room. For even though Godfrey had proven himself to be a better actor than an assassin, there was no telling whether the curse would revive itself. If ever the fates decided to curse her again, Rosalind couldn't help but believe, they would surely do so when she had finally found the man with whom she wanted to spend the rest of her life.

Drake scoffed at her talk about the silly curse, but he agreed to make up for lost time by spending a week in bed. Or until the fruit nourishing them grew soft . . . as he himself surely would. Surely!

In the meantime, he assured her, he would spend all his might, and all his nights, romancing the rose.

Epilogue

❧❧❧

Four months later Drake escorted Rosalind to the Globe Theatre for the premiere of her play. It was being staged in its entirety, but Rosalind would not be listed as its author. She did not care. She was simply honored that Shakespeare thought enough of her skills as a dramatist to present it. He always said his goal as a writer was to fill the theatre, and he would consider it an honor this once, for a special friend, to lend his name to a new work that promised to do that very thing.

By the time she and Drake entered a back door to the tiring-house, where the players attired themselves, the theatre was nearly full. Patrons standing in the yard were busy dancing their jigs and eating their fruit and bread. More dignified patrons waited patiently in the galleries and the lords' rooms in the balconies. The players were dressed and anxiously whispering their lines offstage, or quietly running through their scenes together in the wings. Among them was Godfrey. With Rosalind's help he'd managed to obtain a walk-on part. He was so busy rehearsing his single line of dialogue that he did not even notice Rosalind and Drake's presence.

She looked around anxiously for Shakespeare, and he appeared moments before the trumpets blared to herald the start of the afternoon show.

"Rosalind! I'm so glad to see you."

"I wouldn't have missed this for the world! I'm nearly daft with worry. How is the play?"

"It's ready for an audience. We had plenty of time to rehearse."

"You should have let me attend some rehearsals. I don't even know the title you've chosen for it. You've kept me in the dark about everything."

"Now, now, Rosalind." Drake gently rubbed her arms. "Master Shakespeare knew what a nervous mother you would be. It's better to see the birth of this child with fresh eyes, as will the audience."

When Rosalind nodded and looked up adoringly at her husband, Shakespeare smothered a triumphant smile.

"Did you have to edit many of the lines?" Rosalind asked him, quickly refocusing on her multitude of worries.

"No, not many. You work was exceptional."

She gave him a bittersweet smile. "What a pity no one will ever know I wrote it."

Shakespeare shrugged. "Does it matter? Who knows? Perhaps one day my plays will be lost. Or if they survive, perhaps my name will be long forgotten. Or, Heaven forbid, perhaps future generations will give credit to someone else for my labor. It does not vex me now. I will always know what truth has sprung from my pen and my heart, and that great gift from the muse is enough."

He reached out and placed a reassuring hand on her shoulder. "Have faith, Rosalind. You have penned a comedy that won't soon be forgotten. Now I must go. The trumpets are blaring."

When he started away, Rosalind called out to him. "William, what did you decide to name my play?"

He glanced to the floor and spotted a playbill that had fallen by the wayside. He picked it up and handed it to her. "Read for yourself." He winked and was gone.

Rosalind righted the playbill in her hands and read the title aloud. *"The Taming of the Shrew."*

She beamed up at Drake, treasuring his proud smile. "I think I like it."